JACK MEREK

BLACKBIRD

WARNER BOOKS

A Time Warner Company

WARNER BOOKS EDITION

Copyright © 1990 by Jack Merek
All rights reserved.

This Warner Books Edition is published by arrangement with Contemporary Books, Inc., 180 North Michigan Avenue, Chicago, Illinois 60601

Cover design by Diane Luger
Cover illustration by Miles Sprinzon

Warner Books, Inc.
1271 Avenue of the Americas
New York, N.Y. 10020

W A Time Warner Company

Printed in the United States of America

First Warner Books Printing: April, 1992

10 9 8 7 6 5 4 3 2 1

For Susan,
Garrett, and Grace

Acknowledgments

THIS IS TO NOTE APPRECIATION for assistance from SSG Jim McLain for his help in ensuring authenticity on nonclassified aspects of special operations. I'm indebted to Capt. Kevin Bradley for his insights on flight in the "high-G" environment. A note of thanks should also be made to Susan Anderson, Mark Mooney, and Steven Levine in manuscript review. I would also wish to thank my agent, Clyde Taylor, and editor, Bernard Shir-Cliff. Any mistakes are the author's.

— 1 —
The Plane

The California Desert

THE BOY CATNAPPED IN THE car, snoring sweetly as his grandfather sped down Sierra Highway in the classic Corvette. The silver-haired man with the brown weather-beaten face drove a 1968 race-circuit model called the L-81. It was propelled down the desert road by a hot tail wind and a rebuilt V-8 engine that crammed 427 inches of pistons and power under its sun-faded silver hood.

The Corvette topped eighty miles per hour, defying any nearby California Highway Patrol cruisers that might be prowling the remote stretch of tumbleweed highway. The boy shifted in his sleep and nuzzled his cheek against his grandfather's cracked leather jacket. The jacket was worn soft with age and had a patch on it that read Ad Inexplorata—test-pilot's Latin, meaning "Toward the Unknown."

The boy shook his head sleepily. He blinked his eyes for a few seconds, blankly watching the blur of spiny Joshua trees and sagebrush next to the black ribbon of highway leading away from Edwards Air Force Base. Momentarily, he sank back into dreamland, snug in the racing safety harness that held him in the bucket seat. Nothing could shake the boy's serene

1

confidence that his granddad, the man behind the Corvette's wheel, was a master of dangerous machines.

The old man, whose name tape on the Army Air Corps vintage leather jacket identified him as Cartwright, drove casually and expertly. With one gloved hand on the wheel and the other on the gear shift, he manhandled the muscle car like someone half his age. Methodically, he pulled two sticks of Black Jack gum from his pocket, popped them into his mouth, and began working his jaw with grim concentration.

Alone on the highway, Cartwright pushed the roadster toward the edge of its performance envelope. But almost as soon as he gunned it, he thought better and throttled back to 68.5 miles per hour and 3,000 rpm's, not wanting to risk a surprise with the boy in the car. He kept one eye on the slender thread of blacktop in front of him and the other eye on the sky that stretched endlessly over the Mojave Desert like a great blue canvas.

Cartwright located the black spot on the eastern horizon, almost at the farthest point of his line of sight. It was coming from nine on the clock and far on the other side of Saddleback Butte, the formation of pink rock that jutted skyward from the desert floor like dragon's teeth.

Next he spotted the flash of colors from the American flag snapping in the wind. The flagpole rose from the desert like a salute. A few watchers were already there, gazing intently at the airfield across the road behind the Air Force security fence, which had a sign posted: Warning. No Entry. Deadly Force Authorized Against Intruders.

"There it is," Cartwright murmured to himself, pumping the brakes with the same smooth application of force he imposed on a braking space shuttle coming home to the dry lake bed at Edwards. He veered toward the flagpole.

The Corvette swerved into a controlled skid, leaving a burnt rubber track sizzling across the lonesome desert highway. A roadrunner's tail feathers fluttered as the little bird barely escaped eternity, skittering away from the path of the superwide performance tires. The boy belted into the passenger's seat tumbled awake as he had many times in his grandfather's convertible. Suddenly, his eyes were wide open and he was looking skyward. His ears pricked, listening for the distant thunder.

The braking Corvette showered sand from the highway shoulder onto the door and windshield of a sheriff's cruiser parked near the flag. The deputy emerged, scowling until he recognized the driver. He put his hands on his Sam Browne belt and sighed. "Oh, hell," the deputy grumbled. "General, if you're gonna drive that thing like an unguided missile, leave the kid at home."

The boy laughed and the white-haired man grinned. "Sorry, Radar," Cartwright said. "It'll never happen again."

"Sure," the deputy sputtered helplessly.

"I'm old enough to ride with my granddad," the boy said happily. "I'm eight and a half!"

The deputy shook his head and grinned. "You're braver than I am, little Scotty," he said. The deputy called Radar turned away from the old man to shade his eyes and watch the sky. "Don't let me catch you horsing it over seventy out on Sierra Highway, Scott, old buddy. On my turf I'm worse luck for you than the CHP. I won't take your autograph. I'll take your license."

"When you're right, you're right, Radar," Cartwright said, shrugging. "Out here, your stars outrank mine. I'll take her easy." Suddenly, Cartwright squinted.

"Here she comes, General!" a tough-looking man in a baseball cap and faded Marine Corps flight jacket declared, adjusting his oversized binoculars carefully.

"Give it to me on the clock, John," Cartwright yelled to the man known as the chief watcher. The man frantically waved two finger stumps in the air and whistled. "Coming in on your twelve o'clock and low," the chief announced.

For a mile up and down the highway, cars appeared. They streamed onto Sierra Highway from remote side streets and dusty frontage roads. As the black spot in the sky grew larger, so did the crowd that gathered around Chief John's flagpole. The drivers were pulling over and stopping. A chorus of slamming doors formed counterpoint to the roar of the approaching engines.

The rapidly approaching wedge of black delta wing thundered directly toward the crowd, looking like a speeding storm cloud, loud as a diesel locomotive and low enough to touch with a fingertip.

"That's it! That's the one, Granddad!" the boy declared victoriously. "Blackbird! Blackbird! Blackbird on the wing!" the boy shouted, jumping up and down as the dark wing passed overhead like a prehistoric bird with a tail of fire.

The great black dagger shape passed directly over the heads of the people, who craned their necks and covered their eyes and gloried in the wind that pasted their hair back like a desert storm and snapped Old Glory like a sheet.

The passing plane cast a shadow over the sagebrush emptiness. Two massive Pratt & Whitney engines roared from the aft end of the ebony aircraft. The people below held their ears and groaned, but none took their eyes off the plane. The boy's word was repeated over and over among the dozens gathered on the ground until it almost sounded like a chant. "Blackbird, Blackbird." Some were the people who built the plane in the secret factory at the end of the airfield. Some were just passing and stopped to see the commotion. The ones who built the plane knew it by another name.

For them it was the SR-71 strategic reconnaissance aircraft, or simply "the SR." Nobody who knew it, or ever caught a glimpse of it, failed to be moved by the sight of it. After twenty-five years, it was still the world's fastest operational aircraft, and the one that flew the highest.

The sleek black plane passed overhead, then climbed suddenly. Both engines on the plane ignited, white-hot like twin candles, sending it nearly vertical.

"Afterburner!" the boy shouted. At eight and a half, he already knew all about afterburners. The plane climbed, rising like smoke or a black butterfly, disappearing almost, then twisting over on its dorsal. Far, far above the desert, it seemed to hover motionless on its back. Then it twisted over suddenly and zoomed toward the eastern horizon, disappearing like a spaceship leaving earth.

Scott Cartwright and his grandson watched the black aircraft vanish. Some people climbed back in their cars, but a few remained, huddled near the leatherneck in the faded Marine Air Wing jacket. They stood still as the spiny trees that dotted the desert, watching the sky like sentries.

An extraordinary silence fell on the desert. The sudden quiet was broken only by the whistle of a quail and the wind singing in the rusting barbed wire that drew a line across the sand and sagebrush, dividing the airfield at Air Force Plant 42 from the rest of the Mojave Desert.

"You just saw the first and the last of its kind, boy," Scott Cartwright said, his voice dropped to a whisper. "You may never see another one like it. It was the real 'stealth' plane before everybody got loose lips and started talking it up. But it's almost gone."

"How come?" the boy cried out plaintively, sensing that something was being taken away that he had yet to touch.

"There's fewer than a dozen Blackbirds left, and when they're gone, they won't make any more."

"How come?" the boy repeated, nearly crying.

"They say they don't need 'em," Cartwright replied tersely. "They say the spy satellites do a better job of watching the bad guys."

"Will we ever see it again?" the boy demanded.

"Watch the sky, boy!" Chief John bellowed. He pointed to the horizon with the finger stump he brought home from Hanoi. "Keep your eyes open and your mouth shut. Don't lose the moment."

Cartwright gripped the boy by the arms and hoisted him up onto his shoulders. The boy sat silently, dangling his legs and watching the aquamarine horizon line. Suddenly, the black plane thundered by again, just below Mach, about three hundred feet off the deck and flying northwest toward Bakersfield. It ruffled the sagebrush as it sailed by. The SR-71 climbed and fired a sonic boom like cannon shot, then pushed away into the upper stratosphere, leaving a second and then finally a third boom in its wake.

The black plane was gone.

"She'll be back from Nicaragua by suppertime," Chief John declared. He adjusted his sun-faded black baseball cap that announced POWs Never Have A Nice Day and gave one last pensive look at the evening sky. Radar joined the leatherneck to help him lower the flag as the sun dropped behind the Tehachapi Mountains, casting gray and purple shadows on the parched land.

"Do you think they'll make more Blackbirds someday, Granddad?" the boy asked eagerly as he swung down from the old man's shoulders and dropped lightly on his Nikes.

"Maybe someday," Cartwright said. "If they're smart." He pulled the pack of Black Jack gum from his leather jacket and offered the boy a stick. The boy took it and began chewing the licorice-flavored gum purposefully.

As the leatherneck and the deputy folded the flag with military precision, a white Ford Taurus with rental plates on it pulled up slowly next to Cartwright and his grandson.

"Good evening, General. That was some show you put on for me," the woman in the car said. She wore sensible tweeds and a wry smile on a dried apple of a face.

"Well, howdy, Professor Murdoch," Cartwright said warmly, taking her extended hand and pumping it. "Glad you were able to get away from that Puzzle Palace on the Potomac. But that was no show up there. It's your tax dollars at work."

"Well, it's going to take more than an air show to persuade my boss that we ought to keep a thirty-year-old spy plane flying," she said, brushing back an unruly forelock of chestnut hair. "I'm afraid the Blackbird is due for retirement."

Cartwright shook his head and put his hands on the hips of his faded blue jeans. Tapping his toes in his Nocona range boots, he said somberly, "When you need it, you're gonna want it. Then you won't have it. Satellites can't fly on a few hours' notice, and they can't go exactly where you want to put 'em. How you gonna get your pictures back from Libya when you want 'em in a hurry?"

Suddenly, the woman and the general noticed that the boy was listening, open eared and wide-eyed, taking it all in. He chewed his gum like a machine.

"This is, of course, an unclassified conversation," the boy said sagely. Madeline Murdoch's raisin-colored eyes widened. "Who is this young man, General?" she asked, abashed. "He's too young for active duty, even in your family."

"I'm Scott the third," the boy said, thrusting his hand at her. She shook his hand, and shook her head in wonderment. Lightly, she said, "I'm Madeline Murdoch."

"Do you work with my granddad on the secret stuff?" the boy demanded.

The general patted the boy's shoulders. "Madeline works for the president, Mr. Big Ears. Why don't you run over there and talk to John and Radar for a coupla minutes."

"I can keep secrets," the boy asserted. Then he darted over to the leatherneck and the deputy, who were busy dismantling the flagpole.

"Why do those men come out here?" Madeline Murdoch asked. "It's a stirring sight, but it seems a somewhat idle exercise. I suppose they drink beer and tell dirty jokes."

Cartwright snapped his gum and snorted. "Those men are just like that black plane you saw today. They're maybe gettin' a bit past their useful service life. But when you need their kind, you're gonna want 'em."

Madeline Murdoch chuckled. "You reduce everything to the basics, General. Do you still want to see the Defense Department analysis for deactivating the Blackbird squadron?"

"You're damn right," he said. "I want to see who plunged the dagger."

Cartwright climbed into the car beside Madeline Murdoch. He paged through the report, reading quickly in the fading light and shaking his head sadly. The boy, the leatherneck, and the deputy carried the flagpole over to a panel truck that the retired Marine used as his headquarters at the magic corner of Sierra Highway and Avenue N.

Cartwright skimmed the pages but got the picture. He was hungry. And he had promised the boy, and Madeline, to grill steaks for them at the Ridge Roost near Gorman. Since Gloria's death, he was lonely, and weekend company was welcome. The new second stars of a major general on his shoulder had been scant comfort. He had seen such memos from the Puzzle Palace before. For all their dithering, they could be short and brutal when they wanted.

CLASSIFICATION: SECRET

DISTRIBUTION: The President, National Security
    Council, DoD, and USAF LIAISON
SOURCE: DoD Reports and Evaluations

SUBJECT: SR-71 Operations vs. Other Reconnais-
    sance Platforms

Stand-down of SR-71 "Blackbird" operations is recommended end of year, latest. Manned aircraft roles are largely superseded at this point by Keyhole, LaCrosse, and other orbiting reconnaissance platforms. Spy plane operations are expensive, especially considering the current budget climate. Also, they are, for the most part, obsolete when compared against satellites.

It is further recommended that a veteran officer from the program supervise the stand-down. NSC Adviser Murdoch has put forward the name of Maj. Gen. Scott Cartwright, who would be appropriate in light of his knowledge of "black programs" and his prestige as a senior member of the astronaut corps.

Quickest action urged to ensure smooth transition to full-time satellite surveillance of world trouble spots, pressure points, and arms control verification targets.

"Balls," Cartwright snorted. "This thing was written by some kid with a brand new Ph.D. and a calculator. Such people never did and never will bring back a smidgen of human or electronic intelligence from a trouble spot, as they so daintily put it."

Madeline Murdoch grinned ruefully. "Actually, the author's identity has been concealed. It was Avery Benedict."

"That skunk?"

"That skunk is likely to be the next director of CIA."

"Have mercy," Cartwright said. "Another egghead analyst." Madeline Murdoch made a face. Cartwright looked at her, the deep lines on his sun-baked face creased with worry. "No chance of going back on this?"

"Afraid not," she said. "Will you do it?"

"Have I got a choice? This suggestion looks like an order."

She smiled sadly and nodded. "It's you, or someone less qualified, Scott."

He sighed. "What the hell, Maddy. I'm a widower with

time on my hands. Might as well get the Blackbird a decent burying. But I'm telling you something, old girl.''

"What's that, Scott?" the national security adviser asked gently.

"You might as well be scuttling the space shuttle fleet," the general said directly. "Those Blackbirds are a national asset."

"Let's hope you're wrong, my dear General," she said, taking his arm as she admired the devastating scarlet sunset.

The desert wind blew tumbleweeds by in the darkness. Cartwright clicked his tongue sadly. He whistled for his grandson, then he and the boy climbed into his Corvette and led Madeline Murdoch a merry chase all the way on the twisting back roads to Gorman. She kept up, deftly following the red dots of the Corvette's brake lights. She had topped her class in evasive driving and security maneuvers at "the Farm." And she had made a point to rent the Taurus with the wicked turbocharged SHO engine. She knew Cartwright's driving.

— 2 —
Space Business

THE AIRSTRIP HAD BEEN CLEARED from the jungle on government land near an old prewar rubber plantation eighty kilometers south of Jakarta. The land within the fenced area had the raw look of a wound on nature. Tractors had bulldozed past the edge of the newly poured concrete, leaving deep cuts in the rich red earth, the earth that gave life to the endless sea of rubber forest beyond the fence. Within the airfield perimeter, the presence of humming satellite dishes and a new Tinkertoy control tower did little to dispel the impression that the verdant growth could roll over the little cleared space at any moment.

Between the barbed-wire fence and the forest was a line of machine-gun jeeps from the Indonesian army. It appeared their mission was to protect the aging silver Boeing 707 on the runway from the encroaching treeline.

"God, it's hot," Dewey Levitz, the copilot, said, wiping his brow repeatedly with an already sodden handkerchief. "We should get in the cabin before we melt in this."

"No can do, Dewey," Taggart, the flight captain, replied. "The protocol says we've got to wait for their officers and that bunch of smart-alecky Dutch scientists that built their little communications satellite."

As Taggart spoke and wiped his own perspiring forehead, he waved cheerfully at the line of machine gunners in jeeps at the end of the runway. The sergeant in command of the security detail nodded cheerlessly from behind his mirror sunglasses.

Taggart smiled tightly. "Those little buggers in the jeeps would kill us and cook us up for dinner if their old sarge told 'em to."

"Relax, Taggart," Levitz said. "We're in Indonesia, not Vietnam. This is a Dixie Airways milk run for an Indo-Dutch satellite consortium. You're not going to be taking any SAM fire when we put the wheels up. That war was over fifteen years ago."

Taggart lifted the soaking wet Dixie Airways cap from his balding head and fanned some wet air in his face. He quickly replaced the cap above his fringe of graying sideburns before the heat could do any more damage to his already sunburnt scalp. The pilot looked out at the jungle beyond the airstrip and turned his gaze again toward the men in the jeeps. One driver grinned at him. The others were as passionless as the sergeant behind the mirror sunglasses.

"There's no more war," Taggart whispered, almost to himself, his teeth tightly clenched. "Then why don't I fuckin' feel like there's no more war?"

Before Taggart could sink deeper into the black melancholy that periodically clouded his mood but never affected his flying, Dewey Levitz clapped him on the shoulder and pointed. "Here come the customers," he said.

A convoy of aged black Cadillacs rolled ponderously through the gate. Inside the limousines was a coterie of colonels draped in colorful ribbons and gold braid, each hidden behind the ubiquitous sunglasses that unofficially completed the uniform of the Indonesian army.

"It's show time," Taggart murmured. He squared his sagging shoulders in an approximation of attention and raised his right hand in an imitation of a salute. Exiting the Cadillacs, the Indonesian officers returned the salutes sharply and marched smartly toward the plane.

The army officers were followed by the blond Dutchman that Taggart knew only as Dr. Van Den Brugge, and Philo Williamson, the only American on the crew besides the pilots.

He was the technical rep from Space Business, the Texas firm that supplied the experimental Orion missile to propel the communications satellite into orbit.

Taggart followed the customers aboard his aging aircraft that he affectionately dubbed the *Silver Sow*. Before he and Levitz boarded, they gave one last glance at the Orion. Each unconsciously wanted to be certain that the contact wires connecting the missile to the wing pylon were secure.

"Looks like a Tomahawk," Taggart observed absently as he climbed onto the ladder.

"Say what?" Levitz asked, scuttling up the ladder behind his captain.

"Ah, it's funny, the line between war and peace," Taggart said as the pair stepped into their domain, the flight cabin. "Here we are launching a chunk of tin that'll help twenty million people talk to each other from an archipelago of remote islands."

"Yeah, so?" Levitz said, as he began the preflight checkout.

"So the missile we're hauling aloft looks like the one we carried on a B-52. It packed one butt-ugly nuke. Could've wasted most of Great Britain with it."

They secured the door and entered the cabin. Soon the airconditioning dried their sweat, freeing them to work. "You're crazy, Taggart," Levitz observed, waiting for the Dixie Air captain to begin his preflight check. "You're a war lover."

"Nope. I just don't trust people to be peaceful." The engines on the aging airliner whined to life.

As Taggart got tower clearance from the sing-song English voices inside the Tinkertoy structure at the end of the runway, the cadaverous head of Philo Williamson popped into the cabin. He was a jack-in-the-box of a man, who wore his pocket protectors full of fountain pens as proudly as any colonel displayed his medals.

"How you boys this fine morning?" he asked cheerfully, his accent heavily Texas and faintly Houston—Johnson Space Center. "Y'all ready for a zero anomaly day?"

"It's nearly noon, Philo," Taggart said acidly. Like many career Air Force officers, he had little tolerance for delay and little patience for civilians.

"Every program has a little slip now and then," Williamson said, his Adam's apple bobbing defensively. " 'Sides, we're almost airborne now. You boys are puttin' the good old U.S. of A. back into space."

"You mean we're hauling a piece of commercial space junk up for a Third World country," Taggart said.

"You got the wrong attitude, Captain," Williamson said, making a thumbs-up gesture common among people who didn't fly. "See you back on terra firma, old buddy."

Taggart rolled his eyes and throttled up, causing Williamson to grab the bulkhead to steady himself as the Dixie charter rolled forward. "Fasten your seat belt, Philo."

Nearly an hour late, the Space Business charter flown by the contract Dixie Airways crew was airborne, leaving the steaming jungle and the teeming multitudes huddled in Jakarta far below. Absently, Taggart wondered if the people of Indonesia would be grateful for the improved television and telephone service delivered by the satellite. Just as quickly, he decided it didn't matter to him.

At an altitude of thirty-five thousand feet, Taggart leveled off from a steady climb. He maintained altitude and the heading given him by Van Den Brugge. Taggart didn't like Van Den Brugge. The Dutch scientist was blond haired, with thin lips—and a white scar on his forehead that looked suspiciously like a shrapnel wound. A diffident man, he showed an evident distaste for Americans. Still, Dixie Airways had provided the best bid to take the Dutch satellite into orbit.

Their navigational course set by Van Den Brugge would take them out over the South China Sea, an area of operations Taggart knew well, having flown it many times on the downtown run to Hanoi. Halfway to Thailand the Orion missile separated from the Boeing wing pylon with a dry whoosh. Taggart heard the applause and cheering through the bulkhead, and he knew it was a great day for Indonesia. The satellite, attached to the missile, would hoist aloft into lower space. Then it would separate on its own boosters, traveling up into geosynchronous orbit about 22,300 miles above the earth. There it would deliver phone service to far-flung islands and television signals to remote villages that had yet to see a box with pictures in it. Somehow, oddly, Taggart was suddenly happy that after all the iron bombs he had dropped, he was finally helping to build a peaceful world. He rubbed his sunburnt neck and nodded to Levitz, allowing him to fly the plane for a while.

— 3 —
False Flag

SEATED IN THE COMMAND CUPOLA of his armored car, Jr. Lt. Viktor Borodin looked for a moment up at the distant stars and sighed as he watched the red glow of the rocket's glare disappear into deep space. At twenty-one, he found the world still full of wonders. It had been a grand day. His unit had acquitted itself well on maneuvers. And almost as a special, secret gift, he had just witnessed the launch of a giant Energia rocket from the Baikonur Cosmodrome, far away on the endless steppe.

"Today, the day we met victory and prevailed like our forefathers," he whispered to himself, utterly pleased with his own poetry. He closed his eyes and popped them open, sharpening his night vision. Before he unsnapped the flashlight from his shoulder harness, he stared long and hard into the night.

In the inky distance he could see the armored vehicles emplaced at their proper intervals. Just a smudge here and there to indicate them. His men observed good noise-and-light discipline. That, or they were sleeping. But no. Borodin was certain his boys were at their sentry posts. He snapped the red-filtered flashlight on, unable to resist the pleasure of examining the checksheet again.

15

For Borodin's armored infantry platoon, all check marks were in the excellent and superior columns. That day, his boys had secured the perimeter around the communications center for the Third All Arms Army. Borodin whistled thinly as he looked at the good marks for the hundredth time.

The gunner's hatch opened quietly, and Borodin turned to see the face of Stepan, his section sergeant. Beneath the camouflage face paint, Stepan grinned. He whispered, "Not a bad day's work, eh, Lieutenant Borodin?"

"Our best evaluation ever," the lieutenant replied. "There were lots of ways we could have balled it up. But we didn't. Even Uzbek conscripts can do a job when they have to."

Stepan nodded wisely. Both men twitched and looked at the hard ground in front of the command vehicle as they saw two dark figures approach. A man and a large dog padded lightly past Borodin's armored car.

"Pssst," the section sergeant hissed. "Where do you think you're going?"

The dark figure halted, and the dog came to heel. The dog handler saluted and whispered in broken Russian, "I go to check perimeter." Few Uzbeks were fluent in the mother tongue. "Get on, then," the sergeant snapped. "And be quiet!" The dark figure of the dog handler nodded and moved off into the night.

"Some tea, Lieutenant?"

Borodin accepted the canteen cup from his sergeant. They sipped the cold tea contentedly as the parachutes descended silently.

Four distinct clumping sounds, like potato sacks dropped in the company mess, announced the arrival of the paratroopers. One such sack landed with a metallic thud on the rear engine grate of the lieutenant's armored car. The lieutenant and sergeant suddenly found themselves staring into two blackened faces that smiled horribly at them.

"Spetznaz," the sergeant gasped as a sharp knife was drawn quietly across his throat, so close that he felt a warm trickle of blood.

"Shut up," one of the black faces ordered. "Don't struggle or we'll kill you. Believe it."

Two incredibly strong pairs of hands lifted the lieutenant

clear from the hatch. A third pair of hands shoved the sergeant back down into the vehicle. Hand grenades clattered into the belly of the armored car as the special action troops slammed the hatches shut.

"You are killing my men!" Borodin cried.

"It's sleep gas, fool," one of the black faces said, hoisting the lieutenant clear from the armored car and dropping him heavily on the ground. "The dog handler belonged to my team, Lieutenant. You should have checked more carefully for infiltrators."

The parachutists marched the lieutenant roughly beyond his outer perimeter of armored vehicles. They walked purposefully and with confidence that the way had been cleared for them. Ahead in the darkness, they heard the quiet hum of satellite dishes. The antennas on the black van buzzed like insects. At the door to the van, a pair of camouflaged paratroopers from the strike team stood sentry. When they saw the group from the armored car approach, they snapped to attention, holding their folding-stock carbines at the ready.

One paratrooper opened the door to the black van, like a chauffeur ushering in a carload of rich capitalists. The trio that pushed the hapless Lieutenant Borodin along strode past. The black-faced paratroopers ascended into the multihued light of the communications van, which was the size of a small house. It sat out on the empty steppe country like the tent of a mongol chieftain. As the paratroopers entered, about half the men and officers in the van rose to their feet. The others sat at their positions in front of a dizzying array of colored tracking screens and illuminated maps.

Some maps showed terrain and troop dispositions, including those of Warsaw Pact, Chinese, and NATO forces. Others were astral navigation charts, displaying in three dimensions the progress of satellite orbits over the Soviet Union and territories beyond the border of the motherland.

One map, a cubic screen with 3-D and color enhancement, displayed the outline of the United States and the Soviet satellites that were passing over it. The territory within the borders was identified by the Cyrillic letters CWA (USA), over the words Glavni Vrag, the Main Enemy. Lieutenant Borodin was wide-eyed with wonder as he gazed upon the complexity of the inside of the facility he had been charged to guard. He had never been inside such a place.

"Lights up!" ordered the parachutist who held the lieutenant roughly by his shoulder. The overhead ceiling lights came on, giving the room a sudden ordinary look. In the dimness it had appeared like a cross between a marvelous toy shop and the control room of one of the giant hydroelectric dams from the news programs.

"On your feet, everyone!" the black-faced paratrooper ordered. Then even those who had been gazing intently at their monitor screens rose to their feet and stood at attention. The paratrooper wore the shoulder boards of a general of the Soviet army and the broken nose and cauliflowered ear of a commando who had escaped his Afghani torturers.

"Look at this man and remember his face," the black-faced general ordered, holding the lieutenant as though he were a fish he had plucked from a stream. "You will not see him again. Punishment battalion. Siberia."

All remained silent. The arrays of machinery buzzed and hummed and occasionally beeped, but no human sound was heard. The men in the van held their breath in the presence of the fearsome-looking general. Borodin, who so recently looked at the stars in wonder, stared at his boots. He murmured something unintelligible.

"What's that?" the paratroop general said, batting the lieutenant on the shoulder. "Speak up, former Lieutenant! You must speak clearly when you address a general, particularly this general. I am Yevgeny Pavlovich Strelnikov!"

"Comrade General Strelnikov, my marks were excellent," Borodin muttered. "The field readiness evaluation went well. It went well, my General."

The black-faced general with the broken nose slapped the smooth-skinned lieutenant sharply on the cheek with his open hand. "You are the reason the motherland is knee deep in shit, former Lieutenant. Everyone believes their excellent evaluations. Everyone meets their quota according to the plan. But nothing ever gets done the way it should be."

"I don't understand," the lieutenant murmured.

"Of course you don't," the general snarled. "Paperwork reports don't matter. You should have stopped my infiltrators."

Motioning to the parachutists who escorted the luckless lieutenant into the van, the general jerked his head.

"Get him out of my sight." The Spetznaz troopers complied wordlessly, ushering the lieutenant out of the black van.

"Lights," the general said. The overhead lamps dimmed and the operators resumed work. As normal activity resumed, a lean white-haired man in the uniform of a colonel in signal communications stepped forward. He smiled and saluted the black-faced general. The general inclined his head and looked at the glowing hands of his illuminated Vostok watch.

"Yes, comrade General, you are on time. In fact, you effected the perimeter penetration thirty-seven seconds early."

"Have you got a kopek, comrade Colonel?" the paratroop general asked in a mild tone. The colonel nodded his equine head and presented a copper coin to the general. It was an old coin, with the somber face of Josef Stalin stamped on it. The general smiled and pocketed the coin.

"Pamyat," the general murmured. The colonel nodded and smiled. "Here's to Memory," he replied.

"I wish to be informed of current operational affairs."

"Then, welcome to Operation False Flag, my General," the horse-headed colonel said with a knowing grin.

"Report to me on progress of the south Asian satellite project."

"Come and see for yourself," the colonel replied. "As I said, you were early. You can see the component separation before the Dutch toy reaches geosynchronous orbit."

The general followed the colonel into an inner chamber in the black van.

— 4 —
The Blue Cube

Sunnyvale, California

THE LOSS OF PICTURE ON the monitor screen was sudden and devastating in its implication. Soon a small crowd of Air Force officers and senior enlisted men gathered around the screen, each muttering or whispering at different decibel levels.

The blank screen that had caught everyone's attention so suddenly was monitored by a young Air Force captain assigned to the Consolidated Space Test Center in the heart of California's Silicon Valley. Nestled between a NASA research center and the Lockheed Space and Missiles Company, the windowless powder-blue building was known simply as "the Blue Cube." Personnel at the Cube held responsibility for monitoring every one of the fifty-plus satellites in the Air Force inventory and for keeping track of every piece of space junk that floated about in lower orbit. No one allowed inside the Cube held less than a Top Secret clearance.

"Gimme a situation report, Captain," demanded the lieutenant colonel who was acting as floor supervisor.

The captain at the monitor display, an attractive young woman with a silver-blond pageboy haircut, tersely responded, "Sitrep follows, sir. We've just lost a significant portion of overhead surveillance from the Middle East operations area."

"I'm aware that I'm looking at a blank screen, Captain Ingersoll," the colonel said. "Draw me a picture of what you think happened."

Captain Eva Ingersoll looked up at the colonel and the press of faces surrounding her. Her own face mirrored their deep concern and alarm. "We've lost a Keyhole-11 satellite, sir. Signal. Power signature. Everything. It's just gone."

"That bird wasn't scheduled to go off-line for a year, Captain. What happened?"

"I don't know," she whispered. "It just bleeped off the screen."

The KH-11 that had so suddenly ceased transmission of its real-time information was an aging but effective solar-powered satellite responsible for supplying the best view the United States could gather from an overhead surveillance platform. It was the spy satellite that snooped on Israel and the half-dozen Arab states that formed the world's hottest crisis region.

"Get me Colorado Springs on the line," the colonel ordered.

"Falcon station at Colorado Springs is getting the same picture, sir," a major called from across the room. "No joy on the Keyhole."

Within seconds, different operators in the room full of bulky IBM mainframe computers called in the same result from tracking stations in Guam, Spain, and Australia, as well as the main ground tracking station at White Sands, New Mexico.

Beads of sweat poured down the lieutenant colonel's closely cropped gray head. His hand shaking, he accepted a gold telephone handed him by one of the half-dozen officers crowding around him. "It's Fort Meade, sir," the major said. "National Security Agency."

"Jesus. NSA knows about this already?" The colonel took the phone.

"Looks like we all know, Colonel. It's the admiral," the major said, trying to warn his colonel. The colonel winced.

"Yeah," he said, taking the phone. "Yeah. . . . Yes, sir. We lost a bird. A big bird. Middle East ops area. . . . No, sir. I don't know how, sir. It wasn't scheduled to go down. It's an anomalous event."

The colonel listened patiently to the barrage of questions from the admiral, the man who commanded the vast intelligence apparatus of the National Security Agency based at Fort Meade in the Maryland suburbs of Washington. The colonel, who wished mightily that a general would appear to intercede for him, gave the admiral the only answers he had about the disappearance of the KH-11.

"Sir, there's nothing we can attribute to the Russians as far as I know. Their last launch took place at the Baikonur Cosmodrome in Kazakhstan. But that was a heavy-lift vehicle hauling one of their own snoopers aloft."

Another question from Fort Meade. The colonel pondered. He gazed across the room, looking for a face with an answer. His gaze came to rest on the young woman with the captain's bars who had initially alerted him to the Keyhole satellite failure.

"What other launch activity have we monitored today, Ingersoll? NSA wants to know, and I want to know myself."

"Nothing significant, sir," the young woman replied.

"Be more specific, dammit, Captain."

"The only launch activity scheduled was an announced project of the Indonesian government. They were putting a communications satellite up using one of the Space Business missiles out of Texas."

"That's not it," the colonel said. "That's a Third World bird with a TV signal on it. I want to know about anything, anything that could resemble launch of an antisatellite weapon. Scan the boards."

The captain shook her head. "Nothing out of the Soviet Union," she answered, surveying an overhead screen that looked like an arrival and departure list for an airline. "Nothing out of China. Nothing out of France by way of Ariane in Guyana. Nothing."

The colonel promised to keep the admiral briefed. Hanging up, the colonel muttered, "I just wonder what the hell I'm going to tell my boss."

The gold phone rang again as the harried colonel was scribbling notes to himself on an acetate pad. It was the president's national security adviser, Madeline Murdoch. She also wanted to know what the hell was going on.

* * *

The Indo-Dutch television satellite began transmitting as soon as it achieved orbit, to the great satisfaction of all parties concerned, including the people in the remote villages of Sumatra and Java.

Not least among those who were thrilled with the project were members of the boards of Space Business and Dixie Air, the American companies that had helped the Indonesian-Dutch consortium to fire the satellite into space, proving the effectiveness of the new Orion missile.

In Houston the men of Space Business and Dixie Air toasted with champagne, hailing a new day for private-sector enterprise in space.

In Jakarta, champagne toasts were delayed because of the strict ritual observed by the Moslem colonels who had footed the bill for the Dutch satellite launch. Fruit juice was served instead.

In the Kazakhstan Soviet Socialist Republic, the Dixie Air satellite-missile launch was celebrated with the spicy Pertsovka vodka. The toast was lifted by the black-faced Spetznaz paratroop general and the white-haired colonel, who celebrated because of what they had seen from their marvelous black van.

The Russian officers drank to success because an hour after the Indonesian satellite went on line, a component separated from the main body of the signals transmitter 150 miles above the earth.

The component, a titanium shaft about the size of an umbrella, boosted away from the satellite and powered itself through lower orbit, following the path assigned to it by the Soviet army operators in the van far below on the Kirgiz Steppe. The kinetic energy weapon, copied from an American "Star Wars" design, flew to its target like a silent arrow.

The ASAT weapon was the brainchild of the man known as Dr. Emil Van Den Brugge, the thin-lipped Dutch scientist aboard the Dixie Air charter, who was actually an operative of GRU, the Soviet military intelligence arm.

The small titanium shaft struck the Keyhole-11 satellite like a jackhammer breaking concrete, instantly blacking out U.S. overhead surveillance of a critical sector of the Middle East.

A small cheer rose from the unit personnel assigned to the

van on the Kirgiz Steppe. The tracking monitors indicated a clean kill.

"To the ultimate success of Operation False Flag," General Strelnikov said, pouring another glass of Pertsovka.

"To victory for the motherland," the white-haired colonel agreed, lifting his glass.

"Pamyat," the general said, toasting again.

"Memory," the colonel said. "And death to all fools on the Politburo."

The men in the van on the Kirgiz Steppe were alone in the knowledge that a Russian-built ASAT weapon carried aloft by an American charter plane had killed a Keyhole satellite, effectively putting blinders on U.S. surveillance of the Middle East for an indefinite period.

For the moment, their secret was safe from the U.S. Air Force, the governments of the Netherlands and Indonesia, and the men of the Politburo. The allegiance held by the black-faced paratroop general and the white-haired colonel was very exclusive indeed. They swore loyalty only to a small group called Pamyat, or Memory. The members of this secret order remained unknown even to the KGB.

— 5 —
The Banya

THE TRIO, EACH NAKED AS an egg, nested around the steam that rose from the grate in one of the great baths of Moscow. They seated themselves delicately on the wooden benches and gazed with sweaty contentment out at the colonnade of Romanesque pillars beyond the gauzy curtain that separated them from the others taking steam in the *banya*. Kolchak, the most senior, sat first; next to sit was Strelnikov, the powerfully muscled paratrooper; and third, Kulitsyn, the skeletal, white-haired colonel of signals.

Strelnikov's physique displayed the soldier's tan—brown to the collar and up to mid-forearms on an otherwise pale body. The lean signals colonel and ample Kolchak, both staff men for many years, wore the pale skins of a cold climate. It fell to the colonel to slice the cucumbers, butter the bread, and pour the spiced vodka, as the steam filtered around them in the All Union Railroad Workers' Bath a few blocks from the Defense Ministry in the Arbat.

"So, Yevgeny Pavlovich, you are satisfied with what you saw down in Kazakhstan?" General Kolchak asked.

"Do you think the KGB has posted this facility with listening

25

devices?'' Strelnikov fired back, a note of genuine alarm in his voice.

Kulitsyn shook his head and flashed a smile that revealed his steel teeth. "They are too busy monitoring the progress of democracy and scratching their asses trying to decide what they are going to do about it," the colonel said. "The committee for state security has so many new enemies in the outlying republics that they hardly have time for us, the old ones. The army is the least of their troubles these days. In fact, we are allied as their cat's paw. To put down riots, you need troops."

Kolchak, still heavily muscled in middle age, laughed hoarsely, making his corpulent belly shake. "There are no listening devices in the railroad workers' baths."

The signals colonel nodded. Strelnikov, somewhat reassured, remained grave in his expression, nevertheless. "What has been the American response to the destruction of their satellite?"

General Kolchak munched his black bread thoughtfully. He held his vodka glass in salute, and the three downed their drinks. "No response at all. Their negotiators appear so eager for an accommodation in the arms race that they have not peeped."

Strelnikov shook his head somberly. "Eventually, they will know how their surveillance platform was destroyed. They will complain. There will be an inquiry."

"That is why we must move soon," General Kolchak said. "I ask you again, Yevgeny Pavlovich. Were you satisfied with your evaluation of security at the Kazakhstan tracking station?"

"As your representative from GRU, the military intelligence arm, I must tell you I fear most the threat of wagging tongues," Strelnikov said, pouring himself and his fellow bathers a second glass of vodka. "Such chatterers ended the hopes of the Decembrists, and even a whispered joke in Stalin's day could send a man to the wall."

General Kolchak nodded. "Remember, I lived through those days. So it is the KGB you fear, then?"

Strelnikov nodded and held up his hands. "Of course. The army is rotten like weevils with Komitet provocateurs."

"But not in Kazakhstan," Kulitsyn said, buttering more

bread for his senior officers and placing delicate strips of cucumber on the slices. "Kazakhstan remains secure."

"You had better hope so," the naked paratroop general said, rubbing the thick wall of cartilage that formed the hump of his broken nose. "If we fail, our heads will rest on pikes along the Kremlin wall."

"If we fail, our heads deserve such a fate," the signals colonel said.

"I fear the consequences of our actions, comrades," General Strelnikov said urgently. "Our army has no history of success in revolt. Recall the Decembrists. They were hanged or shipped to Siberia. Or both."

Kolchak stared at Strelnikov as though he were trying to read his soul in the sweat that streamed from the paratroop officer's forehead onto his lips. Kolchak's brown eyes, the deep brown of a true great Russian, held shrewd peasant humor in them. Burly, hairy, and great in size, the senior staff general leaned forward conspiratorially and winked at Strelnikov.

"Strelnikov, did you by chance fight in the Great Patriotic War to defeat the Hitlerite fascists?" the senior general asked.

"You know, General Kolchak, that I did not. I am too young. My wars were wars of national liberation."

Kolchak nodded reflectively and ran his sweaty fingers through his damp hair that remained black as it was the day he rode his tank into Berlin. "Yes. Wars of liberation. You paratroopers always had a taste for quick combat. Hit and run."

The senior general picked up the vodka bottle himself and poured it for his officers. He raised his own glass, and the trio downed their liquor together. "Let me tell you how it was for me, Strelnikov," Kolchak said. "When I was a lieutenant, we raced into Berlin sure in the knowledge that we had defeated the foe. After we leveled the city, punished the fascists, and took their women, we felt confident that the Red Army would raise its flag from the Urals to the Atlantic."

"But that would have been impossible," Strelnikov said. "Not without another world war."

Kolchak nodded. "Yes. But we victorious soldiers of the Red Army believed it possible. Then we discovered who the real enemy was."

The signals colonel busied himself with the bread. Steam poured into the alcove and all three men exhaled deeply as the clouds of boiling water rose about them. "The real enemy, of course, were the little tsars on the Politburo," Kolchak said.

"And Stalin?"

Kolchak spat in the metal grate beneath their feet where the steam bubbled from. "For the man himself, I say he was a monster. He executed the ablest of his generals. He also murdered most of the brethren in your service arm, the intelligence service of the military. Lavrenti Beria did it for him. He killed all the GRU men."

"So, General, why then do we swear by the coin that bears such a hated name?" Strelnikov asked, his tone honestly perplexed.

"Because he was a man, at least!" Kolchak growled. "He did not give victory away. Ruthlessly, he took what he needed and used it. Our so-called leaders in the Kremlin have forgotten how to do that. Thus is our great nation fading on the world stage."

"Pamyat," the white-haired signals colonel said, raising his glass. "Memory. The memory of great deeds." The three men drank.

Kolchak gazed out into the steam. Feeling confident that they were alone, he poked Strelnikov in the chest with a great cigar of a finger to emphasize his point. "Every time we gained the upper hand, the political hooligans gave it back. The missiles in Cuba. Afghanistan. When we could have prevailed, Khruschev or some other little tsar gave it away."

"It won't happen again," the colonel said.

"Not if we succeed," Kolchak added gravely.

"And if we fail, we go to the wall at Lubyanka," Strelnikov said.

"Here's to luck," Kulitsyn said, pouring a fresh round from a new bottle. "Luck and the devil."

Kolchak stood up heavily, standing on his great hairy haunches. "We'll need luck and the devil—and a bit of help from the fucking fascist Germans to pull this one off."

"What's that you say?" Strelnikov said, his ears perking. Kolchak shook his large head heavily. "Nothing you need to know yet, dear General. Just keep your Spetznaz troops ready to move when they are called on.''

The general marched his bulk from the alcove to the great blue-tiled pool that formed the center of the colonnade in the All Union Railroad Workers' Bath. He stepped heavily into the cool water, looking all the while as though he were a bear attempting to grab a salmon and rend its flesh with his sharp teeth. Returning from the bath, he allowed the signals colonel to beat his flesh with a birch switch until he was as red as a battle flag. He grinned, accepted another vodka, and raised his great hairy arm in toast.

"So that is our plot, then?" Strelnikov said. "A soldiers' revolt? A coup d'état?"

Kolchak spit in the grate, where his spittle sizzled. "Nothing so crude, dear Strelnikov. Soviet soldiers are not traitors. We would not revolt against the very state that we serve."

Strelnikov asked, "What, then?"

"We are soldiers. Soldiers need wars," Kolchak replied. "To remain strong, nations need wars. If we find the war, the state will give us the laurels and stop their nonsensical flirtation with so-called democracy."

"What war? With the United States?" Strelnikov asked.

"Of course not," General Kolchak sneered. "That's the endgame."

"Then, where?"

General Kolchak grinned his peasant grin, showing his own teeth, adorned in gold instead of steel. "General war in the Middle East. That will put the Red Army back in the saddle and let those thumbsuckers in the Politburo take a backseat for a while."

Paratroop General Yevgeny Pavlovich Strelnikov whistled, and the signals colonel sighed as he poured more water on the hot rocks, raising the temperature in the baths to a nearly unbearable level of heat.

— 6 —
Keyhole Whisperings

FOLLOWING THE PRESIDENT OF THE United States into a lead-lined secure room a hundred steps from the Oval Office, Madeline Murdoch found it hard to remain silent until the electronic door sealed itself. As she hurried along, the rubbery squeak of her Bass Weejuns walking shoes was picked up by the microwave monitors in the Soviet Embassy on Sixteenth Street a few blocks distant. The door shut.

"God, Mr. President," she exclaimed with uncharacteristic emotion. "We've got to do something."

"Calm yourself, Madeline," the president said, waving his hand airily and beckoning her to sit at the small conference table.

"Mr. President," she blurted. "Do you realize the import of the Keyhole satellite loss? We are blind in the Middle East."

Settling himself in his leather conference chair, the president worked hard at fiddling with a pipe nail that he'd inserted into the bowl of a favorite briar. With studied care, he scraped the carbon cake from the inside of the pipe bowl. Then he began filling the briar with Georgetown Burley.

"Mr. President," Madeline Murdoch persisted. "You heard me, sir? I say we are blind in the Middle East."

Lighting the pipe and puffing with satisfaction, the president waved the match out. "Geez, Madeline, don't you think you're overdramatizing a bit? It's not like we haven't got CIA out there."

"Mr. President, CIA is a weak asset at the moment," Madeline Murdoch asserted. "Beirut station is on life support, and Jerusalem is hobbled as usual by its proximity to Mossad. The Egyptians don't trust us. We need overhead reconnaissance."

"You're not trying to revive the Blackbird thing, are you, Madeline?" the president said, studying his nails as he smoked. "That's a dead horse. Spy planes cost too much money and cause a ruckus over at State. Besides, Avery Benedict doesn't want the Air Force getting onto CIA's reservation. Why make waves?"

"Good God, sir!" Madeline Murdoch nearly shouted. "We have no satellite. Its loss may have been a hostile act."

The president looked up at his security adviser, displaying the first hint of curiosity. "Avery didn't tell me that," he said. "A hostile act by whom?"

Madeline Murdoch bowed her head. "I don't know. But we've got to find out."

"Well, that's CIA's job," the president said with finality, tamping the tobacco in the bowl of his pipe. "They'll study it and get back to you."

"We need the Middle East coverage, sir," Madeline Murdoch said urgently. "Without it, something nasty could sneak up and bite us."

The president nodded, ran his fingers through his thinning hair, and packed some more tobacco into his pipe. "Yes, yes, I see. You go ahead, then. Do what you have to with the means at hand. Just don't break the law, don't spend too much money, and keep me informed." In order of importance, the president cited the priorities of his administration.

—— 7 ——
The Wolf's Lair

Rastenburg, East Germany
(last medium-range missile site in East Germany)

THE SMELL OF CORDITE HUNG heavily in the woods outside the concrete bunker. Bulky figures in rubber suits and gas masks weaved in and out of the smoke, some in pairs carrying the body of a comrade. Sporadic machine-gun fire could be heard from the woods as the smoke cleared, giving way to a gray dawn in East Prussia.

In the woods surrounding the bunker complex, a mist hung from the trees, leaving drops of moisture on the pine needles. A slight breeze kicked up, pushing the mist away from the control complex. The bulky figures in their nightmarish rubber suits walked among the bodies that lay on the ground just outside the low-slung bunker. Some of the bodies twitched and convulsed. They were being tagged.

A klaxon sounded a long blast, and a disembodied voice from a bullhorn announced, ''All clear,'' in German and then in Russian. The electronic gate to the complex swung open, and a sealed staff car with smoked-glass windows and battle flags of the Soviet general staff rolled onto the gravel road that led to the main building.

The car halted in front of the building, and two men in rubber protective suits emerged from it. They accepted the challenge of two gas-masked guards who stood with their folding-stock carbines at the ready. The men from the car displayed a pair of identity cards, and the guards, soldiers of the disintegrating German Democratic Republic's crack army, came to attention in their bulky suits.

The Soviet officers saluted and entered the bunker. Once inside, they removed their hooded masks. As they climbed out of their rubber suits, a dozen East German staff officers and men who had been busily working away at the map tables and microwave equipment came to attention. The only sound in the room was that of boots clicking and some static from the radios.

The Soviet officers hung their suits on a hook and turned to face their rigid hosts. General Kolchak wore the field dress uniform of a Soviet general of armies, complete with medals, the Order of Lenin, Order of the Red Banner, and Order of the Red Star. He was attended by the signals colonel Kulitsyn.

Walking stiffly toward the Soviet officers was an older man in a general's uniform with a destroyed face and shaven skull. Half his face was covered with a metal plate held in place by elastic bands. He did his best to disguise his limp with a precise marching step. He came to a halt and saluted. Then, in a gesture that seemed out of character in an age of missiles, he bowed deeply.

"Herr General Yuri Stepanovich Kolchak," the shaven-headed officer said grandly, rising from his bow. "All that you see before you is at your disposal."

General Kolchak nodded sagely. "I know that, General Grunfeld. Or else I would not be commander of Soviet forces in the German Democratic Republic." He returned the salute perfunctorily. "Your men gave my men a bad time today. I think you actually killed one or two of them."

"A realistic training environment is essential to maintaining security at missile sites," Grunfeld said, evenly. "We fought the way that committed socialists defending their fatherland should fight."

"So you don't mind the idea of a live-nerve-gas drill, eh?" General Kolchak queried.

"It was not my men who died, General," Grunfeld replied.

The Soviet general smiled thinly. "Did you execute any partisans during our little security drill?"

A ghastly crack of a smile turned up at the edge of General Grunfeld's steel face plate. "The Soviet army has taught the army of the German Democratic Republic how to adhere to the Geneva Convention."

The staff men surrounding the three officers stood still as statues—unblinking and, to all intents and purposes, unhearing. It seemed as though the missile communications center was a waxworks.

"I'd like to see you in your office, General," Kolchak said, speaking Russian and so requiring Grunfeld to answer in kind.

"Of course," Grunfeld said. He executed a half-bow and pointed to the steel door. Peering at his staff, General Grunfeld nodded, and they returned to work as though the attack on the missile site's perimeter and the Soviet general's arrival had never happened.

Grunfeld's office was spartan. Inside reinforced concrete walls there was a wooden desk, an ancient chair, and an intercom. The desk contained neat file stacks and a single text, Clausewitz's *On War*.

The room was absent of medal citations or plaques from previous commands. The walls were bare except for two maps. One of the border area that still separated the German Democratic Republic from the West Zone. A second map adorned with blue pins showed where East German soldiers were deployed as volunteers assisting socialist governments worldwide. Libya, Angola, Vietnam, Nicaragua, and half a dozen other outposts of the Third World displayed blue pins. Many pins had been removed recently, with the crack GDR troops coming home to an uncertain future.

Grunfeld waited until Kolchak seated himself before taking his own place behind his desk. As the two generals seated themselves, regarding each other like card players, Colonel Kulitsyn removed an electronic wand from his uniform smock. He ran it up and down the walls of Grunfeld's office.

"Your caution is admirable, comrade Colonel," Grunfeld said. "But the room is clean. My own people are responsible for detecting listening devices."

The colonel nodded but continued his probe. Finishing his inspection, he remained standing until General Kolchak pointed to a wooden chair. Finally Kolchak spoke.

"You were captured not far from here at the end of the war, were you not?"

"You know that. I was the rear-guard, last-ditch defense on the Wolf's Lair, the madman's forward outpost at Rastenburg."

"So long ago," Kolchak observed. "Yet it seems like yesterday. I was just a boy with Fifty-seventh Tank Army. How we wanted to get to your precious Berlin."

"And so you did," Grunfeld said.

"We fought so ferociously. There were causes then that a man could give his life for gladly," Kolchak observed. Grunfeld said nothing.

General Kolchak crossed his knees and regarded a speck of mud on his boots, which were made of fine German leather. "We had such energy then," he continued. "I can hardly believe now that I am the man who shot your face to pieces."

"I believe it," Grunfeld said. "We were soldiers. It was war. I was trying to escape. You did your duty."

"And now we are friends. Is that not strange, comrade General?"

"Now we are allies," Grunfeld said, correcting him. "It is not strange if one studies history."

Kolchak snorted. "You became such a student of Marx after we offered you the choice to become a communist or face the wall. Were you as determined a Hitlerite?"

"A man who is shot like a dog and survives becomes a good listener. Perhaps he becomes wiser. Particularly in an Ivan work camp."

Kolchak laughed. Grunfeld shuffled papers on his desk and gazed placidly at the Russian general. He could wait all day. It was the stoicism of the work camp combined with Prussian discipline.

"They are going to shut this facility down," Kolchak said finally.

"Who is?" Grunfeld asked, puzzled.

"The Combined Commission on Arms Control, convened in Vienna. They put the ink to paper this morning. And Warsaw

Pact high command affirmed that the dismantling of the Rastenburg medium-range missile launch platforms would begin by the start of the new year. It comes as no surprise that the East German army will be demobilized with the signing of the treaties.''

Grunfeld rose from his chair, seized by emotion. He walked to the map and put his hands on it. ''Warsaw Pact high command decides nothing!'' the German general snarled. ''Such a decision could only be taken in Moscow.''

Kolchak shrugged his bearish shoulders. ''And, of course, it was. That is the way of it these days. By the new year the size of the combined Soviet forces will be shrunk by a third. Thousands of officers, from general rank on down, will be cashiered or pensioned off.''

''For what?'' Grunfeld demanded, genuinely angry.

''For peace,'' Kolchak said wryly. ''It seems our masters in Moscow believe peace is breaking out all over. Peace with honor. Peace in our time.''

''So this is what it comes to,'' Grunfeld snarled, ''an accommodation with the West?''

''So it would seem, unless we do something about it,'' Kulitsyn said, speaking for the first time.

''What is your man suggesting, comrade General?'' Grunfeld demanded, his ruined face wrinkling in bewilderment.

''He is proposing a change of command,'' General Kolchak said. ''Such a change of command would be accompanied by a change in thinking at the top, the very top of the Politburo.''

''You are speaking madness,'' the German general said. ''In Stalin's days such words would precede a bullet in the neck.''

''But Stalin is gone,'' Kolchak said softly, almost in a whisper. ''Today we serve a very different bunch.''

Grunfeld shook his head mechanically. ''If this is a provocation to test my loyalty, I would have expected more from you after all these years, comrade General Kolchak.''

Kolchak sniffed. He removed a pack of Troika cigarettes from his pocket. The signals colonel lit the loosely packed tobacco for the general, who leaned back in his uncomfortable wooden chair and puffed contentedly. Evidently he was enjoying his German counterpart's confusion.

''How long since you've seen combat, Grunfeld?''

The German general shrugged. "The last time was Angola."

"How would you like some real fighting?"

"What are we discussing, comrade General?"

Kolchak puffed on his cigarette and spat a few loose flakes. "I am proposing that we deploy your unit in the Middle East forthwith in an advisory capacity near a border with the fascist Zionists."

"My men are ready to travel on an hour's notice," Grunfeld said. "But for what purpose?"

"I propose that, instead of allowing your crack troops to be disbanded or absorbed into the West, you deploy your brigade of missiles, tanks, artillery, and ground attack aircraft near the Solomon Heights and that you make preparation to invade the state of Israel."

Grunfeld put his hand on his shaven head and rubbed it on some of the pink scar tissue above the steel plate. Finally he looked at the Russian general in disbelief. "What do the Jews have to do with the Warsaw Pact?"

"May I remind you, General, the Jews now possess missiles that can hit Kiev," Kolchak said brusquely. "There are grounds for a preemptive strike—the Soviet Union would be within its rights. But that's not my worry. And that's not my plan."

"You have my complete attention, comrade General," the German general said coolly.

"Every day I read the news on the *TASS* printers. Troop cuts. Disarmament. Failing agriculture. Nationalism in the Soviet republics. Elections. Confusion. Religion!" The last word Kolchak spat out.

"We propose a remedy for this," the Soviet signals colonel said.

"Please continue," Grunfeld said.

"A socialist military government," Kulitsyn continued crisply. "Replacement of the Politburo is the only way to ensure the Soviet Union will reach the next century intact."

"What's that? A putsch?" Grunfeld asked, his scarred face coming alive with interest.

"Less than that—and more," Kolchak said shrewdly. "A short and nasty Mideast war to bring the Politburo to its senses. To show it that it cannot disregard the Red Army."

Grunfeld stared long and hard at the man who had shot him so many years before. He stared, fascinated, his emotions caught between admiration and loathing. "I can see now why Stalin purged his generals," Grunfeld said slowly, rolling each word from his tongue. "Hitler did the same."

"We could do worse than Stalin these days," Kolchak said somberly.

"So you say," Grunfeld said wryly. "And my part in this mad Bonapartist scheme, comrade General?"

"You're my iron fist, Grunfeld," Kolchak responded, his teeth flashing in a feral grin. "You will lead an armored and airborne raid on the Israeli missile sites in the Negev. War breaks out. The Red Army takes charge—at home and abroad."

Grunfeld squinted narrowly at the commander of Soviet forces in Germany. "How well have you worked this out? The German general staff tried such a stunt once. The Führer hanged them from meat hooks."

"Like yourself, General, I am a student of history. My comrades have studied their lessons."

"And who are your comrades?"

Kolchak chuckled dryly and said nothing for a moment. When he spoke, he spoke confidently. "My people have already disabled an American surveillance satellite. That should give you time to get your men deployed to the Federated Socialist Republic of Tarak, the country of choice for your staging area. It commands high ground above the Zionist fortifications."

"And if I refuse to become a conspirator?"

Kulitsyn smiled, his steel teeth flashing. "The comrade general will have you shot."

"Dear Colonel," Grunfeld said, almost wearily, "the comrade general has already done that once. It made me a better soldier. What am I offered if we succeed? I know my reward if you fail."

"Command of all armed forces in the east zone of Democratic Germany. And greater autonomy with the enhancement of trust between our two nations," Kolchak said, offering his hairy hand. "So, General, you are with us, then?"

Grunfeld nodded precisely, as he gripped the Russian general's hand. He nodded his ruined map of a face vigorously.

"At my age there's not enough important work to do," Grunfeld observed. "And if I do nothing, my army will be disbanded in the madness of reunification. But tell me, comrade General. How does a single combined arms brigade invade the best-equipped and combat-proven nation in the Middle East? The Jews are no longer meek. They fight. They make a habit of beating your client states in the region."

Kolchak rose. "You'll need to increase your chemical warfare drill. You need an equalizer. I'm going to give it to you."

"My men will acquit themselves," Grunfeld said, his voice filled with somber certainty. "They are German soldiers. They are not like the weak ones streaming West to sell their honor for a few consumer goods." Grunfeld's lips curled in disdain beneath the metal plate. "I built the Berlin Wall, brick by brick. Now the politicians take it away."

"Just so," Kolchak said, smiling. "It will be different when we take charge."

"You will need this," Kulitsyn said, approaching the German general's desk. "It will help you when you request matériel and in getting your orders processed."

The Russian colonel handed Grunfeld a coin with the face of Josef Stalin on it. Grunfeld regarded the dictator's face, both fascinated and repelled by the visage of the man who had inflicted such misery on his homeland, had imprisoned him, then promoted him to general's rank.

"What does it mean?" Grunfeld asked.

"Pamyat," the colonel said. "Our old Russian word for memory."

"Our order stands for memory of the way things were, and the way they should be," Kolchak said. "And so it stands also for the future. A disciplined future," he added, squaring his massive bearlike shoulders.

Grunfeld stared at the copper kopek. "Old dreams die hard," he murmured. The Russian general and his aide rose and took their leave.

— 8 —
Blackbird Sweep

Airborne over Kabul

LT. COL. ADAM GLASSMAN MADE a precise input adjustment on the controls of the sleek black airplane he was piloting eighty-five thousand feet above the earth. He handled the stick of the SR-71 like a surgeon would a scalpel. At Mach 3, slightly faster than 2,300 miles per hour, a one-degree pitch change could plunge the Blackbird three thousand feet or buck it into an equally severe climb.

Glassman loved the Blackbird, even though it was a severe mistress, demanding his attention every second even on autopilot with the astral inertial navigation system functioning. He loved the plane as though it were a haughty, beautiful woman who demanded—and got—the full attention of her suitors. "Where are we, Wolfman?" Glassman asked his reconnaissance systems operator.

"About thirteen nautical miles above the lovely tourist capital of Kabul. Would you like to drop down to sample the local color and maybe try the native brew?"

"Stolichnaya?"

"Probably something they fermented from goat's milk."

"The locals don't drink. It's against their religion."

"Good thing. Hang out long enough with the Russkies and

you pick up bad habits. We probably wouldn't be welcome anyway.''

"Gimme a system status report.''

"Cameras and sensors are nominal,'' replied the RSO, whose real name was Maj. Ed Rogers. "We are nearly over target and ready to align sensors on other targets of opportunity.''

The mission called for the Blackbird to make a one-minute pass over Kabul. During that minute the black plane's sensors would sweep a sixty-mile-wide area that was forty miles long, photographing the tank parks with their armored columns, the helicopter landing fields, and the airstrips for the MiG interceptors that were scrambling even as the Blackbird passed over. Especially wanted were clear, high-resolution photographs of the missile launchers emplaced on the dusty plains outside Kabul. Were Russian crews manning them, or locals?

"How much longer in sweep mode, Wolfman?'' Glassman inquired, as the black plane pitched its shovel nose delicately at three times the speed of sound.

"About another two-zero seconds, good buddy. You should know—my systems indicate a radar attempting to lock on.''

"Would it be a MiG?'' Glassman asked.

"Nope. Probable SAM battery launch. Gimme five more seconds over the objective,'' Rogers demanded as his scopes lighted with the firefly indications of hostile approaches. Still, Rogers kept the ultrasensitive nose-mounted cameras humming.

On the ground far below, the SAM battery crews shouted instructions to one another and looked in rapt fascination at the sight on their radar screens. Though the blip was small, they knew it was a large plane to fly so high and still be seen.

One gunner, with superstitious awe, murmured it might be the American "Stealth bomber.'' Yet the plane they tracked was older than many of the gunners, having rolled off a small, secret California assembly line in 1962.

The surface-to-air missiles cleared their launch tubes with a dry blast and sailed toward space. In a few seconds they left only white fiery tails that looked like comets in the pale blue sky.

"Wolfman,'' Glassman announced, "it's time to go.''

"Affirmative.''

The SR-71 radar tracked the missiles hurtling furiously skyward in pursuit of its glowing tailpipes, and Glassman opened the throttle, the G forces flattening his body like a pancake. But the flier whose call sign was "Bookworm" got what he ordered, pushing the Blackbird beyond Mach 3 and up to the edge of outer space, where, like a descending astronaut, he could watch the earth's curve.

"Did we get what we wanted?" Glassman inquired.

" 'Course we did," the RSO replied confidently.

The Soviet battery commander whistled quietly as he watched the blip vanish into the classified region of the upper atmosphere, somewhere above ninety thousand feet.

—— 9 ——
The Sabrina Knot

London

THE DARK SKY THAT HAD lowered all morning made good its threat. The fine mist that dropped from the grayish black clouds turned to showers, and the showers soon became a downpour on the rich rolling green of Hyde Park. Even the shaggy Marxist on the soapbox was chased indoors. As raindrops the size of fingerlings hit the busy street outside, a ripple of thunder rumbled. Adam Glassman smiled and straightened the collar of his damp Burberry's trench coat, glad to be inside among the bookshelves, looking out at the wet streets as Londoners scurried for the Hyde Park tube station or bravely popped their umbrellas.

Glassman persisted in his hunt of the shelves, picking up novels, inhaling the musty smell of the books gratefully. Sighing with the indecision of the serious browser, he wandered the shelves to the history section and pulled down *The Proud Tower* by Barbara Tuchman. He read the introduction with the same intensity he applied to preflight check on the Blackbird.

The bookstore began to fill with refugees from the cloudburst, the little bell at the door tinkling insistently. Each among the collection of raincoats, black bowlers, and porkpie hats murmured, "Sorry, sorry." Glassman read, ignoring the sound of the bell.

When Glassman looked up from Tuchman's summary of the calamity that befell the twentieth century, he saw the woman staring at him. The smile radiating from her fine-boned, creamy olive face would have been perfect, except for her marginally overlarge lips and a light overbite. Raindrops had beaded on the richly toned copper hair that fell to her shoulders from a gypsy scarf. The weather also had mussed the eyeliner above her large green eyes. She smiled warmly and shivered, digging her hands deeper into her own sodden raincoat.

"Sabrina," Glassman said quietly.

"Hello, Adam," the woman said, smiling. "Still the same old Adam with his nose in a book."

The colonel grinned. "You know I'm sensitive about me nose," he said, patting his prominent proboscis tentatively.

Her smile bloomed and caught in her throat as a small laugh. She touched his forehead lightly. "I know," she said. "Sensitive about that fine, proud nose and your crinkly Jewish hair. So unlike an American Air Force major."

"Bottle-cap colonel, lately," Glassman said, a touch of pride in his voice. "It wasn't easy being the only Jewboy in a WASP military academy," Glassman said, snapping the book shut crisply and brushing his lips against hers.

"You were born in the wrong country, Adam," Sabrina said, returning the light kiss with one of her own. "You should have been a Sabra. You would have been a general by now. All we have are young generals, and every sexy girl in Tel Aviv would love your fine rawboned face."

"At least one of the girls," he said, grinning. "That fine dark half-naked wench on the beach at Eilat."

She shook the rain from her hair and returned the grin. "We had to meet somewhere, Adam. Why not somewhere you could oil my back?"

"It was your front I was thinking about."

"Your modesty fails you, Colonel," Sabrina said, laughing. "All Americans are obsessed with breasts."

"We don't have topless beaches."

"Silly."

"Not if you're raised orthodox."

She pouted and made a face. "That, too, is silly."

"Better be careful what you say," Glassman said in mock serious tones. "The god of Abraham is strict."

"So am I," she said, eyeing him playfully.

He raised his eyes helplessly. "You're not strict, Sabrina. You're just bad."

"Give me a chance, and I'll show you."

The crowd of cloudburst refugees began to shuffle back out into the street, some with their heads wrapped in the *News of the World*. Through the shelves, the lady clerk at the counter scowled at Glassman and the girl from behind her pince-nez. Sabrina, grinning at the lady clerk's disapproving stare, grabbed hold of the steel belt rings on Glassman's trench coat and pulled him to her. The book held fast between them.

"Oh dear," the lady clerk gasped, turning away, then staring surreptitiously from behind the pages of the *Economist*, which she used to fan herself.

Sabrina, like a copper-toned cat, hugged herself to Glassman. "Same old Adam," she said, huskily. "Always with a stack of books to read just before you fly."

"Helps me sleep," Glassman murmured.

"I can help with that," Sabrina said huskily, nuzzling her hair against Glassman's proud chin. Abruptly, he pulled away and smiled. "You know I can't talk about flying. I'm not military attaché in Tel Aviv anymore. Besides, I'm not on flight status in merry old England, anyway. Just pushing paper."

Sabrina smiled and nodded, still holding tight to his belt rings. "Okay, Adam. Have it your way. Tell me nothing. But unless you've got to fly tomorrow, let's get out of here."

"I've got the afternoon free."

"Good," Sabrina said, smiling up at him and running her fingertip down the line of his prominent Levantine nose. "I can put you to sleep better than that book, you know."

The Proud Tower fell to the floor, and Colonel Adam Glassman held the copper-haired woman's hand, following her into the receding storm outside. The bell tinkled as they stepped into the street and the lady clerk rushed to tidy up.

Glassman followed the woman in the gypsy scarf at about ten paces across London. After three tube stops he followed her into a shabby hotel in Piccadilly. An Indian desk clerk stared at Glassman as he gave the woman the key. Glassman hurried up the stairs after her, his nostrils filled with the powerful aroma of curry. The ancient key turned over in the lock, and they were in darkness that smelled of freshly starched sheets and the never-ending battle between mildew and disinfectant.

Sabrina pulled a cord by the window, exposing the gray shadows of the black clouds. "I want to see you," she whispered, walking forward and grabbing hold of his coat. Roughly she freed the large military buttons. Then she bit his earlobe fiercely and pushed him against the ancient flower pattern on the wall in the dark room.

"You want me, you've got me," Glassman whispered back fiercely. She had the coat down around his shoulders and was pulling open his trousers. She got her hand on his penis and rubbed hard, making him spring to attention.

"I've got you all right, Adam," she said, taking him in her mouth and pulling hard. She grabbed hold of him, massaging him tough and tender. "And dammit, this time you're not getting away." She pulled him to the bed and threw him on it, pulling off his trousers, socks, and shoes in a swift and savage movement.

Her own clothes fell in a pile as she jumped on the bed and pushed herself onto him, her nylons still about her ankles. All that was left in the gray blackness of the room was the splash of color from her gypsy scarf, which bobbed up and down as she moved on him. He reached for her breasts and planted each in his mouth, tonguing first one nipple, then the next. First tenderly, then with insistence, he sucked on them, and she moaned. They moved like horse and rider while the storm outside mounted and the raindrops pounded the window like bullets.

As they lay together, she moved her hands roughly across the matte of black and silver hair on his chest. Playfully she bit at his nipples.

"We're not finished, I take it?" Glassman whispered.

"I'm never finished with you, Adam," she said, running her fingers through the hair on his chest and nuzzling him. "I like this woolly patch. It's like a map of Africa."

"What do you know about Africa?"

"I worked there."

"Do tell. Where?"

"Can't tell. But I think your Colonel North called it Country Three."

"Probably some backwater my country shouldn't have any dealings with."

"You can't avoid it, Adam," she said, gently removing her scarf. "Your country is too big. You're engaged everywhere."

"And getting screwed most everywhere."

"Isn't that what being engaged is all about?" she said, nipping him lightly. "We were almost engaged once, weren't we?"

"Just like our countries, Sabrina," Glassman said ruefully. "We were in bed, but we weren't about to get married. What the hell are you doing?"

"Try this," she said, slipping the silk scarf under the starched sheets. Carefully and gently, she wrapped the scarf beneath Glassman's scrotum until he came fully erect again. With expert dexterity, she knotted the scarf until it pulled exquisitely, giving Glassman only a gentle sensation of tightness.

"Keep you from coming too fast, my darling," she said, kissing his inner ear with her tongue.

"I come too fast?" he said in slight bewilderment.

"Every man comes too fast, silly. I want you for a while."

He sighed and let her take the lead again. In some things, Glassman realized, Sabrina was more than his match.

When they finished, she reached awkwardly from the bed and fumbled with a handbag. She retrieved a silver lighter and a packet of Players Export. Sitting up in the bed, she lit the cigarette and blew a puff of smoke toward the yellowed lace curtain.

"Yuck," Glassman said, moving away from her in the bed. "You should quit that."

"Everyone in my country smokes," she said.

"Eight years off your life."

"I don't even know where I'll be next week."

"That's what all the suckers say."

"Not a bad idea, Colonel. Let me blow some smoke around your delicious cock," she said, lifting the sheet. He pushed her away.

"You're incredible," he said, laughing.

"I know," she said, rearing back on the bed so she was in a kneeling position. She traced her finger across the fringe of hair on his belly, and helplessly he found himself getting hard again. He glanced from his erection to Sabrina's large green eyes.

"Look, Adam," she said, holding on to him gently but firmly. "You know how we have never violated one another's confidence. Our relationship has been special, you know."

"I know," he whispered.

Looking at him, and then looking up at his eyes, she said, "My country is in trouble, Adam. That means I am in trouble. How much do I mean to you, really?"

"What are you talking about, Sabrina?" he asked uneasily.

"My people want some pictures we cannot get with the satellite. My people tell me you are among those who get that sort of picture."

Lt. Col. Adam Glassman pulled his knee up and kicked her suddenly from the bed. Rolling off the sheets, the woman rolled over deftly and hit the floor in a weaving stance of a martial arts fighter. She looked at the knifelike shape of her hands and dropped them; standing suddenly naked and forlorn before the undressed colonel.

He watched tears begin to fall from her face and continued to eye her warily. "Do you know what you've done, Sabrina? To us?"

She nodded, her arms helpless at her sides as he hastily pulled on his sweater and trousers.

"I hated it, Adam," she gasped. She looked at him helplessly. "We need the pictures, goddammit to hell! For us it is life or death."

He looked at her and shook his head. "You think I'd screw my country because I got laid?"

"Some people do things for love, Adam," the woman said mournfully.

"And most honorable people would never do what you did

to me, if there ever was any love," Glassman said, grinding his teeth.

Something deep within him made him groan like a wounded animal. His underwear lay forgotten on the floor like a flag of surrender. Hastily, he grabbed his trench coat and turned the key. As he strode into the hallway, Sabrina, still unclad, ran to the door and half screamed, "Adam!" He was already down the stairs.

"Adam, I'm sorry," she whispered to the walls.

— 10 —
Frightfulness

Porton Down, England

THE DIRECTOR CIRCLED THE EXAMINING table slowly. Methodically, he packed his pipe and lit it. "Sir," the supervising examiner whispered, "it wouldn't do to light that here."

"Do you know who you're talking to, young man?" a thick-necked fellow called Billy Chesterton demanded. Chesterton was chief aide to Sir Alfred Whittlesey—director of MI-6, following the most recent scandal.

"The director will smoke if he so desires," Chesterton said, puffing his chest like the first-class toady he was.

Waving the wood match until it was extinguished, the director smiled crookedly, the pipe suspended in his teeth beneath the salt-and-pepper Guards moustache. Gently he said, "It's no bother, Billy." Chesterton sniffed, ever angry at being muzzled.

"It's the chemicals in here, sir," the examiner explained patiently. "They are volatile."

Chesterton snorted, lifting a handkerchief to his mouth as he turned away from the olive-colored corpse on the stainless steel examining table. Sir Alfred leaned closer. He sucked on his unlit pipe and gripped the lip of the table. He sniffed the strong odor of disinfectants and formaldehyde, the rubbery tip of his fine-boned nose moving like that of a bloodhound's.

"I wouldn't get too close, sir," the young examiner said.

"Why weren't we given protective clothing?" Billy Chesterton said. "If there were a danger, you should have told us."

"We believe the subject is clean following the treatment we administered. But you can never be too careful."

"That's right," the director said, placing his arm round the examiner's shoulder and giving him a paternal squeeze. "Doctor Barney knows his trade, as we hope that we know ours, Billy. Now, Doctor, share with us your expertise." The pathologist adjusted his white coat, squared his shoulders, and adopted the lecturer's tone he used when addressing the tape recorder at inquest.

"Subject is male, aged about twenty-five years, whom we might well say was in the full blush of health," Barney said. "Prior to exposure to the toxic agent, he would have been a prime specimen of Mediterranean manhood. Quite robust."

"And after?" Whittlesey probed gently.

"As you can see, we have points of contact on the arms and legs," the examiner said, circling the table with pointer in hand and calling the director's attention to several black blisters on each of the subject's extremities, each blister several inches across.

"These coal-black malignant skin ulcers have caused a poisoning of the blood where the exposure occurred," the examiner said.

"That's it, then," Billy Chesterton said. "Blood poisoning."

"Nothing so simple," the examiner said. "The skin ulcers and the blood poisoning are secondary. If anything, they only emphasize the horror the subject experienced before death."

"Now, please, Doctor, the cause," Whittlesey pressed.

"It is likely that subject encountered the most fleeting of doses, sir. This produced a cough. There were plaguelike symptoms. The subject retained consciousness after a round of bleeding and vomiting. It is likely he wandered about for a bit, out of his head. Death occurred soon after."

"This is unusual, then?" the director inquired.

"Not unusual in the history of our experiments here at Porton Down, sir, or of the general history of chemical warfare. We have nearly eighty years of data stored here, sir, measuring the effects of anthrax poisoning, blood agents, nerve agents, Tabun, and the like. All the stuff that Tommy called the 'Frightfulness' in the first war, sir."

"You scientists!" Billy Chesterton declared. "How could you make such horrible stuff?"

"They make the stuff because we tell them to, Billy," the director said mildly.

"Right, sir. I've only seen photographs from the war years," Barney said. "But during the last war, we prepared anthrax munitions here, at the direction of Sir Winston. For use against the Nazis, of course. I wasn't born then, but I am quite familiar with the history. Everyone here is."

"What would be unusual about the case before us, then, Doctor?" the director asked.

"Rapid mortality. Death in minutes. What's worse, though, was that the viral effects were persistent. The subject took a good deal of cleaning up before it was safe for us to enter this room."

Chesterton moved reflexively away from the table and placed a handkerchief over his mouth.

"This stuff is a rogue agent, much deadlier than anything from the war, sir," the examiner said. "The chemical breakdown is simple. Anyone who could make fertilizer could do this. Frankly, I'm surprised it hasn't been done before."

"Thank you, Doctor. You've been most instructive," Whittlesey said, waving his pipe vaguely and turning to leave. Billy Chesterton nearly pushed past his chief in his hurry to leave.

"A moment, sir," the examiner called out as the men were halfway through the door. "If I may be so bold, where did you get him? The subject, I mean. Can you tell me?"

Whittlesey turned sharply, causing his aide to nearly stumble over him. His lips spread across his teeth in a crooked grin, and he regarded the examiner for a long moment. He took his time lighting his pipe as he stood in the hallway outside the lab. The lit briar formed thick clouds of gray-yellow smoke about the director's head. In answer to the physician's query, Whittlesey's serpentlike eyes merely glittered.

"Not a word about this. Right?" Whittlesey said simply.

"I understand, sir," the examining physician replied.

Whittlesey turned and walked down the hallway with Billy Chesterton close at his heels.

"Do we tell the cousins?" Chesterton whispered.

"I should say not. The Americans will be mucking things up for as long as there's an England," the director said.

"Mossad, then? Surely, they already know."

"All we need is for the Zionists to run off on a tangent and launch some insane mission that would poison the well for all of us. Right?"

"Right, D."

"We'll prepare a brief for the minister. Put it out to committee. That sort of thing. Meanwhile, we'll maintain surveillance through our man on the ground, right? Bloody marvelous, those SAS types."

Stepping into the clear cold air, Billy Chesterton and the director breathed deeply for the first time since entering the redbrick building that housed the Royal Defense Chemical Establishment at Porton Down. The director looked around and wondered what it was about the surrounding woods and rolling green country that bothered him. With a life spent in observation and analysis, it took him only a moment. No birds. He heard a cricket chirping. But there wasn't a bird to be seen from horizon to horizon.

— 11 —
The Plant

The Federated Socialist Republic of Tarak

SGT. MAJ. COLIN DAVIS OF the Twenty-second Special Air Service swatted at a fly. The fly stopped its buzzing occasionally to nibble the goat. The goat swished its tail, batting the buzzing creature back toward the massive figure of the heavily bearded Davis, who sat on the hillside, clad in Bedouin garb. The sergeant major munched halfheartedly on his Arab flat bread. He had been living on the stuff for weeks, augmented by a few dates. There was also milk from the goat. An unvaried diet, though, will eventually tire even the toughest operative. But his mission was to get the job done, displaying that particular élan that distinguished SAS as the world's finest deep reconnaissance and counterterrorist unit.

Finishing his austere ration, Davis whispered, "Who dares, wins," in the little goat's soft ear. Then he chuckled and brushed aside his flowing Shemagh headdress. He lifted his field glasses and continued his observations. The flower-strewn hills and valleys west of the capital at Karmat would be a breathtaking sight to a visitor, but there was little tourism in the Taraki federation. In any event, Sergeant Major Davis was no tourist. Like his predecessors, Lawrence and St. John Philby, he was scouting for Her Majesty's Secret Service. He scratched his beard, lifted a goatskin, and rinsed his mouth thoroughly before taking a tiny swallow. Then, he focused his glasses on the factory grounds, where steam pipes and smokestacks rose grotesquely from the ruins of a mountaintop Crusader castle.

The plant, he knew from all published accounts in the Arab English-language journals, was a triumph of socialist progress. Built next to the new oil refinery, it utilized the petroleum by-products for the manufacture of pesticides that would aid the region's agriculture, particularly in the curbing of weevils that plagued the cotton crop.

Nevertheless, the plant near the Taraki coastline was not open to visitors. So Sergeant Major Davis did his job and spied on it.

"It's a nice goat, isn't it," Davis cooed. The little animal bleated as it munched contentedly on the low scrub. Davis counted six buff-colored Mercedes Benz trucks on the coast road leading up to the plant gate, with its high, electrified fence. They were preceded and followed by drab green trucks of Russian manufacture. The Russian trucks were filled with Taraki troops.

"Bingo," Davis murmured.

The trucks rolled through the gates, and the soldiers jumped down and began unloading steel drums from the lorries. The drums were placed on skip loaders, which hurried them inside a warehouse. Next, a curious thing happened. Davis watched a Bedouin shepherd guiding his flock onto the coast road. As the shepherd urged the sheep on, a helicopter made a low pass over him.

The helicopter landed on the roof of one of the plant buildings, and its occupants, except for the pilot, hurried down a gangway that connected the roof to the ground level. Two men of Middle Eastern origin in officer uniforms of equal parts tan and gold braid trailed behind a pale blond European in a white lab coat. As they reached ground level, one of the officers gestured and shouted orders at the soldiers unloading the drums.

Some ran through the gate. They overtook the shepherd and carried him inside the gate, which closed electronically. The flock scattered. In a few minutes, more troops emerged from the plant to round them up. Davis clucked his tongue. He raised himself up from his haunches and ambled down toward the valley as purple dusk dropped quietly on the hills. The goat followed him faithfully toward the little cave where he'd secured his long-range radio.

Before he reached the next valley, however, he was surrounded by troops who marched toward him purposefully, like a closing net.

—— 12 ——
TDY–FOL*

RAF Mildenhall, England

MAJ. GEN. SCOTT CARTWRIGHT SAVORED the rich coffee they served in the officers' club mess at Mildenhall. It jabbed his memory of the bitter acorn brew the English served during the war. He smiled to himself as he remembered the instant celebrity he earned when he brought his English host family a pound of GI dark roast that he'd hustled from the mess. His "host mother" reminded him tea was the national beverage, but she clearly relished the Hills Brothers. He looked at his steaming brew and wondered that half a life disappeared as fast as a second cup.

"You there, Scotty? You look like you wandered off there, old buddy," said Lt. Gen. Ned Deighton, the three-star who commanded the American contingent at Mildenhall. "You need some more mud?"

Cartwright looked up from his woolgathering and said, "Sure thing. Send it on over."

General Deighton motioned his aide to fetch more coffee. The captain moved quickly, knowing his only shot at stars was to serve them well.

*Temporary Duty–Forward Operating Location

"Shoot, I remember how it was," Cartwright reminisced. "Load up on java before mission and have to pee all the way home from Berlin. I wonder why it is we can't do without this stuff."

"We need it like a Phantom needs JP-4, Scotty. It's 'go juice.' "

"It keeps us edgy," Cartwright grumbled. "But maybe that's the point. Keeping the edge."

"Hell, Scotty. You're probably the only officer your age drawing flight pay."

"And that's the way I aim to stay. Until I'm so old all I can do is go fishing. But until then, I guess I'm an airplane driver."

"The oldest and boldest," General Deighton said, accepting his fresh cup from the young captain and raising it in a mock toast.

"Here's to victory," Cartwright saluted back, downing the full cup of coffee in nearly one swallow and smacking his lips. "Wherever it may be found."

The generals put on their blue forage caps, zipped up their flight jackets, and stepped out into the misty fog that was morning in East Anglia. Behind the fog curtain whined the siren call of military jets taking off and landing.

"You got anything else going here, Scotty? I just like to know what's what when I've got a two-star walking around my base, even if he is the most senior two-star in the entire goddamned Air Force."

Cartwright kept walking at his steady gait and squinted at his friend. "Ned, do you have a need to know?"

"It's my base and I'm a three-star, Scott."

"I'm here to supervise a phased shutdown of Blackbird operations."

"You're bullshitting me," the three-star said incredulously. Cartwright nodded somberly. "I'm told by on high that if we're gonna get a new bomber and sustain our NATO commitment, the spy plane's gotta go. It's expensive."

"Not as expensive as Pearl Harbor," Deighton snapped.

Cartwright put his hand up. "I know, I know. Pearl Harbor hasn't come up lately, I'm sorry to say. And the Puzzle Palace says they can connect the dots with the satellites. This time, CIA agrees."

"Jesus. What if a satellite blanks on us? What are we gonna do if we don't have a spy plane we can put up in a hurry?"

"I agree," Cartwright said. "But we don't set policy. We implement orders."

Deighton checked his watch, shaking his head sadly. "Gotta go, Scott. Staff meeting. I should keep this to myself, I take it?"

"That would be wise. Decision's not final." The men shook hands and the base commander marched off, shaking his head. Cartwright turned to face into the cold, wet wind and watch the sky, the way he had done forty years before, waiting for the Jugs to return from bomber escort. Long before he could see it, far up and away in the gray cloud cover, he heard the roar of the engines, the big Pratt & Whitney ramjets that powered the Blackbird. The inky outline of the great dark delta-shaped wings descended through the mist.

The SR-71 Blackbird dropped onto the airfield and raced down the tarmac like a prize filly on victory stretch. An orange drag parachute popped, bringing it to a gentle stop. A few minutes later, the cockpit raised like the visor on an ancient knight's helmet and, with assistance from the ground crew, the pilot and RSO emerged.

The crewmen wore gold pressure suits and helmets like the astronauts. One flier lowered himself awkwardly down the step and hurried toward a hangar. The other walked gingerly, raising his visor and looking around him while the ground crew hurried to service the plane. He seemed to be searching for someone, until he spotted Cartwright. Then the man in the bulky gold suit shuffled toward the general, removing his helmet and holding a salute as he approached.

Cartwright returned the salute snappily, extended his hand, and said, "Hello, Adam. I see that they finally gave you a proper airplane."

"It's the most cerebral plane I've ever flown, sir," Lt. Col. Adam Glassman said, taking Cartwright's hand. "Did Doctor Murdoch get my memo?"

"She did, and she's taking it under advisement. But it doesn't look good at the Pentagon or the White House. I'm here to evaluate costs and methods for shutting down the forward operating locations."

Lt. Col. Adam Glassman's scowl was nearly as dark as the Blackbird's titanium skin. He brooded. "It's a blunder," he said. "Did you know we lost a Keyhole satellite over the Mideast?"

"I know it," Cartwright replied. Then, rattled, he looked long at Glassman. "How did you know that? Deighton here runs half of NATO and he didn't know it."

"I used to be Defense Intelligence, remember?" Glassman said. "Everybody talks."

"Well, don't you go talking. Bottle-cap colonels that write memos and hear about satellite blackouts make the Pentagon nervous." Clucking his tongue, Cartwright observed, "Can't say I disagree, though. The Blackbird shutdown's a bad business."

"But they'll do it anyway," Glassman said bitterly.

Cartwright nodded somberly. "It's hard to talk sensible strategy in a cost-cutting season."

"Buy you a beer, sir?" Glassman asked grimly.

"Let me buy," Cartwright said. "There's a pub in the village. Serves King's Green."

"Think it's still there?" Glassman asked wryly. "The pub, I mean. It was only about two hundred years ago when you were chasing skirt."

"Likely it is. This is the mother country. Things don't change so fast over here."

Cartwright helped Glassman carry his gear to the hangar. From a distance he looked like a father carrying his son's helmet and kneepads into a locker room before the big game.

— 13 —
The Discoverers Club

London

THE SILVER AND FINE BONE china clattered in a muffled sort of way as fine-liveried waiters cleared tables at the Discoverers Club. Luncheon was nearing its end, and the members were returning to their duties, fiduciary and parliamentary. Sir Alfred remained, however, fidgeting with his knife and attempting to avoid the keen gaze of the man who sat across the table from him.

"You're not going to use that thing, are you?" inquired Whittlesey's guest, David Ben Lavi, as he eyed the knife. Whittlesey looked at the knife and smiled. He held the steak knife lightly, only for an instant, as though it were a commando dagger.

"I suppose if I were to use my knife in anything other than a friendly way, I should have done so long ago," Sir Alfred said, his smile tightening across his teeth, giving him a slightly feral appearance.

"You mean after we blew up the King David Hotel?"

"You should have been hanged for that."

"I nearly was. I escaped."

"You mean your pals from the Stern Gang came and got

you. Jolly terrorists they were. Your whole lot should have been hanged.''

"But we got elected to the Knesset instead," David Ben Lavi said, chuckling. "We're the only democracy on the books in that barren region your people have such a romantic attachment to. You should think more kindly of us, but instead your heart is with those reactionary monarchies that would push us into the sea.''

"And that's because you're the most troublesome bloody country out of the whole lot, too, I might add," Whittlesey declared. "Your little democracy has almost lit the fuse on World War Three a time or two. A stiff-necked people, indeed.''

"You didn't mind our help at Suez in fifty-six.''

The waiter wheeled the dessert cart over, and Whittlesey pointed to the trifles. David Ben Lavi, who was given to thickness at the middle in recent years, demurred and reached instead for his cigarette case.

"Good God, man, don't light that thing," Whittlesey said with alarm. He had an honest hatred for French cigarettes, and most things French.

"What am I to do, then? I must smoke.''

"Let me get you a decent cigar," Whittlesey said, raising his hand again to signal for help. "Something that won't spoil the meal.''

The waiter returned and displayed a box of cigars. Whittlesey selected a pair and presented one delicately to his guest. "Havana," the Israeli said, smiling. "You don't mind buying tobacco from communists?''

"Not a lot of choice, have we? Fidel's a rogue all right, but all that stuff about the Havana leaf declining since the great proletarian revolution is a lot of Yank nonsense.''

Sir Alfred pushed the dessert plate aside with an air of annoyance. He cut the tip of his cigar and graciously did the same for Lavi. Soon they were blowing contented puffs of thick gray smoke. Silently, the waiter delivered the brandy balloons.

"So let's get to it, you old terrorist. What is it you want?''

"You've got something of ours.''

"Balls. We've got no operations in your bailiwick as of

present, and that better go both ways,'' Whittlesey said, tapping the fine gray ash of his cigar lightly in the tray.

"Let us maintain that convenient fiction in the general sense, but I am addressing specifics, and in that area there must be truth between us," Lavi said.

"What are you dancing around? I can't bear all this Levantine palaver."

"You are in possession of a body. He is our man. We want him back."

"A body. What body?"

"Ten days ago a detachment of Her Majesty's Special Boat Service effected a landing some thirty kilometers south of the Syrian port of Latakia. A man operating in the area, presumably attached to one of your special operations groups, performed the handoff of a package—which was large, I might add. It would take a man of enormous strength to deliver it."

"Are you daft? We conducted no such operation, and I might add we have no such interest in what the sodding Tarakis are up to. That's your end of the street, old pal."

"I did not mention the country," Lavi said. "But our regaining the package you took delivery on is of sufficient interest to my government that we would deliver film of this operation to certain of your back-bench friends in Parliament and let them continue the inquiry in public. Downing Street would love that, I'm sure."

"Film? Utter madness."

"The film is of high resolution, with excellent detail even in the near total darkness that cloaked your highly professional recovery."

"Tell me about this package," Whittlesey said, fencing.

"There is nothing to tell, except to say our relative was engaged in observation of the same target your man was surveying some distance to the north, near the coastal plain of the Taraki federation, the chemical plant in Tarak."

"The little shepherd boy? He was yours—bloody Mossad?"

"Sir Alfred, please, if you would not raise your voice, even in your own club," Lavi said, finishing his brandy.

"Is there any spy in the Levant who isn't a bloody shepherd?" Whittlesey snorted.

"We want the remains of our man. We promise their mothers

we will bring them home. We come, asking your help, as friends.''

"His mother won't want to see him. He was a stinking mess.''

"We must talk of that, also. The works in Tarak are a matter of concern for all.''

The waiter returned to replace the ashtrays and collect the remains of Sir Alfred's dessert.

— 14 —
The Kola Wars

RAF Mildenhall, England

ED ROGERS, AN AIR FORCE major known as Wolfman because of a perpetual five-o'clock shadow, trotted under the wide belly of the black SR-71. His usually somber face was clouded with fresh tension. Rogers's equipment—his radars, cameras, and sensors—all were folded into the Blackbird's belly and the knifelike fuselage edges, known as chines. He felt he owned the plane. Running beneath it made for heavy going in his pressure suit, but he was in excellent shape. Still, he panted as he lugged his portable air-conditioning unit.

Adam Glassman stood atop the loading platform, accepting the help of a chief master sergeant who was disconnecting Glassman's portable air unit. The units were used by spy plane fliers to keep the suit cool until the plane's life-support system kicked in. Occupied as he was with the preflight checklist, Glassman failed to hear Rogers's shouts. He only looked up when Rogers tapped his helmet as Glassman settled into the black plane's cockpit.

"Where the hell do you think you're going, Adam? Dammit, didn't you hear me?" Rogers shouted at his partner.

"Take it easy, Wolfman," Glassman said, shaking free of

his partner's grip. "You're not on the flight manifest today. It's not a big deal."

"The hell you say, Adam. You don't take the bird up without an authorized reconnaissance systems operator. You know that! I'm your crew dog, for Chrissake."

A visored head popped out of the RSO's cockpit to the rear of the pilot's office on the big black plane. "I'm the RSO today, son," the helmeted head said.

"And who the hell do you think you are, pal? No hitchhikers allowed on an SR flight. You hear?" Rogers asserted.

"Loud and clear, Major," the voice in the helmet said. "Now adopt a civil tone of voice when you address a general officer." Glassman's partner snapped to attention and fought for balance on the platform.

"Aw, cut it out, Major," General Cartwright said. "You look silly trying to maintain your position while you're in a bag suit. Stand at ease."

Wolfman's shoulders slumped and he looked down, wonderingly, at the general sitting in his airplane. "I may not be a red-hot RSO, but I am an authorized hitchhiker," Cartwright said, grinning easily. "Your crew dog here is just going to take me up on a checkout flight."

"Begging the general's pardon," Wolfman said, sounding a note of concern. "The Blackbird is a young man's airplane."

Cartwright laughed and said, "Don't worry, son. I'm cleared for space flight. I've pulled a couple of Mach 27 shuttle launches, with a Mach 6 landing at Rogers Dry Lake."

"Begging the general's pardon, and with all due respect, you might find this a bit demanding," the major said solicitously.

"Be at ease, Major," Cartwright bellowed. Then he grinned and said, "Check yourself into the officers' club and go have a cold one on me. I'm confident your partner will bring me back in one piece."

Reluctantly, Rogers climbed down the platform. He lifted his helmet from his shoulders and decoupled his ACU as he stood dolefully on the tarmac, watching his airplane.

"Who in hell is the general in my airplane, Sarge?" Rogers asked as the master sergeant finished directing the ground crew. "How'd the Air Force let such an old son of a bitch in my perfectly good airplane?"

"When were you born, sir?" the sergeant asked gently.

"Nineteen fifty-seven. How come?"

"Well, Major," the sergeant observed. "When you were a Mouseketeer, that man was walking on the moon. That's Scott Cartwright."

"Cartwright, the astronaut? The test ace?"

"The only one I know."

"Jesus. I'm a horse's ass."

"Knowledge of self is the beginning of wisdom, sir," the sergeant remarked sagely.

Rogers hurried past the ground crew preparing the Blackbird takeoff operation with the precision of a space launch. His wife often lectured him that all fliers were little boys. Like a little boy, Rogers found himself winking back tears at the prospect of being left behind.

The canopy lowered, sealing shut like a clam. Adam Glassman moved efficiently through his preflight preparations, quietly calling out the checks as he completed them over the radio for his mobile crew. His gloved right hand moved precisely across the myriad of toggle switches and circuit breakers, while his left hand rested on the throttle quadrants. Each switch, each of the dozens of dials and gauges had to check perfectly. Fuel pressure. Oil pressure. Control surfaces. Electrical systems. There were no yellow warning lights on the console. Good. He relaxed, watching the mobile crew truck that would monitor takeoff drive out onto the tarmac like an actor in a play. He looked up at the gray sky and sighed. He inhaled, sucking the air in through his teeth, his lips licking at the slightly ammoniated taste of the sterile helmet.

Adam Glassman knew his plane. He knew it was good as gold. In fact, the thirty-two-thousand-pound-thrust J-58 engines were sprayed with fine gold coating to deflect heat. Glassman knew this—as he knew every detail of the history, capabilities, and wondrous engineering of the spy plane that succeeded the U-2—for Glassman was a scholar as well as a pilot, a poet as well as an engineer. He loved the plane the way a great rider loves a great horse.

For an instant, a vision of Sabrina crossed his mind. Thinking of the woman's treachery brought pain, so he immersed himself in the plane. He glanced from side to side, checking position of the engine inlet spikes protruding from the wing nacelles. The spikes were in forward position, ready to ram air into the angry power plant once aloft. The movable spikes enabled the SR-71 to suck air into the unique turbo ramjet engines and blow it out in a fiery tail blast in excess of three times the speed of sound. He gazed at the sleek lines of the plane, knife-blade sharp and coal black against the gray concrete of the runway. The huge engines looked like wing-mounted rocket motors.

The poet in Glassman reflected on the Blackbird colors, black and gold. Black for the ferrite "ironball" paint coat that reduced the aircraft's reflectivity so it could fly stealthy and confound enemy radar. Gold for the pressure suit that kept his body from exploding fifteen miles above earth. Real gold to coat the Blackbird's heat-resistant engine surfaces. A plane worth its weight in gold for the intelligence product it brought home at March 3-plus to a safely sleeping America. Glassman was ready to fly.

In the aft seat Scott Cartwright conducted as rigorous an inspection ritual as the pilot. As reconnaissance systems officer, he was responsible for the Blackbird's avionics "suite," the singular package of electronics, radars, cameras, and "black boxes" that made the SR-71 the world's most awesome spy plane. Delicately, he adjusted resolution on the glowing circle of radar screen, which looked like the wicked queen's mirror in Snow White. He turned the switch to Standby mode and moved down the list.

Cartwright's history with the aircraft went back to the day Lyndon Johnson misnamed it during a hasty press conference the Texan president called during the '64 election campaign to debate Barry Goldwater's claim that he was "soft" on defense. As a young, bottle-cap colonel, Cartwright stood horrified as the president unexpectedly revealed the top secret Blackbird's existence to the world. Its original name was RS-71, for "reconnaissance strike." But Air Force brass couldn't tell the president he was wrong at his own press conference. Once LBJ dubbed it SR-71, the Air Force magically transformed the airplane's mission title to "strategic reconnaissance." Thus it became, forever after, the SR-71 Blackbird.

Cartwright flipped toggle switches and turned knobs, getting the affirmative responses he wanted from the aircraft's powerful radar system, an advanced and many-times-enhanced version of its ancestor, the original Hughes AN/ASG-18, in its day the most powerful aircraft radar ever built. Later versions were installed in the Navy's F-14 Tomcat. This latest version surpassed all that came before. Its powerful beams could look up, look down, and identify mothlike targets on its green screen that were hundreds of miles away. Some of its attributes were classified even from the men who flew the Blackbird.

His fingers moving like those of a gloved pianist, Cartwright next conducted system checks on the Itek optical barrel camera that could search a hundred thousand square miles in an hour, looking for hidden missiles, troops, tanks, fortifications, or any other form of strategic threat. Finally, Cartwright threw the switches and punched the buttons for the systems check that would inform him of any glitch in the electronic countermeasures suite, the ECM black boxes that would throw out deceptive images or intense blasts of radar energy to foil ground control units, enemy fighters in pursuit, or surface-to-air missiles. The Blackbird's ECM suite could also generate false or "ghost" targets. It all checked out okay. The general's view in the rear seat was somewhat limited by his smaller canopy window, but unlike a lot of stick-and-leather jockeys, Cartwright was a pilot who enjoyed equally the challenge of electronic warfare. He was a charter member of the fraternity of electronic warfare experts nicknamed the "Old Crows." Satisfied his long list checked out, he relaxed. Scott Cartwright was ready to fly.

"You are clear for takeoff, Viper Seven-three," the mobile crew announced from the truck rolling slowly alongside on the runway.

"Viper Seven-three, roger," Adam Glassman answered. A shot of green trichloroethylene gas ignited the awesome Pratt & Whitney engines, and the SR-71 was surging forward on the eleven-thousand-foot runway, its black magic catching the breath of all watching it from the ground.

Adam Glassman's left hand pushed the throttle forward gently as his right hand jockeyed the stick with the poise of a cellist, and the black plane's nose pointed skyward. The landing gear retracted into the black plane's belly as the engines blasted white fire at the disappearing runway. The floating ball of the artificial horizon on the console panel facing Glassman bobbed sky blue as the plane darted into the clouds like a black marble fired from a slingshot.

"Go at full throttle," Glassman grunted, igniting the afterburners on full military or "wet" thrust, spitting nearly seventy thousand pounds of thrust from the Blackbird's tail. Gravity pushed him back, deep into the ejection seat, constricting his chest, crushing him and at the same time challenging him to his physical and spiritual limit as the dagger nose of the Blackbird sliced through the cloud cover into the world above of blue sky and bright sun.

The Blackbird was airborne, leaving earth to the poor, foolish mortals below. And it was the Blackbird that gave Glassman his chief reason for living. It was itself a living thing that propelled him from the fogginess of life on the ground into the azure clarity of a life elevated in the wild blue.

"We're back," Scott Cartwright declared happily on the internal "hot mike."

At twenty-six thousand feet altitude and three-hundred-fifty knots indicated air speed, Glassman prepared to rendezvous with a KC-135 "Silver Sow" refueling tanker off the Scotish coast. The tankers were the black plane's mainstay and one of its principle limitations. Despite its awesome performance, the SR-71 was a thirsty bird, needing several refuelings per mission. For safety reasons, it took off with half-empty tanks.

The black plane approached the tanker head-on in radio silence. The SR-71 crew got its bearing by a tactical air navigation transmitter beam from the tanker. At a distance of about two dozen miles, the KC-135 swung into a turn, so the spy plane fell behind it. As Glassman sighted the silver plane, he positioned his craft beneath the fuel boom in a delicate maneuver.

"Contact!" he announced, completing the aerial mating dance.

Once mated, Glassman communicated with the tanker crew via secure link intercom in the boom. Within fifteen minutes, the SR-71 took on seventy thousand pounds of JP-7. Glassman then steered his craft toward the Kola Peninsula on the northern edge of the Soviet Union.

Climbing rapidly to a ceiling in excess of seventy thousand feet, Adam Glassman punched computer inputs for high-altitude cruise and set the azimuth heading to a course that would eventually put them north of the Arctic Circle. This course would be continuously monitored and corrected by the space telescope that was part of the celestial navigation system that guided the black plane. The SR-71 sometimes caught fire and sometimes crashed. But it rarely got lost. Unless it strayed "accidentally" over some denied territory the way Gary Francis Powers once did in a U-2.

High over the North Sea, Glassman nudged the throttle through the sound barrier a second and then a third time, leaving a sharp crack in the shattered air that sent the plane sailing effortlessly toward its accustomed ramjet cruising speed of Mach 3-plus.

"I'd like to know how you were able to swing this one, General," Glassman said, his voice tinny and disembodied in the microphone.

"What do you mean, old buddy?"

"Wing never breaks up a Blackbird team. How'd you rate the flight?"

"Sonny, I helped form Ninth Strategic Recon Wing. Besides, I do pretty much what I want these days."

"Like getting me assigned to SR-71 flights."

"Shoot, Colonel. You did it yourself. You earned it."

"Until our last outing they had me grounded with a psycho profile."

"Ain't many men could do the piece of flying you turned in. And no other's got a confirmed kill on a hijacked Stealth bomber. There was zero margin for error on that one."

"So what puts you in an SR cockpit today?"

"I got this job 'cause I wanted it. If there's a way to save the Blackbird wing, I've got to be the one to come up with it. And if there's not. I wanted to be the one to supervise the stand-down."

Glassman threw more toggles and punched more inputs, increasing speed and altitude as the plane crossed the Arctic Circle. "You can see the northern lights ahead, sir."

"Damn," Cartwright said, marveling as he watched the rainbow dance of transatmospheric luminescence. He looked back over his shoulder through the small RSO port to see the aft end of the Blackbird's engines glowing white-hot in the high, thin aquamarine air. "You don't get a sight like that even from space."

"I've only got a few quiet minutes before we turn hard right at Finland," Glassman announced.

"Well, Adam. That's all I wanted—a few quiet minutes. This is probably the most secure location we could find. No bugs. No parabolic microphones. No microwaves."

"So, sir. What's the proposition?"

"Just this, Adam. I want us to bring back a packet of high-resolution pictures today that are so sweet that we might yet persuade the wienies inside the beltway that it's a good idea to keep the old Blackbird airborne for a couple more fiscal years."

"Maybe we can do that, sir," Glassman said confidently.

Glassman handled his controls with surgical precision, guiding the plane toward its maximum classified ceiling, in the vicinity of a hundred thousand feet. He pointed the big black plane on an easterly course to cross over Murmansk and the Kola Peninsula.

"Next stop, the sub pens at Northern Fleet Base, Polyarnny. Ivan's front yard. Mission profile calls for a coastal sweep with sensors and cameras running. It should keep us in international airspace, and we'll still get some nice shots of the boomers. Defense has wanted a clear picture of the replacement for the Typhoon-class submarines."

"Well, as old Frank Powers said, just tell me when to throw the switches," Cartwright said dryly. "And I'll watch for Soviet Air Defense Command activity."

"You can throw the switches. And fire up the electronic countermeasures package while you're at it. We're going to be going into a stealth mode once we pass Murmansk over the Barents Sea."

More than a dozen miles below, swimming among the ice floes of Kola fjord was a long cigar-shaped leviathan, a Soviet missile-firing sub. While the keen eyes of Glassman and Cartwright were locked on screens and gauges, they could not behold the reason for their trip. But the high-altitude cameras the Blackbird carried were capturing the priceless imagery of the Soviet sub for them. Such pictures, delivered in timely fashion, could settle an arms control debate or evaluate whether a treaty violation existed.

The Blackbird, a nearly thirty-year-old aircraft forged in the intellectual hothouse of the Skunk Works, was uniquely designed to combine the often mutually exclusive characteristics of human intelligence and electronic intelligence. Unlike a satellite, the plane could flutter through cloud cover, loiter for a long look, and then flee hostile air space at speeds greater than that of a 30.06 bullet fired from a rifle. The Blackbird put assets of a spy satellite under the control of human hands.

The SR-71 plane's sensors and cameras hummed, and the general took quiet pleasure in the technical mastery he still possessed as he monitored some systems and activated others. In any ordinary aircraft he would want the stick.

Far below, officers of the Soviet Air Defense Command were angrily aware that the Blackbird loitered tantalizingly in the acquisition scopes of a cluster of SA-6 missile batteries. Even as the sub was moving through the fjord, three formations of MiG-29 Fulcrum interceptors were scrambling, each Soviet pilot hungering for a Blackbird kill.

"I've got bandits, three o'clock and low," Cartwright announced as the Blackbird moved through its sweep. "We've got a SAM launch, approaching at six on the clock at about three-zero miles and closing."

"Let's call it a day," Glassman responded.

"Good idea. The board is lighting up like one of my grandkid's video games."

Glassman fired the afterburner on the Blackbird's unique J-58 engines and pushed the SR-71 to the edge of space. Two SA-6 missiles ignited at the Soviet battery's estimated ceiling and buffeted the plane as it sailed away from a brace of Fulcrums that were attempting to chase the plane by climbing vertically.

"My screen indicates a lock-on from the Fulcrum," Cartwright said. "It's faint, but this is new. What have you got left on the throttle?"

"Let's go find the edge of the envelope. Right now."

Glassman pointed his great black plane west toward Finland

at full throttle. Within a minute the SR-71's positioning system screen indicated that the black plane was in Finnish air space, but as the plane descended, the Fulcrums still had not waved off. In fact, they pressed their pursuit.

"We're going back upstairs, General," Glassman said calmly. "Mach 3-plus mode."

Making a delicate adjustment that flattened his body deep back into his cockpit seat, Glassman fired the Blackbird back toward the spy plane's classified upper region. Its nose section glowed like a red-hot iron. Cartwright watched and listened in quiet wonder as the Soviet acquisition tone faded. He also watched the earth's curve moving gently more than a dozen miles beneath him.

A half-dozen miles below, one Soviet interceptor maintained its climb rate, leaving the others behind. It was a modified swing-wing Foxbat, piloted by Capt. Max Immelman, attached to Soviet Air Defense from East Germany's Baltic Command. Like his grandfather in the Luftwaffe, he wanted the kill—badly. His thumb on the weapons trigger, with unconsciousness tearing at the edge of his face, he whispered, "I'll get you, my black beauty!" But the Blackbird eluded him as well, its tail burning white-hot at the edge of space.

"That got randy for a minute," Cartwright observed cheerfully. "But I bet we got some dandy pictures."

"Let's hope the Puzzle Palace appreciates the film."

"Roger that. Hope nobody moved while we were gettin' the focus. Where are we headed on the return route?"

"We'll overfly Sweden. We've got fuel for a straight shot back to the forward operating location at Mildenhall."

"Sweden, huh? I ever tell you I got interned there once? It was for about a month during the big show. Kept us in the same town as a bunch of Luftwaffe types. But the locals didn't take to Jerry. They seemed to like me, though. Some woman hit me with a pine switch whilst we shared one of them sauna baths."

"They probably wouldn't be as friendly this time out. We've got another scramble indicated on the board."

"What, Ivan? He's not gonna violate Swedish air space."

"Nope. It's Swedes. New Grippen squadron probably wants some target practice."

The Blackbird's defensive avionics indicated a solid lock by the lead pilot in the Swedish flight. The Grippens flew a vertical welded-wing formation and closed at a greater rate than even the Fulcrums had achieved.

Miles below, a Volvo salesman who was doing a bit of gardening at his holiday cabin by the Baltic looked toward the extreme edge of the sky. He smoked his pipe and watched in appreciation as he saw the Grippens climbing. He was an aviation buff, and he knew his homeland's interceptors would never catch what they were chasing. He listened intently, then smiled as he heard the triple sonic crack that was the Blackbird's signature.

The Blackbird flared down through the low cloud cover over Mildenhall. The big tires bumped on the tarmac, and Cartwright sighed. He wanted out of the pressure suit. Like any combat flier, he looked forward to a shower and the first cold glass of beer. The ground crew from the Blackbird's special hangar rolled the boarding ladder forward. They were followed by two pale men in trench coats. Glassman exited his end of the cockpit first, and Cartwright followed him down the steps.

One of the trench coats waited at the foot of the ladder, and the other stood by the ground crew, surveying the base with suspicious eyes.

The trench coat at the foot of the ladder held out a wallet as the fliers descended. "You are Colonel Adam Glassman," the man in the trench coat said.

"Yes," Glassman said, looking puzzled. "Who let you out here? This area is military only. Civilians are off limits."

"My name is Tom Grandsen, special agent, FBI. I'm going to read you your rights and place you under arrest."

"What is this?" Cartwright demanded angrily.

"The charge is espionage, General. It would be best if you were to avoid personal involvement."

"You're full of shit," Cartwright snorted. "This man's a dad-gummed hero. He's no traitor."

"Very interesting, General. The charge is espionage for the state of Israel," the FBI man said, taking Adam Glassman gently but firmly by the arm. Cartwright balled his hand into a fist as though to strike the FBI man, but Glassman shook his head.

"General! Don't do it." The Blackbird pilot turned to the FBI agent and gazed levelly at him.

"I'm ready," Glassman said, turning toward a waiting car with an Air Force security police officer at the wheel. "Whatever you think you've got, I'm sure we can clear it up, so let's get a move on. But you've got to let me out of the suit. It weighs nearly fifty pounds."

"Adam, what the hell is this all about?" Cartwright demanded.

"Make a phone call for me, will you, General?" Glassman said as the agent helped him down the ladder. "Get Doctor Murdoch. It's a Barf and Rowf priority message."

Cartwright stood staring as the FBI men assisted Glassman down the crew ladder. Suddenly, the pressure suit felt like lead, and Cartwright felt like an old man.

— 15 —
Rendezvous with a Renaissance Man

Karl Marx-Stadt, East Germany

THE LITTLE GAZ TRUCK RUMBLED cautiously through the deep fog that shrouded the isolated airfield about one hundred kilometers south of Leipzig in the German Democratic Republic. Its powerful headlamps poked just a little ways into the ground mist hugging the farmland that stretched up into the hills and pine forests of the Czech border country.

The GAZ was counterpart to the American Jeep, and both little vehicles had done sturdy service in all the wars, big and little, hot and cold. The usual passengers in a GAZ consisted of driver and sergeant, or at most a captain. This morning the GAZ driver was Kulitsyn, Soviet colonel of signals intelligence. Seated next to him was General Reinhard Grunfeld. Sharing the bumpy ride over the rear axle was General Kolchak, commander of Soviet forces in the German Democratic Republic. Seated next to him was a man with blond hair; liquid blue eyes; pale, translucent skin; and a half-moon scar over his eye that looked like a shrapnel wound.

The blond man wore the uniform of a captain in the signals division of the Soviet army. The East German general turned to face the captain and let the full effect of his steel mask sink in. But the signals captain returned his stare without emotion. This pleased Grunfeld.

"So then, despite your uniform, you are of German descent, Herr Kapitan," General Grunfeld asked conversationally, following a life's habit of interrogating junior officers.

"Volga German, Herr General," the man in the captain's uniform replied formally. "I am an ethnic German but am first a Soviet citizen. Forty-five years ago, I was born Ivan Ilyich Kurtz on a collective near the Volga. There were many of us. Some welcomed the Germans as liberators and were shot for their mistaken allegiance."

"So, Herr Kapitan, you are an interesting combination of all things German and Russian," the German general in the steel mask remarked. Almost as an afterthought, Grunfeld said, "I've been to the Volga."

"I know," the pale man replied stonily. "You probably put my collective to the torch before I was weaned."

"Perhaps," Grunfeld said. "It was a hard time."

"Kurtz also is a hard man, Grunfeld," General Kolchak said, patting the captain on the shoulder and grinning with his large yellow teeth. "Like us, he is a good communist and a good soldier. There's no pity in him. He is a virtual war machine. He invents weapons systems, then proves them in combat."

"You look more like a poet or a scholar than a war machine, Herr Kapitan," Grunfeld declared.

Kolchak laughed. "He is the best offensive systems designer in the Defense Ministry's weapons directorate. He insists on conducting his own tests. Ballistics. Fuses. New shells. And experimental things."

"Yes, I am a scholar," the blond man replied, brushing his blond locks back on his wide forehead. "I studied in Angola. I studied also in the Congo, in Cuba, and in Afghanistan," he said, a curious, taut intensity in his thin, high tenor. He continued to speak, his red Adam's apple bobbing insistently as he related his background.

"I also learned lessons—and taught a few—in Vietnam and Cambodia, and also in Laos. You should see some of my pupils. Among them, some American fliers. They learned some hard lessons from me."

"So," Grunfeld said. "Then we are both scholars."

"But not poets," Kurtz replied.

The signals colonel pulled the GAZ jeep off the blacktop and onto a gravel frontage road. Suddenly, out of the mist, a great gray shape, like a ship with wings, loomed before the vehicle. It was a huge Antonov transport. Its giant Soloviev engines were turning over with a high-pitched whine. The flight deck up in the three-story-high cabin was illuminated like a flying saucer, and the aircraft's running lights turned like candy canes in the fog.

The GAZ jeep rolled to a halt, and Kurtz leaped lightly over the rear wheel. He gave a wooden salute and turned to board the aircraft.

"Good luck upon your return to the Federated Socialist Republic of Tarak," General Kolchak said, waving cheerily.

"A moment, Captain," Kulitsyn said. "I require all your outdated documents. They are needed for burning."

The blond captain nodded automatically and handed the signals colonel a Dutch passport. As he handed over the passport, a small photograph fluttered to the ground, and Kurtz retrieved it, pocketing it. Kulitsyn busied himself examining the visa stamps—and the name, Marinus Emil Van Den Brugge. He grinned as he lit a match to the passport. The blond captain marched to the waiting aircraft.

"He's a bit on in years to be a lowly captain, isn't he?" General Grunfeld asked, turning to Kolchak, who had adjusted his ample bearlike frame to fill the space occupied by the passenger.

"Kurtz doesn't give a damn about rank," Kolchak said. "He's had more different ranks and names than we would care to list. He sheds them like a snake drops his skin. He only cares about his work."

"Then, he will work with me?"

"Just so," Kolchak said, nodding his huge head. "In Tarak."

"And what is his specialty, in addition to shedding his skin?"

"Anything with a sharp point on it," the Soviet signals colonel observed. "It was he who killed the American satellite. But the beauty of it was that he used an American charter aircraft to do it. The man is an artist, a Renaissance man. Were he Italian, he would have been a Borgia.''

"And what black arts will he conjure in Tarak?"

General Kolchak smiled. His deep brown eyes twinkled. "Lately he is interested in chemical warfare and the modification of ballistic missile systems," the Russian general said. "He thinks he has conceived the equivalent of a poor man's atomic bomb. He thinks the Israelis can be beat. Anyway, he is aching to try. He has a sympathy for Arab peoples.''

"You mean he hates the Jews?"

"Sometimes that is the same thing," Kulitsyn admitted. "The Zionists can be a dangerous people. Like so many of those fresh faces ringing the bells for change in the Kremlin, the Jews are not to be trusted. Mostly, though, he hates the Americans. Since the Jews are friends of the Americans, it fuels his hatred all the more.''

"I have no love for the Amis," Grunfeld grunted. "My parents died under American bombs. Why does comrade Kurtz hate them so?''

"Who knows?" Kulitsyn murmured. "He never liked them. Hated them more after Vietnam." Grunfeld nodded as though he understood. Hesitantly, Kulitsyn said, "He had to be recalled from Vietnam. He was involved in some unspeakable things." Kolchak grunted as though it did not matter.

"So this man of yours, Kurtz, the German from Great Russia, you think he is capable of lighting a fuse that will burn all the way to the Kremlin wall?" Grunfeld asked.

The Soviet signals colonel nodded knowingly. "Impeccable credentials. Moscow State University in chemistry. The Frunze academy in military arts. He pioneered use of chemical weaponry against the rebels in Afghanistan. If anyone can start a war—nasty, brutish, and short—Kurtz is the man.''

"And after that?" Grunfeld asked.

"Chaos," Kolchak said, grinning. His red eyes gleamed. "And opportunity.''

"If the KGB doesn't find us first," Kulitsyn said.

Kolchak's great frame listed toward the edge of the GAZ jeep, and he spit on the ground. "That for the KGB," he said. "Bunch of damned political police. If we win, I'll put 'em all under military tribunal. Every single Chekist, I promise you.''

''Then,'' Grunfeld said, ''we had better win.'' Kulitsyn smiled wryly and nodded.

The sun burned through the fog shrouding the runway, and the Antonov transport lurched forward, rolling down the tarmac on its twenty giant wheels. The Antonov's jet engines screamed to life, and its giant wings soared airborne, carrying Kurtz the Renaissance man toward his mission in the Middle East.

— 16 —
Doctor Kurtz

Kharmat, Federated Socialist Republic of Tarak

PRESIDENT HASSAN KEMAL SNAPPED THE powerful shortwave set off. He cursed the British Broadcasting Corporation report, accurate as always. To the everlasting rage of Kemal, Israel had announced it was prepared to defend itself with nuclear weapons. Kemal, a fighter pilot, swatted the model of a MiG interceptor from his polished desktop and immediately regretted his temper. He prided himself on his emotional control, and he was fond of the model.

Tea calmed his nerves but did not assuage the rage he felt. Turning the shortwave back on, he discovered every broadcast in the Middle East was filled with the news. In a half-dozen languages, the dreadful message repeated itself. The Zionists had joined the nuclear club.

The telephone rang. Mustafa, his bodyguard, answered and informed his leader the call was important. "It is General Walid. He has heard the BBC report and wishes to see you," Mustafa said gently, the telephone receiver dwarfed by his massive hand.

Kemal accepted the receiver. A few minutes later the president could hear the clicking of heels and the rattle of assault rifles and bayonets in the hallway. General Walid was the man tap-tap-tapping his way to the president's office. President Kemal waited, one hand on his desk and another near the open drawer where the Walther PPK automatic lay. Being president for life meant exercising caution.

Walid, a jolly-looking man of middle age and wide girth, entered, a cryptic smile on his lips. Like the president, Walid eschewed military dress for a gray suit of expensive cut from France. But everyone knew his rank. Walid commanded the intelligence apparatus that made his boss one of the most feared leaders in the troubled region. The men embraced, kissing quickly on both their cheeks, and Kemal bid the general sit on the comfortable divan reserved for state visits and guests not facing arrest or immediate execution.

"You appear happy for one who has heard such terrible news, my brother," Kemal said, seating himself.

"We knew the Zionists had their bomb. It is not the end of hope," Walid said, forming a small temple of his finely manicured fingers atop his crossed knees.

"Tell me why this is not the blackest day in the history of Arab peoples," Kemal said, rising from his desk and striding to a wall-sized map of the region. Kemal pointed to a finger of land to their south on the map, then hit it with his clenched fist. "Every day, their strength gains at our expense."

Clasping his hands behind his back and pacing angrily, the president for life declared, "They threaten us. They make friends with our enemies and there will be no peace. They mean to take our land one day. And the Americans threaten us. Even the accursed Russians threaten us while they play the benefactor. Are we to be isolated?"

Walid dabbed perspiration from his forehead with a silk handkerchief. "Your wish, my President, would be for our small revolutionary state of Tarak to gain possession of a bomb?" Walid asked gently.

Kemal glared. "Brother, you know the search for the Islamic weapon is more than a wish. It is the fulfillment of a destiny. Why should the superpowers and their lackeys possess such a monopoly?"

"But the Russians will not aid us," Walid said, gazing out the window, his soft features shaped into a dreamy smile that belied his profession.

Kemal snorted. "We would sooner get plutonium from the Americans. And if we got the plutonium, the Zionists would take it away—or bomb us as they did the Iraqis."

"Dear brother and esteemed president," Walid said unctuously, "what is called for is not a big bang, an explosion that would turn us into cinders and ash for seven generations. Something more precise is needed."

Kemal stared at his intelligence chief with annoyance. "Don't toy with me, Walid," he snapped. "A president for life is open to ideas. If you've got one, speak up."

"I would like you to meet a man, a man who can help us wipe out the stain of Zionism and guarantee the federation its proper role in the governance of the region."

"Who is this man?"

"A European researcher. He calls himself Kurtz. And he comes to us by way of a weapons-testing unit of the organs of military intelligence from the Soviet state."

"I've heard nothing from their embassy on this."

Walid smiled delicately and dabbed his forehead. "I don't think that their embassy is fully informed. Nor would we want them to be."

"And what would he be doing for us, without approval from the patron state?"

"He is at our disposal, for tasks that we might wish to undertake on a unilateral basis. Already he has helped modernize production methods at our coastal plant, the one engaged in special projects."

"You speak in circles, Walid," the president growled. "What are you getting at?"

"I think the man can build us a missile that will hit Tel Aviv so hard that they will feel it in America," Walid said simply.

Kemal nodded vigorously. "Yes, well. Let's meet this Kurtz."

Walid rose and bowed. He turned and rapped sharply on the door with his knuckles. Into the office stepped a man wearing the loose-fitting European clothing of a professor on Mediterranean holiday. He brushed back a lock of blond hair, revealing a white scar.

He bowed with old-world formality and Kemal rose from behind his desk and offered his hand, diffidently. In impeccable

French the Taraki president asked, "Doctor Kurtz. How is it that you can help us?"

"Generously, I hope," the visitor replied in equally mellifluous French.

— 17 —
The Case Against Glassman

RAF Mildenhall, England

MAJ. GEN. SCOTT CARTWRIGHT PACED restlessly in the outer office. In his personal rule book, two stars waited only for three stars or higher. Yet he found himself in the outer office of the base Office of Special Investigations, cooling his heels like any lieutenant. Two hours passed and a grim-faced OSI major emerged. As Cartwright drew himself to his full height of six feet three inches, the major saluted crisply. Cartwright waited a long minute and returned the salute.

"I want to see my man, Major," Cartwright said grimly.

"I'm afraid that's impossible, General. The FBI could not allow it at this stage of the initial inquiry, and I am afraid that neither could OSI."

Cartwright squinted, placed his hands on his hips and barked a sharp command. "Major, ten-hutt!"

Even a security man knew his place in the presence of general's stars. The major snapped to, and Cartwright circled round him. Cartwright stopped to make a minute adjustment in the oak leaves on the major's shoulder boards.

"I understand why those civilian gumshoes sent you out into my hallway, Major," Cartwright said, fiddling with the major's rank insignia. "They figured, 'Let's us send out a member of the club to talk to the woolly old general.' But those civvies just don't understand, do they, Major?"

"Understand what, sir?" the major replied, maintaining his rigid position.

"They don't understand that as wienie civilians, they are merely guests at my air base. *You* understand that, don't you, Major?"

"Yes sir," the major replied crisply. "I might add that I tried to communicate that to my civilian counterparts."

"Major, I want five minutes alone with Colonel Glassman. Take care of it for me, will ya?"

"No can do, sir. I regret to say the matter is out of my hands. It's not a matter of rank or protocol, General. It is security. Surely, after the Jonathan Pollard business and the Walker family affair over at Navy, you can understand the severity of the situation. This is an espionage case."

Cartwright regarded the security officer as he might a very small but oddly shaped insect. "Stand at ease, Major." The security officer relaxed the slightest bit and placed his arms in a position of parade rest. He had not had his heels locked since academy.

The general stepped over to a gray steel desk that had been occupied by a staff sergeant he had shooed away during his vigil. He picked up the black phone marked Secure and punched in a long series of numbers. The other end of the line rang three times, and Cartwright's face brightened slightly when he heard the prim voice on the other end.

"Hello, Professor? This is Scott," the general said in a warm tone. "Look, I don't want to crowd your inside line, but this is important. I'm over here in the U.K. on TDY, and security is holding a man of mine I need to talk to, a mutual acquaintance."

Cartwright handed the telephone to the major triumphantly. "Take it," he ordered. "It's the president's assistant for national security."

The major's face changed color to a whiter shade of pale than most officers assigned to duty in Great Britain. He accepted the phone. "Yes, Dr. Murdoch," he said. "Yes, I understand,

Dr. Murdoch. No, ma'am, there's no need to put the president on the line. If I need any further clarification, I will call you, Dr. Murdoch.''

The security officer replaced the receiver on the hook. ''You've got your five minutes, General.''

The general grinned. He patted the major on the shoulder and walked past him into the denied area.

Adam Glassman sat quietly at the steel-gray desk, looking out the window at the steel-gray skies that surrounded the huge RAF base. He tapped his fingers on the desk, ignoring the pin-striped FBI men. As Cartwright entered, the senior agent scowled at Cartwright. Cartwright smiled.

''Son, you're a civilian, but I imagine you know what an order is, and as of the moment, you're taking a couple from me,'' Cartwright said.

''Our orders come from Justice Department and the director, General.''

''I know,'' Cartwright said gently. ''But I imagine you'd like to make it back stateside without a complaint in your file that you personally messed with the president of the United States. I've got White House–level clearance. I'm not gonna help this man escape. Now why don't you just go wait outside a couple of minutes. If I got to get the big boss to talk to your boss, everyone's gonna have a case of the ass. Know what I mean?''

The junior of the two agents urged his partner toward the door, and finally the senior man assented, murmuring, ''Just five minutes.''

As the agents left, the general turned to Glassman. ''So what gives, hotshot?''

''They think I'm the new Benedict Arnold,'' Glassman said dryly. ''Or perhaps more appropriately, the new Jonathan Pollard, as though one weren't enough.''

''Bullshit. Have they seen your two-oh-one file? You've damn near got as many decorations as I do.''

''The Distinguished Flying Cross doesn't matter to these guys. They think I worked for Mossad because I'm an American Jew.''

''Adam, it'd have to be more than that,'' Cartwright said

gently, sitting down in the steel chair across the desk from Glassman. "Level with me."

"They don't need a lot more," Glassman said sharply. "It's always been this way. We're Jews, so we must be different. Right? Ever hear of Dreyfus? Our loyalties are divided, you know."

Cartwright held up his hand and said, "OK, that's enough. What do you think they've got on you?" Glassman fidgeted. He picked up a paper clip and bent it back and forth until it broke.

"Colonel," Cartwright said sharply, "you can screw around with the crimebusters out there. You can screw around with OSI. But don't get my nose outta joint, or you'll wish Mrs. Glassman never had a baby named Adam. I ask you again. What do you think they've got on you?"

Glassman looked at the general and shivered, even though he was wearing one of the blue pullover sweaters the Air Force had appropriated from the Royal Air Force a few years back. As talented a flier as he was, Glassman always looked ill-suited to the tailoring of his uniform.

"My guess, General, is that it was the woman," he said, running his fingers through his curly shock of black hair.

"Yeah, it usually is. What woman are we talking about?"

"She was an Israeli air force captain. At least, that's what she said she was."

"Did she have a name?"

"Captain Sabrina Rabin. She was briefing officer at Tel Nof Air Base when I was flying test on some modifications for the Lavi prototype."

"Did you nail her?"

"That's not a gentleman's question, sir," Glassman said quietly.

"I may be an officer, son, but I am not a gentleman," Cartwright said sternly. "You should've known better. You've done intelligence work. Honey trap's the oldest trick in the book."

"My lack of continence doesn't make me a spy."

"But it makes you look like an easy mark."

"I know it," Glassman said miserably, staring at the broken paper clip.

"I will do what I can for you, but you've just made it damn difficult."

"I realize that, sir," Glassman said. The major from OSI popped his equine face through the door. "Time's up, General," he announced before placing himself at attention until Cartwright saluted him down.

"I'll be in touch," Cartwright said to Glassman. He placed his blue forage cap on his head, zipped his flight jacket, and marched smartly from the OSI office in the security police building.

The general strode into the officers' club, searching until he found Ed Rogers, the mournful-looking Blackbird crewman known as Wolfman. "I'm gonna make use of your airplane, Major," Cartwright announced.

"Where's Adam?" Rogers asked.

"Don't ask me questions, sonny. Just go draw a bag suit."

"You can't take an SR plane without a twenty-four-hour postflight check."

"We're gonna manifest it as one day's operation, sonny. Did it all the time out of Okinawa. She's airworthy. I just flew in her."

"General, where is Colonel Glassman?" Rogers demanded, his voice rising as the two men marched toward the Physiological Support Division, where the gold suits were stored.

Cartwright turned and faced Rogers. "How often do you break the balls of a general officer, son? Sounds like a file item to me, if you decide to persist."

"Sir," Rogers said, squaring his shoulders, "a recce flier depends on his crew dog. I had heard there was an arrest, sir. Sir, with all due respect, I am asking you to enlighten me on the status of Colonel Glassman, sir."

Cartwright grinned at the major. "You've nearly got me pissed off, Major Rogers. Fact is, your crew dog is in a world of hurt. Now if he matters to you half as much as you say, you will go draw a gold suit and meet me on the flight line in five-zero minutes."

Cartwright and Rogers mounted the crew ladder for the Blackbird at 1700 hours. During transatlantic flight they overtook and passed a Concorde SST as though it were standing still, without raising a blip on the SST's radar.

One hour fifty-five minutes and forty-one seconds after departure from Mildenhall, the great black plane touched down at Andrews Air Force Base in the suburbs of Washington, D.C. Cartwright made a point of breaking flight speed records whenever he swiped an airplane.

It was early evening when Cartwright arrived at Madeline Murdoch's office in the old Executive Office Building next door to 1600 Pennsylvania Avenue. The blue class-A uniform he wore had been retrieved from a locker at Andrews and smelled of mothballs. Cartwright's ribbons formed a pyramid from his breast pocket to the shoulder tabs with the two stars on them.

Dr. Murdoch's office occupied a spacious corner with a commanding view of the White House south lawn and the Washington Memorial. It reflected the national security adviser's elevation in status since the basement days of Iran/Contra. The adviser's office was light and airy, with curtains from Paris and mementoes of her tenure as United Nations ambassador. There were African fertility masks and Arabic calligraphy scrolls. But if her quarters reflected her taste, her desk reflected her keen sense of organization. The incoming tray remained full, and the pending tray remained empty. In matters of paperwork, she did her own tidying. At day's end the material went in the safe, or the shredder and burn bag, depending on classification.

Her lace-cuffed and ring-laden hands moved with the speed of a blackjack dealer as she moved paper from the incoming stack to the final tray that read simply Done. She looked up at Cartwright in mild surprise.

"General, we spoke a couple of hours ago. I thought you were in England."

"I was. I flew back."

"By yourself?" she inquired wryly. "I'd have thought you'd need a cape for that."

"A buddy of mine from the Ninth Recon Wing lent me his plane."

"Oh, the much-discussed Blackbird plane. Of course," she said, reaching for a stick of nicotine gum, stored in the silver box on the antique French desk. "Your mode of transportation seems to indicate this visit is a matter of some urgency."

"You know it is, Madeline. FBI is holding my ace wingman on a bum beef."

"You mean Colonel Glassman?"

"You know it's Glassman, Maddy. I would have imagined you were briefed on this before they moved to pick him up."

"Honestly, Scott, I was not," she said, dropping the gum wrapper in a small shredder at the edge of her desk.

"It appears to be one of the usual government shuffles of the left hand not knowing the right. But after you called I phoned the FBI director. I have the file on the investigation here," she said, offering it to Cartwright.

The general accepted the dossier, leafed through it, and grunted a couple of times. Finally, he threw it on her desk. "This is bullshit."

"Are you so certain, General?"

"Come on, Maddy. They make this guy sound like a deep-cover mole. He never took a job the Air Force didn't send him on, including the Israeli attaché job. I might also add that he saved this country once. The whole damn country. That's not in the file."

"I understand, General. But he accomplished that particular maneuver after his duty assignment in Israel. If he were guilty, his action in the Stealth bomber affair would, of course, be a mitigating circumstance."

"Mitigating circumstance, my granny. That young man probably saved that precious Western civilization you're always touting in your books."

"You've read my books, General? I'm flattered."

"I read a book once. Look, Maddy. I want this thing with Glassman cleared up."

"So do we, General. Believe me, no one would be happier than myself to learn the young man is innocent. I, better than most, know what a brave flier he is. What an odd pair you two make, like salt and pepper."

"So what do we do, Maddy?"

"General," she said, chewing her gum carefully, "I want you to arrange transport for yourself to Beale Air Force Base in

California. You will join up with Colonel Glassman's crewman there.''

Cartwright regarded the national security adviser quizzically. She always appeared to be two moves ahead and he would have hated to take her on at chess or poker. "Take young Major Rogers into your confidence," Murdoch said.

"That's a taciturn young man, Maddy."

"All the better. I will inform Defense and the base commander at Beale that your services are required for a reconnaissance to be staged out of the southern European forward operating location. Major Rogers will accompany you."

"What have you got in mind, Maddy?"

"I want you to go to Cyprus, General. I have a reliable report that a young woman named Sabrina Rabin is working there."

Cartwright's eyes narrowed at mention of the woman Glassman had named. "What's the cover mission going to be?"

"It is not a cover mission, General. I expect you to find out the truth about this young woman's involvement with Colonel Glassman. You've done this sort of thing before, haven't you? Of course you have."

Cartwright nodded vaguely, trying to keep pace with Madeline Murdoch's train of thought. "Additionally, you will have an urgent strategic mission to fulfill."

"What might that be?"

"With Major Rogers, your reconnaissance systems operator, you will perform an overflight of Israel, effecting a complete photographic and sensor sweep of a nuclear research facility in the Negev Desert at Dimona."

"Madeline," Cartwright said, gently. "Have we lost a Keyhole satellite over the Middle East?"

The national security adviser scowled. "Where in hell's name did you hear that, Scott?"

"A birdy told me."

"Well, if I find out who the birdy is, his ass is in a sling. No one's supposed to know that!"

Cartwright whistled low and shook his head.

"Our Israeli friends must be convinced of our intent to keep close tabs on their weapons program. Meanwhile, I've got to keep the cost cutters on the Hill from gutting the Blackbird squadron until we get another satellite up.''

"Do the Russians know that Keyhole bird is out of commission?''

"I would think that they do, Scott. Their systems know what's up and what's down on a continuous basis.''

"Did they do it?''

"Damned if I know,'' the national security adviser said, examining her nails. "But while I'm trying to find out, I've got to have up-to-date material from the region. It looks as though we're going to need that damned black plane of yours.''

"How soon do I get going?''

"You must be tired, General,'' Murdoch said sympathetically. "But can you leave immediately?''

"Hey, if the Air Force wanted me to have a personal life, they'd have issued me one,'' Cartwright said.

"Sometimes I think I love you, General,'' Madeline Murdoch said, grinning. "Take this along, for luck, won't you?'' She handed him a small coin that looked like a gambling token, on a chain. On one side it had a horseshoe. On the reverse, a four-leaf clover. Cartwright held the medallion in his leathery hand and frowned.

"This, Professor, frankly ain't the kind of luck I'd want to use,'' he said, pocketing the medal. "If Gary Powers used that lucky silver dollar the CIA boys gave him, he'd have been dead before his parachute opened.''

"Still,'' Madeline Murdoch insisted gently. "It may be of some use to you, if things go sour. I'm told the shellfish toxin is painless.''

"Don't believe everything they tell ya,'' Cartwright said. He saluted smartly and marched out of her office.

—— 18 ——
The Aerie

Beale Air Force Base, California

CARTWRIGHT EXTENDED HIS HAND TO Maj. Gen. Pete Rawlinson, commander at headquarters of the Ninth Strategic Reconnaissance Wing, located in the flat farming country near Sacramento. Rawlinson took Cartwright's hand gingerly, as though he were nursing an old wound. He looked upset, and he was.

"I guess you know this place has gone fairly well nuts in the last few hours, Scott," Rawlinson said, his irritation evident in the deep creases on his bulldog face.

"It couldn't have been a pleasant time for you, Pete."

"Jesus, Scott. First those bastards in Washington are trying to pull the plug on Blackbird ops, and now they tell me one of my best spy plane drivers is a spy. Christ. What would you think?"

Cartwright grimaced, the grin wrinkles around his eyes folding into the worry creases on his broad tanned forehead. He popped a piece of Black Jack gum on his tongue and chewed it as delicately as a desert tortoise munching a leaf. "I'd say you've had better days."

"You're goddamn right," Rawlinson said, pacing across his standard base commander's office, which was decorated in standard Air Force walnut. "Can you imagine? My God, man, we've had OSI climbing all over the place today. FBI was with them. Jesus. Civilians loose in the Blackbird tank."

Cartwright ambled over to the venetian blinds and peeked out into the night, watching the lights of nearby Marysville wink in the distance. Outside, a floodlit Blackbird crew was working feverishly on the dark plane's postflight checks.

"You know how these things work, Pete. We're in another intelligence panic. Everybody's got ants up their ass."

"An Air Force spy. And out of the SR-71 program. God almighty," the base commander said, rubbing his forehead. His shoulders sagged.

"Goddammit, Pete, compose yourself," Cartwright snapped. "Colonel Glassman is innocent. He never peddled secrets to Mossad—or anybody outside the U.S. intelligence community. Something deeper is going on."

"You want to tell me what you think it might be, Scott?" Rawlinson said. "Because I don't particularly care for a bunch of J. Edgar Hoovers trying to rifle my desk."

Cartwright put his hands on the hips of his flight suit and chewed his gum thoughtfully. "I dunno," he said, running his hands through his shock of silver hair. "Lemme ask you a hypothetical, Pete."

"Shoot."

"What if those boys in space division over in the Blue Cube at Sunnyvale lost a surveillance platform over the Middle East? How would we cover for it?"

"You know the answer to that one, Scotty. We'd have to get the spy planes airborne around the clock. Otherwise we'd be flying blind."

"What have we got flying out of Cyprus?"

"Couple of U-2s flying familiarization. Routine operations."

"No Blackbirds?"

"Nope," Rawlinson said. He produced a cigar and offered it to Cartwright, who shook his head. Rawlinson bit the end, lit it for himself, and started spewing clouds of semipoisonous smoke in the close air of the office. "What are you driving at, Scott?"

"Seems like a funny time to shut down Blackbird ops," Cartwright said.

"Have we lost a satellite, Scott?"

"I didn't say that." He looked long at Rawlinson, who immediately began looking nervously about his office, wondering if someone had planted a mike. Rawlinson puffed on his cigar, removed it from his lips, and regarded the glowing ash. "You need one of my airplanes, Scott?"

Cartwright nodded somberly.

"Got something to do with clearing your young colonel friend?"

"It might."

"Well, I hope the bottle-cap colonel didn't sell us out," Rawlinson said, chewing his cigar as he joined Cartwright at the window. "You two are a close pair, and a funny one at that."

"I'll bet a doughnut he didn't sell anyone out. He's American as apple pie."

"Kosher apple, maybe," Rawlinson said, chuckling. Cartwright scowled at him.

"You should know better than to make a remark like that, Pete."

Rawlinson waved his cigar. "Yeah, yeah, Scott. No more ethnic jokes. Everybody's lost their sense of humor."

"Some never thought those jokes were much fun, Pete."

Rawlinson puffed his cigar, as though deep in thought, or just to change the subject. "Frankly, Scott, I'm puzzled about the Blackbird deactivation, even with the cost cutters running the Hill these days. Those black planes are more valuable than a Stealth bomber squadron. We may never nuke the pukes, but we use the spy planes every day."

Rawlinson offered his hand to Cartwright. "Go ahead and take the plane and a crew dog, Scotty. But be careful with my aircraft. There are no more where they came from."

"You know me, Pete," Cartwright said, grinning boyishly despite his years. "You know I'm a careful guy."

"I know you'd give the devil a hotfoot and think it was a reasonable idea," Rawlinson said. Cartwright chuckled as he saluted breezily and let himself out the door.

The base commander settled heavily in the chair behind his desk. He pulled open a drawer and gazed with indecision at the white plastic bottle of Kaopectate and the fifth of Jack Daniel's. Finally he sighed and reached for the stomach liner.

— 19 —
The Outline of History

The Plant in Tarak

PRESIDENT KEMAL DROPPED LIGHTLY FROM the helicopter onto the roof of the coastal plant. Kemal and his bodyguard walked briskly in tow behind the intelligence chief Walid and the blond European called Kurtz.

A guard admitted them through a rooftop doorway, and they descended a metal ladder. Mustafa the bodyguard was left like a faithful dog to guard an outer door. In the hallway of the main plant building, Kemal heard a haunting melody in the music that was piped in. Kurtz ushered Kemal and Walid through a series of doors, each of which he unlocked with keys suspended from an enormous chain. Inside a dressing room, he bid them don white laboratory coats that hung on wooden pegs. Kemal turned around, as though he were searching for the source of the music that filled the hallway.

"Mussorgsky," Kurtz declared. His Adam's apple bobbed, and he waved his fingers through the air in rhythm to the music as though he were conducting with an imaginary baton. His pale eyes were a bit wild. "*Night on Bald Mountain*," he said, "I find the music helps my work."

President Kemal smiled uncertainly, staring at the European as though he were slightly mad. To Kemal, the clinical smells from the rows of beakers and glass tubes that surrounded them reminded him unpleasantly of a year wasted at university before he joined the Taraki air force.

"So," Kurtz said, clasping his hands together, "we may begin. But first I have the question I must ask your president, General Walid."

"And what question is it?" Walid inquired mildly.

"The president for life has a strong stomach, yes?"

"Doctor Kurtz," Kemal said. "I am a head of state. Do not address my intelligence chief. Speak directly to me. As for my stomach, I am a soldier. I have fought in five wars and got as many wounds."

"Of course," the blond man said, half bowing.

"*Bon*," Kemal said. "Now, show us the purpose of this visit, as I have affairs to attend to in the capital this afternoon."

Somewhat chastened, Kurtz said, "There is much to see. There are photographs. These must be followed by a familiarization with the chemicals. After that, we will visit the subjects."

He led Kemal and Walid into a small office and bid the officials be seated. Then he pulled down a screen and plugged in a slide projector. Each of his motions was considered, almost mechanical. When he observed that Kemal and Walid were comfortable, Kurtz dimmed the lights.

"The base work for the program here at Tarak was accomplished in Germany, in the late nineteen thirties," Kurtz said. "When the victorious Red Army captured the I.G. Farben chemical works in East Prussia, our scientists learned that the fascists had developed a potent nerve gas. They called it Tabun. Inexplicably, they never used it. Its battlefield application would have been devastating. It could have turned the tide of war.

"The Nazis developed Tabun, but Soviet scientists refined it, in the Caucasus," Kurtz continued. "Once the formula was known, its manufacture was simple enough. If you can manufacture fertilizer or insecticide, you can make chemical weapons."

Kemal listened intently but said nothing. Kurtz fiddled with the slide projector, then clicked a hand control. The first slide was a grainy black-and-white aerial photograph of a factory, which resembled the works at Tarak except for its location in a forest.

"This was the complex at Dyhernfurth, liberated in forty-five. The pictures you see were also liberated from the fascists."

The next few slides revealed pictures of humans in various stages of physical distress. Some were ragged, wretched creatures, their death-camp tattoos marked on their emaciated arms. Others were young and strong, soldiers apparently. When photographed, all were plainly near death. In a second sequence of photos, close-ups of the eyes showed the subjects' pupils contracted to pinpricks, and hideously discolored blotches of skin. Kemal whispered a question to Walid, who told Kurtz to stop the slide show.

"My president asks about your experimental subjects. Who were these people?"

"You see, they were not really people to the Nazis. The strongest among the research subjects were Russian prisoners. They took the longest to expire."

Kemal clapped his hands. "Enough," he said. "I have seen enough. Tell me, Doctor Kurtz, your reasons for bringing your work to my country. I must hold a man in deep suspicion who has no emotions about such work."

Kurtz ran his hand through his blond hair. He looked directly at Kemal, his pale blue eyes almost disconcerting the president for life. "Like you, I am a soldier," Kurtz replied tersely. "I would hazard to say I have probably killed more imperialists than you, Abu Hassan Kemal, President for Life."

"And so?" Kemal demanded. "I want your opinion on the work you do."

Kurtz shrugged. "The climate for such weapons development as I am interested in is not good in my country at the moment." With mounting intensity he added, "In fact, there are insane proposals to do away with such weapons altogether. But such weapons are needed, wouldn't you agree?" His eyes burned through the darkness with an eerie intensity.

"Needed for what?" Kemal asked pointedly.

"For your struggle, my President," Kurtz said smoothly.

"If you should decide to wage war on the Zionists. A decisive war. And I can assure you—in that matter your struggle is my own."

Kemal got up and abruptly strode from the office. Walid followed him into the outer laboratory. "My President, you are troubled," Walid said, seeing that his leader was, in fact, livid.

"This has no honor, Walid! This filth that you have brought me is not a man. He is a satanic creature!" Walid pursed his lips and crossed his arms. He coldly returned the gaze of the man who could have him executed at the snap of a finger.

"Your responsibility is to your people, my President. Let me say this. I think I need say it only once. The Zionists have the bomb. As we speak, they could reduce our homeland to smoking ruin that would not bear fruit for a thousand years. We must use the tools at hand to defeat them."

"This man that you call a scientist is a lunatic, Walid."

"It is not for us to judge the sanity of his ideas. We must regard his work." Walid took his president gently by the arm and led him back into the office.

"Please tell your president that I am sorrowful if he is offended by the graphic nature of my presentation," Kurtz said tonelessly. "Science must be presented without letting decadent sentiment get in the way."

"This form of warfare is distasteful to him," Walid explained.

"I understand," Kurtz said. "Our great leader Lenin also was a kind man." His eyes came strangely alight as he became more animated. "Please, President Kemal, believe me when I say that I am sympathetic to your plight."

Pacing, with his hands behind his back, Kurtz said, "When I was a small child, my village was sacked by the fascists." He stopped and turned abruptly. "Do you understand what that means?" Kemal nodded silently.

"I spent my young life studying the science of war and the science of socialism," Kurtz said. "It leads me to conclude that Zionism is fascism."

"We would agree," Walid said perfunctorily.

Kurtz looked at Kemal imploringly. "Even my own government is losing its taste for the fight with the imperialists! But a few of us see the need to continue the struggle. We can help you if you let us.'' He clenched his fists in front of him as he spoke. Suddenly, the mechanistic Kurtz was convulsed with emotion.

Kemal slumped in his chair and folded his arms. "How do you come to be here, Doctor Kurtz? Under what authorization? Candidly, you sound like a madman, and your operation sounds like treachery to your leaders in Moscow."

"Judge my work to see if I am mad," Kurtz said. "I represent a group that will reshape the face of socialism. And I guarantee—the weapon we offer you is a bargain at any price. Is your personal loyalty to Moscow?"

"It is not for you to ask where my loyalties lie," the president for life said cryptically. Kemal shifted uneasily in his chair, then waved his hand, bidding Kurtz to continue his presentation. The scientist returned to his slides.

"It was by relentless research that we came upon that which we were seeking. There had been many gases. Mustard, lewisite, chlorine, phosgene. Although deadly, they lacked persistence. A change in wind could blow them away—or in the wrong direction, at the troops that launched them."

Abruptly Kurtz ended his presentation, plunging the office into momentary darkness. He turned on the light, blinding Kemal and Walid for an instant. He opened the office door leading to an inner laboratory chamber and beckoned them to follow. With their eyes still blinking, Kemal and Walid followed.

The room was dark and cool. Kurtz switched on a lamp. A large mongrel stood panting in a cage. It was the sort that wandered the back streets of Kharmat, seeking scraps. This one was large and well fed. Kurtz pressed a button and a laboratory assistant entered, carrying a damp cloth and an eye dropper. The assistant opened the cage and shaved a patch of the animal's fur with electric clippers. The animal, apparently sedated, did not object.

The assistant nimbly placed a drop of liquid on the dog's shaven skin. Immediately the animal quivered violently and collapsed. An instant later, the dog lay on its side, still shaking but already dead. Kurtz crossed his arms triumphantly and beamed at President Kemal and General Walid.

"You see? The effects are immediate. There was a time when it took hours or minutes for such a toxin to work. Gentlemen, this is progress."

Kemal grunted a question in Arabic to Walid. The intelligence officer asked Kurtz in what quantities the toxin had been prepared.

"We need more research," Kurtz replied. "I must make use of the other experimental subjects you have been so kind to supply me with. And, of course, we will need to improvise a delivery system." Producing a sheet of paper from a manila folder on the desk, Kurtz showed it first to Kemal, then to Walid.

"I have asked Moscow for these in the past," Kemal said, pointing at the diagram on the sheet of paper. "SCUD-B. An old missile, but reasonably accurate and with a five-hundred-kilometer range."

"More than enough range to hit Tel Aviv," Walid agreed. Kurtz smiled. He rubbed tentatively at the scar on his forehead and said, "Maybe this time we can get them for you, Honored President."

—— 20 ——
The Needle

The Plant in Tarak

SGT. MAJ. COLIN DAVIS TWITCHED his leg muscles and flexed his arms, testing the strength of the straps that bound him to the gurney. They were snug and strong. Regaining consciousness after his capture, the SAS man could only guess what lay ahead. He shivered. He heard the bleating of the sheep nearby.

Still groggy, he blinked furiously, fighting to regain his sight. The white light of blindness subsided to a muddy blur. He tasted bile on his swollen tongue. The doping was doubly unpleasant because while he was awake, he was coherent enough to understand what was said, but he couldn't move. He had a nightmare memory of a man with a scar staring at him.

As he worked to clear his head, the dopiness subsided enough that the sergeant major could drool. He could raise his neck a fraction of an inch. As Davis practiced rolling his head from side to side, an enormous medical orderly entered the room, reeking of body odor and hair tonic. In Istanbul, Davis knew, such men worked at the baths as masseurs. Realizing that he was not in Istanbul but was captive in a dungeon, strapped to a table, the groggy sergeant major recognized the evil-smelling man for what he was—a goon.

The man leaned over and leered, adding garlic breath to his repertoire of odors. Having done most of his duty tours in the Middle East, Davis's olfactory senses were seasoned, but this goon was truly exceptional. The huge orderly wheeled the gurney around and out into a hallway that was lit by bare bulbs. Foul-smelling water dripped from creases in the wall.

The giant pushed the gurney down a long stone ramp, then around a corner, and Davis found himself in yet another examining room. Davis gritted his teeth in cold fury at his own helplessness. A nurse entered the examining room. She wore a surgical mask and carried with her a tray of hypodermic needles, which gleamed with cold elegance.

The nurse methodically filled one syringe with an evil-looking fluid that resembled urine. She turned to Davis. The SAS man watched the goon who wheeled him in fold his arms and grin like a dog waiting for a treat. Davis looked into the nurse's brown eyes, attempting to read them for some sign of compassion, regret, or excitement. They registered only professional detachment. The goon peered over her shoulder as she prepared the injection site.

Using a cotton ball, she swabbed Davis's arm with alcohol and raised the syringe, preparing to plunge the needle deep into his skin. He looked on helplessly and pushed against the straps so he would not flinch. Thunderstruck, he watched her stick the goon instead.

Suddenly the evil-smelling orderly fell to the floor, like a tree trunk falling in the forest. The woman extracted the needle from the goon's arm and pulled down her mask. "Can you walk?" she whispered urgently. "If you cannot, it is better that I kill you right now so it will not be slow and terrible."

"Put it to me that way, miss, and I think I can fairly well fly," Colin Davis grunted.

The woman went to work loosening his straps. Davis eased himself off the gurney. His legs nearly buckled beneath him, but he willed himself to stand. For a moment he leaned on the gurney, breathing heavily and sagging under his own weight. The nurse worked furiously at pulling the sweat-stained khaki shirt off the back of the unconscious orderly.

"Help me," she demanded. "If we delay, we will both die in this place."

Davis sucked in a deep breath and helped her pull the man's shirt off. He examined it with distaste, then shrugged and put it on. They took the orderly's pants and boots and his pistol belt. The nurse tossed Davis her sterile mask and motioned for him to put it on, which he did.

"You must help me put him on the table," she whispered. Davis sighed, glad that the mask barred at least some of the man's smell from his nostrils. Stealthily, he pocketed the half-empty syringe.

With all the strength he could gather, he helped the woman lift the goon. The woman worked efficiently, with a man's strength and speed. She peered into the hallway, then bid him to follow, pushing the gurney. They rolled it back up the ramp and onto a floor just below ground level. Davis heard the bleating sheep above. The sergeant major and the woman pushed the gurney until they came to a steel door with a mesh window grate. A guard peered through the grate. Seeing the nurse and her aide, the guard opened the door.

Both guards at the door carried AK-47 assault rifles. One glanced at Davis, then looked at the gurney. Muttering an oath, the guard reached for his rifle, which lay beside the wall. With a quiet snap his neck was broken by the knife edge of Davis's hand. The nurse brought the other guard to his knees with an eye gouge and kick to the crotch. She silenced him by pressing on his windpipe until it cracked.

The SAS man and the nurse caught each other's eyes in momentary appraisal, finding each other competent. The woman picked up one of the assault rifles and hid it under the sheet next to the goon.

They pushed the goon through the door and out into the evening air. The two walked briskly, attempting to maintain a clinical deportment, but the sounding of an alarm klaxon signaled that they had been seen. Troops poured out the door they had just exited, and another squad ran around the building, making toward them. Davis pulled the pistol he took from the goon and dropped two of the soldiers on the run with a sharp *crack, crack.* The nurse pulled the assault rifle from under the sheet. Soon rounds were popping throughout the yard. Davis felt the sharp sting of a ricochet and a warmth on his right arm.

"This way," the woman urged, stopping only to fire as she ran.

They turned the corner of a building, and Davis shot a truck driver in the face as the man wheeled his vehicle forward. The woman handed the AK-47 to Davis and pulled the slain driver from the cab. She climbed in and gunned the engine. Davis jumped onto the running board of the vehicle as it lumbered toward the gate and dropped his pistol through the driver's window into his rescuer's lap.

Bullets whizzed by as the woman crashed the truck through the barricade at the plant gate. Davis heard sirens screeching and saw searchlights come ablaze in the truck's mirror as they bumped onto the coast road. He saw the headlights of other trucks and heard a heavy machine-gun chatter as they drove away. A heavy tire blew as the woman careered down the highway. Luckily, the Russian trucks were built for rough travel.

Less than a mile from the plant on the coast road, the woman turned hard right and shouted to Davis, "When you see the airfield, start shooting!"

Davis, still weak, clung to the wildly veering truck. But when he spotted the helipad with the little Russian helicopter, he gritted his teeth and fired, dropping two guards on the concrete with the AK as the woman mashed gears and stopped the truck.

"In your interrogation you said you could fly, Sergeant Major. I hope you were right."

"I'll fly anything in NATO. Never flew one of Ivan's egg-beaters before."

"Now is the time to learn," she gasped as they raced toward the cockpit. They heard the convoy in pursuit from the plant turning onto the road to the helipad.

Clambering into the cockpit, they found themselves looking down the barrel of a pistol held shakily by a Taraki pilot. Davis smiled and dropped flat as the nurse shot the top of the flier's head off with her pistol. Davis pushed the pilot aside roughly and hit the chopper's ignition.

"You know the way to Cyprus?" the nurse asked.

"By dead reckoning, maybe. My mates are there."

"Mine, too, Sergeant Major."

As the helicopter soared aloft over the moonlit whitecaps of the Mediterranean, he noticed that his rescuer was a copper-haired Levantine beauty.

— 21 —
Proud Bird Under Glass

Arlington, Virginia

FROM THE EIGHTEENTH FLOOR OF the Best Western hotel in Arlington, a guest with a corner room possesses a commanding view of the Capitol dome, the gleaming obelisk of the Washington Monument, and the stately box of the Lincoln Memorial. The corner room also offers views of the silvery USA Today Building and the stately gothic architecture of Georgetown University on the Potomac.

That day, all Lt. Col. Adam Glassman wanted was a commanding view of an escape route. Lacking that, Glassman would have liked a shave and a shower. He had a pitcher of water, but coffee was denied him by his three guards—an Air Force security man, the FBI counterintelligence man, and most recently, a young sandy-blond CIA officer attired in a faultless Navy blazer as though he were still prepping at Exeter.

A muffled knock at the door was answered by the CIA man. He allowed in a middle-aged woman in a brown tweed suit. She removed her court-recording equipment from its carrying case. Seated at her keyboard, she looked up expectantly. When the CIA man began talking, her fingers sped across the keys.

"So let's try it again, Major," the CIA officer said. "When

did you decide Israel's interests superseded those of your own country?"

Glassman replied, "I would have thought you needed permission from an adult to come all the way here from Langley. You're younger than a flight surgeon. I guess it's like cops."

The roses bloomed in the CIA man's cheeks, causing the FBI man and the Air Force major to smirk. "Let's try it on again," the CIA handler repeated, stuttering slightly on the *t*. "When you decided to sell out your country, was it for money, like Pollard, or are you some kind of true believer?"

Glassman shook his head and chuckled bitterly. He eyed the trio of investigators and folded his arms. "I want to know when they're going to send in the A team," Glassman said. "You guys should be playing in the Carolina League."

"Tell us about the Arabs, Major," the Air Force interrogator said. "Did they light you up after they shot you down in eighty-five? Put the electrodes on your nuts? Did that piss you off enough to make you work for your friends in Tel Aviv?"

"Major, I will say for you what I have said previously. I was assigned by the U.S. Air Force to act in the capacity of air attaché in the nation of Israel. Standard diplomatic coverage."

Glassman reached for the water pitcher, poured himself a glass, and took a few sips. Tonelessly, he repeated his recital. "Pursuant to those duties, I evaluated Israeli combat aircraft for the United States Air Force. During that assignment I was shot down and captured by forces of a government that more often than not is hostile to the interests of the United States."

"And hostile to the interests of the Israelis, you might add," the FBI man interjected.

"Don't interrupt me, pal," Glassman retorted. "You want to ask questions, then let me answer. As previously, I state that I was captured and was, in effect, a POW. I acquitted myself honorably and was decorated by the president. How much of a spy do I sound like to you, really?"

"Try not to wrap yourself in the flag, Major," the CIA man sneered.

"Suit yourself, youngster. You've got my statement. I don't see how much further we can go."

"You realize of course, Colonel, that this inquiry is being

conducted deep in the black,'' the young CIA man asserted. ''We don't ever have to let you go.''

''I can't tell you how much I treasure the thought of us growing old together,'' Glassman said acidly.

The Langley man glared at him, and the Air Force major kept himself busy scribbling notes on a yellow legal pad, even as he stubbed his cigarette out in an overflowing ashtray.

The FBI agent stood up, stretched, and took off his coat. Slinging it over his shoulder, he paced for a few moments. Then, folding his arms, he approached Glassman and squinted at him. ''There's one thing I don't understand, Mr. Glassman.''

''Address me by my rank.''

''Okay, okay, Colonel,'' the FBI man said. ''Have it your way. The thing I don't understand is if you're so squeaky clean, why won't you go on the box?''

''It's simple. If I take a polygraph, this inquiry becomes formal. I've got a flying career, and I don't want this in my two-oh-one file.''

''You think this isn't a record?'' the CIA man said angrily, waving toward the stenographer.

''You'll shred it when you find out how badly you fucked up, sonny,'' Glassman said, grinning. ''That's what you guys are good at.''

The Air Force investigator stood and adjusted the wrinkles in his civvy suit. ''We want to hear it again about this girl, Sabrina Rabin,'' the Air Force man said.

''Anything you want about her, you're going to have to clear at a higher level than what I see in this room right now,'' Glassman said, pouring himself some more water.

''At what level?''

Glassman said, ''Talk to the main guy at Langley. The director. Brady Daniels. He knows about Miss Rabin.''

The young CIA agent jerked his head and marched over to Glassman. ''You lying son of a bitch,'' the CIA agent hissed. ''Typical asshole stunt to pick a dead witness.''

''What are you talking about?'' Glassman demanded, rising from his chair.

''Director Daniels died of a stroke in New York two days ago. The deputy director for operations is in charge until they get a new chief.''

Glassman gazed through the eighteenth-floor window at the planes taking off from National Airport. He stared into space for a moment, then turned to the CIA man. "This is true?" he asked.

"You lying sack of shit," the CIA officer said, mimicking a phrase learned from an older case officer. "You know it is."

Glassman put his head in his hands and sighed deeply. The CIA handler grabbed the FBI man by the arm and ushered him beyond the earshot of Glassman and the stenographer.

"This isn't getting us anywhere," the CIA man whispered. "I want the Air Force out of this, and I'm going back to Langley with a recommendation for hostile interrogation."

The FBI man shrugged his shoulders and muttered, "He thinks he's a hard guy."

The FBI man looked up and saw Glassman staring at him coolly, as though he were measuring him for a suit or a casket. Suddenly, it occurred to the FBI man that Colonel Glassman was, indeed, a hard guy.

— 22 —
Enter the Dragon

Beale Air Force Base, California

CARTWRIGHT PACED OFF THE 101-FOOT length of the SR-71 aircraft, checking its expensive black skin for dents, scratches, or other flaws that could interrupt its unique aerodynamic form. He executed an about-face and walked nearly halfway back beneath the spy plane's spade-shaped nose. Trailing him was the maintenance crew chief, the lanky Senior Master Sgt. Tom T. Ellsworth, and Major Ed Rogers.

Approaching the aft section, Cartwright led the anxious pair in a column left, slowly passing under the fifty-five-foot span of black titanium wing. As they made their circuit, a dripping echoed in the hangar. It was the special JP-7 jet fuel forming droplets as it seeped from fuel bladders in the wings. In another plane such leakage would constitute danger. A spark could cause an explosion and fire. Blackbird fuel, however, was designed to propel an airplane at Mach 3-plus. No ordinary seal could hold it. Rubber soon turned brittle on a superheated plane hugging the edge of space. So the high-temperature combustion fuel leaked harmlessly through the cracked seals, and a bold or foolish man could throw a lit match in the puddle of fuel without fear of blowing himself to hell. None had ever tried it though.

"Is she ready, Tom?" Cartwright inquired quietly.

"She's my airplane, General," Ellsworth replied. "Until you take the stick, that is." Cartwright took him at his word with a nod.

"Major Rogers and I will retire to officers' mess, where we will consume a high-carbohydrate breakfast consisting of steak, eggs, and one optional cup of black coffee," Cartwright declared. "Following that, we depart for a classified destination."

"Affirmative, sir," Ellsworth replied.

"Until Major Rogers and I are airborne, you, Sergeant Ellsworth, are not to take your eyes from this strategic reconnaissance aircraft."

"Understood, sir," Ellsworth answered.

"You done good, Tommy," Cartwright said, clapping Ellsworth on the shoulder. "It's not easy to live up to a reputation."

The lanky senior master sergeant from Texas grinned. Cartwright turned about-face and strode from the hangar with Major Rogers in tow. Their boots clumped across the concrete hangar floor, echoing into the starlit darkness outside.

Inside the SR squadron mess, Cartwright wolfed down his steak, chewing with gusto. Rogers sipped disconsolately at a Pepsi. "Major, is there something wrong?" Cartwright demanded as he sawed a piece of steak with a wicked slash.

"No sir."

"You look pale, son. A man doesn't like to fly with a man that looks like he's got a bug up his hindquarters." The major, a husky young man with a linebacker's neck and an advanced degree in physics, looked up helplessly at Cartwright.

"Sir, I am not entirely happy to be flying with the general."

"And why would that be, Major?" Rogers's cheeks flushed as he stared silently at his untouched steak. "This isn't the officers' wives' club, Major Rogers. Spit it out," Cartwright ordered.

"Sir, begging your pardon, but the SR-71 operation is a close-knit crew. I have flown thirty-three missions with Colonel Glassman. With all due respect for your rank, sir, I know you only by reputation and some testimonials in magazine ads."

Cartwright chewed his steak carefully. "I appreciate your candor, Major. And I understand. Now, listen up."

Rogers took a stab at his steak and gulped down a mouthful of scrambled eggs. The high-carbohydrate breakfast was designed to sustain the fliers on missions of many hours and thousands of miles, but it seemed to catch in his throat. He swallowed hard and made a show of listening.

"You may not be aware that I helped build the strategic reconnaissance program, Major."

"No sir, I was not."

"That's good. It means people in the program still keep their mouths shut. That is as it should be. Are you aware of your partner's current troubles?"

"I am not, nor should I be."

"That, Major, is also an acceptable answer. Chicken-shit but acceptable. I will be frank. Your airplane driver is in some deep shit."

"I understand," Rogers said glumly.

"You probably don't. But I want you to know some small part of my involvement. I am actively engaged in attempting to extract him from the honey dip he finds himself in. To do that, I need to get back in the cockpit of the SR-71. That means that for the next little while, I am your airplane driver."

"Yes sir."

"Can you live with that?"

"Yes sir."

A moment later Major Rogers looked up in surprise. General Rawlinson, the base commander, entered the tiny mess area set aside for Blackbird preflight. Automatically, he rose. Cartwright got up more gingerly and extended his hand to the base commander.

"General, you're up early."

"I'm not getting much sleep these past couple of days, Scott," he said, shaking Cartwright's hand. "At ease, Major." Seeing the major's pained expression, the base commander said, "Major, go get yourself another cup of coffee."

Rogers hurried away gratefully, belonging to the flier's school that wanted as little contact with generals as possible.

"You've got a change of plans, Scott. You've got a short hop to Southern California before you deploy to your TDY station."

"What's up?"

"A huddle with a couple of Lockheed tech reps at Palm-dale," Rawlinson said.

"Why are you telling me this, Pete? You could've sent a lieutenant over here and got some shut-eye."

"I'll be brief, Scott. On this base I am the only man jack in the chain of command who has knowledge of your eventual destination."

"I'm not entirely aware of it myself, Pete. We'll check in at RAF Mildenhall and play it by ear," Cartwright said, grinning easily.

"Don't play games with me, Scott. I'm too old. Besides, I'm ringmaster on your refueling operations. You're going to Cyprus."

By the time Rogers and Cartwright completed the elaborate series of final checks on their gold space suits and their airplane, rose-hued streaks of dawn stretched over the low, brown country that surrounded the air base. Twirling lights on maintenance vehicles turned like barber shop candy canes as the rosy sky turned gold and the two men in space suits clambered aboard the black plane.

The candy cane lights twirled, the ground radios chattered, and the myriad of ground crew voices chorused the singsong of Blackbird preflight ritual. The SR-71 swung onto the runway, graceful as a black swan.

Easing the throttle ahead only slightly, Cartwright propelled the dagger-shaped Blackbird forward. Once the plane was airborne, the afterburners of the J-58 engines fired, and the black plane took off like a bullet. The Blackbird flew the distance from Beale, near San Francisco, to Los Angeles in a little more than twelve minutes, descending on a guarded airstrip in the Mojave Desert before its ramjets hit cruising speed.

"Hardly seems worth the waste of an 'E ticket' to take her up and bring her down so fast," Cartwright remarked as he eased the plane down onto the runway at Air Force Plant 42.

A tow vehicle rolled forward, hooking itself to the nose section of the Blackbird. Cartwright and Rogers stepped clumsily down the metal ladders.

"Stay with the airplane, Major. I'll be back."

"Yes sir."

"And, Major—"

"Yes sir?"

"Loosen up."

Cartwright clumped away toward a civilian who waved a clipboard at him. The Lockheed man wore the button-down shirt and pocket protector that were the uniform of the tech reps who installed the "black box" sensor gear on the spy plane. Cartwright followed him into a hallway adjoining the hangar. They passed through a maze of doors, each activated by a keyless entry pad and opening with a little electronic thud. Finally they stopped at a door where a red light flashed like a traffic signal. When the light turned green, they moved on.

They entered a room bathed in red light. There was a conference table with three or four chairs. Near the back wall of the concrete chamber was a room divider designed for muffling office noise. The tech rep vanished.

A portly man with a salt-and-pepper beard stepped from behind the divider. On the lapel of his dark blue suit, the old man wore a little pin about the size of a dime. The pin was an enamel skunk. The bearded man carried a multilock high-security briefcase in one hand and offered his free hand to Cartwright. "Hello, Scott. Long time, no see," he said, grinning impishly.

"Benjamin Johnson!" Cartwright said, pumping the man's hand vigorously. "Too damn long." Cartwright noted quickly the bulge of an automatic pistol in Johnson's ample waistband.

"So how's my black plane holding up?" Johnson asked, seating himself.

"Not bad for a girl of thirty," Cartwright replied. "You built her to last."

"She could turn tricks well past forty," Johnson said.

"Tell that to the Pentagon," Cartwright said. Johnson snorted.

"You didn't bring me to Palmdale for a testimonial, Ben. What's in the case?"

A high-pitched whine pierced the white noise of the generators pumping air into the underground chamber. It was the sound of an electronic speaker box, adjusting pitch.

"You are correct, General," a tinny, disembodied voice

announced from behind the room divider. "Your presence here is mission essential."

With a puzzled expression, Cartwright glanced at Johnson, who busied himself fiddling with the locks and latches on his briefcase. Cartwright started to walk toward the room divider.

"Make no attempt to identify me, General Cartwright," the tinny voice ordered. "To do so would constitute a grave national-security breach."

"I like to know who I'm talking to," Cartwright said. "Suppose we get acquainted by me walking around your little wizard curtain."

"If you should do that," the electronic voice beeped, "the only thing you could depend upon would be your immediate separation from service and cancellation of your mission. Do you want that?"

"Nope," Cartwright said softly, forming his lips into a soundless whistle. He seated himself at the table across from Johnson and, like a good poker player, waited the next move. Johnson gazed levelly at Cartwright, his eyes gray pools of steel. "You've been invited to a very special briefing, Scott. They saw fit to bring me out of retirement for it."

"Sometimes it is better to put trust in experience," the tinny voice said. "Recall the efforts of Colonel North. All that youthful zeal yielded little benefit for the national security. Don't you agree, General?"

"It wasn't my call. I don't believe I got your name, stranger."

"That is because I didn't give it, General. I gave no name. But for the purposes of organization, you may call me Dragon. Just so you are aware of your circumstances, General, consider me a superior officer of flag rank."

"Okay, Dragon, sir. You got this rusty knight in your castle," Cartwright said, gesturing toward Johnson. "So what do you want?"

"It is not what I want," the tinny voice beeped from behind the divider. "Mr. Johnson will give you details on a new piece of equipment you are to carry aloft on your deployment."

Johnson methodically spread a series of schematics and diagrams before him. To a layman they were incomprehensible.

To Cartwright, an engineer in addition to being a test pilot, the drawings represented the language of genius.

"The Dragon wanted me to carry these and deliver them by hand," Johnson said proudly, running his fingers across the drawings and adjusting the pistol in his waistband.

"Okay, Benjamin. You got a new black box. What does it do?"

"The new box achieves a degree of high-resolution photography never before dreamed possible. My boys are installing it in your plane even as we speak. In fact, it's not even photography. It's radar imagery."

"It looks neat. But look here, Ben boy. I can only take so much ribbing. Who's the guy back there?" Cartwright asked, indicating the screen.

"Give your undivided attention to Mr. Johnson," the tin-box voice beeped. Cartwright frowned at the screen that shielded the voice from his sight. He sighed finally and turned to Johnson.

"Okay, it's your move. I thought we'd taken high-resolution photography about as far as it could go. We can detail on anything down to the size of a golf ball."

"Not under reinforced concrete," Johnson said portentously. "Until now. That's why they gave me the chained suitcase and the gun."

"Capability for surveillance through concrete? X-ray vision, like Superman? C'mon."

"Listen, Scott. They poured billions into the Strategic Defense Initiative when it was at high tide. You didn't think I'd let them spend all that Star Wars money without my guys getting some use out of it?"

Cartwright whistled roundly this time, running his fingers through his shock of silver hair.

"You are looking at the specifications for a camera that makes use of combined technologies, taking advantage of advances in radars, lasers, and use of the electromagnetic spectrum."

"So what do we get for our taxpayer dollars?"

"An imaging device that works better than an X ray. It will give us precise verification of enemy installations by technical means."

"I thought the only thing we flew over Russia lately was satellites."

"No overflight of Soviet territory is planned, General," the metallic voice behind the screen asserted. "You will be flying over the Middle East. That is my part of the briefing."

"Why tell me about all this?" Cartwright asked. "If you brief me on this technology, I could be opened up like a can of peaches if I get shot down."

"If you get shot down, General, the plan is for you to die," the tinny voice said. "Surely you must realize that. The means will be provided."

"That's what they told Powers," Cartwright snorted. He found his hand in his pocket, unconsciously fingering the lucky charm given him by Madeline Murdoch.

"General, before we continue, let me preface myself," the voice box beeped. "Up to this point, you are not witting. Should you opt to proceed, you will be in possession of operational knowledge. This is an 'off-the-books operation.' "

"Clarify yourself, Mr. Dragon," Cartwright demanded.

"There will be no further clarification. Do you accept this mission?"

"I have accepted every damn mission my government ever gave me."

"You have been chosen because of your years, your seasoning, your experience. Younger men might be more physiologically ideal, but our belief is that it is your experience that will provide mission insurance."

"Skip the saddle soap. What's the deal?"

"The deal is you are to overfly the nuclear reactor at Dimona, Israel. You will conduct a reconnaissance of the suspected nuclear weapons stockpile there."

"Sweet Jesus," Cartwright whispered. "Madeline wasn't kidding. We've got no satellite coverage. That's it, isn't it?"

"Silence!" the Dragon said peremptorily. "During overflight the Blackbird reconnaissance operator will effect a sensor sweep of a coastal factory in Country Six, otherwise identified as the Federated Socialist Republic of Tarak."

"You think that's enough for one day?" Cartwright asked dryly, eyeing Benjamin Johnson and his pearl-handled pistol.

"It is not enough," the tin voice replied. "During your deployment at the RAF base on Cyprus, you will effect contact with an Israeli national. She is called Sabrina Rabin, a friend of your protégé, Colonel Glassman. You will determine the extent of their relationship and attempt to verify Glassman's loyalties."

"Anything else?"

Johnson interjected, "Should your aircraft be destroyed, your data will separate from the Blackbird via a D-21 drone. The remotely piloted vehicle will be recovered."

The tinny voice adjusted pitch. "More to the point, General, let's hope the pilot gets home safe and sound. We want to know about Colonel Glassman's loyalties. We also need to know about the Dimona reactor and a potential problem in Tarak. In short, we have need for quality in human intelligence and technical intelligence. Good hunting."

An automatic door snicked open, and Cartwright listened to the whir and rubber wheels of an electric wheelchair receding into the hallways. The general stared quizzically at Johnson. The aircraft designer gave him a cryptic Mona Lisa smile by way of an answer and shackled the black-box briefcase to his wrist.

— 23 —
Charlotte's Web

SITTING IN HER WEST-WING OFFICE at the White House, the national security adviser was chewing nicotine gum and reading a transcript of a National Security Agency satellite interception in its original Russian. In Madeline Murdoch, the president possessed an aide of such commanding intellect that rather than being swamped by data, she sculpted it.

It also aided the president that damn near all the men on Capitol Hill were intimidated by the Nobel laureate he recruited and that his military men were simply scared of her. Although married to a pleasant economist known as the "Denis Thatcher of Georgetown," her own nom de guerre on the Potomac was "the Duchess." She never heard it to her face, but she relished the knowledge of it, just as she relished her faint resemblance to Katharine Hepburn.

At the moment, she was reading raw transcript of cockpit conversation preceding the departure of an Ilyushin transport from Iraq, just outside the passover pattern of the lost Keyhole satellite.

"Dr. Murdoch, the president will see you now," her secretary announced on her speaker box.

"Send Charlotte ahead," the security adviser replied. "I'll

be along in a minute." She deposited the nicotine gum in the ashtray. Her attempt to quit smoking was going on three weeks, but even so, she knew she could not chew gum while briefing the president. She closed her eyes and breathed deeply, sinking back in the inviting arms of her antique New England reading chair. It was in such moments of fleeting meditation that she would weld her briefing into a single thought, like a complete act in a play. She rose from her favorite chair and marched gamely, her Bass shoes squeaking all the way.

She entered the elevator and rode it to the basement level that housed the White House Situation Room and the Secure Room. As she marched toward "the Tank"—the lead-lined Secure Room—civilian and military staff cleared a path for her as though there were an invisible red carpet rolling out. Madeline Murdoch marched past the junior officers who tracked the electronic maps and three-dimensional data displays that lined the walls of the Situation Room. Charlotte Duncan, Murdoch's planning aide, stood by the bank of wire service printers, holding a folder full of briefing material.

A Marine colonel heard to gripe about "all the skirts at NSC" had vanished from the Situation Room staff recently. Charlotte Duncan was one of the many female faces on Dr. Murdoch's handpicked staff of academics from George Mason and Georgetown universities. Murdoch's "old-girl" network was rapidly replacing the "Beltway bandit" consultants.

"Charlotte, dear, this is your first Sit Room briefing, so naturally you are tense," Dr. Murdoch said briskly. "But since there is no substitute for experience, conquer your emotions and jump right in. Nobody can give this presentation better than you."

"Yes, Doctor," Charlotte Duncan said gratefully. Praise from Murdoch was rare and usually reserved for pep talks before battle.

Smiling, the national security adviser said, "Just be ready to run for a goddamned pack of cigarettes if I get a nick fit."

"With your willpower, Dr. Murdoch, you can do anything," Ms. Duncan said reassuringly.

"Easy for you to say, dear. Try it sometime," Dr. Murdoch said formidably. The national security adviser adjusted the fit of her Harris tweed coat and businesslike, yet frilly, peach-colored silk blouse.

Seeing Madeline Murdoch, the Marine sergeant at the desk outside the Secure Room rose to attention. Making a white-gloved usher's gesture, the sergeant motioned her toward the combination-locked door, all the while keeping his other hand on his sidearm. The sergeant inspected Charlotte Duncan's badge, then keyed the electronic pad to the lead-lined, bug-free inner sanctum.

The president waited within, along with Avery Benedict, acting director of the CIA; James Scott, director of the FBI; and Richard Nunn, secretary of defense. Minutes of the meeting would reflect the secretary of state was in Brussels, attempting to shore up NATO, again.

She was not late, Dr. Murdoch observed, checking her Rolex. They were early. All rose to greet her, and each man smiled politely at Charlotte Duncan. "Coffee, ladies?" the president offered. His informality was linked to his popularity.

"Thank you, no, Mr. President," Madeline Murdoch said. "I am trying to kick the tobacco addiction and caffeine seems to aggravate the need. My aide, Ms. Duncan, might like a cup, however."

In a courtly fashion, the gaunt director of the FBI, known to all as "the Judge," walked over to the coffeemaker and poured a cup for Charlotte Duncan, who was maintaining her composure by standing regally erect, waiting for the president's men to sit. She took one small sip, then set the cup on the table that held twin projectors and an IBM personal computer.

"Well, let's get to it, Dr. Murdoch," the president said. "I get about three briefings like this in a normal lousy year. What's up?"

"Mr. President, I fear that we are facing a Hydra, a monster with many heads, a complex and dangerous situation."

"You're at your best when you're blunt, Doctor," the president said.

"In fact, sir, I do not intend to speak until the briefing is finished, so that we may consider options. My aide, Ms. Duncan, will give the presentation."

"Please proceed, Ms. Duncan," the president said.

Holding a mouse control in her hand, Charlotte Duncan gathered her wits. Manipulating the mouse, she illuminated the screen.

"Gentlemen, today we present a complex web of events. What you are viewing is a nuclear explosion in the South Atlantic. The blinking light in the map portion of the graphic displays the longitude and latitude where the detonation took place."

"How did we come by this?" snapped Avery Benedict, acting director of the CIA. Benedict was half the age of his predecessor, the late Brady Daniels. "I want to know your source," Benedict demanded, forgetting he was talking out of turn with the president in the room. "I'm supposed to get the satellite stuff first."

Charlotte Duncan looked to Madeline Murdoch for guidance. The security adviser frowned and nodded, as though to say, "Get on with it, girl!" Ms. Duncan flicked her wrist, displaying a satellite picture overview of a barren desert landscape with a shadow on it that formed the shape of a dome.

"Gentlemen," she said, "for years we have known the true purpose of the Israeli reactor at Dimona. Its existence as a power station is, of course, fictional. It is the equivalent of our own weapons plants at Oak Ridge and Rocky Flats."

The camera image zoomed closer to better define the dome sitting in the wasteland, with its surrounding city and inhabitants frozen in stop motion as they went about their business during this particular fly-by of a Keyhole satellite.

"Unfortunately, in the Middle East the situation is subject to continuous change," Ms. Duncan said. "The meaning of the Israeli ambassador's recent United Nations speech was plain enough. Their government has decided to introduce operational nuclear weapons into the region."

"Balls," Avery Benedict snapped. "If they had done it, or were about to do it, CIA would know."

"Oh, really?" Madeline Murdoch said, just the least bit maliciously. "You mean, you would know it the same way that you predicted the revolution in Iran?"

Benedict flushed uncomfortably and scowled. "If I may continue," Ms. Duncan said. "We know the Israelis maintained deniability, keeping their weapon components separated in underground storage chambers. We know if they felt the need, they would assemble the weapons quickly. The greatest fear is that they might use them before they could be deterred."

"Ms. Duncan," the president said, clearing his throat. "What indication have you that our friends contemplate such a disastrous move?"

Charlotte Duncan placed her hands together as if praying and paced. "We know that for years the Israelis have possessed a nuclear potential. But their announcement, coming at the same time that we have lost satellite surveillance capability over the region, is a frightening coincidence. Couple that with the flash in the South Atlantic, and Dr. Murdoch and I fear more than coincidence may be involved."

"What are you suggesting, Ms. Duncan?" the president asked.

"We fear perhaps the Israelis decided to take our satellite down to blindside us over Dimona."

The FBI director and the secretary of defense shifted uncomfortably. Avery Benedict rose and declared, "Frankly, Dr. Murdoch, I grow somewhat weary of this dog and pony show. This is outrageous. The Israelis wouldn't and, for that matter, couldn't take a potshot at a Keyhole. That's nuts."

"Avery, sit down," the president ordered. "You are out of turn."

The acting CIA director complied, crossing his arms. He continued to speak, however. "Sir, what we have seen here is a parade of assumption after assumption. It's an exercise in feminine intuition, and I am not prepared to give it a stamp of official approval."

"That's uncalled for, Avery," Dr. Murdoch said. "It is also sexist and fatheaded, and everyone else sitting in this room is quite aware of that."

"None of this so-called information was conveyed by CIA," Benedict complained. "This is all outside-source stuff, Mr. President. I suggest that your national security adviser is free-lancing, and as director of central intelligence, I resent it."

Madeline Murdoch said, coolly, "That, Avery, is why you were invited to hear our case. We need your help, but unfortunately we haven't been able to get it."

"What are you talking about, Madeline?" Benedict snarled.

"Simply that since the illness and death of your boss, Brady Daniels, you appear more consumed with jockeying for his job than with providing timely intelligence."

"Cut that out," Benedict shouted. "That's damned unfair."

"*You* cut it out, Avery," the president ordered grimly. "I will not have my national security staff going at each other like barking dogs. We are civil in our war councils." Turning to Dr. Murdoch, he smiled easily and asked, "Madeline, what are you driving at?"

Madeline Murdoch rose and took the mouse from Charlotte Duncan. "Mr. President, there are a variety of factors in play, and we need a unified effort. It is for this reason that I asked FBI and Defense to be present as well as CIA."

She adjusted the resolution on the computer graphic of the Dimona reactor. "It is my wish to make use of the Air Force. I want to mount a manned reconnaissance over the Negev Desert."

"Dr. Murdoch," Secretary of Defense Nunn said, his every word a liquid Alabama utterance, "what yoah asking is damned risky. We don't generally overfly our friends."

"Nonsense, Dick," Madeline Murdoch said peremptorily. "We do it with satellites all the time. Only now, we haven't got a satellite, and we need timely information."

"That's what Allen Dulles said before the Russians shot down the U-2," Avery Benedict snapped.

"Avery has a point," the president said. "What would we gain from an overflight, Madeline?"

"Much greater detail on our photography, with new equipment that is being installed on an SR-71 today. From that, our information would give us some cards to play."

The men all looked at her. Clearly, she held the floor. "What else do you need, Madeline?" the president asked.

"Get FBI and CIA to resolve the matter of Adam Glassman's guilt or innocence," the security adviser said, inclining her brooding head toward the Judge. "You do remember Glassman's role in thwarting the Stealth hijack, Mr. President? He is a formidable man. If he is innocent, he must be cleared. If guilty, he must be tried." The president closed his eyes and rubbed his forehead. Finally he nodded.

"Who authorized a Blackbird preparation?" the Defense

secretary demanded testily. "We've been preparing to shut that operation down."

Smiling, Dr. Murdoch said sweetly, "It was done at the wing level, Mr. Secretary. All very harmless."

"Dr. Murdoch, nothing you are involved with is harmless," Nunn declared solemnly. "Thanks to you all, they're gonna throw open the Gridiron Club to the fair sex. Shoot."

"Mr. President, do we have authorization for the Blackbird overflight?" Madeline Murdoch persisted.

"Go ahead. But keep me informed. Let's not have any of this 'Why didn't the president know?' nonsense. I can't bear that." Signaling the end of the briefing, the president touched an electronic keypad, and the door to the Tank popped open. Avery Benedict whirled out in a huff, with his hand on his neck as though he had a pain.

— 24 —
Nitrogen Dreams

Plant 42, California

CARTWRIGHT LAY BACK IN HIS gold spacesuit and watched Ed Rogers nod off to sleep in one of the deep reclining chairs provided for SR crews in preflight prep. It would take about an hour to extract the nitrogen from their bloodstream. The suit, the same used for space shuttle operations, was a second skin that kept the blood from boiling and the head from exploding in the thin air on the edge of space. Cartwright disliked any period of vulnerability, but this quiet hour comforted him, knowing he was among friends, protected by the good guys in physiological support division.

The general looked at Rogers's sleeping face behind the visor and saw a baby, really. When Cartwright had been that age, he was already blooded, a hunting eagle roaming the angry skies over Europe. As the content of his bloodstream transformed to a safer mixture for the upper regions, he looked up at the soft warm light of the PSD chamber and saw the Messerschmitt dropping out of the sun. But he smiled, dopily, knowing it to be a dream Messerschmitt, a sleepy mirage, a memory of youth. The dream pilot gave him a ghostly wave as he passed by. His cannons must have jammed, Cartwright observed drowsily.

The general's eyelids were so heavy, yet he felt himself floating amid the womblike silence of the suit and hoses. He nodded off and dreamed of space, of the shuttle deck and the spurt of rocket motors. Finally his dreams were peaceful, the dreams of deep space.

He awoke to the gentle but insistent pressure of a PSD aide shaking his arm. "It's time, General," the strawberry blonde sergeant said cheerfully. She represented the new Air Force, and he liked it. "The PSD van is ready for you and Major Rogers."

Cartwright and Rogers looked at each other uncertainly, as though they were preparing for a moon walk. They hooked up their portable oxygen systems in the suitcase-style carriers and marched awkwardly to the PSD van outside. The van held more recliner chairs, with ventilation hoses that would keep the fliers from sweating profusely until they reached the black plane, a mile distant on Runway 22.

As streaks of pink knifed across the velvet blue sky in the east, prehistoric Saddleback Butte's jagged peaks defined the horizon. Blackbird, with the sun rising behind it, looked more spaceship than airplane.

Mounted piggyback atop the spy plane was a contraption that looked like a black cruise missile. As Cartwright and Rogers clambered down from the PSD van, Benjamin Johnson walked forward to greet them. "I haven't seen a drone mount in a dozen years," Cartwright remarked to the bearded engineer.

"We reactivated a few after Challenger blew up and we lost all those Titan boosters," Johnson said. "I always said if you could fly a plane without a pilot, why risk the valuable pilot?"

"And you were always wrong," Cartwright said, poking Johnson playfully with his heavy-gloved finger. "You'll always need the man. He's the brains in the plane—and the guts."

Rogers started walking toward the crew ladder.

"My rizzo is impatient," Cartwright remarked. "Probably thinks he's on a doomed mission with an old coot like me at the stick. Any last helpful bits of advice, Ben?"

"A few," Johnson replied. "The drone's your backup. If the bad guys get you, you must destroy the plane according to protocol. The drone will carry most of the mission data to a programmed pickup point. But we want you home in one piece, Scotty, because the D-21 can't code in the advanced imaging data from the new box. We haven't got the software yet.''

"I guess I'll just plan for success, then," Cartwright said, grinning.

"Luck to you," Johnson said, shaking the general's gloved hand.

"No such thing as too much luck," the general said, mounting the crew ladder.

The engineer shivered in the chill air of the desert dawn as he watched the ground crew pull the chocks from the tires. A green flash ignited the plane's mammoth J-58 engines. Before it used half the ten-thousand-foot runway, the black plane was racing skyward. And just as suddenly, the Blackbird vanished like a time machine, a vision of things to come.

The spy plane refueled three times en route to its forward operating location. Once over Arizona and once off the East Coast between Boston and New York, the Silver Sows fueled the Blackbird. Another airborne tanker flew from RAF Mildenhall to deliver JP-7 to the fuel-thirsty plane just north of the Azores. Thousands of miles passed in a blur. Two hundred miles east of their destination, Cartwright throttled back on the massive Pratt & Whitney engines, slowing the SR-71 for descent over the citrus orchards of Cyprus.

25
Landfall

Cyprus

THE RUSSIAN HELICOPTER FLEW LIKE an iron pig. Skimming the waves and flying a serpentine pattern, Colin Davis evaded Taraki coastal radar. The Tarakis had no talent or desire for night flying. But each second, the Moscow eggbeater threatened to dump into the sea. Davis grappled with the control yoke.

"I thought you said you could fly!" Sabrina Rabin cried out.

"I'm not fixing tea, if that's what you mean," Davis shouted back. "Sod off and let me work, woman."

"You're a dangerous fool!" she shouted over the popping and tweaking racket of the twirling rotors and the engine roar.

"Any suggestions, miss?" Davis demanded, fighting the yoke. An odor of smoke and burning oil drifted into the cockpit.

"I will call my friends," the woman shouted.

Davis nodded his head vigorously. "Now's the time for friends, if you've got 'em. We're about fifty kilometers short of landfall. Meantime, I'd don that bleeding life jacket."

As he struggled to keep the shuddering aircraft above the spray, Davis observed Sabrina Rabin remove a device about the size of a pocket calculator from her tattered nursing uniform. She uttered some commands in German, then donned the life jacket and handed another to him. He shrugged it away, unable to take his hands from the controls.

"You will see the fires," she told him simply. "They will be on the bluffs above the coast at Yialousa. Fly toward them, and I hope you can land this thing."

"That makes two of us, missy," Davis snarled. The SAS man flew straight, taking a chance that he was out of range of Taraki radar and hoping they had not scrambled their East German "adviser" pilots. Davis watched the needle on the fuel gauge bouncing against the red of the empty mark. A red light illuminated on the panel and began buzzing.

Straining to see ahead, Davis sighted the dark mass of the Cypriot coast. He sighted the fires on the cliff. Sabrina Rabin, also seeing the lights, clapped her hands and squealed in delight, despite the insistent buzzing of the alarm light.

They flew on, Davis closing the gap between the night and the lights by sheer force of will. Finally the smoke entering the cockpit could not be denied, with its rancid, sweet scent of plastic and rubber burning. There was a shudder of buckling metal. "Sorry, miss," Colin Davis cried out, attempting to free himself from his seat straps as the helicopter plunged toward the waves, short of the beckoning signal fires.

The blunt nose of the Moscow eggbeater plowed heavily into the foam, and all was black-and-white and seaspray, accompanied by a seashell's roar inside Colin Davis's ears as his head smashed into the instrument panel. Within a minute the waves washed over the helicopter, and it was yet another war relic, sinking to the bottom to join the wreckage of conquest once bound for Carthage.

When Colin Davis awoke, he sensed a familiar ache and cold beads of sweat popping on his forehead. Even though he was groggy, he was in a room he recognized. He knew he was to be interrogated again and it was only SAS discipline that kept him from beating his head against the damp wall. Instead, he lay quietly and listened. Was he back in Tarak? Had the woman and the escape been a dream? He ran his fingers along the dank limestone.

A bare light bulb popped on. He squinted, taking in the three-meter by four-meter space quickly. Furniture began and ended with the simple wooden bed he was trying so hard to raise his head from. Still, he was not bound. Sabrina Rabin descended the steps, carrying a tray of pastries and a bottle of retsina, the resinous Greek wine. This development prompted a grin from the sergeant major.

"You are feeling better," the woman said, setting down the tray and pouring the wine into a pair of earthen cups.

The change in her appearance was startling from when he had first viewed her during his tour as a laboratory specimen. At that time his eye had mostly been on the needle she brandished. Now, instead of the shapeless nursing dress, she wore a khaki safari shirt that accented her pert breasts and a smart green skirt that displayed her fine, tan legs to advantage. Her reddish bronze hair was captured in a bun that accented the line of her high cheekbones and strong straight nose. She smiled and handed him the cup of wine.

He downed it quickly. "Better," he said, resting his head against the wall. "Hair of the dog."

"My friends pumped a lot of water out of your lungs," the woman said.

"I've still got a gallon or two in me, I'll wager," he said, shaking his head like a big dog. "I feel all in."

"You will need more rest," Sabrina Rabin said, handing Davis a square of baklava. "But before too long, we hope you will be able to tell us some of the things you witnessed at the Taraki chemical plant."

He appraised her, popped the pastry in his mouth, and chewed with relish. "Thanks for the sweet, miss. And for the drink, too. Now we've dined, but we don't even know each other's name, do we? Wouldn't be proper for me to tell all to a complete stranger, would it?"

"It's not enough that I saved your life in the laboratory?" she asked, affecting a pout. "Many would be grateful."

"And I returned the favor, didn't I, miss? That why we're here in this den of iniquity, isn't it? Now, come on. Give us a name."

"You can call me Eva."

Davis barked out a short laugh. "You mean like Eva Braun? That why you talked like a sodding kraut? All right, Eva. You can call me your uncle Bob. Now what do we talk about?"

"The gasworks in Tarak."

Davis shook his head solemnly, snatching a second pastry from the basket. "That, miss, as you likely know, is of proprietary interest."

"Let me tell you, English. Our interests are in common."

"That may be your way of seeing it, miss. But I've got to look out for my own interests, don't I?"

"Then I suggest you do exactly that," Sabrina said, setting the tray aside. "Consider your present position. You cannot leave this place. We are not enemies. What would be wrong in having an exchange of views?"

Davis laughed bitterly and handed her the cup. He folded his large cord-wood arms and regarded her slyly. "We are not enemies, but that's not to say we are exactly friends. What do your pals with the microphones in the walls think of that?" he asked, inclining his head toward the wooden beams in the low ceiling.

"I think you had better reflect," the woman said soberly.

"I might be wrong, miss, but I don't think your Mossad pals upstairs have the same stuff in them as that old boy you dropped at the plant in Tarak. You might do a lot of things to sweat me, but cold-blooded murder of a soldier of the queen probably ain't one of them, now is it?"

"No one has said Mossad, English."

"Right," Davis said, chuckling.

"Still, we might do things to raise the sweat from you, if we felt it expedient. Do not underestimate us."

"Now the cards are on the table," Davis said, scratching his salt-and-pepper beard. "Well, let me tell you something, missy. I've been shocked with a cattle prod in Derry. I even took a dose of gas, fighting in the bloody Oman. My old bones have known pain you couldn't imagine. If it's going to be rough, so be it. But make sure you kill me. I've been told I've got nine lives."

"Maybe you've used most of them," she said, collecting the tray and cups. She got up to leave but glanced back at him with a trace of sadness in her eyes as she walked up the steps leading from the basement.

She stepped into the upstairs room where her teammates waited. Abraham, who had been monitoring the microphone, picked up the retsina bottle by the neck and took a long swallow. He tossed the bottle to Ephraim, who sat by the window watching the road to Larnaca. The lights of the Cypriot city winked in the distance.

"He is going to be difficult," Abraham said, removing the earphones. "We'll need a team to work on him in relays."

"I hope not," Sabrina Rabin said. "He is a good soldier."

"We are all good soldiers," Abraham said, wolfing down the last pastry. "But we do what we must do."

Sitting at the window, staring into the night, Ephraim gazed at the stars. As he watched the heavens, a black shadow passed overhead, the silhouette of a dagger-shaped plane.

—— 26 ——
Coldwell Integrated Armaments, Inc.

Alexandria, Virginia

MADELINE MURDOCH FOLLOWED BILLY CHESTERTON out of the light and smoky noise of the Fish Market Pub on King Street in the Old Town section of Alexandria. The national security adviser and the emissary from British intelligence walked two short blocks along the dimly lit banks of the Potomac until they reached a bank of low brick warehouses. Low-wattage lamps illuminated the flat black letters: Coldwell Integrated Armaments, Inc. A gray steel door clicked open. As Madeline Murdoch stepped inside, the surveillance cameras anchored to the ceiling whirred quietly.

"I've known about this place for years, but I've never been here," Dr. Murdoch said.

"Coldwell still does a favor or two for us, now and then," Chesterton said absently. "When he's not too busy counting his money in Liechtenstein."

"He's a British subject now, isn't he?"

"Brother Coldwell is a citizen of the world."

Chesterton opened a last door, and Sir Alfred Whittlesey, the director of Her Majesty's Secret Service, rose to greet Madeline Murdoch from his seat behind a modern Swedish desk of plain blond wood.

"Dr. Murdoch, what a pleasure it is"—offering his hand. His clipped military moustache bobbed above a tight smile.

"Let us hope so, Sir Alfred."

The desk Whittlesey occupied sat in a glass booth at the center of the open floor in the warehouse, which was stacked high with crates the size of small coffins. Some were stamped with the stenciled fiction Oil Drilling Machinery. Others were more descriptive: Fabrique Nationale; Heckler & Koch; or Colt. The crates stretched as far as the eye could see. Machine guns. Rocket grenades. Mortars. The Third World's arsenal. The desk where Whittlesey sat was decorated on either side by a highly polished antique Gatling gun and an early Vickers on a tripod, collectors' prizes treasured by the unseen host.

"That will be all, Billy. Secure the outside office and take a look round. That's a good fellow."

Chesterton was crestfallen at being shooed away. He sighed and departed with the dignity of the offended obese.

"He's strictly second-rate, but that's what you want in a good lackey," Whittlesey said as soon as Chesterton had left. "I can't abide that lean and hungry look of every young Cassius who comes along."

"We don't agree on management styles, Director," Madeline Murdoch said, seating herself in an uncomfortable-looking Swedish chair.

"Better to have 'em at your feet than at your throat, dear lady."

Dr. Murdoch smiled sweetly and said nothing. Whittlesey packed his pipe, lit it carefully, and blew clouds of smoke that were sucked away by the ventilation system. Fire warnings were everywhere along the wall. Madeline Murdoch reached into a pocket of her Burberry's coat and extracted a fresh pack of gum. Whittlesey gave her an odd look.

"Forgive me, Sir Alfred," Madeline Murdoch said. "While you are indulging your addiction, I am trying to give mine up. Thus I am chewing this damnable nicotine gum until I lose the jitters."

"Commendable, Dr. Murdoch. But I find my vices are antidote for my excess of virtue."

"How nice of Mr. Coldwell to lend British intelligence the

use of this excellent facility—and so close to Washington," Madeline Murdoch said acidly. "Convenient."

"He helps his friends. Perhaps he'll help you one day."

"He will, or he'll find getting the required export license for his more exotic product lines difficult."

"Exactly. Now, dear lady, how can I be of service?" Sir Alfred smiled tightly with his lips pressed across his yellowed teeth as he spoke.

"I want some British help in the Middle East."

"That's strange. Certainly you have the full use of CIA."

"At the moment I would personally prefer not to involve the agency."

"Egad," Whittlesey said, clamping down on his pipe and frowning. "You're not Johnny Poindexter going round the back door again. Got a mole, have you?"

"Certainly not," Madeline Murdoch snapped. "I merely want discreet assistance. It must be compartmented."

"To use your coppers' expression, you're not leveling with me," Sir Alfred said, his lips fixed in his reptilian grin.

Madeline Murdoch sighed. She folded her arms and rested her prominent chin in one hand. "When Director Brady Daniels of CIA died, he unfortunately took with him a great deal of knowledge about Israeli operations. Knowledge that only he possessed, up here," she said, tapping her forehead.

"That was Brady, all right," Sir Alfred said, nodding approvingly. "Close to the vest, always. And he was a good friend."

"To those he trusted, he certainly was a good friend. To those he didn't trust, he was the riddle of the sphinx. He trusted me."

"And me," Sir Alfred said, puffing his pipe contentedly. "What is it you require?"

"We wish all the information that can be gathered on a Mossad agent known as Sabrina Rabin. We believe she could solve a problem for us."

"What's in it for the queen?"

"Gratitude," Madeline Murdoch said, smiling sweetly. Whittlesey puffed and then examined his highly polished nails. Finally he nodded.

"We'll track the lady down if we can. But there's something I need."

"What might that be, Sir Alfred?"

"Brady Daniels's sudden demise was a blow to intramural cooperation between Her Majesty's service and the Company. He was a good Atlantic man. I am being candid with you, madam. CIA has shut us out since that young Turk name of Avery Benedict took over."

Madeline Murdoch sighed. "I don't think I could influence that, Sir Alfred. The president is undecided about what to do at CIA. Benedict could be there for months. He could even get the job."

"Right. Meanwhile, there is a piece of technical intelligence we are keen about. It does fall within the Middle East theater. Maybe you could get it?"

"What might that be, sir?" Madeline Murdoch asked smoothly.

"We would wish an aerial photo reconnaissance of the Israeli reactor at Dimona and the hundred or so square miles surrounding. Something that could be obtained with the U-2 or whatever it is you've got."

"Director, I am a brazen and nosy woman," Madeline Murdoch said, speaking quickly to cover her alarm. "Suppose I ask you why you want that piece of data."

Sir Alfred coughed. "Well now, I don't want to tell tales out of school, but we fear a transfer of British nuclear technology to Israel via the South African channel. We wish additional proofs, and then we intend to stop it."

Madeline Murdoch folded her elegant hands in her lap and considered the fine cut of the De Beers diamonds that graced her long fingers.

"And you say an aerial reconnaissance would help you?"

"Indeed it would, ma'am."

"I believe it can be arranged discreetly."

"Thank you kindly, Doctor. I had understood you were formidable. Now I know it. Care for a drink?"

"Thanks. Got a brandy?"

"Certainly. Too cold for gin," he said, reaching back to a portable bar behind the desk. They toasted like pirates, and

Whittlesey buzzed for Chesterton. The aide escorted Madeline Murdoch back to the Fish Market, where she called for a cab. Chesterton then quickly returned to the Coldwell warehouses, finding his boss lost in thought among the antique machine guns.

"Are the Americans aware of the chemical plant in Tarak, do you think?" the owlish aide asked his master.

"It seems not. And we'll not tell them before we are ready. Find this Sabrina Rabin woman, will you? She seems important enough to get us what we want if we should find her. Bloody women. Suddenly they're thick as shepherds."

Chesterton nodded agreement and reached for the brandy. Seeing his boss's pronounced frown, he chose the whiskey instead. The boss hated to abuse Steve Coldwell's hospitality.

A few miles away, Adam Glassman was being treated to the hospitality of the CIA's counterintelligence "sweeper" team. As he regained his senses, he felt sick from the lurching van. He was encased, mummylike, in a roll of carpet the sweepers had wrapped him in as the drugs took effect and they hustled him from the hotel safe house. Quality control on the dosage had failed, however. Adam Glassman was coming around. With the characteristic reflex of the downed airman, he assessed his survival prospects. He knew that hostile CIA interrogation could put him in limbo for years, maybe forever.

He guessed the van to be rolling through the northern Virginia suburbs on its way to a new safe house somewhere in the isolated rolling green country between Langley headquarters and the Farm at Camp Peary. The twisting back roads that darted off Chain Bridge Road were better suited for horse-drawn coaches than for cars. Glassman tested the carpet. His hands were stuck, but he could move his legs some. He looked through the tunnel of fabric and saw a big man at the wheel.

His head aching and his stomach wrenching, Glassman focused on his anger. The best opportunity to escape was soonest after capture. But how?

He heard the driver call out to someone in the back of the van. The man came forward as the vehicle rolled slowly down a steep incline to a stop. In the dark, red lights from a railroad crossing funneled through the hole in the carpet, and bells clanged. Glassman heard the rumble of a train in the distance. He could see the driver was talking to the preppy CIA handler from the hotel. Dimly, Glassman recalled his single summer before academy, working as a carpetlayer's helper. He remembered the edge of the carpet, sharp as a knife, cutting his fingers often. The bells clanged. Glassman made his move.

Pushing with all the force his legs could muster, Glassman lunged, the carpet roll hitting the driver on the side of the neck, near the carotid artery. The driver shrieked, and the van rolled forward, crashing through the railroad-crossing guard. The train horn blasted. The pulse of diesel engines was deafening as the van slid across the tracks and caromed off the cab of a semi tractor rig on the far side of the railroad crossing, then rolled onto its side. Glassman slid free from the carpet roll and pushed himself, bleeding, through the twisted rear door of the vehicle. The train thundered by.

Glassman staggered into the forest. He couldn't help it. He had to look back. Regardless of what they'd done to him, they were still Americans. Resisting his first impulse to flee, he ran back to the van and turned off the ignition. He found the driver unconscious. The preppy CIA handler was trapped under the big man, bleeding from a gash on his head. "You bastard," he snarled at Glassman.

Adam Glassman looked around for the driver of the tractor rig but found him nowhere. Glassman spotted the syringe from the dope kit lying in the shattered glass of the van's windshield. He snatched it and injected the preppy CIA man. "Bastard!" the preppy repeated.

"You won't burn, but you'll sleep through the shock," Glassman said. "I'll call nine-one-one. Just remember, the Lord helps those who help themselves."

Adam Glassman clambered back into the woods. This time he didn't look back. Having survived, he was hell-bent on escape and evasion.

—— 27 ——
Small World

Larnaca, Cyprus

THE ANCIENT ENGLISH FORD RACKETED through the narrow streets, the cab's grizzled driver blasting his little horn at the black-clad peasants heading to market. Ed Rogers clung precariously to the door handle, his expression that of a condemned man.

"Buck up, Major. We'll be there soon," General Cartwright said cheerfully.

"Not soon enough, sir," Rogers said, gazing at the door grip as though it were an ejection handle he wanted to pull.

"What's the matter, son? Haven't you ever taken in the local color?"

"I usually stay on base when I'm on TDY, sir. I don't mind a Mach 3 ride, but I'm damned if I want to get killed in a taxi."

"When I was a young buck, we used to get off base every chance we could."

The cab lurched as it topped a hill above the deep blue of Larnaca Bay. "With all due respect, sir, sightseeing is hazardous for American troops in this part of the world."

"Just be glad Uncle Sam bought you that new sport coat, son. You look like an *Esquire* cover."

"With this haircut, I look solid GI. You, too, sir. Despite the best polyester fashion statement."

Cartwright snorted. "Just try to keep a low profile while I do my business, Major, and we'll do fine." The breeze blowing through the Ford's windows smoothed the general's shock of close-cropped silver hair as the cab slammed to a stop in front of a white building with an orange sign that read Mediterranean Produce Co.

"I'll keep as low a profile as I can, with this," Rogers said, gripping at the .38 revolver that made a bulge in his BX sport coat. "You never said what we'd need it for."

"Best you don't ask. It's a need-to-know matter."

"Great," Rogers said.

"I'm your wingman, Major. If you see me come runnin', you open up with that thing just like it was a Sidewinder missile." The general unfolded his wad of Cyprus pounds, making certain to overtip. The ancient driver tipped his Greek fisherman's cap and sped away.

The general clapped Rogers on the shoulder and said, "Sit yourself down at the little café across the street and buy yourself an ouzo. Just remember," Cartwright said, winking. "Keep your back to the wall and watch the street."

The Mediterranean Produce Company's door rattled open and the general stepped inside to witness a whirl of Levantine business. Aged typewriters clattered. Clerks in sweaty open-collared white shirts with the sleeves rolled up argued ceaselessly, arms akimbo. A plump receptionist with a beauty mark eyed Cartwright suspiciously.

"You are American," the lady declared, flashing a hint of gold at Cartwright's infectious grin.

"Honey, how could ya tell?"

"You are big like Clint Eastwood. What you want here, American? You want to buy some fruit? Maybe some Jaffa oranges."

"I need to talk to Mr. Bouchet," Cartwright said, pronouncing the name "boo-shet."

"I don't know," she said doubtfully. "It's maybe possible. Do you have some American cigarettes, Clint?" She pronounced it "Cleent."

Cartwright pulled a hard pack of Marlboros out of his rumpled sport coat and tossed it to her. She caught it nimbly. Marlboros traded better than local currency. She flashed him a broad gold smile and moved gracefully as a destroyer into the sea of mercantile pandemonium. She reappeared, followed by an older, worried-looking man who ran his fingers over a shiny bald dome. Ben Lavi's jaw dropped in surprise. "Scotty?" he said.

Cartwright, equally surprised, looked at the exporter and said, "Davy?"

David Ben Lavi hugged his receptionist, then rushed Cartwright and hugged him. "How long, old friend?" the Israeli asked.

"Since the Suez business in seventy-three."

Lavi slapped Cartwright on both shoulders. "You don't look so bad," he decided. "I'll buy you a drink. Come to my office."

"Let's go to my office," Cartwright suggested. "There's a taverna across the street." The receptionist surveyed the reunion with the practiced eye of a Levanter, never taking her left hand more than a few inches away from a button that would summon help or her right hand from a drawer that held a Walther automatic.

Lavi shook his head at her. "It's okay. Scotty is a good friend. I will go with him." She smiled her gold smile, but as soon as the two men were out the door, she pushed the button.

The pair strolled across the street. Cartwright led the way, guiding the Israeli to a table at the rear of the taverna, walking past Ed Rogers, who looked uncomfortably oversized at his tiny table. As they seated themselves, Lavi nodded toward Rogers. "He is yours?"

"He's a good lad."

"You should get more-experienced help."

"There isn't always time, Davy."

"Still flying by the seat of your pants," Lavi grunted. He shook his head sadly. "When are you Americans going to learn planning is everything? You do so many things ad hoc."

The waiter brought ouzos. Seeing the big American—and his ominously bulging jacket—at the streetside table, the waiter withdrew behind the counter.

"You think the Americans are all bulls in a china shop, but you know, sometimes we manage to muddle through," Cartwright said, raising his glass. "Like the big war."

"Ah, yes. Your good war," Lavi said, returning the toast and tossing back the fiery ouzo. "Since Hitler, you've tied, lost a big one, and retired early in countless others."

"How about Grenada? How about Panama?"

Lavi shrugged dismissively.

"You may be right. Headline victories and body counts are bullshit," Cartwright said. "But it so happens I'm looking for a body right now."

"Is the body alive?"

"I hope so. Elsewise she'd be no good to me."

David Ben Lavi looked out toward the street outside Taverna Olympus, and his eyes met those of the uneasy Major Rogers. To Lavi, the Americans always looked so freshly scrubbed and wholesome. They had no business in the Middle East. He gazed neutrally at Cartwright with his liquid brown eyes.

"Who is this woman?"

"Madeline tells me her name is Sabrina Rabin."

"Madeline should have been secretary of state," Lavi said.

"Sabrina Rabin is one of yours, Madeline says."

Shrugging his shoulders in the traditional gesture of the Levanter, Lavi replied, "I really couldn't say."

"Davy, don't kid a kidder," Cartwright said, grinning. "I want to talk to her. It's important."

Suddenly several men emerged from a Citroën across the street and began striding toward the wine shop. Another car screeched to a stop in front of the café, and other men emerged.

"Tell me what's on your mind, Scotty, before my friends kill your friend," Lavi said, his voice level but taut. "My men seem to think you are abducting me."

"From neutral Cyprus, Davy? Everybody's here. Brits. Russians. Arabs. PLO. Even the bumbling Yanks."

"Athens Street is my territory, and my receptionist is over-zealous." Casually he waved the gunmen away. "She has the hots for me," Lavi said apologetically.

The Cypriot waiter, watching the gunmen, held his heart and hyperventilated. When they retreated, he poured himself an ouzo and drank it down. Rogers took his hand away from the bulge in his jacket, never realizing how close he had been to death.

"Tell me what you want to know, Scott, and I will see if I can find out," Lavi said evenly.

"I need to talk to the woman, Davy. She was involved with a friend of mine, name of Adam Glassman, who's in deep shit on the Potomac."

"The air attaché in Tel Aviv. He was a talented boy."

"My guys are afraid he donated some labor to the Israeli account. Unless I can prove otherwise, he may break rocks in Leavenworth for about thirty years."

"Tell your friends, I will swear on any Bible they choose, that Adam Glassman never worked for us. Mossad would never use a Jewish national of another country. It's trouble for everyone."

"Pollard?"

Lavi shrugged. "A mistake. I told them so. It would never happen again."

"I've still got to talk to the woman, David. Mission essential."

"I know you, Scotty," Lavi said, a trace of a smile curling his thin lips. "It would take an H-bomb to stop you once you say it's your mission."

Cartwright crossed his arms and leaned back in the frail wicker chair. He watched the street, trying to count heads in the little cars parked on the narrow thoroughfare.

"I will try to find the woman, Scott. My government would wish no harm for Colonel Glassman."

"I'm relieved, Davy," Cartwright said, offering his hand to Lavi, who shook it firmly.

"Where can I find you?"

"The RAF base at Akrotiri."

Lavi rose. Cartwright nodded and Rogers moved his chair aside so the Israeli could pass. Lavi walked across the street and vanished behind the rickety door of the Mediterranean Produce Company.

—— 28 ——
Crash Meeting

YEVGENY PAVLOVICH STRELNIKOV, GENERAL OF parachutists, handed a watery glass of Pepsi-Cola to his superior, General Kolchak, as they took their seats in Moscow Stadium. Both wore the rumpled clothes of party bureaucrats. They pretended to watch as though they had an interest in the soccer match. The Dynamos led Army by one.

"My information from the ministry gives me a sense of foreboding," Strelnikov muttered.

"Well, what?" Kolchak demanded, waving a Dynamo flag somewhat halfheartedly as he sipped the soft drink. "Meetings like this are dangerous."

"I've seen a GRU report that maintains the Israelis are prepared to launch a surveillance satellite," Strelnikov whispered urgently.

"And so?"

"If they launch, they will see the enhanced fortifications at the Taraki plant. They may take preemptive action or inform the Americans. We could be exposed should the Americans complain to the Politburo or, worse, personally to the chairman. There will be inquiries. We will be undone."

General Kolchak bared his teeth as he watched the Army

149

team even the score. "Preparations in Tarak move forward. It is too late to stop. What would you suggest, Yevgeny Pavlovich?"

"Hit the Israeli satellite when it launches."

"Impossible," Kolchak growled. "Kurtz is engaged in Tarak. A feat like the Indonesian gambit cannot be duplicated."

"I fear exposure of the Kazakhstan operation," Strelnikov whispered. "The Chekists are everywhere. Perhaps within Pamyat."

"In less than a week, it won't matter," Kolchak said. "I will be promoted to Moscow military district commander. When war breaks out, the Politburo will be too busy to ask how it happened."

"So," Strelnikov whispered, "the satellite-kill capability goes no further than Kurtz?"

"You have no need of that knowledge," Kolchak said curtly. "Just prepare your troops."

"For the Middle East," Strelnikov asked. "Or Moscow?"

"I will decide," Kolchak said. They left through separate subway exits without waiting to see Army get beat by one goal.

— 29 —
A Cypriot Truce

RAF Akrotiri, Cyprus

THE RANGE ROVER SPED DOWN Athens Street, leaving a cloud of dust and scattering small groups of puzzled Cypriots, who had not seen such a rush since the Turkish invasion. Colin Davis sat flanked by the battered giant, Abraham, and the suddenly solicitous Sabrina Rabin. She was dabbing a wet cloth over some of the lumps and patches of purple and black that formed a map of the Middle East on the sergeant major's face. "Thank you, miss. You are too kind," he grimaced.

"You are right," the bloodied giant called Abraham grunted, massaging the pulp of his torn ear. "She never shows such concern for her teammates."

Abraham and his rangy counterpart, Ephraim, had attempted to interrogate Colin Davis. The fresh cuts, purple bruises, and dried blood on their faces testified to the failure of the attempt.

"When you learn a little tenderness, maybe you will get some, Abraham," Sabrina said sternly, wiping a patch of grime from Davis's cheek. "You were wrong to coerce this one. Anyone can see that."

"Save your tenderness for the debriefing," Ephraim said, driving the Range Rover as though it were a Ferrari, scattering chickens and peasants as he drove.

"Ephraim, you are a pig," Sabrina declared, giving Davis a comradely hug. "Working with you has been a pleasure, Sergeant Major. You almost took these two," she added contemptuously, gesturing at her teammates.

The Rover careered toward the Union Jack that waved in the distance at the gate to the Royal Air Force base at Akrotiri on the southern tip of the island.

"Next time we meet, maybe we can skip the roughhouse," Davis said grimly.

"Do not be bitter," Sabrina said, smiling. "It was business. I am glad our superiors have discovered another way to reach an understanding."

"Don't let her sweet-talk you," Ephraim sneered, wheeling onto the base road. "I'd like to try to mix it up again sometime, with or without the knives."

"Me, too," the giant called Abraham said, suddenly cheerful. He clapped Davis on the shoulder, almost affectionately, as though they were soccer mates.

"Super," Colin Davis said, grinning and cracking his split lip. "Next time for the title."

Ephraim turned left at the perimeter fence outside the base. He drove a hundred yards and screeched to a stop, wheeling the light truck around 180 degrees as though he were dodging a roadblock. He stopped suddenly and parked.

"Now what?" Colin Davis asked.

"Now, we wait for our bosses to finish the deal," Ephraim said, turning around so that Davis could see the Uzi submachine gun. "If nothing goes wrong, I don't have to shoot you."

Davis smiled but winced at the pain from his still-fresh wounds.

"Don't do anything stupid, English," Abraham said, patting Davis on the leg but opening his shepherd's vest far enough to display a large Browning automatic.

They sat by the fence, watching the flight line. A squadron of RAF Tornadoes took off, their needle noses edged skyward. Colin Davis spotted a black dot on the far horizon. He watched it grow larger. It was a C-130 Hercules transport.

"Have you got field glasses?" Davis asked Ephraim.

"Sure."

"Mind if I use 'em?" Ephraim sneered and shook his head

slowly, but Sabrina Rabin slapped him on the shoulder. "Don't be such a pig. Let him watch."

"He could hit me with them. He could start trouble."

"Word of honor, mate. No trouble. I just want to see the sodding plane."

Ephraim shrugged and handed Davis the binoculars. Davis raised them to his eyes and found that he could look out only through his left eye because his right was swollen shut. The C-130 was feathering its engines on the tarmac. A jeep towing a small cart pulled out to the cargo aircraft as its ramp lowered. A sandy-haired officer was wearing the earth-colored beret of the Special Air Service. With him in the jeep was the bald-domed figure of David Ben Lavi.

Colin Davis watched as a team of pallbearers in SAS kit carried a flag-draped coffin from the transport. The flag showed the blue and white colors of Israel. "What's this?" he muttered.

"Let me see," Sabrina Rabin said, taking the glasses from him. She looked through the glasses and held her breath. Then she gasped, handing the glasses back to Davis.

"Military honors," he said, watching. "Do you lot have any idea what this is?" he asked the Mossad men, who sat stonily silent.

Sabrina Rabin's face was buried in her hands. She sobbed quietly. Davis urged quietly, "Look here. What's up?"

"I think it is her brother," Ephraim said quietly. "Avi Rabin conducted a reconnaissance on the plant in Tarak. He vanished, just like you, old chum."

"What was his cover?" Colin Davis demanded, looking through the field glasses.

"Like yourself, he was a shepherd. Your people found him when they came looking for you."

Colin Davis lifted one of his muscled arms and placed it around the quietly sobbing Sabrina Rabin. He squeezed gently. "Sorry, old girl. Really."

The vehicle with the casket sped through the gate and turned onto the perimeter road. Sabrina watched the approaching vehicle and dried her tears. "You can get out now, Sergeant Major," she said tonelessly. "You are free."

Abraham stepped out of the vehicle and supported Colin

Davis as he clambered out. He was still not quite steady on his feet. He watched four of his mates from B Squadron, Twenty-second SAS lifting the casket. They carried it to the Rover and elbowed it in on the cargo gate. Despite his injuries, Sgt. Maj. Colin Davis marched toward the Rover where his mates waited. He saluted Major Mellors.

"Well, Sergeant Major Davis. It looks like you beat the clock this time," the officer said, his eyebrows arching and his sandy cropped moustache twitching.

"Walk in the park, Major," Colin Davis said. Then he fainted.

The truck carrying the Israelis sped away. As the British vehicle drove onto base, the SAS troopers' eyes were drawn to the sky. Overhead, they heard the roar of a daggerlike black airplane climbing quickly.

"What's that thing, Major?" a trooper asked. "Sounds like the end of the world."

"Bloody beautiful aircraft," Mellors said.

— 30 —
Overflight

Airborne over Israel

THE BLACKBIRD SPED TOWARD THE Israeli coast like a storm cloud with wings. Cartwright accomplished the sharp climb that brought the SR-71 to its preferred operating altitude of eighty thousand feet, with the black plane's angry engines belching fire in afterburner at a speed slightly in excess of two thousand miles per hour.

"Time to go to work," the general said. "We are beyond abort point. Approaching decision point, over."

"Affirmative, Eagle driver," Rogers replied.

"How are you feeling, young Eagle?" Cartwright asked cheerfully over the internal microphone. "I feel better when the rizzo is happy."

"I'll feel better when I'm hoisting a pint of King's Green back at Mildenhall."

"Understood. Well, let's bring this one in for Adam."

The Mach 3-plus airplane raced to the east, its radar screens taking in an overview of the coastlines of Syria, Lebanon, Israel, Egypt, and the Republic of Tarak. Each nation's air defenses posed a continuously evolving threat to the black plane, but none had ever caught a Blackbird yet.

Rogers, his fingers working with the speed of a seamstress,

threw toggles and switches. He pushed buttons and turned dials that would transform the Blackbird from an aircraft into an electronic sponge for data. As they approached the target coastline of the collection area, Rogers activated the optical barrel camera, which would take in a horizon-to-horizon sweep from the Sinai to Aleppo, scanning a hundred-thousand-square-mile area, with the capability of focusing on objects the size of a soldier's helmet. Meanwhile, he began manipulating the keyboard functions that would activate the look-down see-through camera, the newest innovation that Madeline Murdoch hoped would yield the secrets of the Israeli weapons plant at Dimona.

A Grumman E-2 Hawkeye, one of four purchased from America by Israel, was the first to spot the American spy plane's high-level approach toward the Sinai Desert. The three-man Israeli Air Force crew in the little turboprop AWACS aircraft tracked the sharp dot over Egyptian territory. For the Israeli radar crew, the sharp dot represented not an airplane flown by an ally but a potential attacker. Ari Goldman, the chief radar operator, prided himself on his instinct as well as his keen eyesight.

"The radar cross-section is tiny and the plane is fast, maybe the fastest I've ever seen. It's flying like a missile. This airplane is American. I'm sure of it," he declared, monitoring his glowing screen.

The Air Defense Command in Tel Aviv radioed back, tersely demanding an altitude, heading, and speed.

"Altitude eighty-thousand feet plus," Goldman responded. "Indicated airspeed in excess of Mach 3. An easterly heading with estimated time of arrival over Sinai, approximately three minutes."

As he spoke, F-16 Fighting Falcons from Tel Nof Air Base were already scrambling to meet the intruder. Deep underground in a secure bunker in Tel Aviv, older men anguished over Ari Goldman's report.

"Shall we shoot down this aircraft?" demanded General Ezer Bar Lev as he watched the array of radar screens and intense young operators in the Air Defense Command complex.

"We need some high-level guidance," his colleague, General Moshe Ben Levi, chief of Fighter Command, said.

"There is no Cabinet!" Bar Lev barked. "We must make

decisions as though the Cabinet has been wiped off the face of the earth. We have two minutes to decide our course.''

"This airplane is American," Ben Levi pleaded. "Would you fire on the aircraft of our closest ally? Their mission could be as simple as a reconnaissance of the Golan or the Taraki frontier.''

"They are flying toward Israel," Bar Lev growled. "Their intentions are not announced. Haven't you heard, Moshe? We have no allies.''

"Will you accept responsibility for attack on an American aircraft?''

"No American aircraft has announced its presence or intentions," Bar Lev said coldly. "I would fire on any unidentified aircraft invading Israeli airspace.''

"God help us if we are wrong.''

"God helps those who save themselves. This plane is big enough to carry one bomb that could extinguish the lamp of Eretz Israel. Do you wish to take responsibility for a second Holocaust, my friend?''

General Moshe Ben Levi, who had received his fighter training in Texas and who still wore a cowboy hat out on the flight line, placed both hands on the bank of radar screens and closed his eyes. Sweat popped on his forehead despite the air-conditioned coolness of the bunker.

"Give the command," he said, grinding his teeth and running his fingers through his wiry salt-and-pepper hair. "Engage and destroy the unidentified intruder.''

As the Blackbird piloted by Scott Cartwright crossed into Israeli airspace, the F-16s climbed toward their maximum ceiling to intercept it.

Inside their space suits Cartwright and Rogers functioned at a cool sixty-eight degrees. Outside the aircraft the air heated from the friction of the Blackbird's progress singed the aircraft's titanium skin at temperatures in excess of eleven hundred degrees Fahrenheit, the kind of heat that burns the tiles of a space shuttle on its reentry into the atmosphere.

The Blackbird cruised in the upper atmosphere, with the high thin air fifteen miles above the earth ramming through its engine inlet spikes and exiting out of the Pratt & Whitney exhaust ports, white-hot. Cartwright turned his eyes toward the deep blue of space hovering above him and shivered involuntarily as he spotted a few stars. Turning his head slightly within his fishbowl helmet, he glanced down, outside the port cockpit window, and gazed at the curve of the earth.

Fifteen miles below, soldiers on the desert looked up to the sky as they heard the sonic crack of the invisible plane. Some of the young men below were Egyptian. Others were Israeli, and a few wore the sandy desert camouflage and scarlet berets of the 82nd Airborne All-American Division, the Sinai Peacekeeping Force that buffered the armies of Arab and Jew.

In the aft seat of the Blackbird, without access to the spectacular view enjoyed by the pilot, Ed Rogers busied himself with the complex demands of managing the aircraft's spying apparatus. Almost as an afterthought, he monitored the threat on the SR-71's defensive avionics systems.

"We've got a sky full of bogeys below," Rogers said, looking at the dots on the Blackbird's glowing green scope. "It looks like we've got the attention of the air forces of four different countries."

"Give me a systems status report and navigational fix," Cartwright said.

"We are on our designated heading, passing over Gaza, with the primary target under surveillance," Rogers answered methodically. "Look-down see-through mode is active. The friendlies are climbing to max ceiling, indicating a hostile approach. Suggest we prepare to evacuate the ops area."

"Roger. Let's throw the switch on our insurance policy," Cartwright said.

Ed Rogers threw a series of switches to activate the D-21 drone that was piggybacked on the Blackbird's dorsal section. "Affirmative, we are a go for drone launch."

"Let's do it, Ed."

Ed Rogers prepared to flip the final toggle switch that would send an electrical signal to separate the drone. The D-21 would loiter within the collection area, duplicating the data collected by the SR-71. Within its software bank it already held most of the coded images generated by the mother ship's systems up to the point of separation. Rogers finished his systems checks, all the while monitoring the green fireflies gathering on the radar screen that were rapidly transforming themselves into a swarm of Mach-2 hornets.

"Preparing to launch drone," Rogers announced on the internal microphone. A red light on Rogers's panel switched to green. He touched the switch with his gloved finger and lifted. As the switch made contact, Rogers and Cartwright felt a slight shudder from the dorsal section of the fuselage, followed by a shiver within the airframe. "We have drone separation," Rogers said.

Suddenly there was a popping sound, like the snapping of a bolt, followed by a shaking sensation in the aft section of the black plane. The popping noises accelerated, like corn in an air popper.

"Sir, I think we have an anomaly," Rogers said. "Uh-oh."

The popping became the sound of bullets firing, then the clackety bang of a rivet gun. "Aw, shit," Cartwright said.

Another popping sound cracked within the titanium frame of the Blackbird. And another followed—and another. "Sir, we have a major malfunction," Rogers declared as the black plane dropped like an elevator free-falling down an endless open shaft.

"I'm losing the right engine," Cartwright said, his own voice under control as he simultaneously wrestled the stick, threw switches, and yanked the throttle. "Starboard engine flameout."

The Blackbird plunged—first hundreds, then thousands of feet, and then a dozen miles, its altimeter needle corkscrewing mercilessly.

"We're going in," Rogers gasped as his vision grayed out. As the black plane fell, the Israeli F-16s climbed to engage it.

Not one Israeli pilot hesitated. As the stricken spy plane plunged toward a forsaken strip of desert bordering Israel, Jordan, Syria, and Tarak, the advanced-design Shafrir Python missiles separated from the F-16s and flew toward their target. Even deadlier than their ancestor, the Sidewinder, the Shafrir missiles suffered no anomalies.

The plane disappeared simultaneously from dozens of radar screens operated by Israelis, Americans, Jordanians, Russians,

Egyptians, Tarakis, and Syrians. In the radar rooms, each located in a complex of underground bunkers, men argued feverishly over the significance of the vanished blip.

As the Blackbird fell crazily from its fifteen-mile-high perch, a golden glove in the cockpit twitched. Scott Cartwright struggled to reach the blast handle of the ejection seat with its detent switch to activate the destruct protocol. Younger, stronger men might have failed to grab across the six inches of empty space, lacking the sheer will developed in almost five decades of flight tests and combat. Cartwright reached and strained and demanded that his golden-gloved fingers close on the yellow handle. Just before losing consciousness, he gave his blurred fingers an order, and they closed.

The cockpit exploded around him, and his body was fired into space.

— 31 —
Tea and Sympathy

MADELINE MURDOCH CLIMBED THE STAIRS in her Georgetown row house as though they were a gallows. Her Bass shoes clumped heavily.

"Is that you, my love?" a gentle voice inquired in the darkened hallway.

Dr. Madeline Murdoch, the president's adviser for national security affairs, slumped against a stand of books. Barely supporting her weight on the fine Persian rug, she gasped once and then made an unfamiliar choking sound in her throat. Her husband rushed forward.

"My dear," the gnomish man in the cardigan sweater declared. "My dearest dear, what's the trouble?"

For a brief moment she leaned against him, inhaling the warmth of the wool and the aroma of Old Spice Leather. His thin arms were home and refuge to her. She braced herself and regained her composure. "Sometimes it's a beastly world, my darling Philip," she said.

"Can you tell me about it?" Philip Murdoch asked, gently guiding his wife into their study. He seated her in the Victorian chair amid the stacks of rare first editions and placed her feet on the hassock.

"It's so secret they don't have a classification for it," she said. "You'll probably read about it in tomorrow's *Washington Post*."

He poured a cup of the tea he had warming on a hot plate placed haphazardly on his rolltop desk. The desk was the antithesis of his wife's methodical order and administrative tidiness. It had so many nooks and crannies that national secrets would have been lost in it.

"I can tell you, Philip, that I believe I have lost a dear friend."

"Nothing is certain until there is proof, my dear," the Georgetown University economist said, handing her a cup of strong tea. "Until there is proof, there is hope. Or at least that is what dear old Art Laffer would say." He caressed her steel-wool hair briefly and seated himself in a leather wing chair. "This imperiled friend is in the government?"

Madeline Murdoch shook her head, saying in her gesture that she could say no more, and her husband nodded. He accommodated her in her work, understanding there was much she could not tell him. He accommodated her needs and, without complaint, put up with the changes that her job imposed on his quiet life. He even accommodated the Secret Service agent stationed in the kitchen, even though the young man habitually refused Philip Murdoch's courteous offer of tea and biscuits.

"God, but I'm afraid we've made a mess of it," Madeline Murdoch murmured into the shadows. "If we are lucky, we are not yet at war."

"It will seem better in the morning," her husband replied.

"Or worse," she said. The national security adviser sat in the darkness, absorbing the shadowy serenity imparted by the library with its hundreds of comforting volumes. There were complete editions of the classics, a crazy quilt of journals on foreign affairs and economics, all of which were interrupted by an occasional Le Carré, giving a splash of color in the gray sea of scholarship. A crash of shattering glass on the floor below and racket coming from the kitchen interrupted her meditation.

"What the devil?" Philip Murdoch gasped, rushing toward the door. He looked frantically to his wife. "Madeline?"

"Philip, stay here and get down on the floor," Madeline Murdoch shouted as she moved quickly toward the desk, opened a drawer, and withdrew a pearl-handled .25 caliber automatic. She yanked back the slide and chambered a round. She listened to the struggle downstairs, and with the pistol pointed at the door, she backed toward the antique table with the two telephones on it, her own unlisted phone and the secure line to the White House.

Still watching the door, she fumbled behind her back for the receiver as she heard the sound of someone scrambling up the stairs. As she reached for the phone, she never took her eyes or the gun from the door. The intruder wrenched open a succession of doors in the hallway.

As the door to the study swung open, Madeline Murdoch fired twice, the small automatic making a sharp cracking sound like a starter pistol. A bleeding man fell forward on the floor next to Philip Murdoch, who rapidly pushed himself backward in a froglike swimming motion.

"Don't shoot again, Dr. Murdoch!" the intruder on the floor shouted. "You might hit me."

"Move again and I'll damn sure hit you, Colonel," Madeline Murdoch shouted. "Lie there on your stomach and put your hands over your head."

Adam Glassman complied, and Madeline Murdoch circled him warily.

"Philip, get up and go to the telephone," the national security adviser ordered. Her husband got up, adjusted his rumpled cardigan, and shuffled over toward the pair of phones.

"Pick up the White House line and tell them there's trouble at the Dragon Lady's house," Madeline Murdoch snapped.

"Who?" her husband asked sheepishly.

"It's a code name, Philip. For God's sake, just do it."

Her husband picked up the phone, and Adam Glassman stared at the national security adviser. His face was a fresco of dried blood and blue bruises.

"My God, Colonel, you look like you've been in a train wreck," Madeline Murdoch exclaimed.

"Car wreck, Dr. Murdoch," Glassman gasped. "Whatever you do, don't call the White House until you listen to me. I'm begging you, ma'am."

Keeping the gun on him, she regarded him with a mixture of puzzlement, fear, and curiosity. "Philip, put down the phone. What did you do with the agent downstairs, Colonel?"

"Gave him twenty cc's of what CIA wanted to give me. Not lethal, but he won't wake up for a while," the colonel grunted. "Don't call the White House, please."

"Why, may I ask?"

"There's trouble there."

"What sort of trouble?"

"General Cartwright trusts you. Only you or Brady Daniels."

"With Director Daniels dead, that leaves only me," Madeline Murdoch said.

Seating herself in the leather wingback chair, she kept the automatic pointed at Glassman. Her collection of senses—what foolish men would call intuition—tingled at the back of her head. "I think I should have you arrested, Colonel."

"Don't, Doctor. Please," Glassman implored. "Not until I tell you about CIA."

"We'll strike a bargain, Colonel. My husband will call the Secret Service, but I will listen to what you have to say."

"I'm begging you, ma'am."

One of the telephones rang. It was the secure phone. Philip Murdoch knew, by habit, better than to answer that ring. He picked up the receiver and handed it to his wife, who listened while she kept the pistol trained on Glassman. She listened and turned a shade paler than her normal porcelain hue.

"Yes, I understand," she said. "Keep me informed." She handed the receiver back to her husband, who replaced it on the antique table.

"Philip, dear," she said gently. "I'm going to have to ask you to leave the room."

"Madeline, have you gone insane? With this thug here? I refuse."

"Philip, you know I love you," Madeline Murdoch said. "But for now, you must leave us alone." The economist buttoned his cardigan with great dignity and brushed the dustballs from it. He walked silently from the room.

"That was the White House," Madeline Murdoch said, clearing her throat so she could banish the tremble in her voice.

"Your benefactor and chief advocate, Major General Scott Cartwright, is confirmed to have been shot down on reconnaissance overflight of the border region above Israel, Jordan, and the Republic of Tarak. A parachute was sighted."

"Where?" Glassman demanded.

"The chute fell on the Taraki side of the frontier. Taraki troops were spotted running toward it."

"Who was his rizzo?"

"I beg your pardon."

"The recon systems operator, the other man in the plane, who was he and where is he?"

"A Major Rogers is in Israeli custody. I'm afraid that at the moment the situation is quite fluid. I'm awaiting further word from State and Defense."

"Don't talk to the White House about Cartwright or the goddamned Israelis until you talk to me," Glassman growled. "And let me stretch my arms. They are killing me."

"Colonel, pick yourself up off the floor and sit on the hassock with your hands behind your head. Attempt a move toward me, and I will kill you. You have five minutes."

With effort, Glassman rose from the floor, first on his knees, then to full height, POW style. He sat himself on the hassock, painfully drew his arms up behind his head, and passed out into the chair behind him.

"Oh, damn," Madeline Murdoch muttered. "Philip, come in here. And bring some water," she called out.

The accommodating Philip Murdoch appeared as if by magic, with a pitcher of water and with a damp towel on his arm. He pressed the towel gently to Adam Glassman's bruised forehead and sprinkled a few drops of water on the colonel's lips. The colonel began to come around.

Philip Murdoch placed Adam Glassman's legs gently on the hassock. Glassman attempted to smile, but his lips were blue and swollen. The economist produced a handkerchief and dabbed at the blood. Glassman took the handkerchief and nodded thanks.

"When you're feeling collected, your five minutes begin, Colonel," Madeline Murdoch said, the pistol resting on her left knee. Her right leg kicked in a nervous tic. "No point in your leaving now, Philip. This is an extraordinary evening.

But bring us some tea. The Morning Thunder. If I have any more caffeine tonight, I shall want to smoke."

Philip Murdoch obliged his wife, quickly preparing the tea and placing it beside her as she sat staring at Glassman. The economist watched the colonel and his wife as he placed kindling in the stone fireplace and lit a match. The fire crackled, and Madeline Murdoch looked nothing so much like a disapproving owl sitting high in a firelit tree. "Everyone except General Cartwright believes you a traitor, Colonel."

"Like Jonathan Pollard," Glassman said.

"Correct."

"What do you think, Dr. Murdoch?"

"I know something of your record, Colonel. I know you and General Cartwright turned back a terrorist attack mounted by the Iranians last year."

"And what should that tell you?" Glassman asked wearily.

"It tells me you are a damn good flier and a national hero, even if your heroics are for security purposes shielded from the bask of media approval. We are grateful and you are decorated. But you, sir, are also a hero of an ill-defined, shadowy sort. And I confess, that disturbs me somewhat."

"Meaning I'm not trustworthy."

"Colonel, I work every day with people in the intelligence community. None of them are trustworthy. Why should you be?"

"Because I love my country."

"Nonsense. Patriotism is the last refuge of scoundrels. You know that. Besides there are those who say your sense of *patria* is devoted more to Israel."

"Dr. Murdoch, are you Catholic?"

"Not that it's your business, but yes."

"Are you loyal to Washington or Rome?"

"Touché, Colonel. Nonetheless, you were under sufficient suspicion to require hostile interrogation."

"Because of Sabrina Rabin."

"You had opportunity and a contact—and more motive than many for taking up a double game, Colonel. She approached you, and you responded. We have ample record of that. Videotape. Beachfront resort hotels at Eilat. There is audio tape as well. As the detestable Avery Benedict would say, the works."

"What if I told you I approached Sabrina Rabin?"

"Meaning what?"

"Brady Daniels was playing a deep game. I was part of that game."

"Tell me more."

"The director kept secrets from everybody, including me," Glassman said. "But we were very close. My upbringing was orthodox, and we shared passions for Talmudic history."

"So what?"

"When I moved to CIA as photo interpreter, our discussions ranged into his management of the Israeli account and his friendship with David Ben Lavi."

"I know Ben Lavi," Madeline Murdoch said. "What did Brady tell you about him?"

"That they were close friends once but had become enemies. It happened not long after the Israeli raid on the Iraqi nuclear reactor. Brady was ordered by the White House to cut the Israelis out of the satellite data. Lavi said it was unforgivable."

"What has that got to do with you, Colonel?"

"After the Pollard thing blew, Brady became obsessed that there was another Israeli penetration of U.S. intelligence."

"Indeed," Madeline Murdoch said. "Do you think you could manage some tea now, Colonel?"

"I'd like that," he said, and Philip Murdoch was quickly across the room with a cup that Adam Glassman accepted. He sipped it carefully from the unhurt side of his mouth.

"And how did this shared passion for the Old Testament lead to your seduction by Miss Rabin? Am I correct, Colonel? The girls don't wear tops on those beaches, do they?" Madeline Murdoch asked, a smile cracking her leathery face. Glassman fidgeted. "Oiled her back or something like that, Colonel?"

"We spent a holiday at Eilat when we weren't on the flight line at Tel Nof."

"The audio tapes Avery Benedict gave me are either plain dirty or incriminating," Madeline Murdoch said. "So many things a convent schoolgirl would never dream of."

"Brady wanted me to compromise her," Glassman said.

"Do try to be a gentleman, sir. I know about these things. It might have gone the other way, though. Even your smoothed out version of events sounds more like a honey trap baited by Mossad to me, Colonel."

"I'm telling you, I made the approach, at Director Daniels's order," Glassman insisted.

"I'm told that fliers love only their planes. Still, it appears from the record that you were the one compromised at Eilat. From the point she had your clothes off, it looked, my friend, as though she had you by the short hairs."

"Madeline!" Philip Murdoch exclaimed. "She's never made a remark like that, Colonel," the economist told Glassman, looking quite alarmed as his eyes blinked owlishly behind his thick spectacles.

"Don't interrupt, dear. This is a serious talk," Madeline Murdoch ordered. The economist resumed poking the fire. "Philip forgets I work in a man's world. Go on, Colonel."

"Brady Daniels wanted to get someone inside the mind of Mossad."

The national security adviser's face clouded with a thoughtful frown.

"I would have seduced a woman I didn't love," Glassman spit out. "I would also have killed her, if that's what Director Daniels asked. I think he is one of the greatest sons of this great nation. I would follow him to hell."

"The director is dead," Madeline Murdoch said softly. "Remember?"

Glassman bowed his head. The national security adviser sighed. "So you seduced Miss Rabin at the order of Brady Daniels. But you were not on assignment with the agency?"

"The director wanted an off-the-books operation. He didn't trust CIA anymore. He suspected the Israelis had penetrated the agency and were going around him."

"And what did the Israelis prize so highly that they wanted to go to such lengths to protect it?"

"Two things. First, any information about the reactor at Dimona."

Madeline Murdoch started up from her chair. "And second?"

"Their man in the agency."

Madeline Murdoch coughed. The cough became a hack. "Philip, I need a cigarette," she gasped.

"Have your gum, my dear. It's a nicotine attack."

"Damn the gum, Philip."

"My dear," the economist said, rising to his full height, a little over five feet. "I will do anything for you, but I will not allow you to smoke."

Her eyes watering, she smiled at her husband. "I love you when you are strong. And you are always strong for me." She squeezed her husband's hand and turned to Glassman, gazing at him like a hunting bird.

"My people seem sure you are the spy that has been aiding the Israelis."

"I was just an air attaché. Brady Daniels feared Mossad had penetrated the agency at a much higher level."

"What triggered such fears?"

"Because they were concealing all knowledge from him that they possessed about the chemical factory near Kharmat in the Republic of Tarak."

Madeline Murdoch fixed her gaze on him. "What chemical factory?"

Glassman's lips cracked into a bleeding smile. "As you say, Dr. Murdoch. It's all a matter of trust. I was going to give my information to the one man I trusted besides Director Daniels when they arrested me."

"Scott Cartwright," Madeline Murdoch said.

Philip Murdoch picked the kettle up from his hot plate and jiggled it. He poured himself a cup of tea, staring in the firelight at the battered colonel and his lovely wife, who at the moment had eyes only for each other. Madeline Murdoch broke her silence after a long pause. The fire had gone to embers.

"I don't know if I believe you, Colonel. It is easy to see from the wreckage in your path that you are a dangerous man."

"Turn me in and the problems you have now will be greater, not smaller," Glassman said.

"My Secret Service man downstairs will be stirring soon, I imagine," Madeline Murdoch said. "I don't know if I believe you, but I'm afraid that for the moment I can't afford not to, Colonel."

"Thank you. I've got to figure a way to get to Cartwright."

"My dear God," Madeline Murdoch exclaimed. "Finding Cartwright will be difficult. First, however, we've got to get you out of here."

"You won't turn me in, then?"

"At the moment, Colonel, I think you are a card that I do not wish to give up."

She strode from the room, marched down the hall, and turned an antique brass knob, which was itself a combination lock. She entered a room the size of a small closet. The room contained her IBM PC, which linked her to the White House, State, CIA, and the Pentagon.

She booted the computer. A list of telephone numbers materialized before her. One was a cutout number for the British intelligence service near Piccadilly. The other was the number in Birmingham, England, for the offices of Coldwell Integrated Armaments.

—— 32 ——
Flight of the Bumblebee

Over the Mediterranean

AN F-14 TOMCAT PILOT ASSIGNED to carrier duty aboard the USS *Saratoga* effected first sighting of the Blackbird drone, which resembled a cruise missile skimming across the sky. The Tomcat's radar officer picked up the Mach-3 blip on his powerful Phoenix radar system as he flew far enough to the north of the Libyan "line of death" to avoid coastal sweeps by Qaddafi's inept but annoying air force.

The black drone streaked eastward until its fuel burned up, triggering an orange parachute. It dropped gently toward the churning sea with its precious data. As the canopy descended, an Osprey tilt-rotor aircraft skimmed the waves, dropping a Navy SEAL team. The frogmen accomplished the drone recovery and fired a flare.

"This is Able Doubloon. We have a clean recovery," the Osprey pilot radioed back to the carrier group.

"Roger, Able Doubloon. Handle the article with care. Over," the Commander Air Group radioed from the bridge of the carrier.

"Roger. Out."

Within the hour the drone was carried to Sicily, where it was transferred to a C-141 Starlifter and sent on its way to Andrews Air Force Base in the Maryland suburbs of Washington.

Four thousand miles away in Washington, Benjamin Johnson surveyed the illuminated display map in the Situation Room at the White House. Johnson sighed with relief at a cryptographic message giving news of the drone recovery. With him in the "Glass House" were Avery Benedict of CIA and General Pete Rawlinson, commander of Blackbird operations.

"It's damn little enough good news," Rawlinson growled. "I've got two men down and no status on them."

"We should have Major Rogers back soon," Avery Benedict said. "The Israelis will turn him loose. State is working to effect contact with Tarak. We'll learn soon enough if General Cartwright was a casualty."

The Air Force general stared disdainfully at the CIA chief. "You think we'll get a straight answer from President Kemal? He makes Assad look like a Boy Scout. If Kemal's got Cartwright, he'll use him as a bargaining chip."

"We've got to find out what happened to the airplane," Ben Johnson said, tugging anxiously at his silver beard.

"It's obvious what happened to your precious plane, Mr. Johnson," Avery Benedict sneered. "It got blown out of the sky."

"Dammit, we've got to find out why," Johnson said, pounding his fist on a control panel.

"We never should have used the damn spy plane in the first place," Benedict sneered. "We should have waited for a satellite pass."

"Except that your CIA boys don't have a damn satellite that carries the camera we mounted on my airplane," Johnson retorted. "And it will be months before you can get one into orbit."

General Rawlinson pushed the men apart, then scowled across the room at the code clerks, cryptographers, data interpreters, and communications officers who were watching surreptitiously on the other side of the glass. "This is a mess all right," the general said. "But at least we've got the drone data coming in. With that we can brief the president."

"Let's call Madeline," Benjamin Johnson said. "My guess is the president will want to hear it from her."

"I would think the president would rather get the news from his director of intelligence," Avery Benedict said haughtily.

"Acting director," Johnson corrected.

"Aw, cut it out, fellas," Rawlinson said, putting his arms around both men's shoulders and grinning like a bulldog. "There's enough bad news for the man to get it from all of us."

"I'll call Dr. Murdoch," Johnson said. "We need her before we inform the president."

"Your airplane has caused an international incident, Mr. Johnson," Benedict snarled. "The only option we've got is to call in State and let them do their sackcloth and ashes routine, for the Arabs, the Israelis, and probably the Albanians for all we know."

Johnson glared at Benedict. "Mister, that airplane was collecting essential intelligence when you were whirling a hula hoop. The Blackbird's record is better than the CIA's over the last twenty years, I'd say."

Benedict swore under his breath, and Johnson picked up the phone. He listened for a moment, his face coloring. Finally his mouth dropped open.

"Benjamin, you look like you saw a ghost," Rawlinson said.

"She's not there," Johnson said dumbly. "I talked to her husband." Johnson turned to General Rawlinson. "That flier of yours, Glassman, the one undergoing the security check—"

"What about him?" Avery Benedict demanded. "He's in custody."

"Not anymore," Johnson sputtered. "He's escaped. He abducted the national security adviser."

"Good God," Rawlinson growled. "Let's get the hell upstairs."

The men raced to the door of the Glass House, all three hitting it like the Redskins offensive line. Rawlinson backed off first while the other two shouldered through, leaving Situation Room staff to wonder what fresh hell had engulfed the White House.

—— 33 ——
The Frying Pan

Kharmat, Federated Socialist Republic of Tarak

CARTWRIGHT BLINKED HIS EYES RAPIDLY on waking. They felt like they had sand in them, but they worked. The room's only light came from a steel grate near the ceiling. The general turned his head in the airman's reflex to determine if he was paralyzed. He wiggled his toes and exhaled with relief. The general shook his head a second time to discover wiring attached to his head. He ached with the injuries of a bad beating, a plane crash, or both.

A door opened, temporarily blinding him. Cartwright slowly opened his eyes, seeing a Middle Eastern man of middle age with an ample waistline and expensive suit, accompanied by a gun-toting goon. "How are you feeling today, General?" the rotund man asked solicitously, his moustache curling up like a happy face.

"I've been better," Cartwright mumbled. "What's the name of this hotel?"

The Taraki intelligence chief slapped Cartwright sharply and smiled. "I will ask questions. You give answers. You may address me as General Walid, General Scott Cartwright."

"So much for military courtesy," Cartwright muttered. "Good thing I got this tube stuck up my nose."

"And why is that, General?" Walid asked.

"That way I don't have to smell your cheap cologne."

In psychological assessments provided by the Soviets, the Americans were described as childish and defiant in early stages of interrogation. "I understand your jargon, General Cartwright. I studied international relations at your own American University in Washington."

"College boy, huh," Cartwright murmured. "Goody." Walid slapped him again. Cartwright lay still this time, staring at the intelligence chief to memorize his features.

Walid tugged playfully at one of the electrodes glued to Cartwright's head, causing the general to clamp his jaw tightly. "The electroencephalogram informed us you were sound of mind," Walid said. "No concussion. I must say I was surprised after the way you dropped in on us. Your pressure suit must be remarkable in its protective characteristics."

"The name is Cartwright. Scott Cortland Cartwright," the general said, slowly and with emphasis. "My rank is major general, United States Air Force. Now you've got it all."

"What we have in you, General, is a big fish," Walid said, pacing. "It's not every day a former astronaut is captured on an aggressive spying mission. The question now is how to use you to best advantage. Perhaps you were here trying to spread the AIDS virus?"

"That's bullshit," Cartwright snorted. "They don't even buy that at the U.N. anymore."

Walid shrugged. He cupped his chin in his right hand, which rested on his left. He circled the bed as though he were thinking. The bodyguard remained motionless, patient as a eunuch.

"General, we do not wish you to betray your country," Walid said. "But would you be willing to sign a statement acknowledging your violation of my country's air space? Then you could be quickly repatriated."

Cartwright smiled. Slowly he raised the middle finger on his right hand. "Sorry," he said. "I seem to have a nervous tic in my writing hand."

The Taraki intelligence chief gazed at Cartwright, puzzled at first, then angry. "So you prefer to play the tough American," Walid said softly. "You think you are Rambo or something?"

"John Wayne was more my style," Cartwright grunted. "More my era, too."

Sneering, Walid said, "That's when you Americans believed you ruled the world. Okay, John Wayne, meet Fouad." He motioned the bodyguard forward.

Fouad moved forward and began vigorously tugging at the wires glued to Cartwright's head, pulling them from his snow white scalp, causing the general to wince and strain against his leather straps. He gritted his teeth and did not scream.

"Fouad has many devices that explore the limits of pain, American. Would you like to test your courage against them?" Walid asked.

"Address me by my rank, you son of a bitch," Cartwright gasped, his scalp bleeding in patches where Fouad had removed the brain-scan wires.

"General Walid, you are being a truly stupid man. You don't want a fight with the Americans," Cartwright said, breathing heavily as the bodyguard retreated, holding the wires and tatters of the general's white hair like a trophy. "Keeping me is more trouble than it will be worth to you."

"How so, General?"

"Sooner or later, Uncle Sam is gonna get me or my body back. Then, you're up shit creek."

"There are ways to do the job without making a mess of your remains, General."

"Think I don't know that? Sure, you can use drugs so old Fouad here won't have to grind me into hamburger. But I can flat promise you I will confuse ya." Tapping his forehead with his left hand, he said, "I've got enough disinformation stored in my gray matter to keep your analysts guessing for weeks what's true and what's false. I'm a born bullshitter."

"So, what in your opinion, General, is our final alternative?"

"A show trial. You can march me out in front of the cameras and rant about the American imperialists. But it won't work. It's been done too often. You'll bore your audience."

"You were in clear violation of our air space, remember, General?"

"So what? Everyone knows we do it. Facts of life."

Walid gazed down at the white-haired general and sighed.

Watching the blood trickle slowly down Cartwright's forehead, he guessed that drugs and torture might indeed yield little benefit. "There is yet another option you have not considered, General Cartwright."

"There's plenty of stuff I haven't thought of."

"My government has not acknowledged your presence here. We could sell you to people who would have better use for you."

Cartwright nodded painfully. "You could do it. But my country would find out. And they will avenge me."

Walid smiled. "Maybe soon we will not be so fearful of your country."

"Don't count on it. You must be talking about your little chemical plant."

Walid glowered at Cartwright. "Already you know too much to ever leave here!" he snarled. He turned quickly and strode from the room, his bodyguard following like a large dog.

Cartwright smiled, happy that somehow he had gained more information from the Taraki general than he had given. The chemical plant had been a shot in the dark, a secondary target in his mission profile.

As Walid stepped down the corridor, the supervising physician at the police hospital in Kharmat called out to him. "My General," the physician said, hurrying to catch up with the republic's second-most-powerful man. "Do we administer the drugs?"

"Prepare the American for transport. Sedate him and have him on the roof in half an hour." The supervising physician hurried to comply with General Walid's order.

As the last of the Ilyushin transports touched down on the ten-thousand-foot airstrip at Kharmat International Airport, the flags of Tarak, the German Democratic Republic, and the Soviet Union were raised simultaneously above the reviewing stand. At first they hung limply, but then whipped in the breeze fanned by the backwash of the giant transports braking thunderously on the tarmac.

Atop the reviewing stand stood President Kemal and General Walid, accompanied by the Taraki foreign minister and the East German and Soviet ambassadors. They saluted as a Taraki band shrieked a parody of the anthems of each nation. Each official wished to retreat to his air-conditioned domicile as soon as protocol and Third World solidarity allowed. Meanwhile, they all sweated like pigs.

A procession of armored vehicles descended from the transports, looking like monstrous beetles. They were BTR-60s, eight-wheel personnel carriers topped by ugly little turrets with machine guns. The Soviet and the East German troops were supplied by the Warsaw Pact as a token of socialist good will, courtesy of General Kolchak, who signed the transfer order.

As they rolled away, the Soviet ambassador put his hand on the arm of General Walid, in a gesture of familiarity that the Arab disliked. Nevertheless, Walid concealed his distaste for the Russian and smiled warmly.

"The Republic of Tarak thanks the Union of Soviet Socialist Republics for its fraternal gesture," Walid said unctuously, offering his hand to the Russian.

The men turned to watch the armored squadron. As the troop carriers formed on line, the vehicle commanders rose from inside their metal hatches. Wearing Russian leather tanker helmets, each commander sweated profusely in the blistering Taraki midday sun, despite the tropical uniforms.

At the center of the formation, one man stood bareheaded, the white sunlight beating down on his scarred pink skull. The man's face was covered from the top of his nose to the bottom of his right jaw with a plate of gray steel. General Reinhard Grunfeld saluted, his gray eyes staring into the eyes of the men on the reviewing stand as though he were searching for an equal.

"I expect that is the tank general you told us about," Walid said, whispering to the East German ambassador in English.

"Indeed he is," the envoy replied in their common language. "He is the finest tactician of armor in the Warsaw Pact. It was wise to seek him as an adviser for your own troops. He is probably the last such adviser to come from the GDR. How quickly the world is changing."

"His war wound must have been serious," Walid whispered. "How did he get it?"

"Who remembers at this late date?" the East German ambassador whispered evasively.

"Just so," Walid said, smiling at the man behind the mask. Grunfeld dropped his salute, barked a single command into his radio microphone, and the armored formation wheeled in a left facing movement, as smartly as tanks on review at an old Nuremburg rally.

As the caravan of troop carriers departed in a cloud of diesel fumes, the dignitaries dismounted the reviewing stand. The men of each country were returning to their respective Mercedes limousines when a new car, a stretch Lincoln bearing American flags on its hood and fenders, lurched forward, with Taraki police sedans screeching after it, their sirens blaring. The Lincoln stopped short of a line of Taraki troops, who lowered their bayonet-studded AK-47s menacingly.

General Walid strode purposefully toward the Lincoln as Kemal entered the Mercedes that edged up beside him and departed the airfield. As Walid stepped toward the Lincoln, the bullet-proof door swung open.

"What brings the distinguished American ambassador Carter Salisbury out in this heat?" Walid asked cheerfully. "You must be wishing a glance at our latest demonstration of fraternal assistance."

"Cut the crap, Walid," the ambassador snorted. "Where's our flier?"

Walid shrugged and held his hands up. "I fear I am ignorant about the circumstances of your inquiry."

"Let me put it to you this way, General. I am making a diplomatic inquiry, which I expect to be answered within the hour. After that, the Sixth Fleet may do the talking."

"Ambassador Salisbury, this is not your way. Surely you know such threats are the idle demonstration of a pitiful giant, not a nation confident of its power. Really, I am unaware of the situation you describe, but I will investigate."

"I'll expect an answer I can relay to Washington. Again, sir, within the hour."

General Walid threw his hands up again and smiled. The embassy Lincoln wheeled around and lurched from the airstrip, leaving tread from its bullet-proof tires on the tarmac. Walid straightened his suit and walked across the airstrip to a helicopter. Within minutes he was airborne and heading toward the chemical factory thirty miles away on the Taraki coast.

—— 34 ——
Truth or Consequences

Washington

HIS HANDS SPREAD ON THE big Oval Office desk, the president stared balefully over the top of his half-frame glasses. To Avery Benedict, the disapproving stare came from the man who held his career in his hands. To General Rawlinson, the president's long face formed the disappointed scowl of the commander-in-chief. For Benjamin Johnson, the only real civilian among the president's visitors, the president's pained expression recalled Eisenhower's on that May morning when Khruschev announced the capture of a U-2 pilot named Gary Powers.

"Director Benedict," the president said, addressing the acting CIA chief in a coldly formal manner. "Would you consider it an accurate statement that this has been the blackest day of my administration?"

"It has not been a good day, sir."

"Mr. Johnson," the president snapped. "What the hell happened with your superplane?"

"We don't know, sir. The SR-71 has never failed in an operational environment. That's a twenty-five-year record, sir."

"Well, it's broken now," the president said, removing his glasses. "The way I'm reading this situation, my only choices are to decide what lies to tell and whom to fire."

"By your leave, Mr. President," Avery Benedict ventured bravely. "If Dr. Murdoch were here, I believe she would advise you not to deceive the media about the material facts that an airplane was shot down. We should go public."

"Well, Mr. Benedict, my national security adviser is not here," the president said acidly. "It seems she was kidnapped because your ham-handed operatives can't hold on to one man who is judged a security risk."

Benedict murmured, "The men guarding Colonel Glassman were injured in an unforeseeable and tragic automobile accident, sir. Nevertheless, Mr. President, I can offer my resignation now, if that is your wish."

"No, you don't, Benedict," the president growled. "Not yet. You'd better alert FBI to get every agent mobilized until Madeline Murdoch is found. And God help you if the press tumbles to this or she is harmed."

The door to the Oval Office swung open. The men gaped. "You needn't mobilize the FBI," Madeline Murdoch said breezily as she strode into the office accompanied by her aide, Charlotte Duncan.

"Madeline," the president gasped.

"We should get on with business," the national security adviser said as she leafed through memoranda she carried. "Suffice it to say I am safe after my ordeal and there are matters before us that must be attended to."

"Where is Glassman?" Benedict demanded.

"I don't know and I don't care, Mr. Benedict," Madeline Murdoch said breezily. "He dropped me near the Orange line stop in Arlington. The FBI can find him. Or perhaps not. He appears to be quite resourceful. In any event, I am here to deliver my briefing, thanks to one of those immigrant cab drivers who delivered me to the White House steps after a ride that I can only describe as the most harrowing point of my adventure. He was from Iran, I believe."

"We're going to need to debrief you intensively on Glassman and his whereabouts, Dr. Murdoch," Benedict snapped.

"Shouldn't we be worrying about the big picture?" Madeline Murdoch said crisply. "Let the FBI deal with Glassman. CIA's already had its turn and muffed it."

As Benedict fumed, the president never took his eyes from the national security adviser. Finally, folding his arms, he laughed. The other men laughed nervously, except for the acting CIA chief who folded his arms and slumped in his chair in a deep funk.

Folding her memoranda neatly, Madeline Murdoch announced, "Miss Duncan has the photographic displays the National Reconnaissance Office just finished processing from the drone."

"How in hell did you get that material, Dr. Murdoch?" Avery Benedict demanded.

"I was kidnapped briefly, not killed," Madeline Murdoch replied smoothly. "As long as I was unharmed, it occurred to me I should see if anything good could be retrieved following the downing of General Cartwright and Major Rogers."

"That film is CIA property," Benedict snapped.

"NRO gave me the film, simple enough, based on the fact that I report directly to the president. *N'est-ce pas?*"

"She's right, Avery. Shut up and let's see what she's got," the president ordered, and proceeded to clean his glasses. Charlotte Duncan busied herself setting up a portable slide projector.

The grainy film showed a variety of buildings, smudges, and shadows that represented the yield from the drone. Pointing at a picture of a nuclear reactor, Madeline Murdoch said, "There it is. Same old Dimona that has troubled us all. But note this." Madeline Murdoch pointed to a corner of the frame. "We know the Israelis guard Dimona with advanced Hawk missiles for close-in antiaircraft protection."

"Right," Benedict said. "So what?"

"These, my dear Avery Benedict, are not Hawk missiles," Murdoch said triumphantly.

"What are you saying, Madeline?" the president demanded.

"I've never seen this sort of rocket in the Israeli arsenal before, and I would wager neither has anyone in this room," she said. "The emplacement looks like a Hawk battery, but the missile itself is longer. It more closely resembles a Pershing missile, but it is longer still.''

"Sweet Jesus," General Rawlinson whispered. "The Jericho II. We've heard about 'em. Glassman gave me a report on them.''

"Precisely, General," Madeline Murdoch said. "A new Israeli missile with enough range to reach Kiev and enough punch to take out any city in the Arab world.''

"They wouldn't try to hide something like this from us," Benedict declared. "It would be madness.''

"Israel is an ally, but she does not trust us," Madeline Murdoch said. "She has little reason to trust her allies. Next slide, Charlotte.''

The aide switched to another patch of barren terrain, this time bordered by coastline and a ruined Crusader fortress. The fortress was ringed by antiaircraft missiles and tanks. "Why didn't we know about this development in Tarak, Mr. Benedict?" Madeline Murdoch asked sweetly.

"Your critique of CIA makes me weary, Dr. Murdoch," Benedict said. "That's old stuff. We know they've been cooking gas there for the Iraqis for at least two years. You knew about it, too.''

"But why has the installation been fortified recently?" the security adviser pressed. "I fear there is an ominous symmetry in the offensive weapons in Israel and the plant in Tarak.''

"Madeline," the president said. "What about the film from the new camera? As I recall, we wanted a look inside Dimona.''

Her arms folded, Madeline Murdoch inclined her head. "We don't have that film, Mr. President," the national security adviser said. "Only the Blackbird carried that camera attachment in its nose pod, which autodestructed when the plane went down. But if we had the pictures, I would bet they would show Israeli preparation for a preemptive nuclear strike.''

"Utter lunacy," Avery Benedict cried out. "That's wild speculation based on evidence you don't possess. Why would they do such a thing and risk annihilation?''

"You are quite right, Mr. Benedict," Madeline Murdoch said. "I am speculating. We need more precise data.''

"What are you suggesting, Madeline?" the president asked.

"Another overflight," she said bluntly. "We need it soon, and we need to duplicate and enhance the data recovered from the drone."

"Just what we need," Benedict sneered. "If the Israelis could shoot down your precious plane once, what makes you think they can't do it again?"

"Young man, I don't have to take that kind of talk from you," Benjamin Johnson interjected. "I am speaking to the president."

"Go on, Ben," the president urged.

Johnson rose and began pacing. "Mr. President, you are of course aware of the research and development project to build the Blackbird's successor? The Mach-5 Aurora prototype?"

"The plane isn't ready, Ben," the president said. "We both know that."

"We can get something ready, Mr. President! If I put the Skunk Works into round-the-clock shifts, I can get you something that will work."

"Mr. President," Avery Benedict said, interrupting. "My earnest advice is to stall. We can position a satellite in the same amount of time. Meantime, State can inform Israel of our suspicions."

"You won't get the look-down see-through capability from a satellite," Johnson said. "You need a long look and you need it soon. Give me a few days."

"I think we need that overflight, Mr. President," Madeline Murdoch said. The president fiddled with a pen on his desk and looked at his advisers.

"If this were the only problem that must be dealt with, it would almost be too much," he said, balancing his pen delicately between his two hands. He put the pen down and began to count off with his fingers.

"There is the diplomatic dimension. The Israelis and Tarakis must be dealt with concerning our fliers," he said. "There is the security aspect. What danger do the regional antagonists pose to the United States?" He pushed his half-frame glasses far up on his forehead. "Finally, there is the goddamned media dimension. What are we going to tell the networks when they find out an American spy plane has been downed?"

"How can we help, Mr. President?" Madeline Murdoch asked.

"If you don't mind, Madeline, I think I've been helped quite enough by you people for one day," the president said ruefully. "Leave me alone so I can think." He smiled weakly. "It's what I get paid to do."

— 35 —
Dungeons and Dragons

The Plant in Tarak

CARTWRIGHT SAT HUNCHED IN THE darkness and rested. He had stepped out a circuit of the damp cell until he was thoroughly familiar with its dimensions, five paces by five paces, and about six inches too short to accommodate his rawboned six-foot frame. For comfort, there was a small tin bucket. But the ventilation was so poor that its stench was overpowering.

Insofar as the architecture dated to the Crusader era, the security technology of the cell itself was dated. The steel door, though, was sufficiently modern to deny prospect of escape. Running his fingers along the door, Cartwright felt the air holes that allowed the minimum amount of air to pass through. Cartwright had been fed once and, mercifully, had emptied his bowels only once.

The steel door swung open. In the darkness he heard the guttural language of soldiers who hunted the woods for him in France a lifetime ago.

"Sit," a voice commanded, in English tinged with a vaguely teutonic accent. Cartwright was already sitting in the corner of his cell. Peering at him in the darkness was a man of about his own height with a shock of tousled blond hair. Cartwright peered back. The man had the strange blue eyes of a Siamese cat and a white scar on his forehead.

"So. You are the American," the visitor asserted. The man assumed an odd posture, hunching down on his knees—reminding Cartwright of Vietnamese peasants on market day.

"Hi," Cartwright said. "Who might you be, stranger?"

"I've met American airmen before," Kurtz said.

"Where was that?" Cartwright said.

"In Hanoi."

"What was a nice German boy like you doing in that dump? Not much of a tourist town." Cartwright could hear the man nervously cracking his knuckles.

"You mistake me," Kurtz said pleasantly. "Many do. I am not German, except by ancestry. We Volga Germans are Soviet citizens. I am, first, a Soviet citizen."

"So that's the Hanoi story," Cartwright said. "You sound like a volunteer."

What passed for a dry laugh dropped from Kurtz's lips. "Just so," he said. "I directed the radar gun crews that shot down your fascist B-52s. We got a lot of them."

"Not so many that we couldn't send a few more," Cartwright said.

The hunched figure nodded. "Yes, American. There were always more. The bombs fell, the bombers came. But we shot down a lot, you see. And then, I would visit the Americans. What was their name for that place?"

"The Hanoi Hilton," Cartwright said tersely.

"Yes," Kurtz said. "That was it. For them, the war was so impersonal, until we dragged them in their parachutes. It got personal when we marched them through the streets and showed them their errors. For me, it was always personal."

"Aw, come on," Cartwright snorted. "You commies never fight for personal reasons. You're supposed to be above all that. Serving history and so on. How'd your grand war of liberation end up getting personal?"

"One of the people your bombs hit was my wife, American," Kurtz hissed. "I took a Vietnamese to bear my child. She was carrying my son in her arms the day one of your impersonal bombs found her on the street without joy."

"Sorry," Cartwright grunted. "Really. It's a shitty business."

"Sometimes it is indeed shitty, as you say," Kurtz declared. "Other times, there is more pleasure. I will enjoy it when I boil you, American airman."

The hunched figure rose and turned from Cartwright. The door slammed shut, echoing down the passageway. Cartwright fingered the horseshoe medallion, the one Madeline Murdoch had pressed into his hands for luck just before he left Washington. The Tarakis had let him keep it with his dog tags.

Cartwright sat in the darkness, wrapping and unwrapping the chain of the medal around his fingers like worry beads. In the blackness it was easy to lose track of time. He heard the clump-clumping of hobnailed boots. The general fingered Madeline Murdoch's horseshoe coin. The steel door edged open, and a hand appeared holding a wooden plate with the rice on it. Cartwright seized the hand and pressed the charm tightly on the soft flesh. He heard a groan and a sigh and pressed the medal tighter yet so that the shellfish toxin in the pin found its way. He pulled the dying man into the cell.

"You're a heavy son of a bitch," Cartwright whispered, moving his hands over the guard and rummaging his way down to his belt and the Makarov pistol. Taking the gun, he hurriedly pulled at the guard's tunic until it was all the way off.

"Bastards probably thought I was too old to kick up a fuss," Cartwright muttered. He wrapped the tunic around the pistol and peered around the door. The passageway was lit by low-wattage bulbs spaced about thirty feet apart. He stepped into the passageway and edged along the wall. Just around a corner, another guard perched on an ammunition crate. He was holding an AK-47 carelessly, by its sling.

Cartwright stepped around the corner. Smiling brightly, he said, "Hi!"

As the startled guard turned toward him, Cartwright fired, the pistol making a muffled crack through the crude silencer of the tunic. The guard pitched back on the floor. Cartwright grabbed the man's belt and felt along it for a holster. He grabbed a second pistol and three spare clips from a leather ammo pouch. He decided against stealing the dead guard's boots. He padded in his bare feet, moving carefully. He turned a corner and sighted another steel door, this one also without a window.

He heard the door beginning to open and ran back the way he had come. As he rounded the corner, running past the slain guard, he heard boots and voices speaking rapidly in Arabic. He raced past his cell, turned a corner, and encountered another steel door. Panting, he stopped and listened. The sound of boots was close behind him.

He shivered and heard the low hum of ventilated air being pushed into the underground chamber. Cartwright looked above his head and saw a grate. Leaping, the old man brushed the grate with his fingers and discovered it was not screwed shut. He dropped the tunic, extra pistol, and clips. He leaped again, using the Makarov to bang the grate into the shaft. It sounded like a cannon going off.

Moving quickly, he wrapped the pistols and clips in the guard's tunic and tossed them up into the shaft as though he were shooting a basket at the old hoop nailed to his garage. He jumped again and chinned himself up into the shaft on the edge opposite the tunic and weapons. As he pulled his right leg into the shaft, it brushed the tunic, causing it to fall.

The pistols clattered on the cobblestoned floor. Cartwright winced. He heard voices, closer, now shouting. He peered ahead into the blackness of the shaft and crawled for his life. The Volga German was right. On the ground, combat became more personal.

—— 36 ——
Dinner at Eight

Washington

THE PRESIDENT'S LIMOUSINE POKED through the crabbed and crowded streets of old Georgetown, making its way to the Murdoch town house like a cruiser navigating the Dardanelles. Despite the treacherous straits of tree-lined streets lined with illegally parked automobiles, the convoy of limousine and Secret Service cruisers inched its way to the Murdoch home in time for dinner at eight.

Unnoticed by the university crowd heading toward the Tombs and evening diners strolling to the restaurants of M Street, a cordon of Secret Service security guards ringed the Murdoch home. The heavily armed agents, who'd adopted the tweed and turtleneck mufti of the Georgetown crowd, were deployed on the leafy streets and Victorian rooftops behind Wisconsin Avenue to prevent a repeat performance of Adam Glassman's coup of the night previous. Three agents were now assigned to the Murdoch kitchen.

A previously scheduled dinner with a particularly tenacious Washington columnist went off without a hitch, giving the president and Madeline Murdoch the useful knowledge that the Beltway media had not yet heard about the Blackbird's destruction. When columnist David McClendon was ushered out by Secret Service, Madeline and the president sighed with relief.

"Will you join me in the Secure Room upstairs, Mr. President?" Madeline Murdoch said, offering the president a balloon of brandy.

"Thanks, Maddy. I needed that." He followed her up the stairs, past the dining room and the library to the last door on the left, a book-crammed study. The office Madeline Murdoch referred to as the Secure Room was the only room in her rambling house that was supposed to be immune to bugs.

Inside the study, Adam Glassman waited at attention, wearing a class-A blue uniform and four rows of medals, topped by the Distinguished Flying Cross. The president dropped his brandy snifter in a crash of leaded crystal. Glassman saluted.

"Dr. Murdoch," the president snapped. "Explain this. And while you're explaining, call the Secret Service."

"Mr. President, there is an explanation, but I beg you to wait on it before we alert the palace guard," Madeline Murdoch said.

"Need I remind you this man is a fugitive," the president growled. Glassman held his salute, waiting for the president to return it.

"Remember also that he is a national hero," the gnomish Philip Murdoch said, stepping in furtively from the hallway behind the chief executive. "Our ties go deeper than Yale, Mr. President. Remember Jedburgh justice?"

"Goddammit, Madeline," the president blurted in a near rage. "Your husband is invoking old-boy ties while half official Washington is looking for this man." For an instant Madeline Murdoch feared an apoplectic president might go into cardiac arrest in her study. "What have you to say for yourself?" the chief executive demanded.

"You didn't hire me for orthodox thinking, Mr. President. Give the colonel five minutes to explain himself."

"At ease, Colonel Glassman, goddammit," ordered the president, returning the salute dismissively. Glassman shifted his stance slightly. "Five minutes, Colonel," the president declared. "Then prepare to leave this house in irons."

"I am so prepared if that is your order, sir," Glassman said.

"Well, that's a goddamned relief," the president snorted. "A soldier who's prepared to follow the commander-in-chief's order. Lately that's a goddamned novelty."

The president settled himself in Madeline Murdoch's wing chair. "I feel a bit like Alice through the looking glass at the moment," the president said.

Affecting the detached manner of the briefing officer, Glassman recounted Brady Daniels's suspicions about Israeli penetration of the agency. When he finished, the president was resting his head in his hand as though he suffered a severe headache. "So you busted loose, did you?" the president inquired, sounding exhausted by what he had been told.

"Yes, sir."

"To clear your good name?"

"No, Mr. President. I escaped to warn you of a potential hostile penetration of our intelligence service at a high level."

"You're not an Ollie North are you, Colonel Glassman?" the president asked.

"No, sir."

"Not a loose cannon? Some right-winger with a hidden agenda? Not some Bonapartist getting ready to ride in on a white horse?" the president said, his voice slowly swelling.

"No sir," Glassman said.

"Because what you're telling me either contains a drop of truth or you are a real nut, mister," the president said quietly.

"He's not a nut, Mr. President," Madeline Murdoch said.

"How do you know, Madeline?" the president demanded. "This country has a sad recent record of policy being formed by junior-grade officers who strung their bosses along long enough to sink the ship of state."

Madeline Murdoch folded her arms defiantly. "Mr. President, do you want an adviser or a sycophant like Avery Benedict?"

"Is that what this is about? You want to deep-six Benedict because you don't like him?"

"Mr. President," Madeline Murdoch exclaimed. "Give yourself the credit for selecting me to do this job. Do I have your confidence or not?"

The president sighed. He fidgeted uncomfortably in his chair and shifted his gaze from Madeline Murdoch to Glassman, still standing at attention, to Philip Murdoch who sat polishing his glasses with the edge of his sweater.

"Of course you have my confidence, Madeline," he said wearily. "You're smarter and braver than the lot of them at Sixteen Hundred Pennsylvania. So what is your advice?"

"A second overflight, sir."

"Oh, dear God," the president said. "Not that again."

"Sir," Madeline Murdoch said, rising from the couch. She paced past Glassman and began to think aloud in her best extemporaneous fashion. "CIA should have informed us of the activity at Dimona. The agency did not. CIA should have informed you of the deployment of the Jericho missiles. Again, the agency failed."

"Madeline," the president interrupted. "You forget that we have one flier in custody of the Israelis and another missing in unfriendly territory. Another overflight could be like pouring gasoline on a fire."

"Nonsense," the professor said abruptly. "The Israelis must quickly return Major Rogers or risk a strain in our alliance, and thorough reconnaissance of Tarak will perhaps aid our determination of General Cartwright's fate."

"Sweet Jesus," the president muttered. "What's to gain?"

"Sir, President Kemal is a rejectionist and a radical. Armed with chemical weapons, he could light a fire that couldn't be put out," Madeline Murdoch said urgently.

"The media will have this story in a day or two, at latest," the president said bitterly. "Someone will leak it."

"Let them chase the story, Mr. President. While the reporters trip over each other, we'll put our second plane in and collect our data."

The president arched his eyebrows and crossed his arms. He stared bleakly at Madeline Murdoch. Finally he said, "Colonel Glassman, will you please take a seat? You make me nervous."

As Glassman seated himself, the president turned to Philip Murdoch and put his hand on his friend's arm. "Phil, can you pour me a brandy?"

The president's old friend patted the chief executive on the shoulder and retrieved a snifter and decanter from the study's small bar. The president tossed back the liquor like a sailor. "Who makes the second flight, Madeline?"

"My recommendation is Colonel Glassman, sir."

"Why did I know that would be your answer, Madeline?" the president asked wearily. "I take it you're planning to cut out Avery Benedict."

"For his own good, Mr. President," Madeline Murdoch said. "If his agency is penetrated, he could unwittingly alert the mole."

"So you propose to send on reconnaissance the pilot whom Mr. Benedict had identified as the likely mole. God, it's insane."

Adam Glassman rose from the sofa and again stood at attention. His dark brown eyes fixed on the president. "With all due respect, sir, it's got to be me."

"Your five minutes were up a long time ago, Colonel," the president said tartly. Quickly he added, "Explain yourself."

"Dr. Murdoch informs me a Blackbird is being outfitted with new, more powerful engines. Simply put, sir, I'm the best high flier you've got.

"Not too cocky are you, son?" the president said.

"There are no pilots equal to my command of the Middle East collection area, sir," Glassman persisted.

"Weren't you shot down there, once, Colonel? What kind of record is that?"

"Begging your pardon, sir, didn't you have a spotter plane shot from under you once?"

"This is about Cartwright, isn't it, son?" the president said. "He helped you once, and you've got a debt."

"That's part of it, yes, Mr. President. I am the most highly motivated pilot in your command, sir." Glassman's eyes glistened in the firelight as he spoke with his usual mix of calm and intensity.

"Why should I trust a wild man like you?" the president said, peering deep into Glassman's dark eyes.

"Director Daniels did, sir. So does Dr. Murdoch."

"You're an odd bird, Glassman," the president said. "But a few people I trust do seem to believe in you."

The president rose from his chair and turned to Madeline Murdoch, who stood before her stacks of books looking more like a New England poetess than a stern guardian of national security. "This course you are charting, Madeline, is fraught with opportunity for fresh disaster, and we have had about our fair share of that for a day or two.''

"Yes, Mr. President.''

"I'm going to sleep on this one. Keep the colonel comfortable.''

"Yes, Mr. President.''

"One thing, Madeline. How in hell did you keep this young man under wraps? Secret Service swept the place this afternoon.''

Madeline Murdoch laughed abruptly. "The uniform was delivered. The colonel came in with Philip, cook, and the Cornish game hens. My caterer took the day off.''

The president shook his head and waved vaguely as he made his way down the stairs to his waiting protective detail. "Hell of a fine dinner, Madeline,'' the president said as he made his way downstairs. "We must do it again soon.''

Secret Service passed the president out the door to his limousine like firemen in a bucket brigade.

——— 37 ———
In the Maze

The Plant in Tarak

GENERAL WALID STARED AT THE body on the examining table. He had run the apparatus of a police state for years and not one of his detainees, inmates, patients, prisoners, interrogation subjects, or other classification of victims had ever escaped. Now, within the scope of a week, two had gotten loose: the verminous Englishman and the arrogant American general. He dabbed perspiration from his forehead.

"My General." A man in a white coat and clinical mask was tapping Walid lightly on the shoulder. Tapping again, to shake him from his reverie, the scientist said, "My General, I believe I have isolated the cause of the guard's mortality."

Walid turned around, his eyes slightly wild. "What is it? What are you saying?"

Removing his mask for a moment and brushing his shock of blond hair, Kurtz grinned. His smile was almost one of admiration for the man who had dispatched the guard so handily. "The guard was killed by means of a potent toxin. An injection of poison. The CIA uses a shellfish toxin. Very deadly."

"How was this possible?" Walid demanded.

Kurtz shrugged as he removed his lab smock and rubber gloves. "I do not know. When I observed the prisoner, he was

196

nearly naked, stripped down to his underclothes, except for his identity chain.''

"This man was a special prisoner, brought here for special reasons,'' Walid groaned. ''We must find him before the president becomes aware he is misplaced.''

"I also want the American caught and killed,'' Kurtz said. ''With pain.''

A lieutenant of the guards rushed into the lab. The officer in charge of the previous shift had already been shot for his ineptitude, so the lieutenant moved with unusual urgency.

"General Walid. We have identified the prisoner's escape path,'' the lieutenant said. ''Discarded pistols were found beneath a ventilation grate. The prisoner is hiding somewhere in the air ducts.''

Walid hugged the lieutenant to him as though he were a long-lost brother. Grasping the officer by the shoulders, he asked, "Have you put a search team into the ventilating ducts?''

"We did not go in,'' the lieutenant said. ''It's a maze. We can leave the prisoner to starve in there. We have started welding all the grates shut.''

"Search the vents, lieutenant!'' Walid snarled. ''That prisoner will be found and brought to me or you will be held personally responsible.''

At the same time the lieutenant was running to save his own life by locating the escapee, General Cartwright spied on the enraged Taraki general from his hiding place in the vent above the pathology laboratory. He felt confident the guards would not brave the maze, just as Americans in Vietnam hated the tunnels of Cu Chi. With patience learned as a boy in Kentucky, trained to hunt with a single bullet, Cartwright watched, waited, and listened.

Cartwright had accustomed himself to the darkness of the venting system. At the joints where the corners turned, there was total darkness. But the blackness was dispersed every fifty feet or so by a grayish light from below. He had nearly suffocated, crawling over the heat of a laundry that must have been organized to serve several hundred men. He clutched Madeline Murdoch's once-lethal lucky charm and silently thanked her for it.

Even though he was exhausted, the general knew he could

not nap. He fought to stay awake. One advantage of the vent system was that it conducted sound throughout the facility. The sound could be deceptive, however, because of the venting joints. Noises that seemed far away could be close. Likewise, sounds that seemed close might have traveled hundreds of feet through the vent. It was like moving through a carnival fun house.

Cartwright heard laughing, and what sounded like a guttural German voice. He moved toward that sound. As he crawled past the gray-lit space of a vent, he was assailed by a gagging odor compounded of disinfectant and putrefying flesh. Suddenly, the room below was lit, and Cartwright lurched back. Grabbing at the threadbare lining of his thermal shirt, he tore a handful of fabric and shoved it over his nose and mouth as he watched.

The blond Russian and a man about Cartwright's age, wearing a khaki tropical uniform, entered. Like the blond Russian, the officer in khaki wore a lab mask. In the chamber, men were lashed to the tables with leather restraints. Each man was gagged at the mouth, but each was conscious, their eyes bugging in terror. They whimpered through their gags. A lab technician stood at a counter filling an eye dropper with a clear liquid from a test tube.

At an order from the Russian, the technician squeezed a drop on the man on the first table, then strode rapidly past the next four tables, squeezing a drop of the fluid on each man. On the first, he placed the drop on the face; on the second, an arm; on the third, a hand. By the time he reached the last table, the first man was exhaling his death rattle, and his skin was coloring to a deep purple shade as though burned by acid.

"There, you see?" Kurtz exclaimed triumphantly. "All dead and dying within seconds."

Cartwright shivered and fought off an attack of the dry heaves.

— 38 —
The Deadly Okinawa Snake

Plant 42, California

BENJAMIN JOHNSON HOVERED OVER HIS design group like a mother hen. The men on his scratch team gazed into the computer-aided—design terminal as though it were a glowing crystal ball. The graying baby boomers who tilted and pitched the three-dimensional aircraft display at various angles on the multicolored screen were Johnson's pride. Most were not yet born when he sent his first airplane to war, but he hoped that someday they would be the ones to send a hypersonic airplane into space.

Adam Glassman brooded a few feet away, arms folded, watching the group anguish over the rush project. He wore the flight suit of a test pilot with name tape removed. The disguise was completed by silver hair dye used to color Glassman's tight black curls, aging him twenty years behind the aviator glasses perched on his hawklike nose.

Len Rudman, chief of CAD sketch, turned to Johnson, an anxious expression on his ginger-bearded face. "I'm worried, Boss," Rudman said. "I fear a no-go. We're months away on an Aurora rollout. Not days."

"That doesn't sound like you, Len."

"It just hasn't been done is all," Rudman said, his cohorts nodding silent agreement.

"Look, here," Rudman said, punching buttons on the CAD screen to give the boss an oblique view of the fuselage that accentuated the Blackbird's unique movable inlet spikes on its ram-air intakes.

"The J-58 engine was tailor-made for the SR-71," Rudman said, "The inlet spikes move in such a way to make a symphonic mix of fuel and rammed air. The engine made the Blackbird unique as a Mach 3-plus operational airplane. I just don't know if the old air frame can sustain Mach 5."

"About the time you were born, son, we built a plane here in six months. It was called the U-2. It accomplished a thing or two. We've had years on the Aurora technology. We can't wait. We need an operational airplane, right now."

"But, Ben," the engineer persisted. "It's so ad hoc. The new engines have only been ground-tested. We don't know what they'd do."

"That's flight test's department," Adam Glassman said, stepping forward. "I'll verify your data."

"Who is this guy?" Rudman asked, jerking his thumb at Glassman. "I didn't think we had any of these seat-of-the-pants fliers left."

"Thank your stars there are a few around," Johnson said. "You can crunch numbers to infinity, but you won't know if it will fly until the right jet jock defines the envelope."

Rudman's colleagues looked at the engineer and shook their heads. That was enough for Johnson. "Thank you, gentlemen, you're excused." Rudman's assistants looked horrified. They were being banished from the sanctum. Johnson shooed them out of the design center. "It's okay, fellows. We'll call you when we need you."

Benjamin Johnson turned to his CAD design chief and sighed. "That's the problem with committee work, Len. No boldness."

"Ben," Rudman moaned. "Those men were not wrong. The engine retrofit on a Blackbird is an ad hoc solution to a dangerous engineering problem."

"We have an ad hoc mission!" Johnson snapped. He stroked his beard and paced. He turned to the younger engineer. Pointing his stubby finger, he said, "You have two kids now, don't you, Len? A boy and a girl, isn't it?"

"Yeah. So?"

"Let me put it to you this way, Len," Johnson said. "Skunk Works isn't some ivory tower for you young da Vincis. We work missions of national necessity, so your kids can sleep safely. You are engaged in such a mission," Johnson continued sternly. "If you are unable to perform it, let me know now, Len. I'll get another guy or I'll do it myself."

Len Rudman stared at the designer, trying to absorb it all. Johnson returned his level gaze and then turned to leave.

"Just a minute," Rudman said, grabbing Adam Glassman's shoulder. "You mean it, don't you? You'd fly something I cobbled together overnight?"

"Yep," Glassman said.

Rudman returned to his screen and entered new data. Johnson pressed the keypad at the door, and it shushed open. Glassman followed. "Will he do it within twenty-four hours?" Glassman asked as the pair marched down the hall in the secure facility.

"Train 'em and trust 'em is the way to build airplanes," Johnson said briskly. "You should drop out of sight. There's fresh coffee in my quarters."

"Great," Glassman said.

"I mean it about keeping your profile low," Johnson murmured quietly. "I think there may be a leak in the security at this plant."

"What are you saying, Ben?"

The Skunk Works chief wrinkled his brow and plunged his hands deep in his pockets. "I don't believe Cartwright's mission failure was pilot error or equipment malfunction. It could have been sabotage."

"That sounds outlandish."

Johnson ran his fingers through his silver-gray coxcomb and shook his head. "We've never logged an operational loss on Blackbird. Now, get yourself buttoned down, and I'll see if I can bring you an airplane."

Glassman keyed his entry card and stepped into Johnson's modular living quarters, painted in peach and toast, decreed by company environment designers to be cheering tones. There was a full pot simmering on a Mr. Coffee. There was also a lean, bald man of middle age dressed in mechanics coveralls working away at opening one of Johnson's file cabinets.

"Who are you?" Glassman demanded.

"Building maintenance," the man said, stepping away from the file and smiling shyly. "Mr. Johnson called and said he wanted the locks changed."

"You don't use a picking device to replace a lock, friend," Glassman said, picking up a telephone. "Don't move."

The man shrugged and said, "Can't blame a fella for trying." Then he fired a wicked roundhouse kick.

Glassman's test-pilot reflexes narrowly saved him. Snapping his head back, he avoided the kick by a bare inch.

The bald man advanced, cutting the air with a vicious series of chops and kicks. Glassman swung a chair in front of the intruder. The intruder grabbed the chair and began pushing it at Glassman.

"I'm going to hurt you," the intruder said.

Glassman swung the chair aside and grabbed at the bald man, but the intruder rolled onto his back and kicked Glassman up into the air, throwing him upside down on a table. The bald man was on him in an instant, landing a punch into Glassman's solar plexus, then another. Glassman groaned, feeling his ribs crack. He fired his hands forward, grabbing at the man's throat, but the attacker wrenched free and stepped back lightly.

Glassman picked himself up painfully, pushing the chair in front of him like a lion tamer. The intruder dropped into a riding horse stance with his legs leaning slightly forward and his open hands weaving like a snake mesmerizing a bird. He smiled.

"You should let me knock you out and leave," the bald man said. "You can't take me. You've flown Blackbirds to Okinawa, haven't you? I got an eighth-degree belt there."

"Simple as that," Glassman asked, wiping blood from his own lips. "I let you get away?"

"Sure," the bald man said, smiling. "Why not?"

Glassman gauged the distance to the door and pushed the chair suddenly. He sprinted the short distance and got his hand on the stainless steel knob just as the intruder landed on him in a whirlwind of kicks, chops, and eye gouges that brought

Glassman to his knees, sobbing and nearly blinded by the blood running off his forehead into his eyes. Like a dancer, the intruder retreated and inspected his handiwork, his smile cracking wide in murderous satisfaction. Glassman backed himself crabwise along the door and wall, watching the intruder circle, his hands weaving.

"Say good night," the intruder said, capering forward. The bald man executed a roundhouse kick, narrowly missing Glassman's head. Glassman snatched the coffeepot and flung it in his attacker's face. The man dropped to the floor, howling. But Lazarus-like, he jumped back to his feet and staggered at Glassman, still shrieking. Glassman snatched Madeline Murdoch's small pearl-handled automatic from his breast pocket and fired four shots. The bald man was still gouging and chopping as he fell on Glassman and died.

Glassman groaned, whispering in the dead man's ear, "I've got a first degree in Beretta, you son of a bitch."

Elsewhere inside Plant 42, Ben Johnson sat in his private workroom, gazing Buddha-like at a glowing computer screen. The 3-D screen that displayed brightly dancing, spidery images of the Blackbird's engine nacelles was plugged into a common data base shared with Rudman's computer over in the design room. Though he could enter Rudman's data base, Johnson had a series of blocks and traps built into the software to keep hackers, spies, and other intruders from breaking the wall of security that shielded the black world of the Skunk Works. From time to time the designer glanced at old drawings of the Blackbird. He always checked his protégés' work against his own data.

Behind the modular screen that divided the workroom, a hunched figure punched away at a personal computer, the keystrokes forming a rhythmic counterpoint to the cricket symphony of Johnson's fingertip calculations. Finally, the tinny electronic voice behind the screen announced, "We've got the bastard!"

Johnson rubbed his forehead and continued his number crunching. After a few seconds' pause the tinny voice demanded, "Mr. Johnson, are you there?"

"Are you talking to me?" Johnson asked crankily, irritated at the interruption.

"I said, we've got him. I found him in the payroll scan."

Before Johnson could ask what his unseen companion was talking about, he heard the crash of a falling body against his office door. Johnson looked up to the television monitor that scanned the hallway outside and saw the crumpled form of Adam Glassman. He rushed toward the door, pressing the button on his desk that would pop it open. Glassman slumped inside.

Johnson pulled the colonel into the office suite. He retrieved a bottle of Bushmill's whiskey from his desk drawer. He passed the bottle under Glassman's bloodied nose and poured a trace of the Irish onto the colonel's lips.

"What's going on out there, Mr. Johnson?" the tinny voice demanded from the other side of the screen.

"Damned if I know," Johnson snapped. "Colonel Glassman has been badly hurt."

Glassman's eyes blinked, and he attempted to focus on Johnson. He cracked a ghastly grin. "I think I found your saboteur," Glassman whispered. "The man who sabotaged the Blackbird is probably the dead guy in your quarters."

Johnson gaped at Glassman. The next man to speak was the unseen visitor behind the screen. "Colonel Glassman," the tinny voice commanded. "Describe the man you have terminated."

"Who's that?" Glassman croaked to Johnson, who was drinking from the bottle.

"Don't ask questions, son," Johnson said, offering him the bottle.

Hauling himself groggily to his feet, Glassman growled, "I want to know who the hell else knows I'm in here." He began lurching heavily past Johnson's office desk.

"Don't walk behind the screen!" Johnson shouted.

Glassman fell against the room divider and stepped around the screen. He gasped at the sight of the shriveled form of Brady Daniels sitting beneath an afghan comforter in an electric wheelchair. Daniels grinned like a parchment mandarin and pressed the voice synthesizer to his throat.

"Damn glad to see you, Colonel," Daniels piped tinnily, manipulating his wheelchair controls. "You look like hell."

"So do you, sir," Glassman said. "You look like death in life." Then the colonel passed out.

—— 39 ——
The Wrath of God

Jerusalem

SABRINA RABIN FOLLOWED HER UNCLE, David Ben Lavi, into the library, where the prime minister waited. Sabrina wore the khaki uniform of a captain in the Israeli Defense Forces. Her uncle wore the least rumpled of his collection of slightly worn and disheveled suits. Sitting in a deep leather chair in the library, Prime Minister Yitzhak Shamir wore an expression of cool disapproval. "Be seated," he said, pointing his finger toward a hard sofa.

Sabrina sat on the edge of the couch, her knees held tightly together as though she were still a schoolgirl. Her uncle, the Mossad operations chief, crossed his legs and folded his arms. He studied the rows of leather-bound books lining the walls as the prime minister studied him.

A soft knocking at the library door interrupted the uncomfortable silence. Both Ben Lavi and his niece shifted as they watched an elderly gentleman in an impeccably tailored dark suit enter the room. It was Menachem Begin.

Shamir rose stiffly from behind his desk and walked forward to grasp Begin's arm. The former prime minister, who walked with a shuffle, bowed curtly. He seated himself in a wing chair and gazed about—aimlessly, it seemed. It was said Begin rarely left his house anymore, except to be with his granddaughter. Begin's milky eyes surveyed the room, studying the faces of Ben Lavi and Sabrina Rabin, his judgment reserved to himself behind his thick spectacles. He inclined his head, his bony chin resting forward on his stiffly starched collar. He fixed his gaze first on Ben Lavi and finally on the young woman.

"So," he said. "You wear the uniform of your nation, Eretz Israel. How do you account for yourself?"

Sabrina Rabin bowed her head. Ben Lavi rested his hand gently on her knee and spoke up. "It is I who should speak and give account, Mr. Prime Minister," Ben Lavi said. "It was my operation."

"In a moment, in a moment," Begin said, dismissing Ben Lavi with a peremptory wave of his hand, which was white as fine bone china. "It is first for your niece to speak—and explain how she had the opportunity to destroy such enemies of Israel as are in Tarak. And yet she let that opportunity slip."

"There were operational reasons," Ben Lavi growled defensively.

"Remember where you are," Yitzhak Shamir said sharply, joining his fingers at the tip of his nose as he sat hunched behind his desk. "Reply to the former prime minister when you are questioned."

"Mr. Prime Minister," Ben Lavi said, rising agitatedly to address Shamir. "Is this a formal inquiry?"

"Sit down, sit down," Begin said. "This is a search for truth. It is the only reason I would answer a call to appear in this room. I've known too much sadness here."

Inclining his birdlike head toward Sabrina Rabin, he said, "Tell me, child, what decided you to evacuate from your assignment at Tarak?"

Gazing at her hands, which rested on the knees of her khaki uniform slacks, she said hesitantly, "I believed that the alarm must be raised. I feared for the nation."

"But that was not your assignment, was it, my dear?" Begin persisted. "Can you repeat to me your operational order?"

Returning the former prime minister's cool and level stare with her sea-green eyes, Sabrina Rabin recited from her order. "For the good of humanity, and of the nation of Israel, it was my vow to liquidate the research team from the plant at Tarak."

Begin nodded and placed his bony hands on his knees. "And why did you fail to complete your mission?" Begin asked, his once mellow baritone recapturing some of its lawyerly authority.

"I feared that immediate termination of the target would pose a graver threat to Israel than if I were to continue my reconnaissance," Sabrina Rabin said.

Begin turned his head, looking to the light that filtered into the room from the high window, and then returned his gaze to the shadow. "But," he insisted, assuming a slightly more prosecutorial tone, "you didn't continue your reconnaissance. You aborted your mission and escaped from the plant with the Englishman."

"It was my belief that the English possessed vital intelligence."

"Then," Begin said, his voice dropping nearly to a whisper, "you were motivated solely by your intuition that rescuing the Englishman instead of completing your assignment would better provide for defense of your nation?"

"Exactly, Mr. Prime Minister," Sabrina Rabin said.

"The fact that by abandoning your orders you might be able to learn more of your brother's fate had no bearing on your action?"

"That didn't enter into it," Sabrina Rabin said, rising from her place on the sofa and pacing with her arms clenched tightly to her sides. "It did not!" she insisted, dabbing her eyes angrily.

"This is most inappropriate," David Ben Lavi said, rising and taking Sabrina Rabin by the shoulders. "Compose yourself," he murmured, and then, turning to the two old men who watched, he said, "I will subject my operative to no further questioning unless it is formal, with representation."

"Of course," Shamir said. "But first, she should hear the result of her work. Be seated, David Ben Lavi."

Begin reached into the pocket of his vest and removed a watch, examining it from habit. Then he chuckled softly. "I find that time is less important to me in recent years," he said, his voice suddenly remote and far away. The old man turned his head, his milky eyes resting once again on Sabrina Rabin. "The man you were to terminate goes by many names, but we believe his real name is Ivan Ilyich Kurtz. Were he not a dedicated Soviet operative, he would be a Nazi."

Rising from his chair and taking a few stiff steps, Begin continued. "Like many in the Soviet regime, his anti-Semitic attitude is a given. Moreover, it seems to be enhanced by his hatred of the Americans. To him, our two nations are the same."

Tiring, Begin seated himself again in the wing chair and stared at Sabrina. "What makes him loathsome—and a threat—is the weaponry he has been working on for many years. At his disposal was the data the Nazis collected in their development of lethal nerve gases. These, seized by the Red Army, still represent some of the most advanced work in the field."

"And so?" David Ben Lavi asked quietly.

"And so this man has been testing these agents on battle-grounds across the Third World. In Cambodia. In Afghanistan and Africa. We now fear the advanced nature of the technology he has developed."

Begin sighed, his shoulders slumping in the chair. "This is the man who continues his work within artillery range of three million Jews," he said. "It is not for me to judge or condemn, but I must ask you, Captain Rabin, why it is that he still lives. Can it be that a Sabra has no historical memory of the fate of the Jews?"

"Do not patronize me, Mr. Prime Minister," Sabrina Rabin said, rising from her place on the couch. Begin appeared slightly taken aback as the woman paced in front of the desk of Yitzhak Shamir.

"You have taught us about these evil people from the cradle," Sabrina said. Then pointing at the two old men, she continued, "You and you—all of you—you never let us forget what was done to our people. And I did not forget."

She ceased her pacing and folded her arms, looking defiantly at the two old men. "If we are to survive, we must watch our enemies with unfailing vigilance," she said. "The blond Russian is supported by the entire weight of the Taraki state apparatus. Something fearful is being planned within that research facility. I needed to know more in order to disable it completely."

She drew herself up to her full height and stared down at the seated Shamir and Begin. "Do you really think I would put even my brother, my little Avi, before the lives of all my countrymen?" Begin and Shamir stared silently at the young woman.

"Had I killed the blond Russian, my own life would have been forfeit instantly. I could not allow that to happen. The security of Israel was my only thought in taking flight. I had to bring you the information that I retrieved. I could not end his work by myself. I needed help."

Finally it was Shamir who spoke. "What was it you saw in Tarak?"

"The production of chemicals for the other front-line states is only a ruse," Sabrina Rabin said. "The true work at the plant concerns perfection of a biological agent, a persistent and deadly toxin."

Begin cocked his head. "And if I may be so bold, what are the characteristics of this biological agent?"

"It is a Jew killer," Sabrina Rabin said flatly. "It is a quantum development of the sickle-cell A virus, coded genetically to destroy semitic peoples."

In a puzzled tone, Begin remarked, "Then it might also conceivably kill Arabs. Yes?"

"Kurtz knows that and doesn't care. The Taraki fools working for him are unwitting and unsophisticated in laboratory theory. All he wants is a weapon to drop on Israel, and the world be damned."

"What is the means of delivery?" Begin asked intently.

"The agent is diabolical. Like the British anthrax poisons, it is mixed with spores that drift on the wind and settle. It can be delivered by artillery shell, missile warhead, or merely set adrift on the wind. It is deadly if inhaled or if it even touches the skin. It spreads like pollen."

"What is its stage of development?" Shamir demanded.

"Kurtz believes it is ready."

Begin inclined his head forward and rested it on his gaunt hand. He closed his eyes and sighed. He turned to Shamir, who sat hunched behind his oversized desk. "My old friend," Begin said. "It is my opinion that Captain Rabin did not fail. Her safe return was vital to Israel."

"Mr. Prime Minister," David Ben Lavi interrupted. "Time is our enemy. With the release of Sergeant Major Davis on Cyprus, and the exchange of his freedom for the remains of Avi Rabin, the English will be aware of our keen interest in the Taraki research facility."

"We should not have let that man go," Shamir observed.

"Mr. Prime Minister, we are not in the habit of holding prisoner the soldiers of friendly Western states. Moreover, there is the matter of the American spy plane pilot, Major Rogers," Ben Lavi continued. "He must be released."

Shamir slapped his hand on the desk. "That I will not do! The American was in clear violation of our air space. We can only assume they were snooping on the rockets at Dimona."

"Nevertheless, Mr. Prime Minister," Ben Lavi pressed. "For every day we hold him, the scrutiny of the Americans increases. He may even endanger our American asset."

"Do you think I am not aware of this?" Shamir said, rising from behind his desk for the first time. He walked to Lavi and placed the papers on his desk in the intelligence chief's hands.

"Here are three notes from the American president, delivered in the past twenty-four hours. Our American friends are unpredictable. They could even turn their precious Sixth Fleet on us. Us! Their closest ally in the region."

"Precisely, Mr. Prime Minister," Ben Lavi said, reading the terse demands of the man in the White House. "It is for that reason that we must appease them."

"Appeasement is not a term that comes to mind when I say the word Israel," Shamir growled.

"Nevertheless, this is the time for secrecy. The spy plane was destroyed. We have reason to believe in the security of our preparations at Dimona. We should release the American."

Begin raised his hand, pointing a gaunt finger in the air as though he were a Biblical prophet. "Ben Lavi is right, my friend. Release the American and you will confuse them for a day or so. Better yet, announce it to the press."

Exasperated, Shamir slapped his broad forehead with his hand. "Do you know what chaos that will create?"

Begin nodded stiffly, and a ghost of a smile crossed his cadaverous face. "Exactly, my friend."

Ben Lavi looked down to Sabrina Rabin, who sat as though she were forgotten. Turning to the two old men, he said, "We must resolve the question of what to do about the plant in Tarak."

"It is a military question," Shamir said curtly. "Intelligence has fulfilled its responsibility. Now, we must plan the destruction of the plant."

Sabrina shouted, "No! You must not."

"What are you saying, Captain Rabin?" Shamir demanded. "We must treat the plant at Tarak with the same high seriousness as the threat from the Iraqi reactor." Begin nodded his agreement.

"If you bomb the plant, there is the potential to spread the virus," she said urgently. "The wind could carry it across the frontier into our cities."

The old men looked at each other, then to Ben Lavi. "She is right?" Begin asked.

"Of course she is right," Lavi retorted. "She is my niece."

"And what course of action does your niece propose?" Shamir asked dryly.

"The Wrath of God," Ben Lavi said.

"The unit was disbanded after termination of the Black September terrorists," Shamir said.

"Reactivate them," Ben Lavi said. "A WOG team will liquidate the blond Russian and his helpers. Such a team also stands the best chance of retrieving the viral agent and removing it to a place where it can be destroyed. We need a scalpel, not a hammer."

"Who will lead this team?" Shamir asked.

"I have been inside the plant," Sabrina Rabin said. "I will lead them."

"And if you should fail?" Begin inquired.

"They must not fail," Ben Lavi said solemnly. "The only other way to decontaminate the plant is a tactical nuclear strike."

Begin sighed. Shamir gloomily sank further in his chair. "You would use the F-16s as we did at Osirak?" Begin inquired, cocking his head.

"Not feasible," Ben Lavi said, rising and pacing with his

hands clutched together behind his back. "We could not guarantee the success of an air raid. The SAM batteries around the facility have been reinforced. And there is another worry."

"Be specific, Ben Lavi," Shamir snapped. "What is the other worry?"

"The Soviets have inexplicably presented President Kemal with a dozen SCUD missiles, a fighter-bomber squadron, and a reinforced battalion of air-mobile infantry from East Germany. I believe those rockets are a delivery system."

"Are the Russians mad?" Shamir demanded, slapping his hand on the desk. "Do they know what they are doing?"

"Who can say?" Ben Lavi said. "There is chaos in their own country at the moment."

"What is the stage of readiness on the SCUD missiles?" Shamir asked.

"A week or less and they will be operational," Ben Lavi said.

Picking up a phone on his desk, Shamir punched the button for the line that would connect him with the Israeli Defense Force's strategic command complex in the Negev Desert. The commander, a major general, came immediately on the line.

"This is Joshua. Do you authenticate?" Shamir asked, immediately getting the counterresponse from the commander of the Negev complex. "Bring the Jericho battery to yellow alert and await target coordinates."

Within two minutes after the prime minister provided the coordinates given him by David Ben Lavi, the Jericho II battery that provided Israel's tactical nuclear punch was aiming a brace of buff-colored rockets at Tarak.

—— 40 ——
End User

Washington

THE BLACK STRETCH CADILLAC IDLED at the end of Runway 4 at Washington's National Airport. An executive jet descended. Its pilot landed with the ease and speed of a Congo mercenary on a supply run. Exiting the plane, the diminutive figure of Stephen Coldwell was dwarfed by his bodyguards, a scarred Belgian legionnaire and a former Royal Marine with a luxuriant handlebar moustache. As Coldwell marched toward the limousine, the bodyguards scanned the tarmac. Inside the limousine, Madeline Murdoch pushed a button on her console, and the door to the Cadillac swung open.

The big Belgian climbed into the spacious interior first, seating himself across from the president's assistant for national security affairs. Coldwell piled in next and the Royal Marine took the front seat next to Madeline Murdoch's driver. The limousine eased itself off the tarmac.

Coldwell, dressed in an elegant suit and Bill Blass designer glasses, offered his hand. Madeline Murdoch subjected the arms dealer to her fabled iron grip, and he smiled wanly, revealing rows of small but highly polished sharp teeth. "Pleasure," he said.

"What have you got for us, Mr. Coldwell?" she asked. "It had better be as good as advertised, or I can promise you this coach will turn around at the Fourteenth Street bridge and you will be on your way back to where you came from."

"You are direct, Dr. Murdoch," Coldwell said. "After years of Third World palaver, it is refreshing. Got a brandy?"

Madeline Murdoch motioned imperiously to the Cadillac's wet bar, and Coldwell obliged himself, pouring from a decanter. "That's better," he said, smacking his lips as the limousine swung past the crawl of taxis crowding into National Airport and lumbered out past the glass towers of Crystal City and onto Interstate 95.

"I've a nugget or two," Coldwell said, returning his brandy balloon to the bar and pouring himself another generous dollop. "My sources in Amman are impeccable."

"Please be brief, Mr. Coldwell," Madeline Murdoch said. "The Fourteenth Street Bridge and then Foggy Bottom lie just ahead. Or we can loop around past the Tidal Basin and head back to the airport."

"It's like that, is it?" Coldwell said. "Try to do a patriotic favor, and you cast me in the role of merchant of death."

"That's about the size of it."

The Cadillac moved into heavy traffic on the bridge. The sky above was turning from gray to black. Coldwell drained his brandy. "I know where your downed flier is."

"Tell," Madeline Murdoch said sharply.

"What's in it for me?"

"I thought you were a patriot," she said, smiling coldly. "You'll have to trust me."

Coldwell removed a silk handkerchief from the pocket of his camelhair topcoat and dabbed delicately at his forehead and graying temples. "I detest dealing with the American government or its agents," he said. "One never knows where one stands. You are not reliable."

"I can be relied on, Mr. Coldwell. What have your impeccable sources told you?"

"The recce pilot is alive in Tarak."

"Thank God," Madeline Murdoch exclaimed.

"He is held prisoner in a coastal facility, a factory of sorts on the Taraki coastline. It's an old Crusader castle, heavily defended, presumably because it is rumored to be a manufactory for chemical armaments. Nasty stuff.''

"Where is he in the plant, Mr. Coldwell?''

"I don't know. Wish I did. American fliers engage my sympathies. But look here, have we got a deal or not?''

The Cadillac was moving past the Bureau of Printing and Engraving and weaving between tour buses filled with visitors craning their necks at the Washington Monument. Madeline Murdoch hesitantly offered her hand to Coldwell. "I keep my word,'' she said.

Speaking into the microphone to the driver on the other side of the smoked glass, she said, "Alex, we will proceed to State.'' The driver turned left on Constitution Avenue. Coldwell smiled, happy as a child, and reached for another dollop of brandy. "I always feel great after a done deal,'' he said.

"Do you always consume alcohol in such alarming proportions, Mr. Coldwell?'' Madeline Murdoch asked.

"Only when I fly. Mind if I smoke, Professor?'' the arms merchant said, reaching for his leather cigar case.

"As a matter of fact, yes.''

He gave her a wounded look and replaced the case in his breast pocket. "In any event, it's good to be home,'' he said cheerily. "If all goes well with your associates in the export controls office, I shall be glad to be returning to my adopted homeland of Liechtenstein before the day is done.''

The limousine descended into the underground entrance reserved for the State Department motor pool and the Soviet ambassador. The coach rolled to a smooth stop next to a line of armored Cadillacs.

Madeline Murdoch pressed the door button, and Coldwell's bodyguards stepped smartly out of the limousine into the parking garage.

Madeline Murdoch smiled coyly. "Mr. Coldwell, tell your aides they must surrender their weapons to my driver, or you will never make it to the elevator for your meeting.''

"They never give up their arms when they are traveling with me, Professor.''

"They will if you wish to dicker with my friends upstairs.''

Coldwell barked, "Jacques, you and Bill give your pieces to the driver.''

Grudgingly, the pair surrendered their automatics. "Wish me luck, Professor," Coldwell said, his lips tightening in a predatory smile.

"I do not approve of your business, Mr. Coldwell," Madeline Murdoch said coldly. "But you will probably get the export certificate for your airplanes anyway."

Madeline Murdoch closed the limo door. She directed Alex to drive her to the Executive Office Building next door to the White House. The fact that Cartwright was alive made her feel alive. She smiled at her own joke that when Coldwell finished his business, he would have to hail a cab and return to the airport with his bodyguards minus their sidearms.

— 41 —

A New Envelope

Plant 42, California

CLOSETED IN BENJAMIN JOHNSON'S INNER office, Brady Daniels watched the Cable News Network broadcast of the news conference in Jerusalem. As he watched, he marveled at how Ted Turner had shrunk the world.

The wolfpack that was the Israeli and international press corps was shouting questions at the beleaguered Foreign Ministry spokesman, who shouted back, assuring the reporters that all was as it should be, even though it clearly was not. Benjamin Johnson quietly stepped up behind Daniels's wheelchair, wincing at the spectacle of cameras and lights focused on a topic too close to his heart, the downed American flier.

"Does anybody there know what it is they're shouting about?" Johnson asked dispiritedly.

"Fortunately not," Daniels rasped through his tinny throat mike. "They're confused. It will be at least a day or two before they know what's happening."

"We need a week," Johnson said glumly.

"We'll have Ed Rogers here for debriefing soon," Daniels said. "Maybe we can have him mission ready in a few days."

"He'll be exhausted," Johnson said.

"Is he a flier or some overpaid ball player with a rubber arm?" Daniels demanded tinnily.

"You can't trifle with an airman's physiology," Johnson responded. "He's going to need rest."

As the pair argued, the broadcast shifted from the fracas of the Foreign Ministry news conference to file tape taken earlier of a convoy of limousines speeding to an air base where a U.S. Air Force transport waited to carry the unidentified American flier home. The CNN voice-over summary reported that an American plane had strayed off course from its Sixth Fleet assignment and had apparently been downed by SAM missile fire from the Arab side of the Taraki frontier. Meanwhile, the Israeli Defense Forces had effected a rescue of the American flier and were returning him to the United States, the reporter intoned gravely. The aircraft type was not identified, he added portentously.

"Good," Brady Daniels rasped. "Shamir and Ben Lavi are playing it close to the vest. No interviews with the flier. And no note of protest to State."

"But why?" Johnson wondered. "They don't owe us any favors."

"Two reasons," Daniels beeped crisply. "By holding their tongues, they will gain leverage on the next aid request to Congress."

"And the other?"

"They are hiding something God almighty fearful in the Negev and throwing Rogers back to us like a half-grown trout. I wonder if they know the Keyhole satellite is down?"

The buzzer to Johnson's office door sounded, and the designer scanned the television monitor. It was Adam Glassman, holding himself awkwardly erect in the bulky gold pressure suit. With him was Rudman, the engineer, also in a pressure suit and with his beard shaven. As the two trudged into Johnson's office, Brady Daniels backed his electric wheelchair into the deep recess of the suite, secreting himself behind the modular room divider.

"I've never seen you without the shrubbery, Len," Johnson remarked, grinning as he rose to shake hands with Rudman and Glassman. "What's the meaning of this?"

"I want one of your silver dollars," Rudman replied, returning the grin. "I figured the engine design modification was worth one. Your Blackbird driver said I could ride with him. The beard had to go to get the right fit for the helmet."

Johnson frowned. "The coin is yours, Len, but I don't think I want you flying."

"You won't lose him," Glassman said. "I've got to talk to your colleague." As Rudman seated himself heavily on Johnson's couch, his portable air-conditioning system making a quiet hum, Glassman stepped behind the divider.

Brady Daniels, the wheelchair-ridden, hollow-voiced spymaster in hiding, looked like a creature out of Dickens, with a few wisps of white hair mussing his forehead. Arranging his afghan comforter, he grinned at Adam Glassman.

"I think I'm entitled to some answers, Director Daniels," Glassman said, seating himself heavily in an oversize chair that Ben Johnson used for catnaps. "These past few days have been a trip through the looking glass."

"Entitled to answers? What makes you so special?" Daniels demanded, pressing the voice synthesizer against his throat. "The great game always has more questions than answers."

"It's no game to me, Director," Glassman half shouted. Lowering his voice, he growled, "I've been arrested. I've been investigated by your agency's bully boys. I've been flung from a speeding van and used as a punching bag. The man who's the closest thing to a real father I've ever had is sitting in some Middle East shit hole. You owe me. I want answers."

Daniels, slumped in the wheelchair, gazed at Glassman with the slackness of a man who had suddenly aged. The spymaster sighed. "I spent a lifetime cultivating the special relationship with our friends in Israel," the director of central intelligence said. Then, resting his throat, he looked at Glassman almost apologetically and, once again, pressed the voice synthesizer to his throat. "I'm not well," he said.

"You were supposed to be dead," Glassman said, his tone accusatory.

"A ruse de guerre," the DCI said, nodding. "It was necessary for me to die."

"So there was a funeral at Arlington, brass band, twenty-one-gun salute, and all," Glassman said. "And a closed casket."

"I needed to disappear for a bit," Daniels said. "The illness was real. Throat cancer. My good friend the briar pipe turned on me."

"That's why you vanished—surgery?"

"It doesn't do to let the opposition know you are ailing," the resurrected director croaked. "They try to take advantage."

"Brady, you didn't just vanish for the opposition. Everyone believes you're dead."

"Almost everybody," Daniels said, winking slyly. His green eyes wandered around the room as though he were having difficulty concentrating. But Glassman watched the battle inside the man and knew he was lucid and attentive, even if close to exhaustion.

"Something is rotten in Langley," Daniels said. "The relationship with the Israelis aborted itself." He sighed again, deeply. "I was cut out without explanation. Yet they knew about all our Middle East operations."

"Mossad knows everything in the region," Glassman said.

Daniels shook his head. "They knew from inside the company. From Langley. So you see," he said, "I had to die. While you poked around, Adam. It was the only way to get a detached look at the thing."

"Do you feel free to share any of your conclusions with me?"

Daniels grinned and tapped his forehead. "There is little that I share, even with those I love."

"You used me, Brady," Glassman said. "Was it worth it?"

"It will depend on the outcome," Daniels said. "It is safe to tell you that whoever is playing this game out felt sufficient fear to sabotage Cartwright's overflight."

Benjamin Johnson stepped behind the screen into Daniels's refuge. He held a gray wire, about a quarter-inch thick. "This was it," he said. "A detent wire for the drone. Telemetry from the flight indicates the airplane's breakup began along the dorsal section. One of the detent wires was sliced. The electrical connection failed, and the drone literally tore itself from the airplane."

Glassman whistled softly. "Who preflighted the aircraft?"

"The fellow you shot was one of the preflight check crew,"

Ben Johnson said. "Pay records indicate his salary was not being issued by the manufacturer."

"Who, then?" Glassman asked.

"Department of Defense," Daniels said, pushing aside a wisp of white hair that dropped into his eyes. "But it goes deeper than that. I think a deeper computer scan will indicate he once worked for the Company as a unilaterally controlled asset."

A green light in the wall popped on and the television set that had displayed the CNN reports changed to a test pattern. Then the test pattern disappeared, and the screen showed the spy plane on the tarmac, looking like a great winged beast.

Digital characters ticked off minutes and seconds in real time at the bottom of the screen. Blackbird preflight was more like a space mission than an aircraft takeoff.

"Your airplane is ready, Adam," Johnson said softly. "And if you don't go soon, I fear my chief design engineer will either have a heart attack from fright or shit his pants in great expectation."

"Who did the preflight checks?" Glassman asked, his face clouded with worry. "No more free-lancers?"

"I know each man working on this airplane personally," Johnson said. "I guarantee their work."

A half hour later, the plane took off from its California base. The flight to England established a classified record for a maiden flight. The black plane averaged nearly 3,000 miles per hour. Rudman had won his silver dollar.

─── 42 ───
Night and Fog

Porton Down, England

TO SGT. MAJ. COLIN DAVIS, the skies over the Royal Chemical Defense Establishment appeared somber and evil. Lightning bolts illuminated a cover of dark clouds, turning the sky a muddy yellow color. Davis and Major Mellors, both clad in the cardigan and tweeds of civilians on holiday, waited in the upstairs conference room. They smoked Players cigarettes and watched the gravel drive below their window perch with the patience of recon men.

The MI-6 director's Rolls-Royce rolled forward onto the drive. Davis watched the driver opening the door for Sir Alfred and his toady. A few minutes later, Sir Alfred Whittlesey and Billy Chesterton entered the conference room. Davis and Mellors rose tentatively, stubbing their cigarettes in an ashtray. SAS men observed the courtesies but were not deferential.

"Well, we're nearly all here, aren't we?" Chesterton said brightly, shaking some papers in a buff-colored folder to establish the proper bureaucratic ambience. At Sir Alfred's nod, the quartet seated themselves.

"Dr. Barney will join us momentarily," Chesterton said, giving minute attention to his cuff link. Whittlesey produced his pipe, then looked at the SAS men, who watched expectantly.

"Well, go ahead, lads," he said, packing his pipe. "Have your smoke. I know I will." Soon, the air was evil with his musty-smelling pipe smoke. Dr. Barney, clad in his white laboratory smock, entered the room and crinkled his nose. He liked his odors clinical. He carried with him film transparencies that resembled X-ray photographs.

Barney's nearsighted eyes roamed the room like those of a mole. Returning his gaze to the transparencies, he said, "All things considered, sir, I should say that your operative is fortunate that he is Anglo-Saxon."

"Get to the point, Barney," Sir Alfred grumbled. "Haven't got all day."

Barney pulled a screen that hung suspended over a schoolroom blackboard. He placed his transparencies on an overhead projector and dimmed the lights. He illuminated the overhead projector, displaying an amoebalike structure in shades of gray and black.

"The syringe your man cadged provided an abundant example of some pretty awful stuff," Barney said. "It's fair to say that if the operative had possessed a trace of Mediterranean heritage, he would have died a quick but horrible death."

Sir Alfred looked up with interest. "What's that?"

"The same fate would have befallen him had he possessed the genealogy of an Arab, a black African, or a Jew," Barney continued, shaking his head with respect for the amoebalike apparition on the screen.

"What are you saying?" Chesterton piped up. "Have the chaps we're watching devised a wog killer? That's a modest proposal."

"Shut up, Billy," Whittlesey said crisply. Then, noting his aide's anguished look, the intelligence chief said more gently, as if to a child, "Let Dr. Barney finish."

The amoeba shifted on the screen, looking equal parts mushroom cloud and Rorschach ink. "You are looking at a virulent strain of bacteria that forms the nucleus of sickle-cell anemia infection. It is opportunistic and invasive, particularly of those who share Mediterranean or African heritage. An Anglo-Saxon or other nordic, or even a slav or Asian, might well go unaffected by it, but in the Middle East it would deliver a plague that would make the Black Death look like a game of ring around the rosie.''

"Lord," said Colin Davis.

"My reaction, exactly," Barney responded. "It is the product of a brilliant mind. This strain appears to be one that could be produced in quantity."

"What is the view of Porton on this stuff?" Sir Alfred asked, scratching a few notes.

"For people of color, this particular toxin poses a threat as grave, perhaps, as a nuclear strike," Barney said. "More grave because it is more likely to be used. I don't mind telling you Porton would like to get hold of some of it—purely for research purposes, of course."

"Of course," Sir Alfred said.

"Balls," Colin Davis muttered to himself.

"What's that, Sergeant Major?" Billy Chesterton piped. Davis gave him a withering glance and turned away in his chair. Chesterton shuffled his papers, and he looked up at the pathologist angrily. "This has gone quite far enough. It is off army's reservation, I should say." Turning to Sir Alfred, he said, "Really, sir. We must insist on a higher level of classification for this debrief or heads will roll. Army really shouldn't be here at all."

Colin Davis slammed one of his large hands on the conference table, startling everyone except Mellors, who smoked and watched his subordinate with interest.

"Just a bleeding minute, you funny little man," Davis said, rising suddenly to his feet. "I may be one of the few of the queen's own who have been gassed in one of your little low-intensity conflicts. I'm old school here at Porton. I mean to hear out the rantings of the honorable physician here. I want to know every bit about what I collected on my journeys."

Sir Alfred stared coldly from his place at head of table. "Sergeant Major, you will remain if you are allowed to remain, and that's the end of it."

Major Mellors also rose from his place at table, saying, "With all due respect, D, my man was doing your men a favor on this outing. He's had a rough time of it, and his confidence is more to be relied on than many in your own service, if I may be so bold."

"Gentlemen, thanks very much," Sir Alfred said curtly. "You are free to dismiss yourself to regiment at Hereford. Army will be informed if your services are further required."

"Will it?" Davis said sarcastically.

"At ease, Sergeant Major," Mellors interjected quickly.

Mellors and Davis turned about and strode from the briefing room. Tapping their way down the steps, Davis fumed, "That's my last party for the fancy boys in London. They can carry their own water from now on without Colin Davis's help."

Mellors clapped him around the shoulder and said, "Come on, Colin. Chin up. It will all come right."

"So you say, Major," Davis said, marching out the door toward the Range Rover parked on the gravel. Climbing in the driver's side of the Range Rover and turning the key in the ignition, Davis drove past the guard post and out onto the highway, but it wasn't so easy to shake the smell of Porton.

"Did you know I was gassed in the Oman?" Davis asked.

"So you said, Colin."

As the Range Rover sped through the green country, the gray sky was turning to the black of night. Davis put on the lights, which threw dancing shadows like ghosts in the vehicle's path. "Major, I can tell you what it's like to be gassed. Not many can. Just me and old Jacob."

"Who the hell is old Jacob?" It was night now.

"Me granddad. Just another poor sod who took a dose of Jerry gas the first time round on the Somme. Poor blind beggar. Tried to warn me off the army because of it, he did. He called the gas 'the Frightfulness.' I told him that were all done with. Showed how much I knew, right?"

"Sorry," Mellors said. "Look here. What are you getting at, Sergeant Major?"

"We should go clean out that nest in the Tarak. I've got friends across the Near East, Bedouin and Jew alike. They don't deserve to be on the business end of that horrid stuff. I'm a fighting man and it near laid me out, sir. Think of the children."

Mellors smiled. Mercifully Davis slowed a bit as he rounded a tricky curve in the dark. He called his skill behind the wheel "driving in tactical mode." His men called it "a fright."

"We'll go if there's orders, Colin," he said gently. "That's our lot."

Davis nodded bitterly. "That's Tommy's lot all right. But it isn't right, Major. We should finish the job."

"Leave it alone, Colin. Regiment are glad you beat the clock and made it home."

They stopped at the Lion's Head for a pint of Best bitter. Colin Davis was not cheered despite his major's best efforts.

Deep in the pigeonholed warren that made up the service's central depot, Sir Alfred sat at his desk, shuffling through transparencies from Porton. It was explosive material. He absolutely didn't want Foreign Office involved. Whittlesey never wanted anyone else involved, a trait he personally instilled in the late Brady Daniels during the American cousins' cradle days in OSS. Good chap, Daniels. Good comrade. The telephone warbled, signaling that it was the transatlantic line. The cousins. Even think of them and they were all over you. It was Madeline Murdoch.

"Is it you, D?" the mellifluous voice of the American president's assistant for national security affairs asked silkily.

"It is he," Sir Alfred said. "How may I assist you, good lady?"

"We have some of the material that we agreed to share, based on our understanding reached at the offices of our friend near the river," she said.

"Ah, yes. Good," he said, perking up. "But my friends at RAF advised me that your spy plane was destroyed."

"Yes, that is true," Madeline Murdoch said somewhat archly. "But the reconnaissance photography was not. A meeting should be arranged for your viewing the materials," she continued. "We have an additional request that is in the spirit of our understanding."

"And what would that be, good lady?"

"We believe a Commonwealth firm subcontracted construction on a certain fertilizer factory located near the coast of Tarak. We should like to see the blueprints and layout of the facility. If your service could obtain those plans, we would be grateful.''

Brightly, but his voice somewhat brittle despite his best efforts, he said, "And why would that be, good lady? Isn't your government spreading enough manure already?"

Madeline Murdoch suppressed a laugh. Then she said, "One of our pilots is being held there. Since President Kemal is intractable and unfriendly, it's my intention to go in and get our man."

"Damn," he said. Then, recovering himself, he added, "Tell us anything you need." He scribbled the name of the firm that Madeline Murdoch supplied him. Suddenly his face brightened, like that of a man who has seen a light on a deserted road.

"Dear lady, would you be interested in securing the services of someone who has actually been inside the alleged fertilizer manufactory?"

"Of course," Madeline Murdoch replied. "Was he a contractor?"

"Actually, he's SAS. First-rate. Had some dealings with the locals there."

"We would welcome such assistance," Madeline said.

"Thank you, madam." The two rang off, and Whittlesey hit his office box. "Chesterton," he half shouted, and the egg-shaped aide waddled in, showing his best expression of perpetual concern.

"Yes, D. What is it?"

"Ring up SAS. I'm going to need those insolent lads."

Chesterton hurried out to do his master's bidding. The master regarded a pencil he had lately been chewing. He substituted it with his pipe and blew rings of smoke at the ceiling.

— 43 —

Operation Werewolf

The Plant in Tarak

IN THE UNDERGROUND PLANS ROOM, Ivan Ilyich Kurtz watched with a gleam of anticipation in his pale blue eyes as General Reinhard Grunfeld spread the battle map before him with the precision of a Berlin waiter. The map made a fine web of grid lines and tick marks until the terrain spread itself into the buff-colored Negev Desert, where the Dimona nuclear weapons plant waited. Grunfeld moved a plastic template from the symbols that marked the Taraki research facility over to the red box marking Dimona.

"Herr General, once again, please," Kurtz said. "Give me the figures on time of missile to target."

"A little more than one minute," Grunfeld said, shrugging. "One minute, eighteen seconds, more precisely. I must know dispersal time for the viral agent."

"After missile impact, dispersal of the Anemia Agent will persist for approximately one hour, depending on the wind."

Placing a callused thumb on the spot that marked Dimona, the old warrior grimaced at the blond Russian. "The reactor at Dimona goes several floors beneath the earth. What is the penetration ability of your poor man's atom bomb?"

Kurtz raised his palms and shrugged. "That problem should

be solved if your missile crews can target a hit within two hundred meters of the plant with an explosive warhead launched concurrently with the chemical agent.''

"*Zwei* hundred meters," Grunfeld muttered. "That can easily be done."

"You have only to hit within two hundred meters of the plant roof. The viral agent will be sucked downward into the plant ventilation system. Can your men do it?"

Grunfeld looked up from his map and said simply, "They are German soldiers." Running his fingers unconsciously across the steel mask that covered his ruined face, Grunfeld added, "I need a casualty estimate inside the reactor complex in order to weigh the proper troop loading on the helicopters."

"Fifty percent within six minutes of impact," Kurtz said. "But by the time your surviving combatants enter the reactor chamber at Dimona, they will walk over the bodies of the dead and dying."

"You can promise this?"

Kurtz nodded. "The Jews who still live, your men should make quick work of, if they are as good as you say they are."

General Grunfeld pounded his leathery fist on the map table. "They are good boys! I can verify. They look like the boys I took to Stalingrad."

"This is good," Kurtz said, rubbing the white half-moon scar. "Everything depends on the first thirty minutes of the operation."

"To summarize," Grunfeld said. He picked up his pointer and swept it quickly from the missile station in Tarak to the Dimona reactor complex. "Missiles one and two to strike the Dimona facility, with our heliborne troops arriving within four minutes of impact. With air cover from the Sukhoi squadron, they will fight their way in, killing the surviving casualties, and seize the Dimona control room and the Jericho missile sites."

Grunfeld sighed. He continued, "That leaves us the rest of the SCUD missile inventory to dispose of. We will have four additional missiles to fire. I need a secondary target."

Kurtz's lips curled up in a thin smile. "That is why the remainder of the battery will be expended on Tel Aviv. We will get all the rats in the trap that we can."

The tank general pursed his lips. "You know what that will mean?"

Kurtz grinned. "General war in the Middle East. Thousands dead. Superpowers at the brink."

"And the Soviet army, under Kolchak's leadership, firmly in command in the war room in Moscow," General Grunfeld said with finality. The general strode to a cabinet. He opened it and produced a bottle of champagne. "I propose a toast."

"*Sehr gut*," Kurtz answered in his native tongue. He accepted a fluted glass. "And what shall we toast?"

"Operation Werewolf," Grunfeld said.

"To General Kolchak," Ivan Ilyich Kurtz replied, raising his glass. "To the victory. Pamyat." The Prussian general clicked his heels and drank with the Volga German.

Cartwright, listening from his hiding place behind the ventilation grate, gritted his teeth and attempted to moisten his tongue. His German was rusty, but he had caught enough of the conversation.

His stomach was shrunken from hunger. He knew he was dehydrating. He needed water. Then food—and a weapon.

— 44 —
Glassman's Charge

RAF Mildenhall, England

ADAM GLASSMAN'S MODIFIED BLACKBIRD SLICED through the gray scud that hovered over the brooding green of East Anglia. The black plane's descent was gentle. It took nearly half an hour of complicated preparation to achieve the docile landing attitude that contrasted so sharply with the spy plane's thundering performance at altitude. Glassman occupied himself with procedure and put from his mind memories of his last trip to the air base, when he had been walked away in irons. "Papa Bear, this is Hard Disk," Glassman announced to ground control. "How's my attitude?"

"Nose up. Wheels down. You're looking good, Hard Disk. Come to Papa."

"Roger, Papa Bear," Glassman said. The black plane bumped onto the runway, the orange drag chute slowing the speed of the heat-resistant tires. The men in the cockpit of the black plane waited as the mobile truck drove toward them, its yellow bubble-gum-machine lights twirling.

"Thanks for the ride of a lifetime," Rudman, the engineer, said. "I'll have something to tell my grandkids."

"Maybe they'll declassify by the time you have grandchildren, but I wouldn't bet on it," Glassman said dryly. "Thanks yourself for the new engine mounts."

"Just don't take it higher than Mach 4," Rudman advised. "The prototype is going to be a Mach-5 machine, but we're not there yet."

"Roger that," Glassman said. "By tomorrow, you should be on your way home to California to collect Johnson's silver dollar."

The mobile truck rolled to a stop and the ground control officer emerged. It was General Rawlinson. He stood with his arms folded and his bulldog jowls wrapped around an unlit cigar. As Glassman and Rudman awkwardly descended the ladder, the general waved Rudman toward a security police jeep. Rudman gave Glassman one last look. "See you sometime," Rudman said wistfully.

Glassman waved. "I'll buy you a beer," he said, and turned to the general, his arm fixed in a salute. The jeep carrying the engineer hurried away. Rawlinson's expression remained grave. "You're Scott Cartwright's protégé, Colonel," Rawlinson said. "Climb in."

Glassman kept his hand up until Rawlinson got tired and returned the salute—glumly. Major Ed Rogers was behind the wheel of the truck, staring silently at his erstwhile pilot. "Yo, Wolfman," Glassman said.

A wan grin crossed Rogers's face, seeing Glassman's premature silver locks. "You've aged, Adam. Musta been some week," he said, rubbing his ever-present five-o'clock shadow. As the truck rolled off the tarmac, the Blackbird was towed to its hangar. The trio drove silently to one of the countless low gray buildings on the sprawling base.

Glassman and Rogers followed the general inside, where they signed an entry roster in the presence of a dour security police sergeant. After Rawlinson and Rogers signed, Glassman hesitated. Defiantly he signed his real name. They walked past the physiological support room, where pressure suits were stored, and Rawlinson said, "Get out of the bag, son. We'll wait."

Freed from the heavy suit, Glassman fell in behind the general and Rogers. The trio descended a flight of stairs, and Glassman felt the English damp in his bones. They approached

a combination-lock door. Rawlinson turned the dials and ushered Glassman and Rogers into the global recce briefing room.

"Be seated, gentlemen," Rawlinson said, indicating a pair
of metal folding chairs that made up the room's only furnish-
ings beside the table with the projector and a screen on the
wall.

Spreading the topo map on the table, Rawlinson moved his
hand in a broad sweep across the disputed borders that Israel
shared with Jordan, Syria, and Tarak. "Look familiar to you,
Major Rogers?" Rawlinson asked. Rogers nodded. "How
about you, Colonel Glassman?"

"I've been shot down there."

The general nodded. "You can swap stories with your partner here," Rawlinson said. Glassman turned to Rogers, surprised. "He was shot down by Israeli interceptors and
repatriated yesterday," the general said gruffly. "Well, you're
both going back. Try to bring the airplane home with you this
time."

"What's the task?" Glassman asked, unruffled.

"Same mission profile that Cartwright and Rogers flew before they screwed the pooch. A pass over the Dimona reactor
site and a broad sweep of the Negev, with one significant
addition."

"What addition?" Glassman asked.

"A good close pass directly over Tarak. We need some high-
resolution stuff of a coastal plant we think the Tarakis have
been using to cook nerve gas."

"I thought our main worry was the Israeli nuke site," Glassman said.

"That's a prime concern, naturally. But we've got a humint
source that indicates Cartwright may be MIA at the Taraki
plant," Rawlinson said. "We want to know about that installation, top to bottom. We'll have to do better than a human
intelligence source report. We need more pictures. All of 'em
we can possibly get."

Glassman stared coldly at Rawlinson. "What's on your
mind, Colonel?" the general snapped.

"Your concern isn't Cartwright at all. It's the plant in Tarak,
isn't it?" Glassman demanded.

Rawlinson chewed his unlit cigar and glowered. "That's

enough, Colonel," he said coldly. "Major Rogers, you're dismissed. You will be in the tank until preflight, zero-three-thirty hours. Colonel Glassman, I want you to remain."

Rogers saluted and left. Glassman rose awkwardly, meeting Rawlinson's attempt to stare him down. Finally Rawlinson said, "Sit down, Colonel." Rawlinson kept staring at Glassman, like a poker player concentrating on an opponent.

"What's troubling you, General?" Glassman said finally.

"I might ask you the same question, Colonel," Rawlinson said, snapping a match with his thumb and lighting the stogie. "How do you feel about going back over there on a mission against your own people?"

Glassman colored. "With all due respect, sir, that question is out of line. I'm an American."

"That's what you say, Colonel," Rawlinson said. "You know, your crew dog had a pretty rough time of it with those people."

"The Israelis do hold the status of U.S. ally. Did they fail to extend military courtesy?"

"You mean did they light him up with a cattle prod? No, but they gaslighted him a bit. Did their best to shake some of that Midwestern stoicism. And, Colonel, before they turned him loose, they asked him a lot of questions about you."

"What are you suggesting, General?"

"Don't you think that's strange, Colonel? Why would they be aware that Major Rogers was your crew dog?"

"Mossad and Israeli military intelligence make it their business to be aware of many things," Glassman replied. "When I left Tel Aviv as air attaché, they probably knew my next assignment before I did."

"Still, it's strange the ferocity of the IAF response to that Blackbird flight, don't you think, Colonel? It's almost as though they knew we were coming."

"They could probably shoot down almost any intruder aircraft, General. Including a Blackbird."

Rawlinson's lips pursed across his teeth. Softly he said, "I certainly hope they don't know this next overflight is coming."

"Speak plainly, sir."

"White House wanted you for this mission, but I didn't. I

would hate like hell to send a hero like Ed Rogers back with someone who would throw him to the lions. Read me?"

"Loud and clear, unfortunately."

"Let me make it easy on you, Colonel. You give me a statement, acknowledging the depth and details of information that you compromised to our friends in Tel Aviv, and I will do my level best to get a deal cut for you. Like you said, they're our allies. We might even arrange a quiet discharge for you, and you can go live there if you want."

Glassman flushed. "With all due respect, sir, you can go straight to hell."

"Even the White House won't save your ass if it turns out you're a goddamn spy," Rawlinson said, waving his cigar at Glassman.

"With all due respect, sir, while I carry the White House imprimatur, I suggest you keep the hell off my back!" Glassman shouted, his brown eyes blazing.

Rawlinson purpled. "What in hell kind of a five-dollar word is that, Glassman?" Glassman grinned smugly. The general stubbed the cigar out. "If it turns out you turned coat, I'll shoot you down myself."

Glassman saluted. He popped the door button on the air lock and strode out. That night, in his quarters, he dreamed of Sabrina Rabin. She faded from his sight like a light around a curve in a dark tunnel as the alarm woke him for preflight.

45

Dawn's Early Light

Tarak

THE YOUNG GRENADIER STOOD STILL as a statue in the dimly lit corridor, his AK-47 held rigidly at port arms. He stood so motionless and formed such a model of East Prussian rectitude that he easily could have held honor guard posting in East Berlin. Cartwright remembered watching them during a tour as military liaison in the East Zone. A little clock beneath their feet would ring on the five-minute mark, and they would goose-step, kicking high in those shiny jack boots as though Hitler were still there to watch.

The old man dropped on the sentry like a spider and pressed his hickory hard thumb into the youth's carotid artery. As the sentry squirmed, the old man held on like he was riding in the Salinas Rodeo. When the guard passed out, Cartwright grabbed hold of the young man's chin strap and gave the helmet a quick twist. No amount of parade ground drill had prepared his young opponent for silent, deadly combat. "*Wiedersehen*," Cartwright whispered. "Next time, look up."

As Cartwright pulled the grenadier's combat smock from his limp frame, the briefest memory of a Wehrmacht soldier in occupied France flashed. Shot down, thirsty, hungry, and bloody, a younger Cartwright had lain flat on his back in the woods while the Nazi bastards beat the brush, prodding with their bayonets. One stopped to take a leak when he should have prodded. His last mistake.

Cartwright pulled on the slain youth's jackboots and donned his shovel helmet. He looked around for a place to hide the body. He had left a trail of corpses, moving through the labyrinth like the grim reaper. He listened, noting that they had placed their sentries too far apart. He heard water trickling beneath his feet, poked his head around a corner, and spotted a grate. An ancient sewer system flowed beneath the complex. He lifted the heavy iron grate and lowered the dead guard into the sewer. *"Guten nacht,"* he whispered.

Cartwright felt tired and filthy from his odyssey in the ventilation shafts. His son, Scott, Jr., had been a tunnel rat in Vietnam. Now he appreciated how his boy must have felt. He picked up the guard's rifle and walked down the hallway. Cartwright marched in a businesslike manner, carrying rifle at port arms as he had seen the East Germans do. He pulled the shovel helmet farther forward over his eyes. He rounded a corner and spotted two East Germans guarding a doorway. One was fiddling with a cigarette. He kept marching and raised his hand in a hurried motion that could have been a salute or a greeting. As he walked past, one yelled, "Hey!"

He stopped and half turned, prepared to open fire. One of the guards walked forward, dangling his cigarette between his lips. *"Feur,"* he said, twisting his lips around the cigarette. *"Haben sie feur?"*

Cartwright fumbled in his pockets and pulled out a box of stick matches. *"Bitte,"* he said, lighting the soldier's cigarette. The guard nodded his thanks and returned to his comrade. Cartwright turned and continued on his way, trying to keep his legs from running ahead of him. He walked to the end of the passageway and opened the same steel door that Colin Davis and Sabrina Rabin had passed through, and found himself in bright sunlight. A whirl of activity surrounded him. Armored cars, with somber-looking crews, patrolled the plant fence around guard stations made from fresh lumber and newly poured concrete.

A tracked radar vehicle carrying an SA-6 missile crew rumbled past, clanking toward the gate with its antenna dish whirling. A hundred yards distant, a battery sergeant was shouting orders at the crew of a 23-millimeter ZSU antiaircraft gun. A brace of Soviet-built MiG-25 Foxbats thundered overhead. Cartwright wondered what the high-performance interceptors were doing in Tarak.

The general kept moving, realizing that his only insurance against quick capture was to look as through he knew where he was going, and avoid notice as the oldest private in the East German army. As he scuffed along, he walked past an uncrated ammunition box. A shiny glint caught his eye, and he saw metal plates used to pack the ZSU-gun ammo. He reached into the emptied crate and picked up one of the plates. Quickly surveying the organized military chaos of shouting and marching that surrounded him, he placed the tin plate on his face for just a moment. Might do in a pinch, he thought.

A siren blared. Taraki and East German troops on the grounds outside the chemical plant began running, manning the newly installed gun positions. Cartwright feared it was the alarm sounded for the slain guard. But as he watched, a pair of tracked AAA missile carriers swung out onto the road outside the plant gate. Air raid? he wondered. Israelis?

He watched the missiles point ominously skyward. The siren blared amid a confusion of German and Arabic commands. Cartwright dived to the ground next to a sandbag emplacement as the first missiles whooshed skyward. He looked high above him, searching the sky for attacking aircraft.

He could see no aircraft, and he heard no high whine of jet engines on attack run. He heard only the insistent siren wail and the hydraulics from the antiaircraft emplacements. A second burst of missiles cleared their launch tubes, zooming skyward like Roman candles. Suddenly, he heard the noise. As quick as it sounded, it was gone. A triple—no, by God—a quadruple sonic boom. *Crack, crack, crack, crack*—like cannon reports. To Cartwright they were as grand as the sight of Old Glory at dawn.

Four sonic booms. It was the Blackbird. They were looking

for him. The whooshes from the missile batteries subsided and
the whirling radar fans wound down as the siren fell silent.
Cartwright knew his job was to stay alive until his buddies
found him. They were coming. His heart was glad. He smiled
for the cameras and said, "Cheese."

—— 46 ——
Sergeant Ellsworth's Airplane

Andrews Air Force Base, Maryland

THE MAINTENANCE SERGEANTS SEARCHED THE sky for the black dot, their ears fine-tuned for the distant roar. They heard the machine before they saw it come sailing in, smooth as a Concorde SST, only prettier and rarer. The Blackbird descending. As the dagger-shaped plane knifed its way toward the runway usually reserved for Air Force One, Sgt. Robby Tucker daydreamed aloud. "Think we'll have time to catch a Skins game, Sarge?"

"Keep your mind on business, Robby," Ellsworth advised laconically as he snatched a fresh chew from his foil pouch of Red Man. " 'Sides, the Skins are sold out four years in advance."

"Well, leastways I can take in the sights. I always wanted to see the 'Nam Memorial. Lost a buddy in a rocket attack."

"No postcards to home, Robby."

"Shit, what do you take me for, Sarge?" Robby said in an injured tone. "I ain't gonna break security."

"You'll be lucky to see the BX snack bar, Robby," Ellsworth said, motioning the SR-71 pit crew into action as the

240

black plane's wheels touched down. Ellsworth's maintenance team moved at a run, rolling out the crew ladder. "We're gonna put in some extra hours on these new engines."

"You got that right," Tucker said.

Maintenance crewmen activated fans to cool the tires. The cockpit canopy raised, but the crewmen inside didn't move. They sat tight until a pair of maintenance crew members helped them out of their seats. Then Colonel Adam Glassman and Major Ed Rogers climbed down heavily from their cockpits.

"Shit, Sarge. Those boys are tuckered out," Sergeant Tucker observed. "And they brung 'em right here to the Pentagon. Wonder what's up?"

"At ease, Robby," Ellsworth said. "You just check the fuel seams on that black plane."

A team of physiological support techs waited anxiously. The mobile truck pulled up and out stepped General Rawlinson, nearly causing Ellsworth to swallow his chew. "Robby, it's the old man himself," Ellsworth whispered.

"Never seen the old man travel on a TDY," Tucker whispered back. "Must be big."

"It's none of our concern," Ellsworth said abruptly. "We've got no need to know." Chewing furiously, he added, "I wonder what the hell is going on."

As Glassman and Rogers put their feet on the hangar floor, Rawlinson marched forward, grinning. He clapped both fliers on the shoulders. "You did some fancy flying, Colonel. You may be all right, after all, son."

Glassman, supported by a pair of buck sergeants, regarded Rawlinson wearily and said, "Thanks, General. That's my job."

"Good, good," Rawlinson said, chewing his unlit cigar. "You can tell 'em about it at the White House." Rogers, whose rubbery legs gave out under him, looked up in genuine alarm. "The White House? Jesus, sir."

"You can get a shower and forty winks, Major. Glassman's to the White House for the briefing," Rawlinson said heartily. "Fancy flying, boys," he repeated, his tone gleeful.

As Ellsworth initiated his spot check of the Blackbird's titanium outer skin, the photo team was opening the nose section, removing film canisters from the optical barrel camera. Ellsworth watched Glassman and Rogers being helped into the medical van. As Rogers climbed the few steps, Ellsworth saw the major's knees buckle again.

—— 47 ——
Collegial Environment

Washington

AVERY BENEDICT CONFRONTED DR. MADELINE Murdoch in the hallway just as she was about to enter the elevator that would take them down to the White House Situation Room. "What a pleasure, Dr. Murdoch, and what a surprise, I might add," Benedict said.

"I'll take it on faith that your greeting is couched in your usual doublespeak, Mr. Benedict," the national security adviser said, smiling. She keyed the elevator with her coded pass card and waited.

"Please don't accuse me of double-talk, Dr. Murdoch, when you've been double-dealing with me through the week," the acting CIA director sneered.

Stepping into the elevator with the slightly rotund Benedict following like a ruffled terrier, Madeline Murdoch said, "Avery, what's on your mind?"

"You are the national security assistant, and I am the DCI. Why was I not informed?"

"You're the acting DCI," she reminded him. "And I am the president's assistant, not yours, Avery. Informed of what?"

"Glassman, goddammit," Benedict said, a blue vein popping in his boyish forehead as he spoke. "You've been shielding Glassman. You've been shielding a fucking Israeli spy.''

"The argument that Colonel Glassman compromised national security has yet to be made, Avery. And it was your team that lost track of him in the first place.''

Benedict sputtered, "The son of a bitch coldcocked one of my men and ran. He's a goddamn federal fugitive.''

"He has yet to be charged formally with any offense. And as I recall, when last he was with your men, they were going to stick needles in him and sedate him into a moronic stupor. I might coldcock someone myself under those circumstances,'' she said, stepping from the elevator.

The security adviser presented her pass to the Marine guard at the entrance to the Situation Room. Benedict flashed his pass and followed her past the Situation Room personnel.

"Who the hell do you think you are, Harriet Tubman?'' Benedict fumed. "You think you're running a one-woman underground railroad for traitors.''

Madeline Murdoch whirled around and said sweetly, "Mr. Benedict, as you are the acting DCI it would certainly be within your range of knowledge and good sense to ascertain that this is not a secure conversation. Shall we continue in the Tank?''

As they showed their passes yet again, the guard to the Secure Room opened the air lock, allowing Benedict and Madeline Murdoch to pass through. As they entered the room, a handsome, towering black man of about forty rose to his feet and straightened his Harris tweed jacket. "Colonel Jefferson,'' Madeline Murdoch said smoothly, "you are early, I see. Could you wait outside for a moment?''

"Dr. Murdoch,'' Jefferson said politely, "hurry up and wait has been my life's work. It's the Army way. No problem at all.'' As Jefferson obligingly stepped outside the Secure Room, Benedict eyed Madeline Murdoch warily.

"Who the hell was that?'' Benedict demanded.

"He commands the Delta unit at Fort Bragg. The president sent for him.''

"You mean you sent for him. Like you cleared Glassman for operations.''

"That was the president's order.''

"The president,'' Benedict sneered. "You shield yourself

behind the presidential seal, Dr. Murdoch. But I promise you, when scandal erupts and it's clear that you protected an Israeli spy, you will be damned for bringing down the chief you profess to serve.''

''You seem confident of your views, Mr. Benedict,'' Madeline Murdoch said, studying her briefing paper. A green light above the door signaled the president was on his way. Madeline Murdoch pressed a switch that opened the door. Waiting outside with Colonel Jefferson was General Rawlinson, dressed in class-A blues and ribbons. Next to him in an ill-fitting pale blue class-B uniform naked of medals or name plate was Adam Glassman.

Stepping through the crowded room accompanied by his cadaverous secretary of state, Willard Gardiner, the president caught Madeline Murdoch's eye and waved. She turned to the acting director of central intelligence. ''Well, it looks like we're all here,'' she said brightly.

Avery Benedict glared at her, crossed his arms, and stepped over to the chair reserved for the DCI. He tugged at his ear, an unconscious habit that reflected ill-concealed anger. As the president and the secretary of state entered, the military men stiffened, including Jefferson in his civilian tweeds. Madeline Murdoch and Avery Benedict also remained standing. The president made his way to General Rawlinson and Adam Glassman.

''Good morning, Colonel,'' the president said, offering his hand to Glassman. ''Be at ease,'' he said. ''Good to see you again.'' The president turned to Colonel Jefferson. ''You're the Delta commander now, right, Colonel?''

''Yes sir.''

''Damn glad to see you,'' the president said, pumping Jefferson's hand. ''Haven't crossed paths since I was at the Pentagon and you were a White House Fellow.''

The chief executive looked around the room and motioned with his hand. ''Please be seated.'' As the president's aides and the secretary of state sat, Avery Benedict remained on his feet. The president produced a briar pipe and began packing it, appearing not to notice Benedict. Finally he looked up. ''Something wrong, Avery?''

''Mr. President, I can't believe you would not be aware of

what is troubling me. With all due respect, sir, I do not believe we should cover any ground that affects national security with that man in this room," Benedict said, pointing a chubby finger at Glassman.

"That's your opinion, Avery. For the present, it does not happen to be mine. Now be seated."

"Sir," Benedict said, continuing bravely. "It has always been my understanding that it's the job of the national security adviser to provide advice and guidance to the president."

"What's your point?"

"Sir, it is my considered opinion as your director of intelligence that Dr. Murdoch is providing pretty poor advice in the matter of Colonel Glassman," Benedict said, his voice quivering.

"Sit down, Avery," the president said. The chief executive walked to his chair beneath a scowling portrait of Churchill, one of the few mementos of the previous administration. He rested his hands against the back of his chair and leaned forward, his unlit pipe jutting.

"You know, Avery, on your strong analytical merits, you've come very far very fast," the president said finally. "But it's not very complimentary to suggest to your commander-in-chief that he is a stooge."

"Sir, I was not suggesting that."

"Put a lid on it, Avery," the president snapped. "Are you tendering your resignation?"

"No, sir," Benedict said, his voice suddenly small.

The president circled behind Madeline Murdoch's chair. She was seated next to Glassman, who sat uncomfortably between her and General Rawlinson. The president stopped behind Glassman's chair and again rested his hands on the back and leaned forward. "This is my room, Avery," the president said. "Even as DCI, you are here at my pleasure. So is Colonel Glassman."

"No one could be more aware of that than I at the moment, sir," Benedict muttered.

"Good," the president said. "Here's a last thing to consider before we begin evaluating a course of action for the Middle East region. There are two men in this room privileged to wear the National Intelligence Medal. Avery, you got yours for being a crackerjack administrator.''

The president walked back to his chair and seated himself. He lit the pipe and puffed thoughtfully. ''The other man who holds that rare decoration is sitting across from you, Avery,'' the president said, indicating Glassman with his pipe. ''He got the medal for stopping a planeload of terrorists on a mission I'm not prepared to discuss even in this select company.''

''Yes, sir,'' Benedict murmured.

''Good. The inquiry into Colonel Glassman's intercourse with Israeli intelligence is not concluded. But for the moment it is in abeyance. Until I order it reconvened. Today Colonel Glassman is the briefing officer.''

Benedict gaped at Glassman. The Air Force colonel stared back, his poker face unreadable. Glassman carried a manila folder to the projector. He pulled a screen unceremoniously over Churchill's scowl. ''This is the freshest material available outside of real-time satellite imagery. Because of operational limitations, I am informed a satellite was not available.''

Placing a picture in the projector, Glassman said, ''Site one is the Federated Socialist Republic of Tarak. Site two is in the state of Israel. Both targets pose hazards for the security of the United States,'' Glassman continued. He adjusted focus. ''This is a picture taken recently by my reconnaissance systems operator, Major Rogers.''

''Rogers!'' Gardiner, the secretary of state, exclaimed. ''You mean the young man that the Israelis repatriated?''

''Precisely. You are looking at an overview from eighty thousand feet of a chemical factory that the Tarakis contend is used for fertilizers. The plant has had time to make the desert bloom, but there has been no corresponding improvement in regional agriculture.''

''The Israelis have complained early and often about it to me,'' Gardiner said, holding his hands up helplessly.

''This is a picture taken yesterday,'' Glassman said. The photograph displayed the sandy coastal plain surrounding the plant in Tarak, the low hill country, and the ominous ruins of the Crusader fortress. The photograph was pockmarked with the black dots of military traffic. ''You are looking at the same site, approximately fifteen hours ago," Glassman said. "I was the pilot on that recon."

"Great," Benedict sneered. "Spy photos from a spy."

"That's enough, Avery!" the president snapped.

Glassman used a collapsible pointer to note changes in the newer pictures. "Within a week's time, the area around this ancient Crusader fortress has been fortified. Heavy antiaircraft defense. SA-6 batteries. Mobile tracked artillery with Russian crews. But mainly, the troops are East German, guessing from camouflage patterns on their uniforms."

"And what are we to infer from this?" the secretary of state asked. "The Russians still have advisers all over the region."

Glassman smiled dryly. "Well, for one thing, the Israelis might not cotton to the idea of heavily armed German troops sitting so close to their own border."

"What else might the Israelis not like?" Benedict asked sarcastically.

Glassman continued unperturbed. "Why further defend an already entrenched location?"

"Why indeed, Colonel?" Colonel Jefferson, the Delta commander asked.

"A partial answer is evidenced by the addition of an offensive capability near the plant," said Glassman, removing the photograph and replacing it with another.

"Here and here," Glassman said, indicating with the pointer. "These missiles could be in Tel Aviv, or Jerusalem, or any single point in the state of Israel within the time it takes to drop an envelope in the mail."

"You've done a fine job of advancing the view of the Israeli government," Benedict observed caustically. "You couldn't have done better if the Mossad gave you the pictures. Maybe they did."

Glassman collapsed his pointer and sighed. He looked at Benedict and said nothing. "Go ahead, Colonel," the president urged.

"Other Arab countries possess SCUD missiles," Secretary Gardiner said cautiously. "Syria for one. Also Iraq."

The president knocked his pipe in an ashtray. "I want to know why we didn't know about these missiles. Where was CIA?"

Benedict's face reddened. "Sir, the agency has been working on an updated Special National Intelligence Estimate. I'm certain that data would have been reflected.''

"If I may continue,'' Glassman said softly. "Those countries identified by the secretary as possessing advanced missiles don't base them next to a nerve gas factory,'' Glassman said.

"Any other bad news?'' the president asked. In answer, another photograph showed an attack helicopter unit, side by side with a MiG-25 Foxbat jet interceptor squadron and some advanced Sukhoi ground-attack jets.

Glassman magnified the photograph. The helicopters each possessed prongs in the nose section and covered gun ports. "These choppers are fitted for combat in a nuclear or biological or chemical environment. They are being assembled as we speak. You may infer whatever you like, Director Benedict.''

"Colonel,'' the secretary of state said. "You mentioned overflight photography of Israel.''

"Gentlemen, what you are seeing is the state-of-the-art from a new technology. Via the use of radar imaging initially developed under the Lazarus project, you are looking at the inner workings of the Israeli nuclear plant at Dimona. More specifically, you are looking at a radar-imaged illustration of a nuclear weapons stockpile. The rouge-colored bullet shapes in the cutaway section of the picture are warheads. They are stored on the third level of the complex, underground, in components that can be easily assembled. A careful count reveals more than fifty of them.''

The secretary of state adjusted his specs, crossed his knees, and pulled at a sock. Benedict shifted uncomfortably in his chair. The Delta commander raised his hand. "I'd like to ask a question,'' Colonel Jefferson said.

"Go ahead, Delta,'' the president said.

"The Israeli policy has been that it will not be the first to introduce nuclear weapons into the Middle East.''

"You are correct, Colonel Jefferson,'' Glassman said. "But by storing the warheads in separate components, they maintain a diplomatic white lie.''

The president sighed. "Fifty warheads,'' he muttered. "Lord.'' He emptied the ashes from his pipe. "I need not remind the acting director the previous estimate was in the area of twenty.''

"There are more, located closer to the delivery systems," Glassman said, placing a new picture on the projector. The picture displayed camouflage netting covering the missiles.

"Avery," the president said, turning to Benedict. "This briefing was not called to lash you, but goddammit, we should have known."

"I'm sure we have this data in one form or another," Benedict said, helplessly. "It's somewhere in the collection loop."

"It's right in front of us," General Rawlinson snarled as he chewed one of his unlit stogies. "My Blackbird crew brought it back. And I suggest we would not have any of this material if Colonel Glassman were in some CIA safe house cooked to the gills on pentothal. I resent your hasty judgment, Mr. Benedict."

Benedict nearly tugged his earlobe loose. "In my mind, the retrieval of this information has not cleared Colonel Glassman," the CIA man retorted. "In fact, the information may be tainted at the source because he was the very one arranging the so-called facts we are looking at."

"Oh, come on, Avery," Madeline Murdoch said. "The pictures don't lie. We're looking at a powder keg. Two well-armed and hostile Middle East nations are at the brink. One's got the bomb and the other's got the poor man's bomb."

Avery Benedict rose from his chair and paced. Speaking deliberately, he said, "It's evident, gentlemen, that CIA is intended to be served up as the sacrificial lamb."

"Nonsense, Avery," the president said.

Benedict raised his hand and said, "Begging your pardon, sir, I mean no disrespect. But when I got this job, the Israelis had carte blanche, and they had shown no reluctance to use it, then embarrass us. I've closed some doors with friendly services, sir, but I felt that we had to."

"Sit down, Avery," the president said, waving his pipe. "Save the rehash of the interagency intramurals. Are there any other indications of a mobilization of either country, Israel or Tarak?"

"I could give you a well-defined answer within twenty-four hours," Benedict said.

"Avery," the president said softly. "I want to know now."

Madeline Murdoch rose from her chair. "Other than the

buildups at Dimona and the Taraki plant, there is no evidence of imminent hostilities. But both countries could go ballistic at any minute.''

Gardiner sighed and turned to the president. ''Do the Russians recognize what they have done to tip the regional balance, do you think?''

''I don't think we want to ask them,'' the president declared. ''Let's not make it more complicated than it already is.'' The president began to pack his pipe, then glanced at Madeline Murdoch, who was evidently suffering the effects of the smoke. Looking somewhat annoyed, the president put his briar away.

In a weak voice the secretary of state asked, ''Mr. President, why is the commander of the Delta force here?''

''There is already a state of hostility between the United States and Tarak,'' Madeline Murdoch explained. ''The Federated Socialist Republic of Tarak is holding an American general officer captive. We believe the site of his custody is the chemical weapons plant at Tarak.''

''Are you certain they are holding our general?'' Gardiner asked. ''And who is he?''

''Scott Cartwright,'' the president said.

''Oh, God,'' the secretary of state said, sagging in his chair. ''The man's an astronaut. He's a national hero. Other nations go to war for less of an affront. Are we dead certain they have him?''

General Rawlinson put his hands on the table and squinted at the secretary of state. ''They have him all right.''

''How do you know?'' the secretary demanded. Rawlinson placed a photograph on the table. The president whistled. ''Is our surveillance photography that good?''

''License-plate-perfect resolution here,'' Rawlinson said.

Quietly gazing at the picture, the president said, ''If we can do it, I want to bring him home.''

The photograph was of a silver-haired man, looking skyward with his ear cocked, as though listening to a high-flying black aircraft. The man in the sandy camouflage kit of an East German infantryman was giving a very American thumbs-up gesture.

— 48 —

Agent Provocateur

Kazakhstan Soviet Socialist Republic

KOLCHAK SURVEYED THE SWIRL OF activity before him with a
practiced eye. Absent a parade in Red Square, a headquarters
move was nearly as satisfying. Kulitsyn, the signals colonel,
was moving the equipment and staff of the mobile van operation that knocked out the American Keyhole satellite.

As part of his new duties in the Defense Ministry, General
Kolchak journeyed by army jet and helicopter all across the
Soviet Union. This day, he supervised transfer of the secret
Kazakhstan Project into the cool concrete caverns of a huge
pyramid housing a radar site the Politburo wanted shut down
to appease the West. The concrete pyramid suited Kolchak's
conspirators.

As the soldiers of the Pamyat conspiracy carried in steel file
cabinets, desks, chairs, map tables, and computer hardware
smuggled from the West, Kolchak lit a Troika cigarette and
blew smoke through his nose. Kulitsyn entered the recently
emptied office, saluting. Together, he and Kolchak peered for
a moment through the one-way glass that overlooked the whirl
of activity inside the radar pyramid. Kulitsyn turned to a pair
of sergeants who carried with them an unwieldy telegraphic
printer.

"As you requested, general, the *Tass* printer," Kulitsyn said. In the rest of the Soviet Union, it would take months to obtain a simple desk and chair. Kolchak got what he asked for. Defense Ministry priority.

When he saw the bulletin on the *Tass* printer, his face darkened. He was reading the internal *Tass* dispatches, sent over wires intended only for state authority. "Here, it is happening again, Kulitsyn," the bearlike general growled. Colonel Kulitsyn took the torn dispatch from the general's hand and hastily read it.

> URGENT
>
> TBILISI, G.S.S.R. (TASS)—Some Soviet army troops today refused to take arms against rebels and hooligans rioting in the streets of the capital of the Soviet Republic of Georgia.
>
> Demonstrators roamed freely through the streets, starting fires and overturning vehicles. Although some illegal protests were scattered by gunfire and tear gas from troops loyal to the state, some troops reportedly surrendered their weapons or placed flowers in their gun barrels, joining the hooligan gangs.

"First the Baltic states. Then the southern republics. Now Georgia. This is enough!" Kolchak snarled, stubbing his cigarette on the bare wood of the desk. "We must make our move soon, or there will be no army to back us."

Kulitsyn frowned and adjusted his steel-framed glasses. Hearing the marching clump of heavy paratrooper boots, he looked up. General Strelnikov entered the office, looking troubled.

Colonel Kulitsyn handed the dispatch to the broken-nosed paratroop general. Strelnikov read it quickly, then crumpled it up in his callused brown hands.

"What do you make of this?" Kolchak demanded of Strelnikov. "What kind of rotten government permits revolt in its streets and fails to discipline the rebels? And what will come of an army not gathered under our banner?"

Strelnikov shook his head and stared at Kolchak, his expression grim. "That is the least of our worries, comrade General. We are penetrated."

Kolchak's face went pale. His chin quivered. "Who? How?" Strelnikov, whirling on Kulitsyn, slapped the old man and said, "Right here. Him."

Kulitsyn was ashen. "Absurd," he sputtered, massaging the red spot on his face. "This is treachery!"

"And you are the traitor, Kulitsyn," Strelnikov said tersely, thrusting a file in General Kolchak's hands. "It is all here. My people in GRU finished collating the data this morning before I flew from Moscow."

The general read the file quickly. It identified Colonel Kulitsyn as a long-serving penetration agent of the KGB. Also in the file was a summarized memo on activities of the group Pamyat. The memo was signed by Kulitsyn and addressed to the official at the appropriate directorate. Kolchak handed the file to the white-haired signals colonel, who read it as though it were a death sentence. Helplessly, he looked at Strelnikov and Kolchak. "This is a provocation," he whispered. "I am loyal to Pamyat, to you."

Kolchak said tersely, "Comrade General Strelnikov, assign a detail."

Kulitsyn straightened his tunic and came to attention. "I will not sink to my knees to beg for my life, General," he said. "I have kept faith with the army and with you."

"You are a liar," Strelnikov said, picking up the file. "I ask you only to tell the truth before you die. Your answer determines whether you die a soldier's death or a traitor's."

Kulitsyn regarded the paratroop officer sullenly. "This will be an interesting question, I am sure."

"Have you betrayed to your KGB masters the existence of the Taraki operation? Have you betrayed comrade Kurtz?"

Kulitsyn squared his shoulders, stared haughtily for a moment at Strelnikov, then turned to General Kolchak. "May I have a cigarette?" Kolchak obliged him and lit it. "How could I betray Kurtz when I am loyal?" the colonel asked with quiet dignity as he puffed. "How could I expose the Taraki gambit, when I am loyal? There is a traitor in our midst, but it is not me."

The paratroop general rubbed the cartilage of his broken nose and looked at Kulitsyn with an expression of disdain. "Agent provocateur. That is what you are." Twisting his lips in disgust, he spit the word, "Chekist."

"We must move quickly with our plan," Kolchak said, speaking as though Colonel Kulitsyn were already gone. The colonel remained at attention, still as a statue.

Finally Kulitsyn spoke. "How will you communicate with Kurtz? I am your link to him." Kolchak waved his hand dismissively.

"Kurtz will act," the ursine general said. "That is why we picked Kurtz. He is independent, like all Spetznazim."

"It will do no good to have comrade Kulitsyn shot," General Strelnikov said. "He commands this detachment. The others will wonder. He should instead be replaced, in a conventional change of command. I will take charge here."

"What do you propose, General Strelnikov?" Kulitsyn asked sardonically. "That I shoot myself?"

"Nothing so crude, Colonel," Strelnikov said, tapping lightly on the steel office door.

A pair of tough-looking sergeants wearing camouflage jump smocks of Spetznaz troops entered. Kolchak and Strelnikov followed the noncoms, who escorted Kulitsyn through the cavernous passageways of the radar pyramid. No one took notice as Kulitsyn was hustled aboard a helicopter waiting on the pad. The helicopter rose vertically about two hundred meters in the air and exploded. One of the noncoms nodded perfunctorily at General Strelnikov and replaced the control box he had removed from his smock. The Spetznaz saluted and marched to another helicopter as men ran to hose down the wreckage.

"Radio control," Strelnikov said to the pale-faced Kolchak, who nodded dumbly. "The Japanese make such excellent radios."

—— 49 ——
The Remorse of Kemal

The Plant in Tarak

GENERAL REINHARD GRUNFELD'S COBALT EYES focused on the maps, which were highlighted with colored inks to mark points of demarcation. Green for the staging area. Yellow for the jump-off point. Red for the target, the Israeli weapons complex in the Negev. Kurtz and General Walid watched him anxiously. "It can be done, then?" Walid asked, dabbing sweat from his forehead with a silk handkerchief.

Grunfeld inclined his shaven head and squinted at the maps. "Flight time to target in the armored helicopters is twenty minutes. By that time, most target personnel at Dimona will be dead or dying." He paused to look at the map again for a moment and sighed. "We will kill the rest."

"What about air support?" Ivan Ilyich Kurtz asked the Taraki intelligence chief, his pale blue eyes alight with anticipation. "You know the Jews have the best air force in the world, General Walid."

Walid smiled. "The intelligence service of Tarak and its air force are as one," he said, pressing his hands together. "On the day of the attack, an order will be given to launch three squadrons. Sukhoi ground attack fighters will screen the helicopters, and your own MiG-25 fighters from Foxbat squadron will provide the high-level screen across the assault corridor.''

"The Zionists will make quick work of your old ground attack fighters," Kurtz said.

"What does it matter, if General Grunfeld's helicopters reach their target?" Walid asked, with ruthless logic.

As he spoke, the map room door burst open. Accompanied by his bodyguard, President Kemal strode into the room and unceremoniously punched his intelligence chief on the chin, bowling him over. "You are arrested, brother," Kemal cried out. The intelligence chief backed away from the president, nursing his bleeding lip with a handkerchief. "You have lied to me and conspired against me, Walid," Kemal said, his face contorted with anger. "It is a good thing that I am my own eyes and ears."

"What are you talking about, my President?"

"The village of Atar. I have seen it myself. This filth you conspire with were responsible for an atrocity there. They sprayed the village with their poison. All are dead."

"My President," Walid said, raising his hands apologetically. "It was you who ordered the village disciplined. They were a rebellious minority."

"I ordered arrests," Kemal snorted. "Not chemical massacre! Their bodies were like the dried husks of locusts. They are unclean."

The blond Russian bowed deeply. Rising from the bow, he said, "I take responsibility, Honored President for Life. A test was needed to assure the effectiveness of the new weapons."

"Silence, you jackal!" the president shouted. "You also are arrested. The work of this place has come to an end." General Grunfeld was moving his hand gingerly toward his holster as the president spoke.

"Touch that weapon and you are a dead man, General," Kemal stated flatly. "As of this moment, you are persona non grata in the Federated Socialist Republic of Tarak. You will be returned to the German Democratic Republic for courtmartial." Grunfeld merely regarded President Kemal with curiosity.

"Take General Walid from the room, Assam," Kemal said, motioning to his bodyguard.

Walid grinned shrewdly and then said, "My President, it is with regret that I inform you that you are the one arrested." He cocked his head toward the bodyguard. The bodyguard obediently put his massive hand on the shoulder of President Kemal, violating his person for the first time.

Kemal's eyes flashed. "What is this? Assam!" The bodyguard tightened his grip and began pulling Kemal from the map room.

"You son of a pimp," Kemal cried as his erstwhile protector pulled him from the room. As he was manhandled into the hallway, Kemal shouted, "You are going to die a slow and painful death, Walid. I will enjoy watching."

"I think we can get on with it, gentlemen," Walid said, as though nothing had happened. "We have a little time before any loyalist officers become suspicious. They know their president often goes to the desert to meditate. Meanwhile, the air force is mine."

As they returned to the maps, a banging in the hallway interrupted them anew. It was one of Grunfeld's men. "Herr General!" Grunfeld opened the door and looked into the frightened face of an infantry captain. "What is it, Kinder? We are busy."

"Two of our soldiers are murdered! The uniform of one was stolen. There is an infiltrator."

"What in the devil's name are you talking about?" Grunfeld asked testily, turning to Walid as his captain stood with his heels locked.

"It was an American pilot spy detained by my security services," Walid said.

"Well, if the son of a bitch is killing my men, General, don't you think I should have been informed?" the East German commander demanded.

"My men were searching," Walid said helplessly.

"A fine job your men did," Grunfeld sneered. "We will use the dogs. Have you got an article of the prisoner's clothing?"

"I think so," Walid said, pressing the kerchief to his forehead.

Grunfeld turned to his captain. "Bring me the Rottweilers. You are going hunting, Kinder. And I want updated status on helicopter and fixed-wing aircraft preparation." The captain saluted and hurried out. "Too many surprises," Grunfeld said darkly. "Prepare your troops for movement to the staging area, Walid. Time is the enemy."

Walid nodded and quickly abandoned the room. Grunfeld folded his map and placed it in the unit safe. "We will inspect the area," Grunfeld said, turning to Kurtz. "Make sure your chemical warheads are in readiness."

Kurtz nodded and grinned. Turning to leave, he said, "I hope you are ready to start a war, comrade."

"Never more ready, comrade Captain Kurtz," Grunfeld replied. "This time I put paid to the Jews."

The Taraki guard had been sitting on a pair of ammunition crates, his head listing slightly to port. Cartwright had caught him in a doze. The general rifled the slain guard's pockets and found a ring of keys and a packet of field ration crackers. Pocketing both articles, he also removed a pair of dust goggles from around the sentry's broken neck before propping him against the crates. He took the guard's pistol.

In the rapid-fire world of air combat, Cartwright's plan remained simple. Kill the enemy and get home. He didn't change his style much down on the ground. But he needed a hiding place. He tried the keys on the door in the dark underground passageway, found one that opened it, and stepped into the cool darkness.

He had entered another part of the underground complex from which he had escaped. But in the area where he'd been held, the cells were filled with prisoners and the subjects of the experiments, and the corridors echoed with a constant groaning, punctuated by an occasional shriek. Here all was silence, a subterranean darkness permeated by the odor of formaldehyde. The general tore the foil off the rations. He hadn't eaten in nearly two days, but he chewed carefully, not wanting to turn his stomach. He took one swig from his canteen and swished it in his mouth. Then he flicked on the flashlight he'd taken from the East German guard and examined the piece of metal he had picked up.

Next, the general unsheathed a bayonet. He stepped on the metal with his boot and spiked the piece of metal twice with the bayonet as though he were punching holes for a child's

Halloween mask. Next he used the bayonet to cut the elastic from the dust goggles. He threaded the elastic through the metal and tied the ends. He used the butt of the Taraki guard's pistol to hammer at the piece of tin and to beat the sharp edges over.

He placed the tin mask over his face. It fit. The odor of disinfectant became overpowering. Cartwright rose to his feet, dizzy. As he shook his head to clear it, the flashlight swung around the room.

The beam flashed on a metal table with a body on it. Or parts of a body, cut cleanly in sections like beef. The head was missing. The blood had drained from the corpse into grooves in the table, leaving the flesh an iridescent white, like a fish belly. White except where the skin was burned. Those places were marked with tape. A chart hanging from the table displayed a diagram of the victim's marks.

Cartwright, who had seen the jellied remains of comrades slain in fiery cockpits and gun turrets, doubled over. He retched and fell to his knees, gasping. Pulling himself to his feet, he looked around and saw a row of similar tables, with more bodies on them. He glanced at the headless horror on the lab table and ran past the body of the slain guard, in search of fresh air and daylight.

Cartwright stepped briskly up the stairway that led outdoors. It was false dawn, with a spangle of stars winking before giving way to purple dawn. Smelling salt air, Cartwright estimated he was about a mile from the sea. But escape in a boat was unlikely, he decided. The only time he had spent in an open boat was a dicey twenty minutes in the South China Sea after he punched out of a Phantom hit by ground fire. He knew he had no talent for sailing.

As pink light streaked across the eastern sky, the general crunched onto the gravel of the motor park. There was plenty of activity, with squads of East Germans marching and shouting. Cartwright heard dogs baying beyond the crumbled turret of the ruined castle walls that ringed the chemical weapons plant.

Donning the metal plate to mask his face, Cartwright marched toward a Russian GAZ jeep that was idling in the motor park. Cartwright spotted a bareheaded lieutenant shouting orders at a squad that was pushing a two-wheeled trailer stacked awkwardly with ammunition crates. The troops pushed and pulled, confused by the young lieutenant's contradictory commands. Cartwright quickly climbed in the GAZ jeep and swept off his helmet. He put on the lieutenant's peaked cap as he drove toward the gate and saw the officer had left a carbine and satchel of grenades on the passenger seat.

"Thanks, young 'un," the old general grunted. As he steered through the formations marching across the factory grounds, he returned salutes from squad leaders briskly. Sitting erect, with a haughty demeanor, the general drove toward the gate, which was manned by a joint detail of German and Taraki guards. The East German guards snapped to attention as he drove by. He returned their salutes and drove out the gate as sunrise warmed the hills.

As he swung onto the perimeter road, a convoy approached. Cartwright adjusted his cap, trying to look every bit the East German officer as the lead vehicle approached. Awaiting the obligatory salute from the officer who led the convoy, Cartwright swallowed hard as he saw that the officer in the leading armored car also wore a metal face plate. Suddenly the officer began shouting. Cartwright put the gas pedal to the floor.

As he raced down the perimeter road, he heard the convoy grinding to a halt. He drove toward an antiaircraft emplacement, a ring of sandbags around a 23-millimeter tracked "zoo" gun. As he sped toward it, the antiaircraft gun crew saluted. Cartwright tossed a grenade at them.

The general heard the whump of the grenade and screams of the gun crew as he sped away toward yet another sandbag fortification. A bewildered crew watched horrified as Cartwright cleared the pin on a second grenade and tossed it among them as he drove by. The grenade exploded before the crew leader dropped his salute. A blast of heat and a shock wave rattled the *kampfwagen* as Cartwright fought for control of the wheel.

Cartwright looked back and saw the black smoke and flames billow from the sandbag ring. The trucks were somewhere behind the smoke. He heard the sharp popcorn cracking of hundreds of rounds of 23-millimeter antiaircraft ammunition exploding.

As he raced toward the coast road, the first round of mortar fire exploded behind him, hurling the jeep forward with its shock wave. Cartwright's ears were ringing. A second mortar round dropped neatly, about a hundred meters in front of the little jeep.

"Bracket," Cartwright croaked. He wheeled onto the coast road as the third round whistled by him and exploded, blasting the jeep off the road and down a ravine. The vehicle bounded down the incline and crashed, pitching Cartwright onto a crag where he lay unconscious and bleeding. Moments later, three soldiers wearing buff-colored East German uniforms clambered down the ravine. One kicked the general in the chest with his scuffed desert boot.

"Do you think the son of a bitch is alive?" the team leader grunted.

"Ja."

"Before he dies, we'd better get to what he was doing here." The trio collected the general's body and began carrying him awkwardly up the ravine. "Heavy bastard," the kicker complained.

50

The Starlifters

Pope Air Force Base, North Carolina

THE C-141 STARLIFTERS TURNED HEAVILY toward the departure line on Runway 5 at Pope AFB near Fort Bragg, the high-pitched whine of their engines announcing their readiness for flight. The huge birds pulsed like living things.

Standing on the tarmac, clad in denims and a black field jacket topped with a woolen cap, the Delta commander looked like a merchant seaman who had lost his way. Adam Glassman wore the same uniform as Colonel Jefferson, with black tape covering the American flag shoulder patch of airborne troops. Jefferson once more scanned the flimsy that he would read aloud to his men once they were wheels up:

> To those charged with the success of Operation Scalpel: The hour is arrived at last to use the Delta option. I have decided to commit Delta and the Rangers to the fray, based on the best information I had at the time. Should there be a failure, the responsibility for it is mine and mine alone. God speed you on your way and keep you on your mission of mercy.

The flimsy, printed on edible rice paper, was signed by the president.

The Delta operators boarded the giant cargo jets silently, followed by the Rangers. They might have been coal miners, but instead of picks and drills, they carried Hechler & Koch machine pistols. From their sturdy shoulders hung custom-designed satchel charges of plastic explosive, hooks, grapples, and nylon ropes.

As Delta and the Rangers embarked, a quartet of black Hercules aircraft were taking off, creating a windstorm in the gathering dusk. Two were AC-130 gunships and the other two were Combat Talons, fitted for refueling, communications, and electronic countermeasures. Watching the Special Ops aircraft lift off, Glassman murmured into the wind, "Here we come, General."

"The last American general officer held by terrorists was Dozier. The Italians brought him home," Jefferson observed bleakly. "My worst fear is that General Cartwright is loose in the chemical plant and acting independently."

"That should help," Glassman said. "He's the most independent son of a bitch I know."

"That makes it even worse," said Jefferson. "With him wearing East German uniform kit, if he makes a hostile move, my operators will take him out."

"Colonel, I sure as hell don't want to lose General Cartwright to friendly fire."

"It's a tall order, fly boy," Jefferson said evenly.

Glassman sighed. Tugging at a grenade on his shoulder straps, he said quietly, "I will verify the identity of General Cartwright once Delta is on the ground. If necessary, I will shield his body with mine."

"You sound like you've been around the block with the general," Jefferson said.

"Something like that," Glassman replied. As the engine whine of the Starlifters shrieked ever higher, a Delta captain approached at double-time. "All present, Colonel," he shouted, saluting.

Jefferson and Glassman double-timed with the captain onto the last Starlifter. Moments later, the mighty four-engined jet roared into the night sky carrying its lethal human cargo toward a rendezvous with destiny.

— 51 —
Operation Scalpel

Washington

THE PRESIDENT'S NATIONAL SECURITY PLANNING Group convened in the White House Situation Room as Delta was departing for its classified forward operating location. The president's mood, usually cheerful even in crisis, was anxious and grim.

"How did it come to this?" the chief executive lamented. "Chemical warheads and ballistic missiles in the hands of the Tarakis. With our principal spy satellite down, Israeli nukes are poised to strike. We've got an American general held captive. What in hell are we doing wrong?" the president asked, raising his hands heavenward. Madeline Murdoch, Avery Benedict, and the cabinet officers kept their eyes on the table.

"Our intelligence system has failed again," the president said, scowling at Benedict. "It was by technical means we discovered the Israeli nuclear arsenal and the Taraki mischief. CIA still doesn't know how we lost a satellite. Without the Blackbird we'd be blacked out."

"The Russians deny any role in loss of the Keyhole, sir," Benedict said.

The president sighed. "It doesn't help that our own damn

spy plane is attacked by airplanes we sold to Israel, which now threatens to blow up the world from fear of its homicidal neighbors, who in turn have been armed by the Russians." The president shook his head disgustedly. "What a world."

The secretary of state turned his gaunt, undertaker's face to his chief. "What do you propose that we do now, Mr. President?"

"Willard, I'm glad you asked," the president said sharply. "First, you will inform the Israelis that any further increase in the state of alert in the Negev will meet with a response."

"Sir?"

"Leave the wording ambiguous, but let there be no mistake about our meaning. If you have to get on the phone to that son of a bitch Shamir, you do it."

Gardiner closed his eyes and began massaging his bony forehead. "I'm not through, Mr. Secretary," the president snapped. "You will inform the Soviet ambassador that the chemical weapons factory secured by East bloc troops is an affront to international law and decency. It will be dismantled."

"It won't wash, Mr. President," Gardiner said. "The Tarakis haven't even signed the Geneva protocols on chemical warfare."

"I don't give a damn what the Tarakis have signed. You will inform the ambassador that a multinational force is en route that will aid the extraction of any foreign forces with the good sense to surrender."

"When am I to do this?" the secretary of state asked weakly.

"Upon notification that the Delta and Ranger elements are on the ground."

Avery Benedict had maintained an uncharacteristic silence. Finally he spoke. "Mr. President, your action could start a war. Maybe a big war."

"I agree, sir," Richard Nunn, the secretary of defense, said, his voice swelling with the basso profundo that marked him as a former Southern senator. "We could be eyeball to eyeball with the Russians. It could risk all our recent gains."

"Doctor Murdoch has already advised me of that possibility," the president said wearily, his eyes bleary from lack of sleep. "I'm going to have to take a calculated risk that we are preventing a conflict, not starting one."

Almost involuntarily, the members of the National Security Planning Group turned their eyes toward the woman at the podium, a mixture of resentment, envy, and respect on their faces. With her calm gray-green eyes, she returned their gaze.

"Mr. President," Secretary Nunn drawled. "Has yoah assistant advised you of what the possible consequences might be if Operation Scalpel fails?"

"Mr. Secretary, after ten years of training, either Delta is able to perform or I will expect your resignation."

The secretary nodded solemnly. "God help them in their righteous cause," Nunn said.

Meeting the eyes of each of his advisers, the president said, "Should failure appear likely, I will commit the full resources of our forces in the Mediterranean to neutralize both the plant at Tarak and the Israeli arsenal at Dimona."

None of the men at the table had guessed the president capable of acting with such decision. "What I am telling you, friends, is simply this," the president said quietly. "Don't fuck up." Seldom given to profanity, he packed his pipe carefully and lit it. "This informal meeting of the National Security Planning Group is concluded."

As his advisers gathered their papers and filed from the room, the president beckoned Madeline Murdoch to remain. Staring enviously at the smoke drifting from the president's pipe, she reached for a stick of gum. "I admire your determination in quitting, Madeline," the president said.

She clucked her tongue ruefully. "The flesh is willing enough, but I'm afraid my spirit is pretty weak."

"Professor Murdoch, I would welcome the luxury of a moment of weakness," the president said, smiling ruefully. "Have we committed another dreadful blunder?"

"It's not too late to recall Delta, Mr. President."

"No, dammit, they're going. But I sure as hell wish I could watch the action. Madeline, I don't want to monkey with the field commanders, but I want to be able to see. Lincoln watched his troops in battle. Maybe if Johnson had, we wouldn't have bungled so badly."

''Let's call Ben Johnson on the coast. Maybe he's got another trick in the Blackbird bag.'' The president's face brightened as Madeline Murdoch picked up the phone, gave her authentications, and waited to talk to the engineer in the California desert.

—— 52 ——
Identify Friend, Foe

The Plant in Tarak

CARTWRIGHT WAKENED IN DARKNESS TO the sharp pain of a steel-toed boot in the ribs. Someone had tied his wrists. In German, a man's voice declared, "He's awake. Let's interrogate the bastard and get on with it." Cartwright held his eyes shut, opening them slowly to adjust his night vision. He made out three shadowy figures, one of them about to kick him again.

Cartwright rolled to shield himself from another blow. A boot shot into his back, firing a blinding shower of nerve signals to his brain. "What can he tell us?" another man's voice demanded. "Kill him now, I say."

"He may know some useful detail of the plant layout," the interrogator said. "First we question him. Then we kill him."

A flashlight blinded Cartwright. Sniffing the mustiness and faint smell of animal spoor, he guessed he was in a cave. He recoiled from the cold prick of a bayonet. "Who are you?" the man poking the bayonet demanded.

"*Frick du,*" Cartwright snarled. In English he added, "Take your toadsticker and sit on it!"

"He is American!" a woman uttered in a surprised tone.

"American? Why would an American be here?"

Slaps and kicks followed. Cartwright groaned and snarled, "Goddamn right I'm American. Who the fuck are you people?"

"Stop!" the woman cried out, slipping into English. "He is not an enemy. Stop beating him."

"I don't give a shit if he's from Mars," the man with the bayonet grunted, dropping the heavy steel haft on Cartwright's knee so that the general gritted his teeth in pain. "He is a threat to mission security. So are you, woman! Speak German!"

"You're killing him!" the woman shouted defiantly in English.

"Fuckin' A," Cartwright shouted. "If you're gonna ice me, get on with it. Skip all the tenderizing."

The flashlight shined in his face and a rough hand grabbed a tuft of Cartwright's brush of silver hair. "Who the hell are you?" the man demanded.

"I don't have to tell you shit," Cartwright spit back. "But just 'cause I always liked the Mossad, I'm gonna tell you. I'm an American airman."

Cartwright was stung by a sharp slap. "Mossad? What do you know about Mossad?"

"It wouldn't take a genius to figure out you're not with those commie bastards down at the chemical works, Fritz," the general reasoned. "You've got me trussed up like a sow, but you don't know my game. Ya talk German and good American. You must be some of David Ben Lavi's little helpers."

"You know Ben Lavi?" the woman demanded.

"Let's kill the cocky bastard," the man with the bayonet suggested. "He's already compromised the operation." The man pulled Cartwright up by the hair and pushed him to a sitting position against the damp cave wall. He grabbed hold of the tin plate still strapped to Cartwright's face. He plucked it and let the elastic snap back on the general's cheek.

"Why do you wear this? You are impersonating the commanding general. Why?"

"Untie me and I'll tell you a story," Cartwright growled. "Kill me and you'll never get inside that lunatic asylum I just escaped from. Those bastards are fixin' to push your tribe back into the sea again, and they might do it, too."

"How do we know this man is not a decoy?" the man with

the bayonet complained. "How do we know he is not sent out here to trick us."

"Don't be an idiot," the woman hissed. "What decoy would say 'fuckin' A'?"

"Damn right," Cartwright said. "Smart woman. I had some engine trouble and my chute opened on the wrong side of the line." The general painfully adjusted his position. "Name is Cartwright. Rank is major general, U.S. Air Force. And that is all you are goddamn well gonna get from me, unless we come to terms."

The man with the bayonet leaned into Cartwright's face. "Listen to me, you American spy bastard," he said. "You are going to tell us anything we want to know, or I am going to kick you to death."

The man with the flashlight set it down, so Cartwright could see the trio of Israelis. Almost affectionately, the big man patted Cartwright on the shoulder. "I am Abraham," he said. "I command this team."

"Pleased to meet ya," Cartwright responded.

Abraham lit a cigarette and passed it to Cartwright's lips, but the general shook his head. Abraham shrugged and returned the cigarette to his own lips. "Your turning up here is not good for us, General. We work alone. Anything threatens security of the mission, we terminate it. It's not personal, but maybe we have to kill you. Okay? We've got no room for you in the plan."

"Sure, nothing personal," Cartwright said, working his jaw painfully. "Except if you kill me, Ben Lavi and the whole Mossad shootin' match are gonna know you killed an American officer. They'll find out. So will the *New York Times*, eventually. They always do. Think about it."

"How do you know Ben Lavi?" Abraham asked.

"We go way back. We've got all kinds of mutual friends. I'll bet you even know some of 'em. Like the air attaché who ran errands for him maybe?"

"What air attaché?" the woman demanded.

"Glassman," Cartwright grunted. "Your man."

The woman gasped. "Adam," she said involuntarily.

The woman pushed by Abraham and grabbed Cartwright by the collar. "How do you know this Glassman?" she demanded.

Cartwright rolled his head back at her. He could see her beautiful Sabra bone structure in the lamplight. It contrasted with the drab ugliness of her uniform tunic. Cartwright guessed at the beauty of the woman beneath the rough cloth. "Hell," he groaned. "You're his girl, ain't ya? You're Sabrina."

"How do you know him?" she insisted.

"Adam's my wingie," Cartwright muttered before passing out.

The Israeli trio sat in the cave, all staring at the unconscious general. Abraham, the team leader, smoked and considered whether to kill Cartwright. Wrath of God did not like interruptions.

— 53 —
Coup d'État

The Plant in Tarak

MAJOR ANDROPOV RUBBED HIS KNUCKLES through his thinning hair and chuckled. He was reading an old copy of *Krokodil*, the Soviet humor magazine. The lieutenant in charge of the SCUD-B missile crew had given it up with a boyish smile. What junior officer would not gladly surrender his mail from home to the KGB man? The three-man missile crew that shared the huge command module of the Zil missile carrier continued their desultory card game while he chuckled and sipped a glass of tea.

"Show your cards, Fedka," Oleg, one of the crewmen, ordered. Fedka displayed his hand and grinned slyly, causing his friends to snort in disgust.

"Fuck your mother," Oleg grunted. The Zil missile carrier, resting on its sixteen heavy balloon tires, was built for the Arctic wastes or the most barren desert. Comfort, never considered a high priority by Soviet designers, was important in the Zil. Its air-conditioning was almost capitalistic. The Zil's central air was cool in the Gobi Desert, and its heaters could withstand Siberian cold.

All told, for the Russians, the Tarak assignment could have been worse. The East Germans did the heavy work of hauling

ammunition and guarding the chemical factory and the mobile
missile sites that encircled the Taraki plant. All the Russian
missile crews needed to do was to stave off boredom and avoid
the bootleg hooch distilled from engine coolant. This night
passed like all the others since Andropov's posting. None of
the troops could like or trust the detachment's secret policeman,
so he was left to his reading and the fading pastime of lectures
on party discipline.

All was quiet, even the curses hurled at cards.

The command module door swung open with a metallic
clank. Pushing his way into the vehicle was the East German
general, the ugly bastard with the plate on his face. Andropov
saw first the Makarov pistol the German pointed at his chest.
"What does this mean?" Andropov demanded, spilling his
tea.

"*Zdrasdi*," Grunfeld greeted Andropov in barely accented
Russian. He grinned strangely and motioned Andropov to his
feet with a wave of the pistol. The missile crew remained seated
by the command console, holding their cards, as Grunfeld's
aide, an East German colonel, clambered in. The colonel
pushed past his general and shot Fedka. The missile operators
screamed as the driver's blood spattered on the windshield.

"You will see that we are serious men, comrade Major,"
General Grunfeld said, standing before Andropov with pistol
in hand. The missile crew stared in dumb horror at their slain
comrade.

"What are you doing?" Andropov gasped. "I demand to
know in the name of the Komitet," he said, invoking the name
of the KGB as though it were God.

"A fine thing for you to say," Grunfeld grunted, pointing
the pistol at Andropov's head. "You are a traitor to socialism,
and this vehicle is commandeered in the name of the people."

"This is madness," Andropov spat out. "I am the KGB. I
command here."

"Sit down, traitor," Grunfeld ordered, slapping the major.
"If you want to live to morning, you will do exactly what I
tell you."

Andropov sat, rubbing his face. He did not want to shame
himself in front of the other Russians, but he could not stop
trembling. "What is it you want?" he whispered.

"This missile battery has been transferred to operational control of the loyal German Democratic forces stationed at site one, Federated Socialist Republic of Tarak," Grunfeld declared. "Red Army staff has informed me that you, Andropov, are an agent in pay of the Zionist forces."

Andropov looked up helplessly. "This is not possible," he said, his voice nearly a whimper. "I am a loyal Soviet officer. You fascist bastard, I am KGB!"

"You are a traitor and spy. We know this, and now these poor bastards know it, too," the German general said, waving his pistol at the terrified missile operators who stared uneasily at Andropov. "Now, listen," Grunfeld barked in harsh Russian. "This missile battery is on a war footing as of this moment. You will prepare your equipment for a launch on order from me as the legitimate representative of Warsaw Pact command. *Ponimayete?* Understand?"

If there was one thing the operators understood, it was Grunfeld's pistol and Fedka's still-fresh corpse. They nodded dumbly.

"During the next several hours, the warhead configuration of this battery will be changed. You will render all technical assistance necessary to the fraternal socialist troops of the Federated Socialist Republic of Tarak. Understand?" Grunfeld demanded. He pointed to Andropov, then indicated the body of the driver with his pistol. "Get this trash out of here," he ordered in Russian.

One of the missile operators, barely out of his teens, began to weep. Fedka had been his friend.

President Kemal meditated in the darkness, his hands shackled. He knew that when the time for screaming came, he would scream. Until then, he wanted to preserve his dignity. The cell door swung open. He smelled Walid. Always too generous with the cologne, Walid. "Greetings, jackal," Kemal said.

"There should not be anger between us, brother," the portly intelligence chieftain said cheerfully. "As of this night, I hold power in Tarak."

"You never held power and never will. Once you were my cat's paw. No more. Now this sovereign Arab land is in the grip of foreigners, heretics, and madmen."

Walid, squatting down, shook his head sadly and smiled. "Don't you see, Kemal? We make use of the foreigners. They give us the tools we need to vanquish the Zionists."

"You are the one who'll be vanquished, Walid," the president said. "You betrayed me and have allowed a foreign army into the land of the Arab. It will be your undoing." Kemal dropped his chin to his chest and said softly, "I know that I am going to paradise. Your fate is less certain, brother. But I prophesy that you will not live out the week."

Boots clumped in the hallway. A light shined into the cell, blinding Kemal. He heard the voice of the foreigner. "General Walid," Kurtz called out as he stepped into the cell. "We have seized the missiles from the Russian crews. We command the entire complex."

Walid smiled triumphantly at Kemal, "You see? I command in Tarak now." Kemal made no reply.

"General Walid," Kurtz said. "You are needed for assistance in final target coordinates for the bacterial warheads."

"Barbarian!" Kemal shouted at the Volga German.

Kurtz stared at the captive president, unconsciously rubbing his half-moon scar. His pale blue eyes were strangely alight. "Why does this one live?" Kurtz asked. "He is of no further use, except possibly for research."

"No, Walid!" Kemal screamed. "Don't let this animal have me for his unclean passions. Kill me!"

"All right, brother," Walid said, removing a small Beretta from his suit coat and firing a single shot into the head of the president for life. "Let us proceed," Walid said, turning to Kurtz.

They stepped smartly out of the cell. Its steel door slammed with a hollow ring, blown by a sudden cold breeze, and the heels of their highly polished boots echoed as they marched to the missiles.

— 54 —
Red Sky at Morning

Airborne over the Atlantic

THE DELTA MEN AND THE Rangers slept to the lullaby of powerful Starlifter engines. After boarding, they ate a high-carbohydrate meal, and the pressurized cabin was heated to a toasty eighty-one degrees to make them sleep. Rest before engagement was mandatory. While Delta slept, Colonel Frederick Jefferson compared high-resolution photographs against diagrams of the Taraki plant drawn up by his intelligence officer. He looked to Glassman for explanation of the pictures from the Blackbird overflight.

"Tell me about this building," he said quietly. "When we land in the UK to pick up the Brits from Special Air Service, I expect to get some human intelligence from inside the plant. But I want to know everything I can learn."

"Radar imaging displays show it's three stories, one below ground. Beneath it all is a labyrinth of tunnels and passageways. Probable activities are chemical fabrication and research," Glassman said. "It also serves as command-and-control headquarters."

"Does it really, or is that speculation?" Jefferson demanded crisply.

"The hostile HQ is in that building," Glassman replied.

Jefferson stared at Glassman. "I hope you're not shittin' me, Colonel. My guys will be outnumbered and outgunned. They've gotta hit the ground running."

"You know as well as I do that the ground situation often changes," Glassman said tersely. "Just remember, I'll be on the ground with you. My mission is to find Cartwright."

Captain Wally Ishimoto, the intelligence officer, approached with Sgt. Maj. Country Walker. They stepped delicately past the web nets that held the sleeping commandos suspended like banana bunches. "What have you got for me, Wally?" Jefferson asked.

Ishimoto was smiling. "We got some downlinked flash traffic. Base says we're going to have a Blackbird pass over target within thirty minutes of H hour."

Jefferson's brow furrowed. "I don't like that. A recce flight could tip off the bad guys."

"It'll be off their radar screens before they can spot a blip," Glassman said confidently.

"Don't soap me, Colonel," Jefferson said. "I was just getting to like you."

"That Blackbird flies at Mach 3-plus. Absolute speed is classified. It's not likely they'll pick it up."

"Balls."

"It's true, Colonel," Glassman said. "I got the photos you're looking at flying that airplane."

Jefferson appraised Glassman anew. The Starlifter hit a pocket of turbulence, and the men braced themselves against the bulkheads. "Maybe the Blackbird pass will verify the gun positions before we hit the landing zone," Ishimoto said hopefully.

"If the Combat Talons bleep the radar and our gunships hose down the plant, we might just mosey on in," Country Walker drawled. Solemnly he added, "On the other hand, it could be a real hot LZ."

The C-141 descended through the low gray ceiling over RAF Lakenheath. As the Starlifter landed, a pair of hitchhikers waited, wearing nondescript mechanic's coveralls. Like the Delta operators, they held canvas bags that carried the lethal tools of their trade. A gray mist turned to rain, but Colin Davis and Major Mellors stood unblinking, indifferent to the weather. Mellors turned his head toward the insistent beeping of a Range Rover driving onto the airfield.

Mellors strode toward the Range Rover. "Half a minute," he called back to Davis. Sir Alfred levered open the rear door of the Rover, and Mellors climbed in next to Billy Chesterton at the wheel. "Thought we'd see you off, Major," the intelligence chief said.

"Right, sir," Mellors said. "What's up?"

"I shall be brief," Sir Alfred said, handing Mellors a canister with a thick rubber seal around it and a canvas gas-mask bag. "Whatever our American cousins do at Tarak is up to them. But your job is to collect a sample of what Johnny Arab is cooking."

"You're joking," Mellors exclaimed.

"Chaps at Porton want a look," Sir Alfred said.

"I've got a sergeant major out there on the tarmac that would probably eat your liver if he heard your idea, sir. He doesn't like gas. It's personal."

"Then he can resign from regiment," Sir Alfred said. "No room for personal complaint in SAS."

"We need him to get into that bloody waxworks," Mellors said. "He knows the way out, too."

"Then don't tell him what you're about, Major," Sir Alfred said. "He's got no need to know."

"Bravo," Billy Chesterton piped.

"Shut up, Billy," Sir Alfred said.

The Starlifter bumped onto the long runway and began turning for quick takeoff. "I've got to be along," Mellors grumbled.

"Mind the sample," Sir Alfred said, waving cheerily. "There's a good fellow. Six is grateful."

Mellors jumped from the Range Rover and ran to the transport to join Davis and Delta, cursing all civilians, scientists, and cloak-and-dagger boys.

The right parachute door of the Starlifter beckoned. Colin Davis and Colonel Frederick Jefferson hoisted the SAS major into the cargo plane, which was already rolling ponderously toward takeoff.

"Damn glad to see you again, Freddy," Mellors said, pumping Jefferson's hand heartily. "Haven't had the pleasure since that hostage op in Singapore."

"Good to see you, Major," Colonel Jefferson replied. "Who was the chap in the Range Rover that held you up?"

As the parachute door swung shut and the Starlifter cleared the runway, Major Mellors grimaced. "Bloody snake-oil salesman from Six." Jefferson nodded, sympathetic to the plight of soldiers who deal with spies.

The Starlifter banked sharply and soared into the clouds to find a red sky at morning.

— 55 —

The View from the Cave

The Plant in Tarak

LYING ON HIS STOMACH AT the mouth of the cave, Ephraim adjusted his binoculars, spying on the Crusader castle that shielded the Taraki plant and its warheads, pointed menacingly skyward like ancient spear tips. More ZSU antiaircraft guns had been uncrated in the night, until the plant fairly bristled with them. Trucks from the airfield east of the plant rumbled up the coast road, bringing in more crates and boxes.

A Soviet Hind "Flying Tank" attack helicopter made a menacing sweep over the plant, and the antiaircraft guns tracked on it automatically, as though drilling for an attack. A pair of MiG Foxbat interceptors zoomed overhead, leaving sonic cracks. But it was the big Zil carriers on the distant hills that held Ephraim's attention. "Abraham, come here, quickly!"

The Israeli team leader took the field glasses. Wiping the sweat from his forehead, Abraham spotted the German troops and Arab soldiers at work beneath the camouflage netting that covered the SCUD-B missile sites. "What is it you see?" Sabrina Rabin demanded. She waited in the recess of the cave, dabbing Cartwright's forehead with a damp cloth.

"They have removed a warhead from the missile launcher,"

Ephraim replied, focusing the binoculars. "They have a long wooden field table and are performing some kind of modification."

"If I was you boys, I'd call in an air strike," Cartwright offered. "This thing is bigger than you."

"Shut up, American," Abraham said. "For years your fucking State Department restrains my government, and now you offer advice."

"It's not his fault," Sabrina Rabin said. "He tries to help."

"My country's been your armorer for damn near forty years, big guy," Cartwright said. "Your attitude is kinda unseemly."

"Shut up, General," Abraham ordered. "Sabrina, come here." She crawled to the cave entrance and took the binoculars.

"They are modifying the warheads for chemical attack," she said bleakly. "A dozen or so hours and they will be operational. Maybe a little more time, but not much."

"We take out the leaders and we cut off the head of this snake," Ephraim snarled. "We must get inside."

"Are you luckless bastards out here without a radio?" Cartwright asked.

"We are not spies," Abraham said matter-of-factly. "Wrath of God doesn't report events. We create them."

"Hit team, huh?" Cartwright muttered.

"If you like," Abraham said. "We call ourselves justice. Sabrina, can you get us inside?"

"It will be difficult," she said.

The team leader grabbed the field glasses and again surveyed the fortress complex. The German troops continued their work unmolested. He lowered the glasses. "If we fail, we are cursed of God," Abraham muttered.

"We have our uniforms," Ephraim said grimly. "We can seize a munitions truck, rig it with explosives, and ram the main building. Those bastards do it. Why not us?"

Cartwright coughed. "I thought you boys had a reputation for improvisation. That sounds pretty lame to me."

"Shut up, Uncle Sam," Ephraim growled. "I may still kill you."

Cartwright laughed. Though he was still bound, he rolled

like the rabbit in the briar patch. Sabrina looked at the filthy and ragged Cartwright. "He said you were crazy. My Adam."

"Your boy wasn't half wrong," Cartwright said. "But I'm at least as sane as you folks. Which isn't saying much."

"Son of a bitch," Ephraim said, rushing at Cartwright, his hand raised in an open-handed chop. "I should kill you now and be done with your noise."

Cartwright grinned. "Do it, sonny, and you'll never get inside that plant." Ephraim dropped his hand.

"How would you get us inside?" Abraham demanded.

"Same way I got out. Sewer pipes. Drains. Air ducts. I lived in that place like a rat."

"Will you do it?" the team leader asked.

"Hell, yes," Cartwright replied. "I'm an American. All ya had to do was ask."

"How can this old bastard help us?" Ephraim complained. "He can't even walk."

"How did I get this far, sonny?" Cartwright demanded. "I'll take you in to target. You can bet money on it."

Abraham gazed solemnly at Cartwright. Then he took a knife from his boot and cut the general's bonds. As dusk fell that evening, Cartwright donned his East German officer's cap and picked his way down the craggy hillside toward the plant at Tarak. Three shadowy figures followed him into the canyon.

—— 56 ——
The Kolchak Sting

ARRAYED IN THE FINERY OF his dress tunic and a peaked cap accented with scarlet and gold braid, General Kolchak returned salute for salute. Light tanks paraded past his reviewing stand at a stately pace, carrying parachute troops atop them. Hard-looking and grim-faced, each paratrooper saluted, hands slicing the air like knives. Kolchak's bemedaled chest swelled with pride.

"They look fine, Strelnikov," Kolchak declared. "Men like these will restore the Soviet army to glory. Soon they will join battle." His voice dropped to a conspiratorial whisper. "Your men should be ready to move on an hour's notice, Yevgeny Pavlovich."

"Is it to be Tarak or Moscow?"

"For your men of the Airborne Forces, it will be Moscow," Kolchak said, eyeing the coterie of aides that stood a few feet below the reviewing stand. "The air assault divisions will secure the Defense Ministry as soon as our fraternal forces from the German Democratic Republic move in Tarak."

"And when will that be?"

"Within twenty-four hours," Kolchak replied confidently as the last formation passed and he began to dismount the

284

platform. Strelnikov nodded curtly, as though satisfied. Ushering General Kolchak down the steps, the paratroop officer walked with him toward the large black Zil limousine that waited at the edge of the airfield. The door to the limousine swung open, and Kolchak seated himself, arranging his bulk comfortably before he noticed the bald man with steel-rimmed glasses seated next to the driver behind the bulletproof glass. Turning in alarm to Strelnikov, General Kolchak growled, "This is not my car!"

The man behind the bulletproof glass opened the small window and smiled. "But it is your car, General," the bald man in steel-rimmed glasses said as Strelnikov settled himself next to Kolchak and the limousine pulled away. "This car gets excellent mileage. It goes all the way to Siberia on one tank of petrol."

Kolchak's eyes bulged as he turned to Strelnikov. "General, I demand an explanation!"

The broken-nosed paratroop officer shook his head slowly as he lit a cigarette. "It is you, General Kolchak, who will give explanations. You have made your last demand."

"Who is this man?" Kolchak said, pointing at the bald man still smiling at him through the window.

"Ask me yourself," the little bald man said cheerfully. "I will tell you. I am your interrogator. We will talk again, at Lubyanka." With that, the bald man turned and shut the window.

At mention of the dread KGB's headquarters, Kolchak paled, and an involuntary shiver passed through his ample frame. "Lubyanka," he whispered, almost to himself. He turned to Strelnikov, who sat smoking impassively as the limousine gathered speed, moving onto the Ring Road leading back toward Moscow. "You, Strelnikov! You were the informant. It was you who betrayed Kulitsyn."

Strelnikov stubbed out his cigarette. Turning his cold-eyed gaze to Kolchak, the paratroop officer said, "You betrayed the Soviet state, Kolchak. I was loyal all the while. The key trait of a counterintelligence man is loyalty to the state."

"How can you surrender a general of the army to the KGB?" Kolchak asked helplessly as the car sped along the highway.

"You are no longer a general," Strelnikov said. "Not even

a comrade. I needed two pieces of information before we could move to shut down your crude conspiracy. It was necessary to know that the Kazakhstan project was isolated and that Colonel Kulitsyn was the link to your provocation in Tarak. You will tell us the rest soon.''

Kolchak rubbed his forehead. Suddenly he grabbed for the door—as though to hurl himself from the speeding car—and then discovered that there were no door handles. Strelnikov smiled. Beads of sweat poured down Kolchak's neck, dampening his stiff, braided collar. ''What will you do?''

''Move quickly to salvage peace,'' Strelnikov said. ''Then find every conspirator in your viper's nest and get them their just deserts.''

The limousine vanished from the streets of Moscow into an underground garage. Kolchak's rebellion had brought him to the doors of KGB headquarters at Lubyanka.

—— 57 ——
Gathering of Eagles

THE STARLIFTER ROLLED TO A halt. Driving up to the C-141 was a pair of passenger vans that SAS had cadged from a friendly air line on the island. The Delta men, teamed with the hundred Rangers, were discreetly ferried in relays from the rising heat inside the Starlifter to the shade of a large hangar. The special ops troops took the Mediterranean heat with stoicism characteristic of their breed. There was little idle chatter. Inside the hangar were cots, no-caffeine soft drinks, and freeze-dried combat Meals—Ready to Eat. Logistics was handled by Air Force Special Operations Command.

In a massive hangar adjoining the troop quarters were odd-looking camouflage aircraft that resembled a hybrid helicopter and transport plane. The unlovely Ospreys represented the first generation of tilt-rotor technology. They would fly to the LZ like airplanes and on approach to target tilt their wingtip engines skyward like helicopter rotors and descend vertically for troop exit.

On the tarmac were two modified Hercules transports. These planes bore as much resemblance to the thousands of conventional Hercules in service around the world as a dump truck would to a Porsche. Like the rest of the Special Operations assets, the crew of the Spectre Hercules gunship rested during the hot daylight hours—except for Colonel Whitley Record, a fireplug of a man who was joined by a maintenance crew chief. Together, the pair made their way from cockpit to aft section, checking bulkheads, fittings, fasteners, lines, seals, seams, and the guns.

The Spectre earned its name in Vietnam where its muzzle flashes, joined by flares and the powerful beam of its xenon searchlights, turned night into day and created hell on the ground for the enemy. The AC-130 was not a cargo hauler, unless Vulcan cannon ammo fired at a cyclic rate of twenty-five hundred rounds per minute was cargo. Later versions carried a 105-millimeter main gun for killing tanks. Special ops fliers called Spectre the fabulous four-engined fighter plane.

While the assault element aircraft and Delta's final transport were being checked by their cadre, the normal drill of a day at RAF Akrotiri masked the unobtrusive activity.

Tornado bombers of the RAF sortied from the taxiway, soaring skyward to NATO exercises on Crete. Transports belonging to the Royal Navy completed mail and supply runs. In the control tower, the air traffic separation officers took tea and biscuits as they orchestrated the comings and goings with British aplomb. The busy life of an air base surrounded and hid preparations that went on in the "guest" hangars.

Inside the troop hangar Jefferson tapped Adam Glassman lightly on the shoulder, waking him. "C'mon, fly guy. We've got to talk to the man."

Blinking his eyes, Glassman asked sleepily, "What man?"

"What man do you think?" Jefferson said impatiently. "Move your ass."

They drove a jeep across base to a nondescript concrete bunker with U.S. and British flags painted on a small sign on a steel door that read No Unauthorized Entry. The door clicked open and a colonel ushered them past a bank of American and British officers manning audio consoles with tape spools recording static or broadcast signals that chattered in a half-dozen Middle Eastern dialects. Virtually all regional newscasts and military transmissions of more than a dozen nations were recorded.

Sitting in an office chair deep at the end of the listening

room was Maj. Gen. Pete Rawlinson, chewing his unlit cigar. "Welcome to Fantasy Island," Rawlinson said, offering his hand first to Jefferson, then Glassman. "You've just stepped through the looking glass."

The trio walked downstairs to a red door. Rawlinson punched a key pad, and they filed through. Captains from the Army Security Agency manned the console. "At ease, fellows," Rawlinson said as the pair rose. The room was dominated by a giant screen monitor. "Have we got the downlink yet?" Rawlinson asked.

"Two minutes, sir."

The television monitor snapped on, displaying a blue test pattern of the presidential seal. A caption read "Please stand by," and a digital clock display counted off seconds. A disembodied voice transmitting on the screen announced, "Gentlemen, the president of the United States." The chief executive appeared suddenly on the screen, his still-handsome face worried by crisis. "Good day, gentlemen," the president said. "You may be seated."

General Rawlinson shook his head, smiling. "Sorry, sir. I think we've got to stay on our toes. No room in here."

"No matter," the commander-in-chief said, clearing his throat. "It's gratifying to see that all command elements are together."

"The security and assault element is assembled, Mr. President," Colonel Jefferson said. "I am unaware of General Rawlinson's role."

"How about the British?" the president asked.

"SAS is ready, sir," Jefferson said. "Their sergeant major has shown us the entry route to the chemical weapons plant. It's been a big help."

"Good," the president said, "General Rawlinson's Blackbird is my eye in the sky, Colonel."

Jefferson, a lonely black face at West Point, had made a career of controlling emotions. With quiet intensity he said, "With all due respect, Mr. President, I would like assurance that I am in sole command once we are on the ground."

"Your point is well taken, Colonel," the president said. "The plane flown by General Rawlinson will not be used as a dead man's handle. You run your mission."

"Yes sir," Jefferson said quickly.

"I'm not finished, Colonel," the president said. "General Rawlinson will be transmitting real-time imagery of the mission back to the White House. I take full responsibility for the success or failure of your mission. Read me, Colonel?"

"Loud and clear, Mr. President," Jefferson said, somewhat chastened.

"Operation Scalpel's objective is to disable the Taraki plant and get Cartwright. My mission on the other hand," the president said, "is to avert World War Three. I need the most timely information I can get."

"General Rawlinson's participation is welcome by Delta," Jefferson said. "He can watch my tail any day."

"Colonel Jefferson," the president continued, his tone becoming solemn, "I want you to tell your men I care about them, each of them, personally. This is, in fact, a humanitarian mission."

"Will do, sir," Jefferson said, saluting smartly.

"I will have a word with Colonel Glassman," the president said. "The rest of you are dismissed."

As Rawlinson and Jefferson trooped out, the army captains sat at their consoles like a pair of sphinxes. Their brief was to forget every word they heard. Glassman stood waiting. The president smiled. "Colonel Glassman, my guess is that you've had a pretty rough week."

"It's been like no other, Mr. President," Glassman said.

"No, I'm sure," the president said. "If I had a wish, I guess it would be that your particular case were not such an enigma for me."

"I will be glad to lay it out for you, sir, in the event that I return."

The president nodded somberly. "You'll get that chance. You see, my CIA director thinks you're the devil. But my national security assistant wants you canonized, if there are Jewish saints."

"Probably as few as righteous Gentiles, Mr. President," Glassman said.

"Touché, Colonel," the president said. "In any event, if you live, I need to be certain you don't become America's Dreyfus."

"That would be good, sir."

The president's features darkened. "But if you've spied against America, even for a friendly power, I'll see you in hell, Colonel."

"The guilty flee where no man pursues," Glassman said. "I'm not running, sir."

"Fine, fine," the president said. "That brings us up to the minute. Before we clarify your status, your commander-in-chief has one request."

"It's what I live for, Mr. President," Glassman said without irony.

"Get Cartwright. If he is alive, get him out. I want to bring one of our guys home." In an anguished tone, the president said, "Just once, I'd like to get one home."

"No one will try harder than me, sir."

"God bless," the president said.

Glassman saluted, and the commander-in-chief's visage blanked from the screen. The display pattern announced Transmission Concluded.

── 58 ──
Anxious Old Men

Jerusalem to Moscow

THE RUSSIAN-MANUFACTURED RADAR-GUIDED GUNS that ringed the plant in Tarak had shot down four Israeli remotely piloted surveillance drones within three hours. The troops under Grunfeld's command worked feverishly to complete transfer of the new warheads onto the hijacked Russian missiles. They looked anxiously to the sky as the "zoo guns" fired at the drones.

In Jerusalem, Prime Minister Shamir's advisers ruled out an air strike, fearing that whatever germ, bacterium or chemical, was cooking in Tarak might contaminate the entire region. "We still have the Wrath of God to consider," advised Foreign Minister Schlomo Ha-Etzni. "They could yet neutralize the threat." Shamir rubbed his hands as though they held a bottle with a genie in it.

Shimon Dayan, the defense minister, counseled instead that the plant be cauterized—immediately. "A Jericho missile," he said. "Just one, with a tactical rather than a strategic warhead."

"You are proposing that Israel initiate nuclear warfare," Ha-Etzni moaned. "Is this what we will be remembered for?"

"Better that we live to be remembered at all," Dayan said

gravely. It was Shamir who issued the order to assemble a tactical warhead at the Dimona complex in the Negev.

Five floors beneath the Kremlin, in a conference room of concrete reinforced against nuclear attack, the Politburo convened to consider the news of Kolchak's arrest and the pending crisis. Soviet satellites indicated the East German troops had taken control of the rogue missile battery. It was a Kremlin nightmare. Mutiny by a highly trained East bloc unit, armed with weaponry of mass destruction. "Exterminate the brutes," Foreign Minister Konstantin Grimov advised President Alexei Maximovich. "Once fascists, always fascists."

"How could this have happened?" President Maximovich demanded of no one in particular, before focusing his liquid brown eyes on Rudenko, the KGB chief.

Rudenko replied, "You want the answer, comrade Chairman? In Stalin's day a disloyal faction within the army would trigger a purge."

"This is not Stalin's day!" the chairman said, smashing his first on the table. "And we will not solve problems in Stalin's way."

"What do you propose to do with General Kolchak?" Rudenko asked mildly.

"He will be executed, of course," the chairman said matter-of-factly. "And the nest from Pamyat must be cleansed. But now we must decide what to do about the missiles in Tarak."

"Attack in force with a parachute drop of Spetznaz forces," the KGB chief advised. "Kill every fascist except their commander. Bring him here and find out what happened out there."

Marshal Rosskovsky, the defense minister, nodded solemnly. The Spetznaz troops belonged to him, or so he believed. "Strelnikov is the man," he said. To his surprise the KGB chief nodded agreement. Marshal Rosskovsky, perhaps feeling his own neck in the noose, bowed his head and shook it sadly. "Who would have thought it of Kolchak?" Slyly he looked at his colleagues. "It's indeed fortunate that comrade General Strelnikov and the GRU uncovered this plot. I recommend decorations."

Looking exasperated, Grimov nearly shouted, "Comrade Chairman! At the moment we have rebellious Warsaw Pact troops in control of a strategic asset of the Soviet Union.'' Rising from the conference table, he said, "The world must not know, at least until the mutiny is crushed. There will be time to assess blame later. Decorations, indeed!'' The foreign minister glared at the defense minister.

Closing his eyes and sighing, Maximovich exercised his prerogative as chairman and asked a final question: "Comrade Foreign Minister, shall we inform the Americans of our intended troop movement?''

"There is a time for openness and a time for action, Alexei Maximovich,'' Grimov said tersely. "This is not the time for *glasnost*. Speed is of the essence.''

Within eleven minutes Soviet paratroops under the command of General Yevgeny Pavlovich Strelnikov were loading onto their Ilyushin transports at Khodinka Airfield. Within the hour they were airborne, headed toward a staging area in Soviet Turkestan. Four hours later, after loading their heavy equipment, the Airborne Forces took flight again.

First information about the Soviet airborne formation was relayed to the White House from the Pentagon via an AWACS aircraft on patrol over Saudi Arabia. It had picked up the Ilyushins crossing the Iranian frontier. Soviet Flogger interceptors escorting the transports shot down an Iranian F-4 Phantom that attempted to radio back information as the IL-76 planes crossed over Tabriz.

— 59 —
Readiness Is All

THE BLACKBIRD RESTED IN ITS dark-winged majesty at the farthest remove of Runway 8. A few minutes after 02:30 hours, the support vehicles moved into position, maintaining radio silence except for squelch checks. The SR-71 was to climb to cruising altitude, hooking a left turn to meet its refueling tanker over Saudi Arabia's Empty Quarter, and loop back toward the decision point over Tarak.

A pair of eerie lime green candles ignited suddenly, lighting the black plane's aft section. Its engine nozzles roared and the dark shape raced down the pavement and lifted from the runway. The afterburners fired, making the tailpipes glow white-hot and transforming the dark aircraft into the futuristic vision of a spaceship leaving earth. Col. Frederick Jefferson watched in awe. "Godspeed," he murmured.

"God give us good recce," Sgt. Maj. Colin Davis rasped. Davis watched the Delta troops loading onto the assault carriers. The Americans were good, he knew, but lacked the experience of SAS. Counterterrorist combat was measured in minutes, or seconds. Cold sweat popped from Colin Davis's forehead, streaming over his greasy face paint. His thoughts roamed to the clock tower at Hereford and the list of names on it of SAS men who failed to "beat the clock."

Adam Glassman watched the Blackbird vanish and wished he were flying, but realized that out there in the darkness beyond the sea Cartwright needed rescue. Still, Glassman's heart and soul were in the cockpit.

"*Di-di mau*. Let's go," Jefferson said simply, adjusting the strap on his H & K machine pistol and marching toward the lead Osprey. As the assault transports rolled forward, directed by Air Force ground guides waving flashlight wands, a huge Combat Talon thundered off the runway, its mission to jam the Taraki radar and fuel the heavily loaded Ospreys once airborne. Minutes later, the Delta formation skimmed the waves on its way to target.

—— 60 ——
Decision Point

Washington

Aﬀer taking on fuel from a KC-135, the Blackbird climbed to eighty thousand feet. Far below, the flinty sand of the Empty Quarter gave way to the hilly, crowded countries of Israel and its surrounding enemy states. At Mach-3 cruise, General Rawlinson announced, "Rawhide, this is Linebacker." The SECOMSAT uplinked his message and bounced it down to the White House more than six thousand miles distant.

"Rawhide here," the president replied from the White House Situation Room. "I need a situation report." The president sat with the secretaries of state and defense, Madeline Murdoch, Avery Benedict, and the chairman of the Joint Chiefs of Staff huddled behind him like children crowding around a video game.

"This is Linebacker. Sitrep follows. We are at altitude. Indicated airspeed approaching Mach 4. We are beyond abort point, approaching decision point, with lateral discretion for target sites one and two. We are ready to illuminate at your order, over."

The president's console in the Glass House consisted of a brightly colored array of imaging screens. Situation Room staff went about their duties, much as they would any other day.

But there was a dry prickly quality to the dust-free air pumped through the underground chamber. Like bees in a hive that is disturbed, the Situation Room staff was nervous. People dropped coffee mugs and cursed. Paper cuts caused small shrieks. Nobody looked at the president behind the glass, and everybody looked at him.

An Air Force image analyst manipulated console dials to adjust color tone and resolution on the radar-imaged landscape relayed from the Blackbird. "Sensors are on line, Rawhide," Rawlinson radioed the president. "In other words, if you want a peek, just say so, over."

"Roger, Linebacker," the president replied. "I will want an overview of site two in the friendly zone."

"Site two magnified," the console operator announced. A moment later he added, "Mr. President, you've got a problem here." He indicated a ring of black video dots surrounding the Dimona reactor complex. "That's an offensive missile site in the Negev, I suspect. Two gantries are up, indicating launch readiness, sir. Warhead type is not identifiable."

The president turned to his cabinet officers and the chairman of the Joint Chiefs, who mirrored his somber expression. "There's no recalling Delta now," he declared. He turned to his secretary of state. "Willard, phone your deputy and deliver the note to the Israelis to stand down their goddamn missiles."

"And if we are wrong, Mr. President, what then?" the secretary asked, his voice filled with anguish. "This could be a crisis of our own making."

"Just deliver the note, Willard."

The secretary picked up the line to State. As he did so, an Air Force colonel bounded into the Glass House, thrusting a ragged slice of computer printout paper into the president's hand.

"We just got this from across the river," the colonel said breathlessly. "Pentagon says there's a formation of Soviet transport aircraft over Iraqi airspace on a heading for Tarak."

"Where did they come from?" the president demanded.

"Turkestan, sir. Their fighter escort shot down a half-dozen interceptors over Iran. Looks like Russki paratroopers or an emergency airlift, sir."

"I've got to talk to Maximov," the president snapped. "I need the red phone and the Soviet ambassador. And fresh coffee."

Madeline Murdoch summoned an interpreter and handed the president his refill. "Sir, whatever the Soviets intend, it must be our first priority to turn their aircraft back," she said.

"I know that, Madeline," the president said, a raw edge in his voice. "Let us pray that the great persuader in the Kremlin is prescient enough to be persuaded." Taking the red phone, the president waited and listened. After a series of authentications, the president heard his counterpart.

An interpreter mimicked the president's calm voice. "Alexei, we must discuss the intentions of your aircraft headed for Tarak."

There was a long pause followed by a terse Russian pronouncement. Maximovich's interpreter said simply, "Mr. President, there is nothing to discuss." The president's Adam's apple bobbed, and a blue vein pulsed on his high forehead.

"All right, Alexei," the president continued, his tone still pacific. "Let us be frank and candid. I have organized a multinational rescue unit that will land on the Taraki coast in less than thirty minutes. Unless my watch is wrong, that is about the time that your troops will be opening their chutes."

Another pause, then the Soviet interpreter, in stiff, formal tones, said, "Comrade Chairman and President Maximovich asks His Excellency the American president, what please are the intentions of your aggressive invasion party?"

"There is no invasion force," the president snapped. "This is a rescue mission. The multinational force will disable the weaponry of mass destruction that the radical regime of Tarak is using to threaten its neighbors. We will not tolerate resistance to this humanitarian enterprise."

The president listened to a hurried exchange in Russian, and he looked to his own interpreter, who shrugged, because too many voices were talking. The Soviet interpreter returned to the phone. "The chairman says the intentions of the Soviet landing force are similar to those of your own troops, Mr. President. He suggests you call back your force and allow the friendly forces of the Soviet Union to resolve the problem in Tarak."

The president was rattled. "What the hell are you talking about?" No translation was needed.

"There has been a misuse of fraternal assistance lent to the Federated Republic of Tarak," the interpreter said smoothly. Without missing a beat, he continued, "The friendly Soviet forces will correct the misunderstanding."

This time the president held his hand over the telephone and searched the eyes of Benedict and Murdoch, who had been monitoring the discussion on a conference line. "Will somebody please translate this mishmash I'm getting from the goddamn Russians?" the president ordered.

"The forces in Tarak must be in mutiny," Madeline Murdoch declared. "The Russians seem to be conducting a police action against their own troops."

"I can't take their word on that," the president said. "This could be prelude to a full-scale invasion of the Middle East." Taking his hand off the mouthpiece, the president said quickly, "Alexei, our best advice is that you turn your aircraft toward home. Once we have finished our operation, we will do the same and restore status quo. That is a sane solution. I implore you to accept it."

Almost immediately the answer came back, "The Soviet forces will implement their fraternal mission. Any resistance will be opposed."

The president closed his eyes. "Alexei Maximovich, the United States of America has no quarrel with the Soviet Union. We have no wish to engage your troops in combat."

Through his interpreter the chairman replied, "The intentions of the Soviet Union are similarly peaceful."

"Mr. Chairman," the president said deliberately, "the American forces will launch their humanitarian assault. They will attack the plant and, as a secondary objective, seize missile sites so Tarak no longer poses a threat to its neighbor Israel. Is there a way you can see to avoid confrontation with our raiding party?"

The Soviet interpreter listened to his boss. Then, calmly, the Russian translator said, "Demolish the plant. Its fate is of no concern to the Soviet state. Abandon the secondary objective of seizing the missiles. The soldiers of the Soviet Union will take control of the missile site."

The president turned to Madeline Murdoch, Avery Benedict, and Bud Kelly, the chairman of the Joint Chiefs. "Can we do this?" the president asked, his tone almost pleading.

"Can we trust them, sir?" Avery Benedict asked.

"Don't give me rhetorical questions, Benedict," the president snapped. "I need an answer."

"Sir, I'm worried," Benedict said. "This could be their own gambit to initiate a missile attack."

"That doesn't sound right, Mr. President," Madeline Murdoch said. "They could launch now and be done with it. Some outside agent has wrested those missiles from Soviet control. It sounds like all they want is their missiles back."

"General Kelly," the president said. "Your reaction to the chairman's suggestion."

"Sir, when Delta hits the ground, they will kill anything that moves. I don't see them holding fire on a second landing force in enemy uniform."

"General," Madeline Murdoch said, "is it not true that the Delta operators are trained to distinguish between hostages and terrorists? Why would they not be able to discriminate between friendly and hostile forces?"

Kelly slammed an open hand on the sensor console. "Madam, the Russians are not friendly forces!"

"And we, General, do not want to start a third world war," Madeline Murdoch said, unruffled. "Is there a signal that could be given to keep the Russian and American ground forces separated?"

The president, holding up the phone, said tensely, "Alexei, is there a signal that could be given to our troops in order to avoid hostilities?"

A rapid exchange in Russian followed. After a long minute the chairman returned to the line with his interpreter providing simultaneous translation. "Parachute troops of the Soviet Union wear a distinctive uniform shirt beneath their battle jackets," the chairman said. "A sailor's jersey of blue and white stripes. Our forces will remove their battle jackets so that the shirts are clearly visible. They will fire green star shell flares. Order your men to refrain from firing at forces arrayed and signaled in this manner."

"Agreed, Mr. Chairman," the president said quickly. "The

American forces are wearing black battle jackets, quite distinct from the desert camouflage worn by the interventionist forces in charge at the chemical plant. Tell your men not to fire at the troops wearing black.''

''It will be done,'' Maximovich replied through his interpreter. ''But you are reminded that your troops must not attempt to seize the missiles.''

''We can prevent a war if we act in good faith, Alexei.''

''For the sake of all mankind,'' the chairman replied. ''Let us hope your troops exercise restraint.''

The president wiped sweat from his forehead. ''Mr. Chairman, you will forgive me if I leave the line to give my order. It is my considered advice that we maintain a contact through my Pentagon chief and your minister of defense, since this is a military problem.''

''Agreed, Mr. President,'' Maximovich replied. ''We have a remaining request. Some troops that are the object of our nations' mutual interest remain under Warsaw Pact command.''

''I'm afraid I don't understand you, Mr. Chairman.''

''Should the American raiding party be the first to engage the Warsaw Pact forces, it would be the wish of the Soviet state that those forces be attacked and destroyed without mercy.''

The president shook his head, as if dumbstruck. He looked first at Madeline Murdoch, then Avery Benedict. Finally he nodded and said, ''Yes, Mr. Chairman, I understand.''

''Should there be any prisoners, of course, they would be transferred immediately to the Soviet commander,'' the chairman said. ''They are our people, you understand. It would be the position of the Soviet state that if we did not get them in a timely manner, we would fight for them.''

''I understand perfectly, Mr. Chairman,'' the president said hollowly. ''I will take my leave now.''

''And I, too,'' Maximovich said. ''May there be peace between our peoples.''

The president's face was ashen as he handed the line to the chairman of the Joint Chiefs. He murmured to Madeline Murdoch, ''That guy is cold.''

''A nice smile but strong teeth,'' Madeline Murdoch observed. "We must contact Delta, sir. They are approximately eight minutes from target."

The console operator opened the satellite link to the assault force. Col. Frederick Jefferson in the lead plane took the earphones from his radio operator. It was the call he was dreading, to recall the raiders. The flight of Osprey transports was two minutes outside Lebanese airspace, following one minute behind the Spectre gunships and radar-baffling Combat Talons. "What's the message?" Glassman asked.

"The Russians are going to drop an airborne regiment near the Delta LZ," Jefferson said, groaning.

"Good God," Glassman said. "Are we going up against the Russians?"

Shaking his head, Jefferson said, "They are to be considered friendlies. So long as we land first, our target remains the missiles and the plant. We take out the East Germans and the locals on the ground. At some point we are to turn the rockets over to the Russkies."

"How in hell are we supposed to separate friendlies from hostiles?"

"We've got to break radio silence and pass the word not to shoot the Ivan paratroopers in the striped jerseys. Looks like this rat-fuck could end as a flag football match between the shirts and the skins."

"Or World War Three," Glassman sourly observed. The task force thundered on, fifty feet above the sea level at 370 nautical miles per hour indicated air speed. The message passed between aircraft forty-five seconds before the Delta formation crossed into the lobe of the Taraki radars.

—— 61 ——
The Dagger Poised

Tel Aviv

THE STATE DEPARTMENT NOTE WAS handed to Prime Minister Shamir as he sat before radar displays deep in the bowels of Air Defense Command, watching Delta's movement into Tarak. The prime minister glanced from the screens to the note and within minutes was on the phone to the Situation Room.

"Please, Secretary Gardiner, no intermediaries," Shamir said in his stilted, formal English. "I must speak with the head of state."

The president came on line. "What is the meaning of this threat to the security of your principal ally in the region, Mr. President?" the prime minister asked crisply.

"Our mission is to remove a threat to Israel, Mr. Prime Minister," the president replied.

"That is an option we reserve for ourselves, Mr. President," Shamir said coldly. "We ask no one to defend us. And we demand that no superpower presume to know best our own interests."

"Mr. Prime Minister," the president said firmly. "You must allow us to act in this matter, or there will be war in the Middle East."

"There could well be war, Mr. President," Shamir replied. "And the people of Israel will prevail."

A brief silence followed. "This is not a threat, Mr. Prime Minister. I promise you that if you decide for the nuclear option, we will destroy your arsenal at Dimona before you can use it."

"So it comes to this? Before that threat is carried out, the state of Israel would destroy its enemies," the prime minister said. "All of its enemies."

"Such talk is counterproductive, Mr. Prime Minister. At this moment, forces friendly to the state of Israel intend to remove a dagger poised at your nation's heart, sir. For humanity, allow that work to be completed."

"Do not speak to me of humanity after what I have witnessed," Shamir snapped. "Forgive me, Mr. President, but my nation has little faith in the ability of your country to carry out its fine intentions."

The president breathed deeply and waited a beat. "Do not underestimate me," he said slowly but distinctly. "If you leave me no alternative, I will destroy your weapons complex at Dimona."

Shamir sighed deeply. Four million lives depended upon his decision. As he paused to consider, his defense minister handed him a fresh note describing the Soviet aircraft crossing the Taraki frontier. "Mr. President," he said angrily, "you have been less than candid with me. As we speak, Soviet transport aircraft are moving to reinforce the Taraki aggressor."

"Mr. Prime Minister, should you move against the Russians, the war begins," the president said. "We are in communication with them. As of this moment, the states of Israel, the United States, and the Soviet Union possess a common interest. My forces can take out the Taraki plant without contaminating the region if they are not interfered with. I beg you, Mr. Prime Minister, for the moment allow the present balance to continue."

In an anguished tone the prime minister said, "Mr. President, it is difficult to perceive any balance. I do not wish to be the leader who allowed a new Holocaust. Understand, additionally, that I have no wish to initiate such a tragedy. Land your forces. We will monitor their progress. But if your soldiers fail, my missiles will fly.''

"I want a commitment from you, Mr. Prime Minister, not to move within the next hour."

"Such a commitment would be worthless, Mr. President," Shamir said curtly. "But please accept my prayer for the success of your men."

Israel's long-sweep radars indicated a near convergence of the American and Soviet aircraft. Shamir shook his head gravely and, for the moment, stayed his hand.

—— 62 ——
Spectre Strike

The Plant in Tarak

GENERAL GRUNFELD PICKED UP HIS field radio mike to order the attack helicopters and the Foxbat interceptor squadron airborne toward Israel. He smiled and nodded first to Kurtz, then to Walid, who picked up a telephone to send the Taraki escort of Sukhoi attack bombers to Dimona. From his perch in the air shaft, Ephraim aligned the crosshairs of his collapsible sniper rifle between Kurtz's half-moon scar and milky blue eyes. Behind him, Cartwright, Sabrina, and Abraham waited still as deer. Ephraim nudged the tubelike 5.56-millimeter rifle off safety and wrapped his index finger gently around the trigger.

The building shook as the first 105-millimeter high-explosive round struck the foundation, knocking Grunfeld to the floor and ruining Ephraim's shot. The bullet struck Walid, shattering his skull like a melon. A second cannon round hit the building as the Spectre gunship roared overhead, its Allison engines sounding to Grunfeld like the drone of a B-17 over Dresden. The East German dropped to the floor, looking at the wild face of Ivan Ilyich Kurtz staring at him in wonder. The old general pulled Kurtz through the doorway. Both men coughed from plaster dust shaken loose in the Spectre's opening salvo. The lights failed as the third round hit. Outside, the sound of gunfire grew louder. The East German antiaircraft battery finally engaged, making a *pop-pop* sound. It was answered by a chainsaw buzz.

"That's it!" Cartwright shouted triumphantly. "Our team is landing. That's a minigun cuttin' loose out there. It's gotta be your guys or mine."

Sabrina Rabin grabbed Cartwright's shoulder. "I smell smoke," she said. A fire had broken out in the complex and smoke was invading the shaft.

"I strongly urge we unass this vent," Cartwright growled. Ephraim abandoned his sniper rifle and used an Uzi to batter open the vent. He dropped to the floor with the others following. Cartwright landed hard. "We're gonna have to find someplace to lay low for a bit," he groaned. Cocking his ear to the sound of the minigun, he said, "That's some terrible shit going on out there."

Ephraim seized his Uzi. "Wrath of God has not finished its mission," he cried out. "We will seek safety when the job is done."

An ammunition dump blew and thousands of rounds popped like firecrackers amid heavier explosions of antiaircraft artillery shells. "You can't kill anybody if you're dead," Cartwright shouted. "Follow me and let's find a hole. We've got to snatch us a couple of these bastards and take their gas masks. No telling what's gonna leak out of this Pandora's box."

Cartwright moved into the hallway, his assault rifle ready. Sabrina waved at her comrades. "He is right," she said. The Israeli assassins looked at each other, then they also followed Cartwright. They heard the ominous chainsaw buzz outside and hugged the wall, coughing dust and smoke as they moved. They heard the steady, repetitive *bam-bam* report of the Spectre's cannon.

Aboard the Spectre, pilot and copilot remained busy at the controls of their fabulous four-engine fighter. The AC-130 Hercules gunship was a big transport, but its crew handled it like a fighter. "The night belongs to us," Maj. Evan "Lucky" Locklear, the Spectre pilot, declared. Taraki radar had been jammed by its sister ship, the Combat Talon. The Spectre lit targets with infrared light as the loader jammed forty-two-pound shells into the breech at six rounds per minute, taking out several "zoo gun" antiaircraft batteries.

The pilot watched the Low Light Level Television monitor that turned night into day. The electronic warfare officer, using the Black Crow set that tracked heat from ignition systems, announced, "I identify tanks in the open. Looks like the Ho Chi Minh trail on Friday night down there."

"Take 'em out," Lucky Locklear ordered, banking his gunship in a left pylon turn to aim the 105-millimeter tank-killer gun. The fire control officer laid the big gun on a tank and activated the 7.62-millimeter rotary Vulcan minigun to hose down ground troops. The Spectre fought like a tank with wings. "Fire Control to Lucky. We are truly death from above."

To General Reinhard Grunfeld, the night looked like the last weeks outside Berlin. The attack had achieved total surprise. But panzer officers were not easily bowed. He heard the roaring of the Spectre engines overhead and angrily grabbed a radio handset from a slain infantryman. "Grenadier Airborne Element, this is Werewolf leader," he announced.

"Werewolf leader, this is Jagdeschwader Ein," the squadron commander of the attack helicopter squadron responded. "We are observing fire at your location. What orders do you have, Werewolf leader?"

"A simple order, idiot!" Grunfeld shouted into the microphone. "Stop observing and start fighting! Neutralize the attacking aircraft, and I will rally the ground element."

Grunfeld looked around the chaos on the plant grounds. Corpses lay strewn about and the light from scores of fires made the factory seem a vision from Dante. A panicked Taraki officer drove by Grunfeld in a GAZ jeep. Grunfeld snapped off a round and the jeep careened into a revetment. Grunfeld shoved the dead officer aside and drove hastily for his field headquarters and the missile sites.

— 63 —
The Look-down War

Over Tarak

THE PRESIDENT GAZED TRANSFIXED AT the screens, eyes roving from the menacing video dots near Dimona to the battle in Tarak. The president's video "eye in the sky" arrived via Spectre gunship relay to the Blackbird spy plane, which uplinked to a MILSTAR satellite. Suddenly, the president realized that if the world were to end, he would watch the Apocalypse on television. His own combat experience failed to prepare him for the sight of the Spectre minigun cutting down infantry like wheat. "That's murder," he murmured.

"Sir, the gunship won't get all the troops at that plant before Delta lands," Madeline Murdoch said. "And it's a damn shame. If they have any fight left in them, they'll be killing our men. Also, the Tarakis have moved up their tanks."

The president nodded. Without looking away, he asked, "Have we any word from the Taraki government?"

"None, sir. It's baffling. No message from the presidential palace or the foreign ministry. No message at all."

"Delta will reach objective in less than two minutes, sir," General Kelly said. Suddenly, the new Osprey transports swung into the range of Spectre's cameras. "That's it," Kelly announced. "Delta's going in."

The lead Osprey tilted its engines from fixed-wing to rotor mode, converting the craft to an assault helicopter. Black night became a ball of flame as the transports hurtled to target. In the cockpit between the pilots, Colonel Jefferson blinked his eyes rapidly. For Delta, night vision would not be high priority. The plant was a ring of fire. Jefferson glanced at the glowing cockpit displays, which showed the other Ospreys flying tight formation. "Here's to Otto Skorzeny," Jefferson muttered to himself.

"What's that, Delta Six?" the pilot asked.

"Just admiring your flying," Jefferson said, grinning, as the pilot initiated a stomach-lurching descent. Jefferson moved aft past the huddled figures of Glassman, Colin Davis, and Major Mellors. "This is Delta Six," Jefferson announced to the blackened faces staring at him in the racketing, shaking darkness of the transport. "All okay?"

In one voice, the Delta operators volleyed back, "Delta Six, Alpha Troop, all okay!"

"Two minutes!" Jefferson shouted. "Don your protective masks. Remember, the masks stay on until the CBN operators effect a complete tox sweep." Jefferson felt his heart pumping and his breath coming in short gasps. "As we initiate contact, I want you people to remember one thing. Airborne troops always face overwhelming odds on the ground. Men of Delta, acquit yourselves." The men of Delta, as one, shouted, "Ho!"

"Good hunting," Jefferson shouted. The operators donned masks, looking like a Martian war party. The transport descended to treetop level and zoomed by the outer ring of the East German air defense. The ZSU guns popped ominously and their muzzles flashed, but Delta flew onward. Sweat streamed down Adam Glassman's face. The aircraft shuddered, the doors opened, and the men of Delta walked into the fire.

— 64 —
Desantniki

STANDING IN THE COCKPIT OF the lurching transport, General Yevgeny Strelnikov acknowledged the radio order from the Defense Ministry with a curt *"Da."* The Ilyushin-76 pilot announced eleven minutes to the dropping zone. Strelnikov checked his watch and saw he had two minutes before beginning jump preparations. As the pilot initiated descent to altitude for jump formation and radar evasion maneuvers, Strelnikov's stomach rushed. Keying the internal intercom, Strelnikov bellowed, *"Tovarishi, desantniki*—comrades, paratroopers—prepare yourselves! We've come a long way since Kabul!"

A battle cry of "Strelnikov!" erupted from the troops. The general stared into the dark recess of the roaring transport. Seeing his boys laden with weapons and equipment, their heads covered in simple leather helmets of airborne troops, Strelnikov's heart swelled with a feeling akin to love. Yet he knew he would spend their lives like kopeks if orders came.

"Strelnikov!" the troops chorused again as the right paratroop door yawned open into the thundering night. Strelnikov tightened his chinstrap and hooked his static line. The altimeter on his reserve pack parachute read five hundred feet. The green light flashed, and Strelnikov's regiment began stepping into the windstream, filling the night sky with hundreds of blossoming parachutes. Within thirty seconds, the *desantniki* hit the ground, moving toward the fire in the distance that was the Taraki plant.

— 65 —
The Gate of Hell

The Plant in Tarak

KURTZ STUMBLED IN THE PASSAGEWAY and fell to his knees, coughing. "Grunfeld!" he cried through the smoke. "Grunfeld, where are you?" The general was gone. Kurtz crawled like a miner in a collapsing shaft, moving toward the noise of a generator. His hand touched something wet. It was the shattered face of a Taraki guard.

"*Horosho*," Kurtz grunted. He tugged the guard's gas mask from his belt, donning it quickly. He snatched the guard's pistol and stumbled toward his lab where tubular steel columns of Tabun nerve gas and the sickle-cell viral agent spoors waited, ready to be loaded onto the warheads that were not yet ready for launch.

Outside, weapons fire screeched and whined, the rounds and bombs slamming into their targets with distinctive *thump*s.

Ivan Ilyich Kurtz, veteran of Vietnam and Afghanistan, didn't care. In battle, only the result was important. He reached a steel door and swung it open. Inside the cathedrallike chamber of the lab, a half-dozen Taraki chemical workers huddled. Like Kurtz, they wore protective masks and their collective breathing made a gargling noise. His assistants ran to him as though to a father, and he shot them one by one.

314

Moving past the dying workers, Kurtz stepped up to a small console. Finding he could not ignore the screams of the dying, he went from one to another, administering the coup de grace until he ran out of bullets. He returned to the console and switched power on. The unit still functioned. He got a readout on prevailing winds and listened to the gunfire outside. Rising from the console, he gazed up at the forty-foot-high canisters of chemical agent with their venting pipes that protruded through the roof. The spoors carrying the sickle-cell agent were lighter than thistles. All they needed was a gentle east wind to travel to Jerusalem.

As Jefferson's ground team rushed out of their aircraft, Adam Glassman watched the roof team rappel down the side of the main building, their silenced H & K machine pistols blasting windows with a quiet plunking noise as the men swung toward them. As the roof team's Osprey flew away, it dropped parachute flares holding chemical detection sensors. Fighting in protective gear was daunting, with each man losing precious body fluids. A team of CBN specialists fanned out, ready to blast an air horn when the tox sweep was complete.

Each trooper scouted for slain or wounded enemy soldiers to see if they wore gas masks. The Spectre roared overhead, its searchlight exposing the T-55 tanks that rumbled toward the gate. Rangers armed with Dragon missiles crawled to high ground above the highway. The lead tank stopped. The tank commander and loader unbuttoned and fired their machine guns up at the droning Spectre. A Dragon missile whooshed from its tube. "Target!" the Ranger shouted.

It was a clean hit on the turret ring. The missile ignited the turret ammo. The exploding tank halted the other two T-55s, which backed into defilade, their tank commanders buttoning up hastily. To Glassman, huddled behind Jefferson at the edge of the vehicle park, the attack was utter chaos. Bodies littered the ground. Occasionally there was a hurried movement in the darkness at the end of the building, and Delta machine gunners would fire a burst. Hunched down next to Colin Davis and Mellors, Jefferson gave a steady stream of commands into a backpack radio connected to his mask.

The chemical team blasted the air horn. Jefferson unmasked

and shouted into his bullhorn, "Delta teams and Rangers, you are clear to unmask and advance." Silently the fire teams moved out. Turning to Glassman and the SAS men, Jefferson barked, "You ready?" The Brits nodded. Jefferson gave a hand signal and advanced. "We've got to unass this area," Jefferson said to Glassman, pointing to barrels filled with oil and diesel. "It's gonna be the Fourth of July when it goes."

"I know," Glassman said. "I've bombed fuel dumps." Jefferson grinned, his camouflaged face demonic in the flames and smoke.

General Grunfeld wheeled the little GAZ jeep up a ravine on high ground overlooking the plant. "Halt," a sharp young voice cried and rounds whizzed by the general's head. Grunfeld mashed the gears on the GAZ jeep and tumbled out, hugging dirt.

"Give the password," the voice bleated.

"Idiot," Grunfeld growled. "This is Werewolf leader. If you are going to shoot, kill me."

"*Jawohl, Herr General*," the sentry said, his voice faltering as he recognized the rasp of Grunfeld's hacksaw voice. Grunfeld strode toward the sentry as though he would walk over him. "They are shooting down there," the sentry said, pointing toward the fires. "I imagined I should be shooting, too."

Grunfeld laughed hollowly. "And so you shall. But at the enemy, not your general."

The ramp lowered on the BTR armored carrier that served as Grunfeld's command vehicle. A colonel ran forward. "All is in readiness, Herr General Grunfeld."

"To hell with readiness," Grunfeld growled. "Let's fight!" Grunfeld climbed aboard the BTR armored car and grabbed the radio, calling out for the attack helicopters. "Shoot down that goddamned bomber, Werewolf air element," Grunfeld shouted into the mike.

Grunfeld keyed his mike several times to activate the unit radio net. "Werewolf panzers, this is Werewolf leader," he announced. "All ground elements except for missile security teams advance. We attack at dawn."

"*Herr General*," the driver cried out. "Who are we attacking?"

"Zionist bastards," Grunfeld growled from under his steel plate. "They made short work of the Taraki tankers. Now it is our turn. German armor will give them something to chew on." The general grinned as though he were on the advance to Warsaw half a lifetime ago. He slapped the driver's helmet, and the BTR groaned forward. All along the hills, tanks and infantry of Gruppen Grunfeld began advancing.

Half a world away in the White House, the Spectre's gunship camera blacked out, and the president turned from the screen, glowering at the chairman of the Joint Chiefs. "Could be a satellite failure, sir," the general said.

"Don't soap me, General," the president snapped. "The gunship is down, isn't it?" General Kelly nodded somberly in the affirmative.

"You've still got a backup relay from the Blackbird," Madeline Murdoch said, leaning forward and putting her hand on the president's shoulder. "We've lost video, but we can get an audio report from General Rawlinson."

"We lost more than video. We lost some good men, goddammit," the president growled.

"And we'll lose more before the night is out," Madeline Murdoch said grimly. Seventy-five thousand feet above the battle zone, the Blackbird loitered with Major Ed Rogers monitoring sensor systems and screens. By satellite relay General Rawlinson confirmed, "The Spectre's gone, Rawhide."

The president ordered General Kelly to commit the fleet air arm to screen the return of the Osprey formation for extract. While the Ospreys were being refueled by the Combat Talon, a squadron of F-14 Tomcats and A-7 Intruders screamed from the flight deck of the supercarrier *Saratoga.*

Below ground in the Defense Ministry, Prime Minister Shamir watched video relayed from the Mastiff drones, model airplanes that carried Sony television cameras. The drones had served Israel well in 1982, enabling the Jewish state to knock out the Syrian SA-6 batteries in the Bekaa Valley.

"Who would imagine such a day?" Shamir observed to David Ben Lavi. "The Americans joining battle with the Tarakis and the Germans."

David Ben Lavi snorted. "The Americans will bungle it."

"You had better hope they do not, my friend," Shamir said. "If they fail, the Jericho missile flies." A general shuffled through the gaggle of cabinet officers. "Mr. Prime Minister, target coordinates are set."

Shamir signed a flimsy, then handed it to the defense minister for countersignature. It was the executive order that would decree a state of military emergency in Israel and authorize a nuclear strike on Tarak.

Col. Frederick Jefferson heard the approaching armor. Picking up the bullhorn, he shouted his battle order. "Rangers, this is Delta Six. I want another Dragon team on the high ground." He turned to Glassman. "Unless we nail the tanks, there will be no Delta force."

The Dragon team scuttled up the hill, joining a skirmish line of Rangers armed with light antitank weapons. It would take a lot of shoulder-fired LAW rockets to stop a Russian tank. Delta's hold on the plant was precarious despite the easy slaughter of Taraki guards. The fire from the downed Spectre sent heat waves shimmering across the disputed real estate. The East German armor advanced, PT-76 light tanks joined by BTR infantry carriers. "Antiarmor teams, engage at will," Jefferson shouted into the bullhorn. "Entry team, prepare to crack the building."

Some thoughtful Taraki guard had locked the door to the main building. Fire teams tossed grenades through a window, and a Delta trooper followed the blast, firing as he leaped. The steel doors swung open from the inside.

"Let's go, fly guy," Jefferson grunted. He abandoned cover behind a smoldering GAZ jeep and ran serpentine. A roving Hind attack helicopter stitched a line of machine-gun bullets. The Hind operator unstitched Jefferson's right leg at the calf, and the Delta commander fell. "Damn," he shouted as he lay exposed, with the Hind turning for a second pass.

Glassman trained his machine pistol skyward with the eye of a fighter pilot and fired a long burst, killing the chopper pilot. The Hind plunged nose down, groaning like a compactor in a wrecking yard as it struck the ground. Glassman sprinted across the open space and manhandled Jefferson to the plant door. "Medic!" Glassman shouted.

"Fuck the medic," Jefferson snarled. "Unsnap my pressure bandage. As Glassman fumbled with the shoulder pack, Jefferson methodically cut his denim open with a fighting knife taken from the boot of his bloody leg. "Missed the artery," he observed professionally. "I'm gonna live if I don't get my ass killed." Jefferson tied the wound off and used Glassman to steady himself. He pulled himself to full height and leaned on the leg. "I'm gimped," he said painfully. "But I can shag ass if I have to."

Joined by the stoic Sgt. Major Walker, the Delta commander rapped out his orders. "Secure the inner perimeter here, Country. Get on the horn to the fence team and try to get a sitrep from the missile site."

"Affirmative, Colonel," Sergeant Major Walker said. "You men," he shouted to an M-60 machine gun team, huddled just inside the door, "I want a one-hundred-eighty-degree field of fire from the far end of the building. Take a LAW team with you." The machine gunners disappeared down the smoky hallway.

"Fly guy and me are gonna link up with the roof team and recon the area to set charges. You are in command at the door, Sergeant Major." As he spoke, another Hind helicopter dropped down, scanning through the windows with its searchlight like an enormous insect seeking a meal. Before it could fire, a rocket smashed into its fuselage.

"Stung him!" Country Walker shouted jubilantly. "I knew our Stinger boys was as good as the Muj if you give 'em half a chance." The Hind dropped to earth, funneling black smoke into the building. Jefferson jerked his thumb at Glassman and hobbled inside.

Capt. Max Schleuter, deputy commander of the SCUD-B missile site, watched the glowing red sky and listened to the explosions from the plant. After endless Warsaw Pact drills, it suddenly dawned on him he might have to fight for his life. He watched his section sergeants and lieutenants hurrying about. Standing inside the missile command vehicle, he felt as though he were watching a movie. A Foxbat interceptor screamed by, leaving a sonic crack in its trail.

Schleuter watched the missile battery commander. He was old, like Grunfeld. An old Hitlerite. Schleuter hoped the bastard knew what he was doing. Volkmann put down the radio mike and turned to Captain Schleuter. "Give the order to raise missiles on their launchers, Hauptmann Schleuter," Volkmann ordered.

Schleuter looked into the officer's coal black eyes and saw something disturbing. A tingling at the back of his neck told him that something was wrong here, desperately wrong. "Oberst, in a Warsaw Pact formation an order to prepare for launch would come from theater level," Schleuter said hesitantly.

The East German missile operators at the controls watched the officers furtively. They had been going through systems checks to verify launch readiness. Now an order was questioned. Extraordinary. "An order has been given, Hauptmann Schleuter," Volkmann said calmly. "We are under attack. Prepare missiles for launch on my command."

Schleuter's throat was dry. He could feel instinct warning him to disobey this strange old man, regardless of his superior rank. "I must have a higher authorization," Schleuter said bravely. "Since we seized the missile battery and imprisoned the Russian crew operators, there has been no communication from higher than battalion level."

Volkmann picked up the microphone and handed it to Schleuter. "We will speak directly with Fraternal Forces Directorate in the capital at Kharmat." As Schleuter accepted the microphone, Volkmann pulled a pistol from his holster and blew the captain's brains out. Turning to the operators, he smiled. "Now," he said, "prepare for missile launch."

The operators turned the knobs and threw the switches activating the hydraulics on the SCUD-B launcher, raising the thirty-foot-high missile to launch position with a metallic groan. The other five rockets in the SCUD battery rose into the night sky. Their launch coordinates and fuse settings were preset. The missiles stood poised like darts, aimed for the Dimona reactor and assigned secondary targets.

— 66 —
The Apocalyptic Moment

The Plant in Tarak

MELLORS AND COLIN DAVIS MADE their way down the passage-way, firing short bursts. Delta sappers unreeled detonation wire behind them. As they turned a corner, Davis searched for Sabrina Rabin's escape route. He threw a concussion grenade around the corner. The grenade whumped, prompting a cry in the hallway. "One more for good measure, Colin," Mellors grunted from his mask, and tossed a fragmentation grenade. The pair waited until the screams subsided, and scurried past the open space. They came upon a large steel door. "That's it," Davis said, diving past the entry. Moving through a small antechamber with rubber suits hanging on pegs, they low-crawled into the lab. They spotted the corpses piled on the floor and looked up to see a blond man with a white scar on his forehead gazing intently at an instrument console.

Seeing the commandos, Ivan Ilyich Kurtz was strangely calm. His pale blue eyes seemed to glaze over at the carnage before him. Spotting the Union Jack patches on their jacket sleeves, Kurtz spoke in stiffly formal English. "You are unwelcome. This is a pharmaceutical research facility on sovereign territory, and I demand that you cease your criminal assault, which violates international law," he said haughtily.

"The bloke's gone potty," Colin Davis muttered.

"You the chap running this waxworks, then?" Mellors asked, looking around at the gas canisters leading up to the venting pipes in the ceiling.

"He's the sod, all right," Colin Davis remarked. "He tried to carve me up like Christmas turkey, Major."

"Please," Kurtz said, raising his hand. "Lay a finger on me and I will release enough gas and combined biological agent in those canisters to kill every Jew in the Middle East, and some tens of thousands of Arabs as well." Outside the building the din of high explosive rounds shook the building anew. Colin Davis moved grimly toward Kurtz.

"I say kill the sod," Colin Davis shouted, aiming his machine pistol at Kurtz.

"Hold off, Colin!" Mellors cried out. "He'll turn the knob while the bloody bullets strike."

Kurtz sat calmly, his left hand on a control knob. He was smiling as the grenades bounced through the door, sliding across the concrete floor like deadly eggs. They exploded in rapid succession, showering glass and splinters across the room.

The filthy, ragged figures of Cartwright and the Israelis staggered in. Cartwright methodically picked up the machine pistol flung from Mellors's hand when the concussion grenades exploded, and fired insurance bursts under the lab tables. He moved past Kurtz, slumped facedown on the instrument console. Coming through the inner door, Abraham grabbed the heavy body of Colin Davis by his battle jacket. Davis, bleeding from the ears and mouth, was facedown as Ephraim prepared to shoot him behind the ear.

Sabrina Rabin screamed at Ephraim, "Look! He is our English!" Sabrina grabbed his gun hand. The gun came free in Ephraim's fingertips, and its hair trigger slipped as he tried to retrieve it. The pistol made a dry *punk* sound as it clattered to the floor. Sabrina's lips formed a startled "Oh," as she stumbled and fell.

Dropping Colin Davis, Abraham stared horrified at Sabrina. He turned in disgust and anger to Ephraim as the blood swelled beneath the ragged khaki of her shirt. "You shot her!" he cried out.

"He was mine to save," Sabrina Rabin gasped, her fingers caressing Colin Davis's rough-hewn face. "I saved him before. And he saved me. We owe one another."

As Sabrina bled, Cartwright used a bayonet to slice a slain chemical worker's lab coat. He cut a good-sized square, folded it, and ripped Sabrina's khaki shirt open. He grabbed Abraham's hand and held it down on the hasty dressing. "Keep the pressure on," he ordered.

Cartwright looked down at the pools of chemicals spilled on the floor. "Drag her out of this stink hole," he ordered. "No telling what witch's brew is spilled out in here." Meekly, Abraham scooped Sabrina up in his massive arms and carried her out.

Ephraim stepped over to Kurtz and prodded his body with a bayonet, then grabbed the blond Russian by the collar. He was still alive. Ephraim shouted triumphantly. "It's Kurtz. We've got the target!"

The lean assassin retrieved his dropped pistol, and Cartwright yelled, "Wait a minute, buddy. You gonna take him out in cold blood?" Ephraim sneered uncomprehendingly at Cartwright and fired.

As Ephraim shot the blond Russian, Kurtz's blue eyes popped open in a sudden twitch, and he clutched the console knob, turning it in reflex, like a snake that strikes after death. The readout display next to the console started spewing pages of data into a high-speed printer.

"Jesus Christ, man," Cartwright shouted. "What have you done? That dingus could be the trigger for the whole operation here."

Transfixed, the two men watched the data roll out of the printer. Cartwright ran around the console, booting Kurtz's body off the chair. He grabbed at the first sheets of paper and looked up in wonder at Ephraim.

"It's a weather report," Cartwright murmured in quiet awe. "It's a sonofabitching weather report." Ephraim sank on his knees to the floor.

Outside the main building the Rangers fired a hail of LAW rockets into the armored carriers and tanks crashing through the wire. Most of the Rangers in the forward positions died in place, riddled by coaxial-machine-gun fire. The ones that didn't blazed away at East German infantry that dismounted from the burning BTR carriers. The East Germans formed skirmish lines and advanced.

Three PT-76 tanks tore through the wire, firing smoke grenades. Emerging through the smoke, the lead tank struck a mine placed by the Ranger sappers. It blew the tank tread, but the PT-76 crew continued firing. The tanks behind the crippled lead track fired their co-ax guns, but they in turn suffered a fresh barrage of LAW hits.

General Grunfeld jumped to the ground from the burning PT-76 and grabbed a rocket grenade and assault rifle from a wounded grenadier who cried for his mother. "Forward, you bastards!" Grunfeld shouted. "Fight like SS men!" he screamed, just as a round struck the steel plate that covered his face, knocking the East German general to the ground. A burst of machine-gun fire stitched his body, making it twitch like a marionette.

At the Delta command post just inside the main building, Sergeant Major Walker huddled behind a barricade of steel desks, watching the fight on ground-surveillance radar. The radar showed a fresh wave of enemy infantry pouring the wire and fanning out on the Ranger flanks.

"We're not gonna make it, Captain," Walker shouted at Ishimoto, the intelligence officer. "We're running out of LAW rockets. We're running out of ammo, and we're running out of Rangers. It's time to dial up the extract team."

Ishimoto put down the radio mike and said, "Delta Six says the charges are almost set."

"Roger that, Captain. But if we don't have some effective air cover, the extract airlift might as well bring mops and body bags." A rocket-propelled grenade zoomed over their heads.

"Linebacker, this is Scalpel," Ishimoto said, giving his call sign to the Blackbird hovering on the edge of space. "Our situation is going critical. Send the cavalry over."

—— 67 ——
Blackbird's Bluff

Airborne over the Middle East

FIFTEEN MILES ABOVE EARTH, THE Blackbird soared, training its sharp electronic eyes on the men who fought in the dirt. As the combatants sucked the dust of Tarak into their parched lungs, General Rawlinson breathed pure oxygen, banking the spy plane with delicate, almost surgical corrections.

"I wonder if you're down there somewhere, Scott," Rawlinson murmured. "And I pray God they can bring you home if you are." Realizing his internal microphone was in the On position, he quickly stopped his musing. If word got out that the old man was talking to himself at altitude, he'd fly a desk forever.

In the backseat Maj. Ed Rogers tracked the scopes, radar screens, infrared detection displays, and alarm lights. The Blackbird fired a blast of white heat from its tail as it sailed at Mach 4, pulsing radar beams earthward and soaking up ground imagery with its sensors. To Rogers, the work of reconnaissance systems operator was like the computer software chess games he played, regularly beating his electronic opponent. Rogers gazed raptly as his scope lit up with little symbols that looked like fireflies dancing. "General, I'm getting sensor hits out of the Negev!"

"On the air or the ground?" Rawlinson demanded.

"The ground, sir," Rogers replied. "I am getting an indication of increased radiation in the same vicinity as site one."

"You're sure?"

"Sir, the radiation is coming from Dimona!" Rogers said breathlessly. "The increase in infrared is coming from site one."

"Jesus," Rawlinson groaned. He radioed the White House. "Rawhide, this is Linebacker. We've got a problem." As the Blackbird banked, Rogers adjusted sensors to illuminate Dimona, where the Jericho missiles were poised, ready for launch.

Deep below the Defense Ministry, orders for the Israeli Defense Forces came rapidly. Map positions of alert units changed by the minute, shifting toward the Sinai, the Golan Heights, the Lebanon Security Zone, and particularly the Taraki border strip. Seated just a few feet from the hurry of the general staff, Shamir cut a lonely figure. Cabinet members were arriving in pairs, their expressions anxious.

"The hour is arrived, I fear," the prime minister said. Pointing to the screen, Shamir swept his hand across the shadowy battle in Tarak playing out in grainy black and white images transmitted back by the drones. "Our enemy is poised to launch medium-range missiles packed with chemical warheads and perhaps a germ agent of devastating lethality," the prime minister said. "And as we monitor the situation, we are watching an earnest but ill-fated American raiding party get chopped to bits by a rump army from the East Bloc."

The prime minister sighed. "We will launch a single nuclear-tipped missile to cauterize the boil. Then, my brothers, there will be war." Immediately, the cabinet members from Likud began vilifying the Labor members, and the Labor minister shot insults at the Likud bloc.

"Enough!" the prime minister shouted, imposing silence by sheer force of will. "This discussion is not political. It is military, and the decision is taken."

"How can you do this?" the senior minister from Labor demanded.

The prime minister's face was suddenly serene. "Would you

have me deliver our families to the fate of the Jews of Europe? I will not do it.''

The Labor minister hung his head and wept. The commander of the strategic rocket forces whispered to the prime minister. The old man picked up the phone. The general whispered to each of the ministers that the president of the United States was on the line.

''Mr. Prime Minister,'' the president said. ''You must be aware of the perilous course you are undertaking.''

The prime minister activated a speaker phone so the cabinet members might hear. ''And you, Mr. President, must be aware that your fighters are outnumbered and your raid is failing.''

''Sir, I was calling to give you new information, new facts,'' the American president said urgently.

''We think we are sufficiently aware,'' the prime minister haughtily replied. ''As a result of your raid, there is a regiment of Soviet troops air dropping on the eastern border of Israel. This is a new and different danger. Still, we will deal with it.''

''You hard-headed son of bitch!'' the president growled. ''Would you start a world war to keep a few battalions of shock troops out of the region?''

''The Russians are a secondary consideration, Mr. President. The missiles of Tarak threaten our survival,'' the prime minister said. ''We will not allow it.''

The president breathed deeply. ''I understand, sir, and I will tell you what *I* will not allow. At this moment, through our reconnaissance platforms, we know your Jericho missiles are launch ready. Unless they are demobilized immediately, we are prepared to destroy them.''

''So,'' the prime minister said. ''Finally it comes to this. The promises of friendship over a lifetime mean nothing.''

''Mr. Prime Minister,'' the president said, ''You are not acting as a friend. You are giving me no choice. Our strike force at this moment is in the process of dismantling the Taraki offensive capability.''

The prime minister eyed the screens. Even he was impressed. But he was enough of a soldier himself to assess that the Americans could not hold out long against the East German armored assault.

''The state of Israel possesses its own reconnaissance, Mr.

President. Our systems show us that the foreign forces in Tarak are on the verge of dismantling your strike force. What you cannot prevent, we must remove. An animal with its back to the wall must defend itself.''

The prime minister continued, ''Your threat to harm Dimona is empty. The missile site is secure, even from an ICBM, for at least thirty minutes. Should we decide to use our much-discussed nuclear option, our missiles will hit their targets before you finish a launch command or order up a bomber.''

''Not so, sir,'' the president responded. ''As we speak, there is a nuclear-armed bomber loitering within striking range of your arsenal at Dimona. It will drop its warload on my command. Within six seconds, your vaunted atomic arsenal will cease to exist.''

The prime minister turned to the Israeli air force chief. ''Can this be true?'' he snapped.

The air force chief shook his head. ''There is no such aircraft. The Stealth bomber is not yet operational.''

The prime minister returned to the telephone. ''Mr. President, with great respect, I must rely on the judgment of my air force chief, and he tells me there is no such aircraft. I do not believe you.''

''Mr. Prime Minister, can your air force chief's radar spot an aircraft moving at four times the speed of sound and an altitude in excess of one hundred thousand feet?''

The Israeli prime minister turned to his air force commander. The officer shook his head. Then he added, ''We do not classify such an aircraft in the American inventory.''

''Mr. President, we are skeptical,'' the prime minister said.

At the president's order, the chairman of the Joint Chiefs radioed the Blackbird. ''Linebacker, decrease your speed to Mach 3 indicated air speed and your altitude to sixty-five thousand feet. Tell your RSO to illuminate the missile site using pulse Doppler radar.''

''This is Linebacker,'' Rawlinson responded. ''Will you repeat message, over? I want to make sure Rawhide understands we will be exposed to SAM fire or fighter pursuit during descent, over.''

The Pentagon chief repeated the president's order. Rawlinson replied, "That's a good copy, Rawhide. Linebacker will comply. Out."

By the time thirty seconds blinked by, the Israeli air force chief looked up from a radar scope, awed by what he saw. "There is an unidentified aircraft on the scope firing a pulse beam, Mr. Prime Minister," he said. "Most likely a variation of the American spy plane that we downed recently."

The prime minister rubbed his forehead with his thick fingers. "Your information is confirmed, Mr. President," the Israeli prime minister said wearily, coughing to clear his throat. "But where does that leave us? You are circling our territory with an unarmed spy plane, nothing more."

"Ask your air force chief again," the president said. "Ask him if we could load the Blackbird with a nuke. Tell him it's a B-77 free-fall weapon in the single-megaton class."

The prime minister whirled, fixing his gaze on the air force commander. The commander nodded his head grimly. "It could be armed in the manner described."

The prime minister returned to the line and said, "The state of Israel will not allow itself to be provoked or threatened."

As he spoke, the air force chief frantically grabbed his arm, "Mr. Prime Minister!" he exclaimed. "The intruder aircraft is in a power dive."

The Blackbird was indeed diving. General Rawlinson was laughing, a hoarse, cackling laugh unheard since he rode the tailpipe of a MiG and killed it high over Haiphong harbor. "General, what the hell are you doing to this aircraft?" Ed Rogers screamed as the black plane dived.

"They want to know what this baby can do, we'll show 'em!" Rawlinson barked back. In its dive the Blackbird, powered by its enhanced ramjets, was exceeding Mach 5 and plunging toward the Israeli terra firma like a black boulder. "It's got the record for climb rate. Let's try for dive."

"Jesus, sir!" Rogers shouted as Mach and altitude indicators blurred. "Jesus wept!" Rawlinson shouted back.

On the streets of Jerusalem, jeep patrols and aircraft observers heard the black plane's roar first. Then they saw the Blackbird, and everyone who witnessed it shivered. Sonic booms from Israeli F-16s knocked holes in the air as they tried to catch up to the dropping dark thing, yet it flew on heedless of them and the air raid sirens it triggered. "We're running out of sky," Rogers yelled.

"Roger that," Rawlinson replied, his voice calm as he throttled back and flared the plane less than five thousand feet off the deck. Stabilizing it, he pushed the nose up and throttled forward again, putting the huge black plane into a steep climb. The G forces nearly crushed Rogers back in the backseat. "We're gonna die," Rogers groaned.

The F-16s were closing, but the Blackbird was climbing faster. "Take evasive measures!" Rawlinson shouted.

Rogers threw every ECM switch he had, to confuse the missile darts that were sure to come. On the ground an Israeli Hawk battery commander tracked the Blackbird's fiery tailpipes. The missile shots came, and the Blackbird outran them.

"It's a Collier trophy job, and they'll never know it, Wolfman," Rawlinson shouted. "But you and I will, boy. You and I will, and God willing, maybe Colonel Glassman and Major General Scott Cortland Cartwright."

As the ramjets of the Blackbird powered it heavenward, a lone Israeli F-16 pursued, its determined pilot firing each of his air-to-air missiles as he climbed to record height at record speed. Frantically Rogers watched and listened for tones, hyperventilating inside his helmet. He hung on as the warning tones faded. Then, he looked in horror at a red light on his panel. "Not again," he whispered. "Please, God. Not again."

The prime minister rubbed his eyes as the Blackbird mysteriously vanished off screen. Quietly, over the telephone, he said, "You made your point, Mr. President. What now?"

"You may choose to nuke the plant at Tarak and cause a general war, but would your people really want that? I have two hundred and fifty million of my own people to consider."

The prime minister held the telephone, his hand trembling. He looked up at the faces surrounding him. At the moment none wanted to argue or advise. Clearing his throat, the prime minister said, "What do you propose, Mr. President?"

"Let my raiders finish," the president said. "My ground team leader has a plan to render the plant harmless. Should the raiders fail, we will make a decision together."

"What if there is not time?"

"If my team fails, I will direct my lone bomber toward the plant at Tarak and communicate with the Soviets personally as to our intentions."

The prime minister furrowed his brow and brushed his fingers across his wisps of white hair. He frowned and snuffled. Then he said, "Okay."

"Okay, Mr. Prime Minister," the president rejoined eagerly.

"We will reassess our situation in twenty minutes," the prime minister said. "Let us pray your mission succeeds."

The president and prime minister returned to their television screens, watching the pieces moving on the board. The president grabbed Madeline Murdoch's lace cuff. "Madeline, do you suppose there's a way they could tell that General Rawlinson's plane is unarmed? It's a bluff I'd hate to get called on."

"Oh, God, sir, I hope not," she said. "One can never tell. What do you think, General?" she said, turning to the chairman of the Joint Chiefs.

"They're good," General Kelly said. "Damn good. And we've only got about eighteen minutes to make good on our end before we're in a new ball game."

— 68 —
Cavalry

The Plant in Tarak

THE HIND HELICOPTERS SPRAYED EXPLODING ammunition, splintering the Rangers' forward defense. Sergeant Major Walker watched helplessly as they flew away. "That's my last Ranger on the wire," he told Captain Ishimoto, who lay bleeding from several wounds to the scalp, arm, and chest. "We'd better hope the bad guy's armor takes out this plant, 'cause the snappers ain't gonna get the opportunity."

Country Walker raised the bullhorn and shouted, "Fire teams right and left, gimme a sitrep on ammo status!"

"Alpha fire teams, down to clips," his right flank responded. "Bravo fire teams, same same," a voice from the left flank shouted back.

"It's gonna be small arms and hand-to-hand," Walker yelled. "Make 'em pay for it."

Country Walker raised his night-vision glasses and surveyed the flanks. All along the line he could see the shovel-helmet infantry advancing. There were hundreds, walking forward at a steady pace with good German discipline. Walker knew the men of the Rangers and Delta were down to rounds that numbered in the dozens. The Russian-built attack helicopters were returning, pouring fresh machine-gun fire into the building as the black sky was turning grayish blue with false dawn.

The East German pilot never saw the Huey Sea Cobras or heard the chainsaw rasp of their cannon as the Marine Corps helicopters buzzed over the hillside, flying nap of the earth. The rockets whooshed and dropped the Russian helicopter to earth in a pillar of flame.

Dozens of East German foot soldiers hit the ground, looking for the moment less like shock troops than roaches sprayed by insecticide from the Sea Cobras. The Marine aviators turned their aircraft in unison and directed their cannon and rocket fire at the scattering grenadier line. From inside the main building a ragged cheer erupted from the defenders. Rebel yells accompanied cries of sheer relief or exhaustion. Country Walker grinned, failing to notice Captain Ishimoto had died.

As the gray light of dawn began to stream into the building, Walker ran to join the rifle team popping rounds at a diving enemy helicopter. "The engines, goddammit," Walker shouted. "Fire at the engines, you turkeys!" As he drew a bead on the intakes, he heard the scream of jet engines that suddenly changed pitch. "I am delivered from evil, and mine heart is glad," he whispered.

Through the smoke Walker could see a pair of AV-8B Harrier attack fighters suspended, nearly motionless as their thrust-vector nozzles lifted them. Walker could see the panicked face of the Hind pilot as he attempted to swing the flying tank to face the Harriers. Rockets from one of the Harriers smashed the Hind, creating a fireball. Walker and his men retreated into the building, shielding their faces from the heat and flying debris. The burning Hind dropped to earth like an elevator with a snapped cable. The explosion made Walker's ears ring and singed his eyebrows off. The Harriers rose vertically, high over the building, and scooted forward, seeking new targets on the ground.

Grunfeld lay flat on the hard ground near the main entrance to the plant. He lay bleeding from shrapnel cuts and showered debris, barely alive as he watched the Harriers. "Jew bastards," he groaned. He staggered to his full height and raised his assault rifle, emptying the magazine in one long futile burst as the Harrier's guns blew him to flying bits. Within minutes, pink streaks of the dawn's early light filtered through the acrid smoke that cloaked the battleground. A half-dozen Delta operators scurried outside the building, stringing det wire over the dead. Medics followed the sappers out, dragging the wounded to cover.

Inside the building Jefferson and Glassman trailed the point man through the smoke-filled passages. Delta sappers followed, stopping to place charges. A trooper fired a short burst and tossed a frag grenade, clearing a hallway. "Demo team forward," Jefferson shouted. Glassman pointed out the steel door. "Point!" Jefferson ordered, dropping to the floor and grimacing in pain from his leg wound. "Toss another egg to clear the room."

The point man pulled the safety ring, holding the grenade close to his ear. He low-crawled tight along the wall. As he cocked his arm to throw, a raw voice from inside the shattered door yelled, "Hold your fire, goddammit! You got an American general officer and a bunch of friendlies in here!"

The point man's hand hung in midair, his pressure still on the grenade handle. "Stop!" Glassman shouted. "Cease fire! Cease fire! It's Cartwright!"

The trooper's eyes widened in alarm. "Hold off, trooper," Jefferson ordered. The trooper stared anxiously at the live grenade. "Begging your pardon, sir, what the fuck do you want me to do with it?"

"Hold it, trooper, just like you've been doing," Jefferson snapped. Then the Delta commander shouted, "You people inside the room, identify yourselves!"

"You got Major General Scott Cortland Cartwright here," the general barked back. "I am in this shitty little space with casualties that need immediate medical attention."

Glassman gripped Jefferson's arm. "No doubt about it. That's Cartwright." A minute passed, with the trooper at point watching the door and his live grenade with equal anxiety. The ragged, towering figure of Cartwright stumbled into the hallway, limping and grinning.

"Would you mind disposing of that thing, sonny?" Cartwright said, pointing at the grenade. "Somebody could get hurt."

The point man scrambled forward to the end of the passage and flung the grenade, which exploded and raised a howl in the corridor. The point man fired a quick burst and the howling ceased. An East German machine-gun team had hidden a few feet from Cartwright and the arriving Delta raiders.

It had been nearly an hour since Grunfeld's last transmission. At the SCUD missile battery, Colonel Volkmann ran his fingers through his brush of white hair and anguished over his quandary—to fire or wait for orders. He sensed panic in the operators, who watched him with barely disguised terror. The SCUD missiles were raised, primed, and ready to launch, with only the final arming sequence and his pull of the contact lever needed to send them on their mission of extermination. "How are you boys?" Volkmann demanded of the missile crew with bluff heartiness. "Medals all around. This time we win."

The crewmen returned Volkmann's smile weakly, wondering what the hell the old man was chattering about. Volkmann took a landline telephone call from perimeter security, but the transmission ended abruptly. There was silence, except for the ominous hiss of the missile's liquid propellant. Volkmann squinted into the gray dawn outside the command cabin. He put down the field phone and lifted a pair of night-vision binoculars to take a better look.

The Delta operators dropped from the roof of the carrier, firing a burst of smokeless rounds into the command module. On the ground the ambush squad tripped a thunderous daisy chain of Claymore mines that sprayed lethal fans of steel balls, perforating the East Germans like game fowl. The Delta men had infiltrated the East German line silent as Apaches and fired from the inside out. The assault lasted eight seconds.

The rappelling team levered the door open and swung inside the Zil carrier's cabin, the lead man firing a clearing burst. Resting his butt on his rope outside the cabin, Sgt. Jack Donaghey stared up at the menacing spire of the thirty-foot SCUD-B missile and shivered, hearing the propellant hiss. "Cabin team," Donaghey shouted. "Give me a status."

"All okay inside," the lead man shouted. "Three kills. There's one on the floor I can't account for, but he's dead, too. But, Sarge, there's beaucoup bullshit we don't want to screw with. We got yellow lights and red lights popping on up and down the console. Looks like a Christmas tree."

"Don't touch anything!" Donaghey ordered, swinging into the cabin on his nylon rope. He stared at the console and began to sweat, realizing he understood as much about the controls as he would about flying a space shuttle. He kept his eyes on the console, ignoring the blood and glass that littered the cabin. "Get these sons of bitches off the control panel," he said, indicating the bodies of Volkmann and the crew.

The assault team lifted Volkmann's body off the console. As they did, the dead man's hand brushed the red firing handle. Donaghey grabbed the dead man's wrist, lifting it gently. The sergeant snapped, "You don't want to work much closer than that!" They lowered the bodies out of the cabin as though they were handling nitroglycerin.

With daylight beginning to warm the hills of Tarak, the Delta troopers looked from the cabin to see Soviet tanks advancing on the missile site, joined by hundreds of infantrymen. A pair of menacing swept-wing Foxbat fighters screamed by overhead, flying low and straight at the missile carrier, so close the sergeant could see the intakes and missiles on the wings. "Shit," Donaghey muttered.

— 69 —
Impasse

Washington

IN THE WHITE HOUSE SITUATION Room, the exhausted president watched the Blackbird data screens, rubbing his eyes. Aides gathered around him while General Kelly remained at the radiotelephone link to Delta. The secretary of state held a telephone line open to Tel Aviv. The secretary of defense remained on the line with his counterpart in the Kremlin. Madeline Murdoch and Avery Benedict watched the president. The president patted the Air Force data analyst on the shoulder and said, "What are we getting from the Israelis?"

"It's cold, sir. No launch signature. Same for the Tarakis."

"Anything else I should know?" The president rubbed his temples and loosened his collar.

"We're getting infrared signatures on trucks and tanks moving toward the plant," the analyst replied.

"Russkies or hostiles?"

"Can't say, sir. It's all Russian built." Watching the glowing vehicle signatures on his screen, the analyst offered, "We've got the forward element of the column surrounding the plant on its flank. It's a pincer movement."

The president turned toward his secretary of defense. "Get

me the chairman," he ordered. "I want a clarification on the location of the Soviet troops."

General Kelly waved urgently at the president. "Sir, I have contact with Delta. It's Jefferson."

Ragged applause erupted from some of the Situation Room staff. The president motioned urgently for the radio telephone. "Delta Six, this is Rawhide," the president announced hoarsely. "What's your status?"

"Rawhide, this is Delta Six," Jefferson replied. "Objective is secured, but I have Russian armor on my flanks and the ridge line to my front."

"Delta, can you identify the opposing force?"

"Delta here. I can see the little sailor shirts. Over," Jefferson's voice crackled through the satellite link.

"Have they made a hostile move, Delta?"

"Negative, Rawhide. But I hope they don't whistle. It wouldn't take much to blow us over. My air cover has returned to *Saratoga* for refueling."

"Mr. President," General Kelly nearly shouted. "Get a casualty count!"

The president glared at Kelly, then abashed by his own thoughtlessness, he asked, "Delta, what are your casualties?"

"Rawhide," Jefferson replied buttermilk smooth. "It ain't the Alamo, but it's close. Killed-in-action count is thirty percent of party. After KIAs, seriously wounded is forty percent. We have nearly zeroed our ammo supply. Wait a minute, sir." Jefferson broke off the transmission. The president gripped the radiophone, his knuckles white.

"Rawhide, this is Delta Six. My Bravo element at the missile site is also facing off the Soviet task force. He's got a problem."

"Spit it out, Delta," the president snapped. As he waited for Jefferson's response, the secretary of defense waved, signaling that he had the Kremlin leader on the line.

"Rawhide, this is Delta Six," Jefferson continued. "My Bravo tells me he's got a hot missile. The hostile rocket crew is dead, but their control panel is lit like Times Square at New Year's. My man fears accidental launch."

The president grabbed the red phone from the secretary of defense. "Alexei, this is the president," the chief executive shouted. The interpreter on the Moscow line rapidly repeated his words and approximated his tone. "One of your goddamn rockets is wired for launch at Israel, and it may go at any minute."

Hastily, the interpreter translated the Soviet leader's answer. "The situation you describe is not the responsibility of the Soviet Union," the translator said. "We implored you to let us seize the missiles. It is out of our hands."

"Don't shout, Mr. President," Madeline Murdoch whispered. "It won't help. Find out if they have a missile team of their own, sir. That's what they came for."

The president returned to the line. "Alexei," he said, his tone moderated. "Get your missile team up the hill to my men's position and disarm your rocket. Then we can all go home."

There was a hesitation on the Moscow end. The translator then said, "It would be best if your raiding party surrendered jurisdiction of the contested area. Then our missile team would be guaranteed safe entry to begin the disarming sequence."

"Goddammit, Alexei," the president shouted. "Quit screwing with me! I am trying to keep your country and mine, and the goddamned Israelis, out of a shooting war."

The Soviet translator assured the president that the chairman was considering his proposal.

— 70 —
Encounters at the Elbe

The Plant in Tarak

GLASSMAN REMOVED THE ASBESTOS HOOD of his fire-fighting suit and gazed through a shattered window up at the hills. The Russians surrounding the plant reminded him of Indians in an old John Ford western, silent, cold, hostile. He knelt down by a stretcher. Removing the fireproof mittens, he gently cradled Sabrina Rabin in his arms, oblivious of the groans in the crowded room. The medics had sedated Delta's wounded down to low moans. Some died. Others called for their mothers.

"Hello, baby," Sabrina said weakly, smiling up at Adam.

"Hi," he replied tenderly. "Long time, no see."

"Where did you get the space suit, Colonel Adam?"

Glassman chuckled. "Grabbed it on the run from one of the labs. Had to help the Delta guys put out some spot fires so you could enjoy this luxurious aid station."

"Oh, my Adam," Sabrina said, sighing. "Always saving other people. Always putting out fires. You are too noble." She clasped his arm.

Cartwright stumbled into the chamber full of wounded. Under the grime and dried blood that caked his face, he looked none the worse for wear. He wore a black Delta field jacket and Navy watch cap that made him look like an old longshoreman. "It doesn't look good for the home team, kids," Cartwright said, removing the watch cap and running his fingers through his dirty silver hair. "We could last about a minute if the Russians made a serious push."

"What about the *Saratoga*?" Glassman asked.

"Air cover is eight minutes out, give or take. And if the Ivans start giving, we're up shit creek, I'd say."

"I guess I'm ready to die," Glassman said quietly. "I'd like there to be a reason, though."

Sabrina Rabin lifted her hand and brushed it lightly across Glassman's lips. "Don't die, Adam," she said, smiling painfully. "Live. You just found me again. It was not for nothing. We stopped the missiles."

Glassman kissed her lightly on the forehead. Cartwright hunched down close to Sabrina's face. "Listen to me, honey," he said. "You may make it out of here, and you may not. There's something I've got to hear in case you don't."

"Leave her alone, sir!" Glassman snapped. "She's got to rest."

"And I've got to have the answer, Colonel," Cartwright said tersely. "Sabrina, honey. Did this man work for your people? The truth now. Truth is best."

A trace of a smile crossed her lips, followed by a sharp stab of pain. "What kind of fool are you?" she asked. "He is an American. He is your hero, not ours." The stab of pain widened into a circle, and her eyes welled wide open.

"Cartwright, you son of a bitch," Glassman hissed. "You're killing her!"

Sabrina gripped Adam's arm. "Don't talk nonsense, Adam," she gasped. "I am dying well enough by myself. He never worked for us," she gasped. "If he had asked, I would have worked for him." She closed her eyes tightly, and her fingers dug into Glassman's arm.

She made a small choking sound, and her grip released. Adam shook her slightly, and her arms fell limp. He gazed stonily at Cartwright. The old man grabbed Adam by the shoulders. The general pulled the sobbing Adam and the body of Sabrina Rabin close to him, hugging them tightly.

In the distance, Cartwright heard the whine of jet engines approaching. As he rocked Adam Glassman and Sabrina Rabin, he gazed out the blasted window. Streaking low over the hill-tops, he identified a brace of MiGs making a low pass over the plant. The Russian air cover had arrived first.

From his vantage point in the missile carrier, Sgt. Jack Donaghey watched the Foxbats screaming across the valley toward the plant. He took a swig of water from his plastic bottle and felt the sweat pop from his forehead. The SCUD-B console light danced in front of him, running new variations of digital combinations. The Cyrillic letters on the control panel meant nothing to him. Outside, he heard the hiss of the propellant leaking. Donaghey stared down the gun tubes of the Russian air-dropped tanks massed below his position.

The Delta fighters lying prone on the hillside had machine pistols and grenades to hold back the Russians. They might as well have had rocks. "Whites of their eyes, boys," Donaghey shouted to his mates.

Donaghey squinted and saw three men dismounting a Russian infantry carrier. One waved a white flag. Suddenly, the Delta sergeant shouted, "Troopers, hold your fire! I say again, hold fire!"

Slowly, the trio made its way up the hill. One was a captain in striped shirt and blue beret. The other two wore heavy radiation suits. Donaghey jumped lightly from the Zil carrier. The Russian officer approached at a gingerly pace and saluted. Donaghey licked his lips with his dry tongue and returned the salute. They shook hands.

The Soviet officer climbed into the command carrier with Donaghey and surveyed the rapidly blinking control panel. "Not good," he said in schoolboy English. His rosy cheeks flushed as he sat in a crew operator chair. The Russian shouted a command to the radiation team, and they ascended the ladder outside the cabin up onto the missile gantry. One of them carried a pair of bolt cutters. "Some guts," Donaghey remarked, watching them through the rear window.

"Please, quiet," the Russian officer demanded as he threw toggle switches. Donaghey couldn't help whistling through his teeth as the Russian played the keyboard. The Delta sergeant sucked his breath in, watching a digital readout display spin like a nickel slot machine. Suddenly, the panel buzzed, and Donaghey heard a sound like an air brake hissing.

"*Tovarishi*!" the Russian officer shouted to his comrades outside the cabin. As he yelled, the men in radiation suits squeezed shut the cutters, snapping a pair of hoses that snaked up outside of the missile tube. The rubber hoses whipped crazily like snakes, and the Russians were blasted from the gantry, vanishing in a cloud of hydrazine fuel. The Russian grinned at Donaghey. "Please, to get up," he said awkwardly. "There is no hurt here. We are finish."

"What the fuck happened?" the Delta sergeant moaned.

"It is fuel in the line that flies my men to the ground," the Russian said. "You have medics, yes? My men are maybe hurt."

Donaghey gazed dumbly out the module window to see that the SCUD-B missile rested silently. At the top of his lungs, he screamed, "Medic!"

The sergeant stared at the motionless forms of the Russian soldiers and shook his head. A Delta medic loped up the hill. Donaghey turned to the Russian in the cabin and began laughing, hesitantly at first. Then uncontrollably. The American sagged at the knees and hugged the Russian as though he were a long-lost brother. The Spetznaz commando returned the bear hug.

— 71 —
The Immelman Turn

Airborne over the Middle East

GENERAL RAWLINSON'S BREATHING QUICKENED inside his fishbowl helmet. The troublesome red light blinked steadily even as the Blackbird attempted to regain speed and altitude. He opened the throttle. Still it blinked.

Rawlinson's eyes remained glued to the panel. It might just be a defective light, the general decided optimistically. Happened all the time, on all sorts of aircraft. The same could happen even on a Blackbird. The great plane climbed.

The SR-71 achieved altitude. Rawlinson's breathing eased. The plane felt OK, he decided. Must have been a faulty light. "What's your situation, Major?" the general asked his back-seater.

"No major malfunctions."

"Roger. I think we've got a bad panel light."

Major Rogers returned to his work, manipulating console knobs that fired a steady stream of reconnaissance data on the battle below to the White House far away. Suddenly, the dark plane shivered. Rawlinson felt the shudder pass through the plane from the intake to the aft section. The general felt the lateral drift, then listened to the *whang*! sound of a rivet popping, then another and another. The racket repeated like rifle fire or popcorn. The aft end of the dark plane dropped, then sank toward the earth like a piano dropped from a pulley.

"I'm getting a fire warning light," Rawlinson announced tersely. "We've got a mission abort."

The black plane lost altitude, with the pilot fighting frantically for control. The altimeter plunged. Periscope and internal rear-view mirrors verified flames from the right engine. Other panel lights indicated what Rawlinson already knew. Total power loss.

"Prepare for bailout," Rawlinson finally ordered.

"Nothing doing, sir," Rogers replied. "I'm staying with you."

"Nobody asked you, sonny. I'm telling you, prepare for bailout!"

Rogers made no reply as the giant spy plane dropped through the high thin air. Rawlinson groaned, trying vainly to make the flight controls obey him.

As the Blackbird fell, a MiG-25 Foxbat interceptor climbed, its pilot consumed with the obsession of bagging an SR-71 spy plane. Capt. Max Immelman's face compressed to a distorted mask, baring his teeth. "Got you this time, you black beauty!"

As he closed, he lost acquisition tone for his Atoll air-to-air missiles. Too close. The Blackbird hurtled toward him. The great black plane filled his cockpit glass. As Immelman's thumb depressed the weapons trigger, he never felt what hit him.

On the ground, the Russians and Americans looked up at the same instant, gazing dumbstruck at the horror and beauty unfolding before them. The giant black plane and the MiG-25 tore into each other a bare three thousand feet above the battlefield. The Foxbat caromed wildly, its wing sheared from the fuselage. It tumbled end-over-end and exploded in a huge fireball, a shower of metal dropping to earth like flaming flower petals.

The Blackbird's titanium air frame dropped like a meteorite. Screams erupted from the Russians, who ran wildly, trying to escape the tidal wave of black metal as the aircraft pancaked, striking the ground with the force of an earthquake and a rumble like thunder. The stricken plane's broken fuselage pointed accusingly toward the Russian lines, flattening the plant fence like a weed. Spot fires erupted in the grass.

"Jesus," Cartwright yelled. "Who was driving?"

"Rawlinson!" Adam Glassman shouted. "And the plane's on the Russian side of the line!"

Before Cartwright could speak, Glassman was up and out through the shattered window, running clumsily in the heavy asbestos suit toward the shattered plane. As he moved forward, he pulled on the fireproof mittens. At the far end of the fence, explosions and fire consumed the wreckage of the Blackbird's massive engines, which had torn loose from the fuselage.

Glassman gathered speed, sprinting toward the shattered cockpit. He bowled over a startled Russian who was running the wrong way and kept running, his breath coming in gasps. He jumped onto the knife blade of the Blackbird's nose and grabbed hold of the shattered cockpit. He stared down through the splintered cockpit glass and saw the battered, lifeless form of Rawlinson. He reached inside and pushed the general's body with his left hand.

"Halt!"

His hand still steadying Rawlinson's body, Glassman turned to look down the barrel of an AK-47 aimed at him by a commando in a striped jersey. Glassman smiled, slowly withdrawing his hand from the cockpit. The Spetznaz trooper stared at him wonderingly.

"*Zdrazdi, tovarish!*" Glassman said, greeting the Russian with a smile. "It's a beautiful day. *Oshen horosho!*"

The commando stared at the yellow metal handle Glassman held in his hand. The colonel's hands were almost over his head when the manual destruct mechanism engaged and blew the fuselage, atomizing the commando, Glassman, and everything that they saw in that last beautiful minute.

— 72 —
Passage of Lines

The Operations Area, Tarak

AFTER THE TRUCE WAS ORDERED from the Kremlin and the White House, the Soviet paratroopers drove into the devastated plant in their air-dropped jeeps and carried off the remaining wounded East Germans. By comparison, Jefferson supervised the handling of Delta's wounded with tender, loving care. Standing amid the wreckage that littered the ruined fortress grounds, Strelnikov and Cartwright huddled over a map. "We can bring your people from the missile site down the road, through the gate there," Strelnikov said, pointing. "It's no problem."

"You talk pretty good American," Cartwright remarked. "Where'd you pick it up?"

"Frunze Academy," Strelnikov said proudly.

"I'm interested in something, General," Cartwright said, stroking his stubbled chin. "There were no Taraki air strikes—at any time."

"We took them out on the ground on our way in," Strelnikov said casually. "They were our planes anyway."

Cartwright shook his head and chuckled. "You leopards haven't changed all that much, have ya?" The Russian general looked at him, puzzled.

"Now, please, I am curious about something," Strelnikov said. "Your man who destroyed the black plane. He had to know, of course, that we would have fought to keep such a valuable intelligence prize, just like we kept your U-2. What sort of man was he?"

"The best we've got," Cartwright said, tight-lipped.

"You were close with him?"

"I'll do my grieving later."

"Well, please, when you recommend the decoration, add my name to the papers. He was very brave." The Russian general offered his hand. Cartwright hesitated, then took it. Jefferson ran up to the pair.

"We've got the extract laid on for zero-five minutes," he said.

Smoke hung in the air from the explosion of the Blackbird. As the Americans labored, separating dead from wounded, the troops of both countries inhaled the lingering odors of scorched flesh, cordite, and burnt metal. Surveying the ruin that surrounded him, Strelnikov turned to Jefferson. "Big fight," he said, offering the American colonel a Troika cigarette. "You have many dead."

"More of them than us," Jefferson said, accepting the loosely wrapped butt. "It was big enough."

Strelnikov lit the acrid-smelling smokes and looked at the long line of Delta and Ranger dead in the yard. He watched Sergeant Major Walker collecting dog tags. "So many," Strelnikov remarked. "My men had a night like this in the Panjir Valley. It was very bad."

"It always is," Jefferson said.

Strelnikov regarded Jefferson thoughtfully and grinned. "One time in Afghanistan, through my field glasses I think I see a negro up on a ridge we were shelling. Probably some CIA imperialist operative. Maybe you were there, no?"

Jefferson's lips tightened across his teeth in a Cheshire cat grin that slowly faded. "Okay, maybe not," the Russian general said, laughing softly as he exhaled smoke through his nose. "Maybe none of us was really there."

"I can't confirm or deny," Jefferson said.

"What about here, Colonel? Did you maybe kill a blond

bastard with a scar on his head, about here?" The Russian general pointed at his forehead.

"Didn't see him," Jefferson said coolly. "There's so many dead, I'm gonna let God sort 'em out. What did the blond bastard do?"

"Crime against the state," Strelnikov said. "Maybe your God, too."

Jefferson grinned mirthlessly. Suddenly, his ears pricked up.

"Extract!" a Delta man shouted joyfully. The rest silently watched the skies, their dirty, streaked faces full of hope as if they were children. Every American fixed his eyes on the approaching formation of tilt-rotor aircraft escorted by the Harrier jump jets.

The first transports carried out the dead and wounded, and the remnants of the Israeli assassin team. They roared away with Swiss-watch precision. Cartwright boarded the last transport, with Jefferson and Sgt. Maj. Colin Davis. The Brit carried his wounded major, still out from the concussion grenades hurled by the Israelis. As Davis manhandled his major toward the aircraft, a small steel canister fell from Mellors's web kit. Davis put Mellors down and picked up the canister, examining it closely. It read: Return by Mail to Porton Down. Do Not Open! Davis chuckled. He pitched the canister back inside the building as though it were trash. "We won't be needing this," he said, and carried his major aboard the transport.

As the Osprey soared away from the blasted plant, Jefferson peered out the right paratroop door. Curious, Cartwright followed him. In a second, so did Davis.

"This ought to give Strelnikov something to tell Moscow Center about," Jefferson said, grinning. As Jefferson pressed the detonator buttons, the plant at Tarak collapsed in a shower of dust and smoke that looked as though a gigantic hand were pulling it to the center of the earth. A cloud of cement dust rippled hundreds of feet in the air, looking like a miniature mushroom blast.

"Bloody hell, Colonel," Colin Davis murmured in awe. "Your Delta bloke's demolition is super."

"Thanks," Jefferson said, proudly. "We never practiced on anything this big. The idea was to take it down like a big building demolition. Collapse it from inside out and implode it. Bury the product under tons of concrete and steel. The site's going to be dirty for years, like Chernobyl. But whatever's in there won't contaminate the region.''

"Right, Colonel," Colin Davis said, scratching his bearded jaw. "You put the Frightfulness back in Pandora's box where it belonged."

"The what?" Jefferson said, quizzically.

"The Frightfulness," the SAS sergeant repeated. "The bloody gas that hurt me granddad's lungs. Old Jacob. He really died on the Somme in '16, but nobody told him."

Cartwright, whose demeanor had been grim since Adam Glassman's charge at the Blackbird, chuckled.

"What's the joke, General?" Jefferson asked.

"I was thinking the Tarakis had better pave over that plant of theirs," Cartwright said. "They'll probably send Uncle Sam a bill."

The aircraft, buzzing like dragonflies, hummed their way to freedom, minus Adam Glassman and Major Mellors's canister.

— 73 —
The Glassman Disposition

Washington

THE PRESIDENT SHUFFLED PAPERS, ARRANGING them as though they might be puzzle pieces. He looked up at General Cartwright, taking in his class-A blue uniform with its ribbons stretching to the stars on his shoulder boards. The president coughed, but otherwise, the secure chamber of the Situation Room remained silent. The president swept his gaze from Madeline Murdoch to Avery Benedict.

"This is a quandary," the president remarked. "My national security adviser and General Cartwright want the Medal of Honor for Colonel Glassman, posthumously. But my CIA chief wants his file closed as a dead spy."

"He was a spy," Avery Benedict said. "Why else would he commit suicide?"

Cartwright's eyes narrowed, and he fought to control himself. "He died keeping the Blackbird out of Russian hands. Is that a spy for you?"

Benedict narrowed his eyes. "No one is suggesting Colonel Glassman was less heroic than any of the Rangers or Delta men who raided the Taraki missile site, General. But there is the real possibility he had an ulterior motive."

Cartwright, squaring his shoulders, said, "I talked to the Israeli woman before she died. She cleared him."

"Of course she would do that," Benedict retorted. "They cover their people to the end."

"That's enough," the president said, looking at the papers. He adjusted his reading glasses, then looked up doubtfully at Benedict, then Madeline Murdoch and Cartwright.

"Mr. President, I want Colonel Glassman's name cleared," Cartwright said through clenched teeth. "And he deserves the medal. If you could have seen him there, sir, you'd know it. The same goes for Rawlinson and Rogers. It's a medal job all around."

The telephone rang. The president picked it up, his face clouded with bewilderment. He handed the phone to Madeline Murdoch. "It's for you," the president said. "It's your husband."

Avery Benedict's lips curled into a sneer, and he rolled his eyes.

"Dear," Madeline Murdoch said, her voice strained but polite, "I told you never to call me here."

She listened for a moment and looked at Benedict, then at Cartwright. Madeline Murdoch leaned over and whispered to the president. He nodded his head vigorously.

"I think we all better sit down," he said. The door to the secure room swung open. Madeline Murdoch's husband, Philip, entered, pushing a wheelchair that carried the shrunken form of Brady Daniels. Like Lazarus, the aged spymaster wore a blanket over his shoulders. Everyone, including the president, came to their feet.

Daniels looked around the room, his parchment face cracking into a mummified smile. He adjusted his afghan comforter with one hand and pressed his other against the electronic box at his throat which gave him a voice. "Please don't get up on my account, Mr. President," Daniels piped through the voice box. "Rumors of my death have been greatly exaggerated."

"My God, Brady," the president said, gaping at the old man. "What in heaven's name have you done?"

"Took a rest cure out in the California desert," Daniels beeped.

"Brady, you were dead!" Madeline Murdoch gasped. "I attended your funeral."

Daniels shook his head. "Just resting," he beeped.

"But why, sir?" Despite the air-conditioned chill of the underground room, Avery Benedict's face was bathed with sweat.

"Had to find the Jerusalem mole," Daniels beeped. "Needed time to look at the big picture."

"Colonel Glassman was your mole, sir," Benedict said triumphantly. "You taught me well, sir. I took it from front to back. I fit the pieces together."

Daniels nodded sagely. "I taught you well," his tinny voice piped. "And you learned." Benedict lowered his head, accepting the rare praise.

"That's why I know that you are the mole, Avery," Daniels continued. "You learned the art of deception at the seat of the master."

In the sudden silence the air-conditioning formed a crescendo of white noise. "What are you saying, sir?" Benedict whispered. "He must be unbalanced," Benedict said hurriedly to the others. "He's lost his senses."

"Don't lie, Avery," Daniels beeped. "I have your account number in Zurich. I have your Israeli contact and his trace to Ben Lavi. I've got it all."

"How," Benedict said weakly. "Where?"

"Voice is tired," Daniels said. He turned his head toward Madeline Murdoch's husband. "Professor?"

Waving his hands helplessly, Benedict stood up and pointed at Madeline Murdoch's husband. "This man is not even cleared to be in here. And this old guy is crazy," he said, pointing at Daniels and rolling his eyes. "Can't you see, Mr. President?"

"Sit down, Benedict," the president ordered. Benedict sank to his chair. Madeline Murdoch's husband spoke, his tone even and smooth. "Brady and I worked together in France during the war," the economist said. "That's why he came to me. We were Jedburgh men. The better-known name was OSS."

"Tell them," Daniels beeped plaintively.

"Brady caught you, Mr. Benedict, precisely because you were his protégé. When you tried to kill Glassman at the aircraft plant in California, you did it the way Brady would have. You went outside the agency. The assassin was— What was he, Brady?''

"A unilaterally controlled asset," Daniels beeped. "Coldwell's man. His payroll anyway.''

"Benedict's assassin was secured from the roster of freelancers maintained by Stephen Coldwell, the munitions dealer," the economist said. "Brady recognized Coldwell's signature in the work—and finally in the record of payment, traceable to the Company's off-books accounts. Once Coldwell knew Brady wasn't dead, he signed on to our team and told all. He wants to keep working.''

Benedict buried his face in his arms. He sobbed, small choking sobs. He raised his head up, his eyes red, his face drawn. "Any spy's work is noble," he whispered. "As long as he believes in the cause he's working for.''

"And you believed in the two million dollars on account in the Credit Bank of Zurich," Brady Daniels added. "What you gave our Israeli allies must have been very valuable.''

Madeline Murdoch removed the pistol from her purse. She moved to the wall and pressed the intercom button. "Sergeant of the guard," she said. "The president needs you.''

Benedict's eyes filled with hatred as he looked at his rival, a small woman of advancing age and advanced intellect. Suddenly, he rushed at her, grabbing her by her tweed jacket. Bowling over the president, he wrestled for the gun. She did not hesitate. She fired before the air-lock door swung open, and Avery Benedict slumped to the floor, bleeding on his president.

As the Marine guard and Secret Service agents piled into the close room, Cartwright fell on them shouting, "Hold your fire! Hold your fire until the president is clear.''

The president then shouted, "Don't shoot, dammit, it's over.'' He pushed the bleeding Avery Benedict from him and picked himself up with great dignity.

"Toss the gun free," cried a Secret Service agent who kept his Uzi leveled at Benedict. Madeline Murdoch pushed her pearl-handled .25 caliber automatic so it skidded across the carpet, then pulled herself out from under Benedict.

The president unconsciously tugged at his suit coat. "Get

the paramedics, Sergeant," he said to the Marine guard. "This man isn't dead."

As the Secret Service men pulled the wounded Avery Benedict from the secure room, a crowd gathered outside. Seeing the body being pulled out, someone shouted that the president was shot. Cartwright quickly slammed shut the air-lock door. "Sir, you better get on the PA system and clear the air, or there's gonna be a riot out there."

"I quite agree, General," the president said. He hit the intercom switch and made a terse announcement that the CIA director had wounded himself in an accidental shooting and that he, the president, was quite well. He turned to his aides surrounding him. Brushing his fingers through his thinning hair and seating himself, the president said, "I believe this resolves our dilemma regarding Colonel Glassman. And now I think I'd like a glass of water."

Madeline Murdoch's husband reached for the pitcher, which had miraculously not fallen from the conference table during the brawl. The economist poured a glass for the president—and spilled hardly any at all. Then he poured a glass for his wife, who was sitting, exhausted, next to her commander-in-chief. Gently, her husband dabbed her forehead with a handkerchief he moistened from the pitcher.

Epilogue

MADELINE MURDOCH LOOKED UP FROM her desk and handed the file jacket to Cartwright. "For the moment, I'm afraid that retirement is out of the question for you, General."

"That's a crock, Madeline," the general retorted. "You know with the years I've got in, I can pull the plug anytime I want."

"Yes, General, but will you? Someone's got to keep the Blackbirds flying. At least until we get the new plane up."

"The new plane?"

"It's called Aurora. It's Mach 5, Deep Black classified, and stealthy. Since the Tarak crisis, the president has taken a sudden interest in reviving the spy plane concept. He sees the benefits of a manned reconnaissance platform and believes that if we scale down the Star Wars project, there might be enough budget money left to get Aurora airborne."

"Mach 5? I'd give my left nut to fill out a test card on a plane like that."

"That might not be necessary, Scott," the national security adviser said wryly. "Someone's got to replace General Rawlinson, you know."

* * *

Cartwright arrived the next day at Beale Air Force Base outside Marysville in the Sacramento Valley. He pulled his new orders from the manila folder and read them for perhaps the dozenth time that morning. He scanned the assortment of acronyms, lines, and blocks that made up the standard-issue form for orders, and shook his head ruefully.

He gazed skyward, watching the twin candles of an SR-71 burn to angry life, soaring away from the brown hills of Sacramento toward the edge of space. He wanted to get in every look that he could before the Blackbird flew into the history books.

AUTHOR'S NOTE: The SR-71 Blackbird served for more than twenty-five years as an advanced manned reconnaissance system, bringing back vital intelligence data not available through other means such as satellites. Late in 1989, after a funding battle in Congress, the SR-71 was retired from active duty. It still holds world records for altitude and speed. No Blackbird has ever been lost to hostile fire while carrying out its mission.

With the retirement of the SR-71, the Air Force said it was evaluating other reconnaissance platforms. Air Force officials decline to comment on the existence of a possible successor aircraft as described in the Aurora project.

Afterword

SR-71 BLACKBIRD: SPECIFICATIONS AND PERFORMANCE

Specifications

Type: strategic reconnaissance aircraft, carrying pilot and reconnaissance systems officer.

Mission: airborne reconnaissance platform, performing tasks outside the performance characteristics of other spy platforms, such as satellites

Length: 103 to 107 feet, depending on modification

Height: 18 feet 6 inches

Wingspan: 55 feet 7 inches

Weight (empty): 76,500 lb.

Gross weight: 172,000 lb.

Powerplant: two J-58 Pratt & Whitney turbo ramjets, each with 32,500-pound thrust

Armament: The SR-71 Blackbird is unarmed. Its defenses are speed, stealth, and altitude.

Reconnaissance systems: classified

Remarks: The SR-71, which began development in 1958 as successor to the U-2, is the highest-flying, fastest air-breathing aircraft in the world. It can survey more than 100,000 square miles of the earth's surface in an hour.

Performance

Maximum speed: Mach 3-plus*

Maximum altitude: 80,000 feet plus

Range: 3,250 miles

Takeoff speed: 230 knots

Landing speed: 155 knots

Minimum runway: 5,000 feet

*Absolute performance limits are classified.